THE
FALLEN
1

THE
FALLEN
1

THE FALLEN AND *LEVIATHAN*

THOMAS E. SNIEGOSKI

Simon Pulse

NEW YORK LONDON TORONTO SYDNEY

SIMON PULSE

An imprint of Simon & Schuster Children's Publishing Division
1230 Avenue of the Americas, New York, NY 10020
This Simon Pulse paperback edition March 2010
The Fallen copyright © 2003 by Thomas E. Sniegoski
Leviathan copyright © 2003 by Thomas E. Sniegoski
All rights reserved, including the right of reproduction
in whole or in part in any form.
SIMON PULSE and colophon are registered trademarks of Simon & Schuster, Inc.
For information about special discounts for bulk purchases, please contact
Simon & Schuster Special Sales at 1-866-506-1949 or business@simonandschuster.com.
The Simon & Schuster Speakers Bureau can bring authors to your live event. For more
information or to book an event contact the Simon & Schuster Speakers Bureau
at 1-866-248-3049 or visit our website at www.simonspeakers.com.
Designed by Mike Rosamilia
The text of this book was set in Adobe Garamond.
Manufactured in the United States of America
8 10 9 7
Library of Congress Control Number 2009941642
ISBN 978-1-4424-0862-3
These titles were previously published individually by Simon Pulse.

CONTENTS

THE FALLEN

For Spenser, gone but never forgotten.
And Mulder, the best pally a guy could have.

I'd like to thank my wife and guardian angel (with a pitchfork), LeeAnne, for everything that she does. Without her love and support, the words wouldn't come, so the stories could never be told.

And to Christopher Golden, collaborator and friend, thanks for the gift of confidence when I wasn't quite sure I could pull it off. It is greatly appreciated.

Thanks to the Termineditor, Lisa Clancy, and her assistant supreme, Lisa Gribbin.

Special thanks are also due to Mom and Dad (for that Catholic upbringing), Eric Powell, Dave Kraus, David Carroll, Dr. Kris Blumenstock and the gang over at Lloyd Animal Medical Center, Tom and Lorie Stanley, Paul Griffin, Tim Cole and the usual suspects, Jon and Flo, Bob and Pat, Don Kramer, John, Jana, Harry and Hugo, Kristy Bratton, and Mike and Anne Murray. An extra-special thanks to Rosolivia Bryant.

PROLOGUE

LEBANON, TENNESSEE, 1995

The Tennessee night was screaming.

Eric Powell ran clumsily through the tall grass behind his grandparents' house. He stumbled down the sloping embankment toward the thick patch of swampy woods beyond, hands pressed firmly against his ears.

"I'm not listening," he said through gritted teeth, on the verge of tears. "Stop it. Please! *Shut up.*"

The sounds were deafening, and he wanted nothing more than to escape them. *But where?* The voices were coming from all around.

Eric ran deeper and deeper into the woods. He ran until his lungs felt as if they were on fire, and the beating of his heart was almost loud enough to drown out the sinister warnings from the surrounding darkness.

Almost.

Beneath a weeping willow that had once been a favorite place to escape the stress of teenage life, he stopped to catch his breath. Warily he moved his hands away from his ears and was bombarded with the cacophonous message of the night.

"Danger," warned a tiny, high-pitched squeak from the shadows by the small creek that snaked through the dark wood. *"Danger. Danger. Danger."*

"They come," croaked another. *"They come."*

"Hide yourself," something squawked from within the drooping branches of the willow before taking flight in fear. *"Before it is too late,"* it said as it flew away.

There were others out there in the night, thousands of others all speaking in tongues and cautioning him of the same thing. Something was coming, something bad.

Eric fell back against the tree trying to focus, and his mind flashed back to when he first began to hear the warnings. It had been June 25, of that he was certain. The memory was vividly fresh, for it had been only two months ago and it was not easy to forget one's eighteenth birthday—or the day you begin to lose your mind.

Before that, he heard the world just like any other. The croaking of frogs down by the pond, the angry buzz of a trapped yellow jacket as it threw itself against the screens on the side porch. Common everyday sounds of nature, taken for granted, frequently ignored.

But on his birthday that had changed.

Eric no longer heard them as the sounds of birds chirping or a tomcat's mournful wail in the night. He heard them as voices, voices that exalted in the glory of a beautiful summer's day, voices that spoke of joy as well as sadness, hunger, and fear. At first he tried to block them out, to hear them for what they actually were—just the sounds of animals. But when they began to speak directly to him, Eric came to the difficult realization that he was indeed going insane.

A swarm of fireflies distracted him from his thoughts, their incandescent bodies twinkling in the inky black of the nighttime woods. They dipped and wove in the air before him, their lights communicating a message of grave importance.

"Run," was the missive he read from their flickering bio-luminescence. *"Run, for your life is at risk."*

And that is just what he did.

Eric pushed off from the base of the tree and headed toward the gurgling sounds of the tiny creek. He would cross it and head deeper into the woods, so far that no one would ever find him. After all, he had grown up here and doubted there was anyone around who knew the woods better.

But then the question came, the same question that the rational part of his mind had been asking since the warnings began.

What are you afraid of?

The question played over and over in his head as he ran, but he did not know the answer.

Eric jumped the creek. He landed on the other side awkwardly, his sneakered foot sliding across some moss-covered rocks and into the unusually cold water.

The boy gasped as the liquid invaded his shoe, and he scrambled to remove it from the creek's numbing embrace. Its chilling touch spurring him to move faster. He ducked beneath the low-hanging branches of young trees that grew along the banks of the miniature river, then he plunged deeper into the wilderness.

But what are you running from? a rational voice asked, not from the woods around him but from his own mind. His own voice, a calm voice, that sought to override his sense of panic. This voice wanted him to stop and confront his fears, to see them for what they really were. *There is no danger,* said the sensible voice. *There is nobody chasing you, watching you.*

Eric slowed his pace.

"Keep running," urged something as it slithered beneath an overturned stump, its shiny scales reflecting the starlight.

And he almost listened to the small, hissing voice, almost sped up again. But then Eric shook his head and began to walk. Others called to him from the bushes, from the air above his head, from the grass beneath his feet, all urging him to flee, to run like a crazy person, which was exactly what he decided he was.

At that moment, Eric made a decision. He wasn't going to listen to them anymore. He wasn't going to run from some invisible threat. He was going to turn around, go back to his grandparents' home, wake them up, and explain what was happening. He would tell them that he needed help, that he needed to get to a hospital right away.

His mind made up, Eric stopped in a clearing and looked up into the early-morning sky. A thick patch of gray clouds that reminded him of steel wool slowly rubbed across the face of a radiant moon. He didn't want to hurt his grandparents. They had already been through so much. His mother, their daughter, pregnant and unwed, died giving birth to him. They raised him as if he were their own, giving him all the love and support he could have ever hoped for. And how would he repay them? With more sadness.

Scalding tears flooded his eyes as he imagined what it would be like when he returned to the house and roused the poor elderly couple from sleep. He could see their sad looks of disappointment as he explained that he was hearing voices—that he was nineteen years old and losing his mind.

And as if in agreement, the voices of the night again came to life: chattering, wheezing, tremulous, quavering, gargling life.

"Run, run," they said as one. "Run for your life, for they have arrived!"

Eric looked around him; the ruckus was deafening. Since

his bout with madness began, never had the voices been this loud, this frantic. Maybe they suspected he was coming to his senses. Maybe they knew that their time with him would soon be ending.

"They are here! Flee! Hide yourself! It is not too late. Run!"

He spun around, fists clenched in angry resignation. "No more!" he yelled to the trees. "I'm not going to listen to you anymore," he added to the air above his head and the earth beneath his feet. "Do you understand me?" he asked the darkness that encircled the clearing.

Eric turned in a slow circle, his insanity still attempting to overwhelm him with its clamorous jabber. He could stand it no more.

"Shut up!" he shrieked at the top of his lungs. "Shut up! Shut up! Shut up!"

And all went instantly quiet.

As intolerable as the voices had become, the sudden lack of them was equally extreme. There was nothing now: no buzz of insects, no cries of night birds. Not even leaves rustled by the wind. The silence was deafening.

"Well, all right then," he said, speaking aloud again to make sure that he hadn't gone deaf. Made uneasy by the abrupt hush, he turned to leave the small clearing the way he had entered.

Eric stopped short. A lone figure stood on the path.

Was it a trick of the shadows? The woods, darkness, and

moonlight conspiring to drive him crazier than he already was? Eric closed his eyes and opened them again trying to focus on the manlike shape. It still appeared to be somebody blocking his way.

"Hello?" He moved tentatively closer to the dark figure. "Who's there?" Eric still could not make out any details of the stranger.

The shape came toward him, and so did the darkness, as if the undulating shadows that clung to the figure were part of his makeup. The comical image of Pig Pen from the *Charlie Brown* cartoons, surrounded by his ever present cloud of dust and dirt, quickly flashed across Eric's mind's eye. In a perverse way it did kind of remind him of that, only this was far more unnerving.

Eric quickly stepped back.

"Who is it?" he asked, his voice higher with fear. He had always hated how his voice sounded when he was afraid. "Don't come any closer," he warned, making a conscious effort to bring the pitch down to sound more threatening.

The figure cloaked in darkness stopped in its tracks. Even this much farther into the clearing, Eric could not discern any features. He was beginning to wonder if his psychosis had started to play games with him, this shadow being nothing more than a creation of his insanity.

"Are . . . are you real?" Eric stammered.

It was as if he had screamed the question, the wood was still so unusually silent.

The darkness in the shape of a man just stood there and Eric became convinced of its unreality. *Yet another symptom of the breakdown,* he thought with a disgusted shake of his head. *It couldn't stop with hearing voices,* he chided himself, *oh no, now I have to see things.*

"Guess that answers that question," Eric said aloud as he glared at the figment of his dementia. "What's the matter?" he asked. "Miss your cue or something? When I realize you're nothing but crazy bullshit my mind made up, you're supposed to disappear." He waved the shape away. "Go. I know I'm nuts, you don't need to prove it. Beat it."

The figure did not move, but the covering of shadows that hugged it did. The darkness seemed to open. Like the petals of some night-blooming flower, the ebony black peeled away to reveal a man within.

Eric studied the man, searching his memory for some glimmer of recognition, but came away with nothing. He was tall, at least six feet, and thin, dressed in a black turtleneck, slacks. And despite the rather muggy temperature, he noticed the man was wearing a gray trench coat.

The man seemed to be studying him as well, tilting his head from one side to the other. His skin was incredibly pale, almost white. His hair, which was worn very long and severely combed back, was practically the same color. Eric had gone to elementary school with a girl who looked like that; her name was Cheryl Baggley and she, too, had been albino.

"I know this is going to sound crazy," Eric said to the man, "but . . . ," he stammered as he tried to formulate the most sane way to ask the question. "You are real . . . right?"

The man did not respond at once. As the mysterious stranger pondered the question, Eric noticed his eyes. The oily shadow that had cocooned him previously seemed to have pooled in his eye sockets. He had never seen eyes as deep and dark as these.

"Yes," the pale-skinned man said curtly, his voice sounding more like the caw of a crow.

Startled, Eric didn't grasp the meaning of the man's sudden reply and stared at him, confused. "Yes? I don't . . ." He shook his head nervously.

"Yes," the man again responded. "I am real." He emphasized each of the words as he spoke them.

His voice was strange, Eric thought, as if he were not comfortable speaking the language.

"Oh . . . good, that's good to know. Who are you? Were you sent to find me?" he questioned. "Did my grandparents call the police? I'm really sorry you had to come all the way out here. As you can see, I'm fine. I'm just dealing with some stuff and . . . well, I just need to get back to the house and have a long talk with . . ."

The man stiffly held up a pale hand. "The sound of you, it offends me," he said, a snarl upon his lips. "Abomination, I command you to be silent."

Eric started as if slapped. "Did . . . did you just call me an abomination?" he asked, confusion and fear raising the pitch of his voice again.

"There are few words in this tongue that define the likes of you better," growled the stranger. "You are a blight upon His favored world, an abhorrence in the eyes of God—but you are not the one that incites me so." The hand held out to silence the boy was turned palm up. Something had begun to glow in its ghostly pale center. "However, that does not change the reality that you must be smited."

Eric felt the hair at the back of his neck stand on end, the flesh on his arms erupt in tingling gooseflesh. He didn't need the voices of the wood to warn him that something was wrong; he could feel it in the forest air.

He turned to run, to hurl himself through the thick under-brush. He had to get away. Every fiber of his being screamed danger, and he allowed the primitive survival mechanism of flight to overtake him.

Four figures suddenly blocked his way, each attired as the stranger, each with a complexion as pale as the face of the full moon above. *How is this possible?* His mind raced. How could four people sneak up on him without making a sound?

Something whined at the newcomers' feet, and he saw a young boy crouched there. He was filthy, naked, his hair long and unkempt, a thick string of snot dripping down from one nostril to cling to his dirty lip. The boy's expression told Eric that there was something wrong with him—that he was touched in some way. And then he noticed the leather collar that encircled the child's neck, and the leash that led to the hand of one of the strangers, and Eric knew something was very wrong indeed.

The boy began to strain upon the leash, pointing a dirt-encrusted finger at him, whining and grunting like an animal.

The strangers fixed their gazes upon Eric with eyes of solid shadow and began to spread out, eliminating any chance of escape. The wild boy continued to jabber.

Eric whipped around to see that the other figure had come closer. His hand was still outstretched before him—but now it was aflame.

His mind tried to process this event. There was a fire burning in the palm of the man's hand, and the most disturbing thing was, it didn't seem to bother him in the least.

Eric felt his legs begin to tremble as the orange-and-yellow flame grew, leaping hungrily into the air. The stranger moved steadily closer. Eric wanted to run screaming, to lash out and escape those who corralled him, but something told him it would be for naught.

Fear overcame him and he fell to his knees, feeling the cold dampness begin to soak through his pants. There was no reason for him to turn around; the feral child growled at his back and he knew the four strangers now moved to flank him. He kept his gaze on the man standing above him holding fire in the palm of his hand.

"Who are you?" the boy asked dully, mesmerized by the miraculous flame, which appeared to be taking on the shape of something else entirely.

The stranger looked upon him with eyes black and glistening, his expression void of any emotion. Eric could see himself reflected in their inky surface.

"Why are you doing this?" he asked pathetically.

The stranger cocked his head oddly. Eric could feel the heat of the flame upon his upturned face.

"What was it the monkey apostle Matthew scribbled about us in one of his silly little books?" the man asked no one in particular. "'The Son of Man shall send them forth, and they shall gather out of His kingdom all things that offend, and those who do evil, and shall cast them into a furnace of fire.' Or something to that effect," he added with a horrible grin.

Eric had never seen anything more unnatural. It was as if the stranger's face lacked the proper musculature to complete the most common of human expressions.

"I don't understand," he said in a voice nearly a whisper.

The man moved the flaming object from one hand to the other, and Eric followed it with his eyes. The fire had become a sword.

A flaming sword.

"It is better that you do not," the man said, raising the burning blade above his head.

The boy watched the weapon of fire descend, his face upturned as if to seek the rays of the rising sun. And then all that he was, and all that he might have become, was consumed in fire.

CHAPTER ONE

Aaron Corbet was having the dream again.

Yet it was so much more than that.

Since they began, over three months before, the visions of sleep had grown more and more intense—more vivid. Almost real.

He is making his way through the primitive city, an ancient place constructed of brown brick, mud, and hay. The people here are in a panic, for something attacks their homes. They run about frenzied, their frightened cries echoing throughout the cool night. Sounds of violence fill the air, blades clanging together in battle, the moans of the wounded—and something else he can't quite place, a strange sound in the distance, but moving closer.

Other nights he has tried to stop the frightened citizens, to catch their attention, to ask them what is happening, but they do not see or hear him. He is a ghost to their turmoil.

Husbands and wives, shielding small children between them, scramble across sand-covered streets desperately searching for shelter. Again he listens to their fear-filled voices. He does not understand their language, but the meaning is quite clear. Their lives and the lives of their children are in danger.

For nights too numerous to count he has come to this place, to this sad village and witnessed the panic of its people. But not once has he seen the source of their terror.

He moves through the winding streets of the dream place, feeling the roughness of desert sand beneath his bare feet. Every night this city under siege becomes more real to him, and tonight he feels its fear as if it were his own. And again he asks himself, fear of what? Who are they who can bring such terror to these simple people?

In the marketplace a boy dressed in rags, no older than he, darts out from beneath a tarp covering a large pile of yellow, gourdlike fruit. He watches the boy stealthily travel across the deserted market, sticking close to the shadows. The boy nervously watches the sky as he runs.

Odd that the boy would be so concerned with the sky overhead.

The boy stops at the edge of the market and crouches within a thick pool of night. He stares longingly across the expanse of open ground at another area of darkness on the other side.

There is unrelenting fear on the dark-skinned youth's face; his eyes are wide and white. What is he so afraid of? *Aaron looks up himself and sees only the night, like velvet adorned with twinkling jewels. There is nothing to fear there, only beauty to admire.*

The boy darts from his hiding place and scrambles across the open area. He is halfway there when the winds begin. Sudden, powerful gusts that come out of nowhere, hurling sand, dirt, and dust.

The boy stops short and shields his face from the scouring particles. He is blinded, unsure of his direction. Aaron wants to call to him, to help the boy escape the mysterious sandstorm, but knows that his attempts would be futile, that he is only an observer.

And there is the sound. He can't place it exactly, but knows it is familiar. There is something in the sky above—something that beats at the air, stirring the winds, creating the sudden storm.

The boy is screaming. His sweat-dampened body is powdered almost white in a sheen of fine dust and desert sand.

The sounds are louder now, closer.

What is that? *The answer is right at the edge of his knowing. He again looks up into the sky. The sand still flies about, tossed by the winds. It stings his face and eyes, but he has to see—he has to know what makes these strange pounding sounds, what creates gusts of wind powerful enough to propel sand and rock. He has to know the source of such unbridled horror in these people of the dream-city—in this boy.*

And through the clouds of fine debris, he sees them. For the first time he sees them.

They are wearing armor. Golden armor that glistens in the dancing light thrown from the flames of their weapons.

The boy runs toward him. It seems that Aaron is suddenly visible. The boy reaches out, pleading to be saved in the language of his people.

This time, he understands every word. He tries to answer, but earsplitting shrieks fill the night, the excited cries of predators that have discovered their prey.

The boy tries to run, but there are too many.

Aaron can do nothing but watch as the birdlike creatures descend from the sky, falling upon the boy, his plaintive screams of terror drowned out by the beating of powerful wings.

Angels' wings.

LYNN. MASSACHUSETTS

It was Gabriel's powerful, bed-shaking sneeze that pulled Aaron from the dream and back to the waking world.

Aaron's eyes snapped open as another explosion of moisture dappled his face. For the moment, the dream was forgotten and all that occupied his mind was the attentions of an eighty-pound Labrador retriever named Gabriel.

"Unnngh," he moaned as he pulled his arm up from the warmth beneath the covers to wipe away the newest spattering of dog spittle.

"Thanks, Gabe," he said, his voice husky from sleep.

"What time is it anyway? Time to get up?" he asked the dog lying beside him.

The yellow retriever leaned its blocky head forward to lick the back of his exposed hand, his muscular bulk blocking Aaron's view of the alarm clock.

"Okay, okay," Aaron said as he pulled his other hand out to ruffle the dog's velvety soft, golden-brown ears, and wiggled himself into an upright position to check the time.

Craving more attention, Gabriel flipped over onto his back and swatted at Aaron with his front paws. He chuckled and rubbed the dog's exposed belly before training his eyes on the clock on the nightstand beside his bed.

Aaron watched the red digital readout change from 7:28 to 7:29.

"Shit," he hissed.

Sensing alarm in his master, Gabriel rolled from his back to his stomach with a rumbling bark.

Aaron struggled from the bed, whipped into a frenzy by the lateness of the hour.

"Shit. Shit. Shit. Shit," he repeated as he pulled off his Dave Matthews concert T-shirt and threw it onto a pile of dirty clothes in the corner of the room. He pulled down his sweatpants and kicked them into the same general vicinity. He was late. Very late.

He'd been studying for Mr. Arslanian's history exam last night, and his head was so crammed with minutiae about the Civil War that he must have forgotten to set the alarm. He had less than a half hour to get to Kenneth Curtis High School before first bell.

Aaron lunged for his dresser and yanked clean underwear and socks from the second drawer. In the mirror above, he could see Gabriel curiously staring at him from the bed.

"Man's best friend, my butt," he said to the dog on his way into the bathroom. "How could you let me oversleep?"

Gabriel just fell to his side among the tousled bedclothes and sighed heavily.

Aaron managed to shower, brush his teeth, and get dressed in a little more than seventeen minutes.

I might be able to pull this off yet, he thought as he bounded down the stairs, loaded bookbag slung over his shoulder. If he got out the door right at this moment and managed to make all the lights heading down North Common, he could probably pull into the parking lot just as the last bell rang.

It would be close, but it was the only option he had.

In the hallway he grabbed his jacket from the coatrack and was about to open the door when he felt Gabriel's eyes upon him.

The dog stood behind him, watching him intensely, head cocked at a quizzical angle that said, "Haven't you forgotten something?"

Aaron sighed. The dog needed to be fed and taken out to do his morning business. Normally he would have had more than enough time to see to his best friend's needs, but today was another story.

"I can't, Gabe," he said as he turned the doorknob. "Lori will give you breakfast and take you out."

And then it hit him. He'd been in such a hurry to get out of the house that he hadn't noticed his foster mother's absence.

"Lori?" he called as he stepped away from the door and quickly made his way down the hall to the kitchen. Gabriel followed close at his heels.

This is odd, he thought. Lori was usually the first to rise in the Stanley household. She would get up around five A.M., get the coffee brewing, and make her husband, Tom, a bag lunch so he could be out of the house and to the General Electric plant where he was a foreman, by seven sharp.

The kitchen was empty, and with a hungry Gabriel by his side, Aaron made his way through the dining room to the living room.

The room was dark, the shades on the four windows still drawn. The television was on, but had gone to static. His seven-year-old foster brother, Stevie, sat before the twenty-two-inch screen, staring as if watching the most amazing television program ever produced.

Across the room, below a wall of family photos that had jokingly become known as the wall of shame, his foster mom was asleep in a leather recliner. Aaron was disturbed at how old she looked, slumped in the chair, wrapped in a worn, navy blue terry cloth robe. It was the first time he ever really thought about her growing older, and that there would be a day when she wouldn't be around anymore. *Where the hell did that come from?* he wondered. He pushed the strange and really depressing train of thought away and attempted to think of something more pleasant.

When the Stanleys had taken him into their home as a foster child, it had been his seventh placement since birth. What was it that the caseworkers used to say about him? "He's not a bad kid, just a bit of an introvert with a bad temper." Aaron smiled. He never expected the placements to last, and had imagined that there would be an eighth, ninth, and probably even a hundredth placement before he was cut loose from the foster care system and let out into the world on his own.

A warm pang of emotion flowed through him as he remembered the care this woman and her husband had given him over the years. No matter how he misbehaved, or acted out, they stuck with him, investing their time, their energy, and most importantly, their love. The Stanleys weren't just collecting a check from the state; they really cared about him, and eventually he came to think of them as the parents he never knew.

Gabriel had wandered over to the boy in front of the television and was licking his face—Aaron knew it was only to catch the residue of the child's breakfast. But the boy did not respond, continuing to stare at the static on the screen, eyes wide, mouth agape.

Steven was the Stanleys' only biological child and he had autism, the often misunderstood mental condition that left those afflicted so absorbed with their own reality, that they were rarely able to interact with the world around them. The boy could be quite a handful and Lori stayed home to care for his special needs.

Lori twitched and came awake with a start. "Stevie?" she asked groggily, looking for her young son.

"He's watching his favorite show," Aaron said, indicating Gabriel and the little boy. He looked back to his foster mom. "You all right?"

Lori stretched and, pulling her robe tight around her throat, smiled at him. Her smile had always made him feel special and this morning wasn't any different. "I'm fine, hon, just a little tired is all." She motioned with her chin to the boy in front of the television. "He had a bad night and the static was the only thing that calmed him down."

She glanced over at the mini–grandfather clock hanging on the wall and squinted. "Is that the time?" she asked. "What are you still doing here? You're going to be late for school."

He started to explain as she sprang from the seat and began to push him from the room. "I was up late studying and forgot to set the alarm and . . ."

"Tell me later," she said as she placed the palm of her hand in the small of his back, helping him along.

"Would you mind feeding—"

"No, I wouldn't, and I'll take him for a walk," Lori said, cutting him off. "Get to school and ace that history test."

He was halfway out the door when he heard her call his name from the kitchen. There was a hint of panic in her voice.

Aaron poked his head back in.

"I almost forgot," she said, the dog's bowl in one hand and a cup of dry food in the other. Gabriel stood attentively at her side, drool streaming from his mouth to form a shiny puddle at his paws.

"What is it?" he asked, a touch of impatience beginning to find its way into his tone.

She smiled. "Happy birthday," she said, and pursed her lips in a long distance kiss. "Have a great day."

My birthday, he thought closing the door behind him and running to his car.

With all the rushing about this morning, he'd forgotten.

Aaron squeaked into homeroom just as the day's announcements were being read over the school's ancient PA system.

Mrs. Mihos, the elderly head of the math department mere months away from retirement, looked up from her copy of *Family Circle* and gave him an icy stare.

He mouthed the words "I'm sorry" and quickly found

his seat. He had learned that the less said to Mrs. Mihos the better. Her edicts were simple: Be on time to homeroom, turn in notes to explain absences in a timely fashion, and whatever you do, don't be a wiseass. Aaron chillingly recalled how Tommy Philips, now seated at the back of the classroom intently keeping his mouth shut, had attempted to be the funny guy. He'd written a joke letter to explain an absence, and found himself with a week's worth of detentions. There was nothing the math teacher hated more than a wiseass.

Aaron chanced a look at the old woman and saw that she was flipping through the attendance sheets to change his status from absent to present. He breathed a sigh of relief as the first period bell began to ring. *Maybe today wouldn't be a total disaster after all.*

First period American Literature went fine, but halfway through second period, while taking Mr. Arslanian's test, Aaron decided that he couldn't have been more wrong about the day. Not only was he blanking on some of the information he had studied, but he also had one of the worst headaches he could ever remember. His head felt as if it were vibrating, buzzing like someone had left an electric shaver running inside his skull. He rubbed at his brow furiously and tried to focus on an essay question about the social and political ramifications of the Richmond Bread Riot. Arslanian's fascination with obscure events of the Civil War was going to give him an aneurysm.

The remainder of the class passed in the blink of an eye, and Aaron wondered if he had passed out or maybe even been taken by space aliens. He had barely finished the last of the essay questions when the end-of-period bell clanged, a real plus for the pain in his head. He quickly glanced over the pages of his test. It wasn't the best he'd ever done, but considering how he felt, he didn't think it was too bad.

"I'd like to give you another couple of hours to wrap the test up in a pretty pink bow, Mr. Corbet . . ."

Aaron had zoned out again. He looked up to see the heavyset form of Mr. Arslanian standing beside his desk, hand beckoning.

"But my wife made a killer turkey for dinner last night and I have leftovers waiting for me in the teachers' lounge."

Aaron just stared, the annoying buzz in his head growing louder and more painful.

"Your exam, Mr. Corbet," demanded Mr. Arslanian.

Aaron pulled himself together and handed the test to his teacher. Then he gathered up his books and prepared to leave. As he stood the room began to spin and he held on to the desk for a moment, just in case.

"Are you all right, Mr. Corbet?" Arslanian asked as he ambled back to his desk. "You look a little pale."

Aaron was amazed that he only looked pale. He imagined there should have been blood shooting out his ears and squirting from his nostrils. He was feeling that bad. "Head-ache," he managed on his way to the door.

"Take some Tylenol," the teacher called after him, "and a cold rag on your head. That's what works for me."

Always a big help, that Mr. Arslanian, Aaron thought as he stepped lightly in an effort to keep his skull from breaking apart and decorating the walls with gore.

The hallway was jammed with bodies coming, going, or just hanging out in small packs in front of brightly colored lockers, catching up on the freshest gossip. *It's amazing,* Aaron thought sarcastically, *how much dirt can happen during one fifty-minute period.*

Aaron moved through the flow of students. He would drop off his books, and then go to the nurse's office to get something for his headache. It was getting worse, like listening to the static of an untuned radio playing inside his brain.

As he maneuvered around the pockets of people, he exchanged an occasional smile or a nod of recognition, but the few who acknowledged him were only being polite. He knew people looked at him as the quiet, loner guy with the troubled past, and he did very little to dispel their notions of him. Aaron didn't have any real friends at Ken Curtis, merely acquaintances, and it didn't bother him in the least.

He finally reached his locker and began to dial the combination.

Maybe if he got something into his stomach he'd feel

better, he thought, remembering that he hadn't eaten anything since the night before. He swung the locker door open
and began to unload his books.

A girl laughed nearby. He looked behind him to see
Vilma Santiago at her locker with three of her friends. They
were staring in his direction, but quickly looked away and
giggled conspiratorially. *What's so funny?* he wondered.

They were speaking loudly enough for him to hear them.
The only problem was they were speaking Portuguese, and
he had no idea what they were saying. Two years of French
did him little good while eavesdropping on Brazilian girls'
conversations.

Vilma was one of the most beautiful girls he had ever
seen. She had transferred to Ken Curtis last year from Brazil,
and within months had become one of the school's top students. Smart as well as gorgeous, a dangerous combination,
and one that had left him smitten. They saw each other at
their lockers every day, but had never really spoken. It wasn't
that he didn't want to speak to her, just that he could never
think of anything to say.

He turned to arrange the books in his locker, and again
felt their eyes upon him. They were whispering now, and he
could feel his paranoia swell.

"Ele nâo é nada feio. Que bunda!"

The pain in his head was suddenly blinding, as if somebody had taken an ice pick and plunged it into the top of his

skull. The feeling was excruciating and he almost cried out—certain to have provided his audience with a few good laughs. He pressed his forehead against the cool metal of the locker and prayed for respite. *It can't hurt this bad for very long,* he hoped. As the hissing grew more and more intense, shards of broken glass rubbed into his brain. He thought he would pass out as strange colorful patterns blossomed before his eyes and the pain continued to build.

The torturous buzzing came to an explosive climax, circuits within his mind suddenly overloaded, and before he fell unconscious—it was gone. Aaron stood perfectly still, waiting, afraid that if he moved the agony would return. *What was that all about?* he wondered, his hand coming up to his nose to check for bleeding.

There was nothing. No pain, no blaring white noise. In fact, he felt better than he had all morning. *Maybe this is just part of a bizarre biological process one goes through when turning eighteen,* he thought, bemused, reminding himself again that it was his birthday.

As he slammed the locker door, he realized that Vilma and her friends were still talking. "Estou cansada de pizza. Semana passada, nós comemos pizza, quase todo dia." They were discussing lunch options—cafeteria versus going off campus for pizza. Vilma wanted to go to the cafeteria, but the others were pressing for the pizza.

Aaron turned away from his locker considering whether

or not he should still see the nurse, and caught Vilma's eye. She smiled shyly and quickly averted her gaze.

But not before the others noticed and began to tease her mercilessly. *"Porqué? Vocé está pensando que una certo persoa vai estar no refeitó rio hoje?"* Did she want to eat in the cafeteria because of a certain boy standing nearby? they asked her.

Aaron felt himself break out in a cold sweat. His suspicion was justified, for in fact the girls were talking about him.

"É, e daí? Eu acho que ele é un tesâo." Vilma responded to her friends' taunts and glanced again in his direction.

They were all looking at him when it dawned. He knew what they were saying. Vilma and her friends *were* still speaking to one another in Portuguese—but somehow he could understand each and every word.

But the most startling thing was what Vilma had said.

"Eu acho que ele é un tesâo."

She said he was cute.

Vilma Santiago thought he was cute!

CHAPTER TWO

At the back of the West Lynn Veterinary Hospital, where Aaron worked after school, a greyhound named Hunter sniffed a patch of yellowed grass with great interest.

"Someone you know?" Aaron asked the brindle-colored dog as he reached out to affectionately scratch him just above his long, whiplike tail.

The dog slowly turned his long neck and wagged his tail in response, before another scent hidden elsewhere in the grass diverted his attention.

Aaron glanced at his watch. It was a little after eight thirty, and he was exhausted. He was hoping that Hunter, who had been constipated since undergoing a procedure to remove a tennis ball from his large intestine, would finally get around to doing his thing so Aaron could go home, have something to eat, and do some schoolwork before passing out.

The dog pulled him into a patch of shadow, nose practically pressed to the ground, turned in a circle and finally did his business.

"Happy birthday to me," Aaron muttered, looking up into the twilight sky. "Somebody up there must like me."

He dragged the greyhound back to the animal hospital, his mind reviewing the strangeness of the day. The business at his locker with Vilma and her friends crept back into his consciousness, and he felt a queasy sensation blossom in the pit of his stomach.

Had he been mistaken? he wondered as he pulled open the door. Had they suddenly switched to English from Portuguese? *No,* he thought, *no, I was definitely hearing Portuguese—and understanding it. But how is that possible?*

Hunter pranced into the cheerfully decorated lobby, his toenails happily clicking on the slick tile floor like tap shoes, excited to see Michelle, the veterinary assistant, standing there.

"So," she asked the big dog, hands on her hips, "did we have success?"

She stroked the dog's pointy snout and rubbed at his ears. The dog was in heaven as it pressed itself against her and gazed up lovingly.

"Well?" she asked again.

Aaron realized she was no longer speaking to the dog, and emerged from his thoughts.

"Sorry," he said. "Yes, the mission was a complete and total success. We'll probably need some heavy construction equipment to clean up after him, but he did what he had to do."

Michelle wrinkled her nose as she went around the corner of the reception desk. "Yuck. Remind me not to go out back for a while." She pulled a folder from a wall rack behind her and opened it. "I'll make a note for Dr. Kris, and our long-legged friend should be sprung tomorrow."

Aaron barely heard the girl, who was as close to a friend as he'd ever had. He was again lost in his thoughts about the impossibility of what had happened at school. There had to be a rational explanation. Maybe it had something to do with his headache.

"Earth to Corbet," he heard the girl say. Her hands covered her mouth to make it sound as though her voice were coming over a loudspeaker. "This is mission control, over. It appears that one of our astronauts is missing."

Aaron smiled and shook his head. "Sorry. It's been a long day and I'm wiped."

She smiled back and returned the folder to the rack on the wall. "It's cool. Just bustin' yuh," she said, pulling her colorfully dyed, shoulder-length hair away from her face. "Bad day at school or what?"

The two had started working at the clinic around the same time and got along quite well. Michelle had said that he reminded her of a boyfriend she'd once had: tall, dark, and brooding, the first of many to break her heart. She was older than he by five years, and explained often that her high school days were some of her most painful, so she fancied herself an expert on teen angst.

"You remember how it was, old lady," he said with a laugh that she reciprocated. "Let me get Hunter back into his cage so we can get out of here."

He hauled the greyhound out from around the counter, where he had been sniffing around a wastepaper basket, and toward the doors to the kennels in the back.

"Hey, Aaron," Michelle called after him.

He turned. "What do you want now?"

For a moment she seemed to be studying him. "You sure you're okay? Anything you want to talk about?"

The idea of sharing the bizarreness of his day was tempting, but he decided against it. The last thing he needed was Michelle thinking that not only was he "dark and brooding," but the equally appealing "psychotic" as well.

"I'm fine, really," he assured her. "Just tired is all."

He pushed through the door and led the greyhound to the kennel. It was a large room filled with cages of all sizes, big cages for the larger breeds and tiny cages for what Dr. Bufman lovingly referred to as the rat dogs. Aaron returned Hunter to his current accommodations, said hello to the other dogs, then went to the staff area where he kept his things. He removed the blue work shirt he wore over his T-shirt, and hung it on a hanger.

He was so tired he felt as though he were moving in slow motion. *Is this what it's like to get old? Just imagine what it'll feel like to be thirty,* he thought. He slung his bookbag over his shoulder and forced himself back through the kennel toward the lobby door, looking at his watch again. It was a quarter to nine. If he made it home by nine, had a quick bite and did the bare minimum on his assignments, maybe he could be in bed by ten thirty. Sleep: It sounded like a plan.

The image of a dark-skinned boy being viciously torn apart by angels appeared before his eyes, and he jumped, startled by the sudden flash of recollection.

Maybe I'll just skip the homework and get right to bed, he thought, a bit unnerved by the dream flashback. *Give the brain a chance to rest.*

He reached the lobby and as he rounded the reception desk, noticed a woman standing there with a German shepherd puppy at her heels. Michelle had a file in her hand and looked at him. From the expression on her face he had no doubt she was annoyed.

"This is Mrs. Dexter," she said, hitting the edge of the folder on the open palm of her hand. "Sheba is being spayed first thing in the morning. Mrs. Dexter was supposed to bring Sheba earlier but forgot."

Aaron closed his eyes for a moment and sighed. He could see his hopes of getting to bed at a reasonable time slipping away.

"I'm so sorry," Mrs. Dexter began. "I completely lost track of time and . . ." The dog had begun to sniff around the floor, straining against her leash, practically pulling the woman off balance.

Aaron stopped listening to the woman's excuses and set his bag down on the floor. He reached across the desk and took the folder from Michelle.

"You get out of here. I'll take care of this," he said.

"Are you sure?" Michelle asked, already taking her purse from the back of a chair. "I could stay a little longer but I've got this thing tonight and . . ."

Aaron shook his head. "I got it. Get out of here. You can owe me."

Michelle smiled briefly and moved around the counter. "Thanks, Aaron. Everything you need should be right there. Have a good night."

He waved as she went out the door, then returned his attention to the open folder. "Okay," he said, removing some papers from inside. "Fill these out for me, please."

Mrs. Dexter took the forms. She let go of the leash and let her dog explore the open lobby. "I'm really sorry about this," she said as she removed a pair of glasses from her purse and put them on. "I was hoping there'd still be someone here." She began to fill out the first form. "Lucky you, huh?"

Sheba approached him cautiously, tail wagging, ears back.

"Lucky me," he agreed as he held out his hand for the young dog to sniff. She licked it and he began to pat her.

It took twenty minutes for Mrs. Dexter to complete the appropriate paperwork and be on her way.

"Sheba will be fine," he reassured the teary-eyed owner as he opened the door to let her out. "The doctor will do her surgery first thing in the morning. You can call around noontime to find out how she did and when she can go home."

The woman squatted in the doorway and gave her dog a last hug and a kiss on the head.

"Thanks for everything," she said as she stood. "I'm sorry for keeping you so late."

Aaron felt a twinge of guilt. It was hard to be annoyed with anyone who showed so much love for a pet.

Sheba began to whine as she watched her master getting into the minivan without her.

"It's all right, girl," Aaron said as he gently tugged on the leash. "Let's get you set up for the night. We've got some lovely accommodations, and you certainly won't be lonely."

He led her through to the kennel. The smells of the other dogs must have been overwhelming, for she tucked her tail between her trembling legs and backed up against him.

"It's okay," he assured her—just as all hell broke loose.

Every dog in the kennel began to go wild, barking crazily,

lunging at the doors to their cages, digging furiously with their paws.

Sheba backed up even farther. She looked up at him nervously and then back to the misbehaving canines, as if to say, "What the hell's wrong with them?" He had no idea. He'd never seen them act like this. Maybe Sheba had gone into heat early, or perhaps shared a home with a more aggressive dog and the others were picking up its scent on her. She began to whimper pathetically and he reached down to stroke her head.

The barking didn't stop, in fact it intensified, and he felt his anger begin to rise. This was all he needed. He was already later than he expected, and now the whole place was going nuts. *What am I going to do?* he asked himself. *I certainly can't cage up this poor dog with the others acting like . . . like a bunch of animals.*

"Quiet," he yelled.

They continued their frenzy. Some of the upper cages had actually begun to rock back and forth from the insane activity within.

Sheba was cowering by the door, desperate to leave. He didn't blame her in the least.

"Quiet," Aaron tried again, voice louder and full of authority.

The shepherd pup started to scratch at the door, digging deep gouges in the wood. He grabbed her by the collar to pull her away from it. The frightened dog began to urinate on the floor—the floor he had already mopped as one of his final duties of the evening.

Aaron's head began to throb with the insane baying; the odor of urine wafting through the air made his stomach roil. He couldn't stand it anymore.

"Quiet, or I'll have you all put to sleep!" he shrieked, his enraged voice reverberating off the walls of the white-tiled room.

The room went completely silent. Each and every dog suddenly calm, as if frightened by his words.

As if they had understood what he had said.

It was close to eleven by the time he finally stepped through the door of his home. Aaron removed his key from the lock and gently closed the front door behind him.

He stopped in the hallway, closed his eyes, and breathed in deeply, wallowing in the quiet. He could actually feel his body beginning to shut down.

The dogs had given him no further trouble after his emotional outburst. There wasn't so much as a whimper as he got Sheba settled in and mopped up her accident. They must have sensed that he meant business. Still, it was kind of strange, how they reacted. Then again, what did he expect after the kind of day he'd had.

Aaron trudged toward the kitchen. He was disappointed that Gabriel wasn't around to greet him, but figured the dog had probably gone up to bed when his foster parents put Stevie down for the night. The dog kept a very cautious eye on the autistic child, as if knowing he was special and needed to be looked after.

The light was on over the stove and a small piece of note-paper was held to the metal hood by a magnet in the shape of a cat's head. The note from his foster mother told him that everyone had gone to bed, and that his supper was in the oven. The note also mentioned a little surprise for him in the dining room. That made him smile.

Using a potholder, he removed the foil-wrapped plate from the oven and proceeded into the dining room. As he sat down he noticed a blue envelope leaning against a chocolate cupcake with a candle stuck in it. He picked up the card, wondering if he was supposed to light the candle and sing "Happy Birthday" to himself. He doubted he had the energy.

The card depicted a young man's dresser covered in trophies for various sporting events, and said, "For a winning son." He opened the card and read something schmaltzy about the perfect boy growing into a man and rolled his eyes. Every year Lori bought the most sappy card she could find. He did the same for her birthday and Mother's Day. There was also a crisp new fifty-dollar bill stuck inside. Aaron sighed. He knew his foster parents couldn't afford this, but also knew it would be pointless to try to give it back. He'd tried before and they always insisted he keep it to buy himself something special.

He finished his dinner of meatloaf, mashed potatoes, and peas and was rinsing the dishes while mentally wrestling with the idea of what he was going to do next. Most of him just wanted to go to sleep, but the more studious part of him thought it best to at least attempt some homework.

Slowly he climbed the stairs to bed, leaning heavily on the rail, and popping the last of the cupcake into his mouth, his tired self busily shoving that academic part of his persona into a burlap sack. The door to Stevie's room at the top of the stairwell was ajar, and the light from a Barney nightlight streamed into the hall. He quietly stuck his head into the room to check on the child. Gabriel lay at the foot of the bed and began to wag his tail wildly when he saw Aaron. He crept carefully into the room and gave the dog's head a good rubbing.

Stevie moaned softly, deep in sleep, and Aaron pulled the covers up beneath his chin. He watched him for a moment, then gently touched the child's cheek before turning to leave.

At the door, he motioned with his head for Gabriel to follow. It was pretty much the same routine every evening. The dog would go to bed with Stevie, but once the child was asleep, he'd join Aaron for the night.

The big dog jumped down from the bed with a minimum of noise and headed down the hall. Watching Gabriel, Aaron fondly recalled when he had first seen the dog, tied up in a yard on Mal Street, his light yellow—almost white—coat of puppy fur covered with grease and mud. He was so tiny then, nothing like the moose he was today.

As he approached his own room, Aaron could hear the soft sounds of a television news broadcast coming from his parents' room across the hall. A timer would turn the television off at midnight. Talk about routine, Tom and Lori had been going to bed early and falling asleep in front of the news for as long as he could remember.

The door to his room was closed and he pushed it open, letting Gabriel in first. The dog hopped up onto the bed and stared at him with dark, vibrant eyes. His bright pink tongue lolled as he panted and his tail swung happily.

Aaron smiled as he closed the door. When he first brought the dog home, he was so small that he couldn't even get onto the bed without help. Now he couldn't keep the beast off it. He often wondered what fate would have befallen the puppy if he hadn't stolen him from the Mal Street yard under the cover of darkness. Rumors were that the rundown tenement housed members of one of Lynn's street gangs, that they stole dogs and used them to train their pit bulls for fighting. With his first gaze into Gabriel's soulful eyes, Aaron knew there was no way he could ever let anything bad happen to the dog. The two had been inseparable since.

Aaron kicked off his sneakers and practically fell on the bed. Never had he felt anything more glorious. His lids, heavy with fatigue, gradually began to close, and he could already feel his body prepare for sleep.

The dog still stood over him, his heavy panting gently rocking the bed like one of those coin-operated, sleazy motel, magic-finger beds seen in movies.

"What's up, Gabe?" he asked, refusing to open his eyes.

The dog bounded from the bed in response and began to root around the room. Aaron moaned. He knew what that meant. The dog was looking for a toy.

He prayed to the god of dog toys that Gabriel's search would come up empty but the ancient deity of cheap rubber and squeakers seldom heard his pleas. The eighty-pound dog leaped back up on the bed. Even though his eyes were shut, Aaron knew that Gabriel loomed above him with something in his mouth.

"What do you want, Gabriel?" he asked groggily, knowing full well what the dog's response would be.

It was no surprise when he felt a tennis ball thump onto his chest.

What was a surprise was when the dog answered his question.

"Want to play ball now," Gabriel declared in a very clear and precise voice.

Aaron opened his eyes and gazed up into the grinning face of the animal. There was no doubt now. The day's descent into madness was complete. He was, in fact, losing his mind.

CHAPTER THREE

Dr. Jonas seemed genuinely pleased to see him.

"You're not someone I'd expect to see waiting out front at eight thirty on a Friday morning, Aaron," the burly man said as he walked behind his desk, removed his tweed sports jacket, and hung it on a wooden coatrack stuck in the corner.

"How long has it been?" the psychiatrist asked, smiling warmly as he began to open the paper bag he'd carried in.

Aaron stood before the chair stationed in front of the doctor's desk. He glanced casually about the office. Little had changed since his last visit. Cream-colored walls, a framed Monet print bought in the gift shop of the Museum of Fine Arts—in a strange kind of way it felt comforting.

Dr. Michael Jonas had been his counselor after his placement with the Stanleys, and had done him a world of good. It was with his help that Aaron had learned to accept and cope with many of the curves life had seen fit to throw at him. The man had become a good friend and at the moment, Aaron was feeling a little guilty for not making more of an effort to keep in touch.

"I don't know, five years maybe?" he responded.

Jonas shook his shaggy head, smiling through his thick salt-and-pepper beard. "That long?" he mused as he removed a banana and a small bottle of orange juice from the bag. "Doesn't seem it, does it? But again, once you hit forty, the dinosaurs don't seem all that long ago." Jonas laughed at his own joke and sat down in the high-backed leather chair behind the sprawling oak desk. He grabbed the banana and juice and held them up to Aaron. "Do you want to share my breakfast? I'm sure I could find a fairly clean mug around here somewhere."

Aaron politely declined as he sat facing the doctor.

"Suit yourself," Jonas said. He twisted the metal cap off the juice and took a large gulp. "If you don't want breakfast, you must've skipped school for some other reason. What's going on, Aaron? What can I do for you?"

Aaron took in a deep breath and let it escape slowly, gathering his wits so as not to spew out the events of the past twenty-four hours in an incoherent babble. How exactly do you explain that you can suddenly understand foreign languages—and, oh yes, your dog has started to speak to you?

"You okay?" Jonas asked, starting to peel his banana. The man was smiling, but there was definitely a touch of concern in his tone.

Aaron shifted nervously in his seat. "I don't know," he answered with uncertainty.

"Why don't you tell me what's bothering you." Jonas broke off the top of the banana and popped the fruit into his waiting maw.

Aaron gripped the armrests tightly, sat back, and began to explain. "I'm not exactly sure what's happening . . . but I think I might be having some kind of breakdown."

The doctor took another swig of juice. "I doubt that very much," he said, "but if you want to explain, I'm all ears."

Aaron was very careful as he talked about what had happened at school the previous day, at the lockers with Vilma and her friends. He was sure to include that he had been experiencing a very bad headache just before he was suddenly able to understand their Portuguese. He decided to stop there, not yet wanting to broach the incident involving Gabriel.

Aaron had been staring at his sneakers through most of his explanation, and gradually looked up to meet Jonas's gaze as the psychiatrist finished the last of his banana.

"It's all right," Aaron said, again looking down at his feet. "If you want to call and get me a room up at Danvers State, I'll understand."

Jonas continued to chew as he picked up the fruit peel and threw it inside the empty paper bag. "This is interesting, Aaron," he said after swallowing. He wheeled his chair over to the side of his desk and tossed the bag into the trash barrel. "Very interesting."

"And I think . . . no, I know I could speak it if I had to," Aaron added, "and . . . and it's not just Portuguese." He thought of the conversations he'd had with his dog since last night. "Definitely not just Portuguese."

The doctor drank some more juice. "Let me get this straight," he said as he wiped the excess from his beard. "You had a headache and now you can understand and possibly speak foreign languages. A skill you've never had before. Is that what you're telling me?"

Aaron felt a flush of embarrassment bloom across his cheeks and leaned forward in his chair, studying his shoes. "I know it sounds really stupid but . . ."

"It doesn't sound stupid," Dr. Jonas said, *"but it does sound a little weird. Do you have any other symptoms?"*

Aaron looked up. "No. Do you think it has anything to do with my headache?"

The doctor had been smiling, but his smile gradually began to fade as Aaron spoke.

"Is . . . is there something wrong?" he asked.

Jonas reached over to a pile of papers at the corner of his desk and removed a yellow legal pad. "You understood what

I just said to you?" he asked, picking up a pen and writing something on the pad.

Aaron nodded. "Sure, why?"

"What exactly did I say?"

Aaron thought for a minute. "You said that what I was saying wasn't stupid, although it was weird and did I have any other symptoms."

Jonas stroked his beard. "I was speaking to you in Spanish, Aaron."

Aaron squirmed nervously in his chair. "But . . . but I don't know Spanish."

"You've never taken it in school?" Jonas asked. "Or had friends who spoke it?"

Aaron shook his head. "The only language I ever took in school was French, and I never got a grade higher than a C."

Jonas nodded and began to write again. Finished, he set his pen down on the pad and looked up. "Describe your headache to me, Aaron—but do it in Spanish."

Aaron rubbed at his temple. "In Spanish?" He smiled uneasily. "All right, here goes." Aaron opened his mouth and began to speak. *"It was like somebody was sticking a knife into my head."* He touched the top of his head. *"Right here. Like somebody put it through my skull into my brain. I've never had a headache like it, I can tell you that."*

He stopped, and a lopsided grin crept across his features. "How was that?" he asked, returning to English.

The doctor was shaking his head in disbelief. "Impressive," he said, failing to keep his growing interest in check.

Aaron leaned forward, eager to know why this was happening to him. "So you don't think I'm crazy or anything? You believe me, Doc?"

The desk chair creaked in protest as the doctor leaned back. He held the pen in one hand and was tapping it against the palm of the other. "I believe you. I just don't know what to make of it," he said thoughtfully. "Let's see. . . . "

Aaron watched as the big man wheeled his chair over to a bookcase against the wall on the other side of his desk. He disappeared as he bent down to take something from the bottom shelf. When he came up, he laid a large text on top of the desk. Aaron could not see what its subject was, and waited nervously as the doctor thumbed through the pages.

"If you . . . can tell me . . . what I'm saying to you . . . right now," he said, struggling with the complexity of the words he pulled from the book, *"I'll have no choice . . . but . . . to believe . . . the incredible."* Jonas looked up from the text and stared with eager eyes.

"I understood you perfectly," Aaron said. "It was Latin, right?"

The doctor slowly nodded, looking stunned.

"It looks as though we're both going to have to start to believe in the incredible," Aaron said.

Jonas's expression was that of a man who had just been witness to a miracle. His eyes bulged as he slowly closed the Latin text. "Aaron, I . . . I don't know what to say."

Aaron was growing a bit nervous. The doctor was staring at him, and he felt like a bug beneath a microscope. "Why do you think it happened?" he asked, to break the sudden silence. "How? . . ."

Jonas was shaking his head again as he combed his large fingers through his graying beard. "I have no idea, but the fact that you had such a powerful headache before this talent manifested suggests that the *how* is likely neurological."

"Neurological?" Aaron questioned, suddenly concerned. "Like there's something wrong with my brain—like a tumor or something?"

The psychiatrist leaned forward in his chair again. "Not necessarily," he said, stressing the words with his large hands. "I've heard stories of neurological disorders that caused individuals to gain unique abilities."

"Like understanding and speaking foreign languages?" Aaron suggested.

Jonas nodded. "Exactly. The case I'm thinking of involved a man from Michigan, I believe. After suffering severe head trauma in a skating accident, he found himself able to calculate the most complex math problems in his head. He hadn't even finished high school, never mind classes in mathematical theory."

"So you think that something like that might have happened to me?" Aaron asked the psychiatrist.

The doctor pondered the possibility. "Maybe something happened inside your brain that's caused this unique capability to develop."

Jonas grabbed his pen again and furiously began to take notes. "I have a friend over at Mass General, a neurologist. We could talk to him—after we've done some testing of our own of course and—"

The sudden rapping at the office door made Aaron jump.

The doctor pulled up his sleeve and glanced at his watch. "Damn it," he said with a hiss. "My nine thirty must be here."

Aaron's heart still pounded in his chest from the sudden scare. He watched Dr. Jonas step out from behind his desk and move toward the door.

"Excuse me for a moment, Aaron," he said as he opened the door and stepped into the lobby.

Alone, Aaron's mind began to race. *What if there is something wrong with me—something wrong with my brain?* He began to bite at his thumbnail. Maybe it would be wise to make an appointment with the family physician just in case.

He thought about missing another day of school and felt himself begin to panic. This business couldn't be coming at a worse time. He'd be hearing from colleges shortly and needed his grades to reflect how serious he was about getting into the schools of his choice. He wondered if colleges looked at the number of absences before making their acceptance decisions.

The door opened. "Sorry about that, kid," he said, moving behind his desk. "Listen, I'm booked solid for the entire day, but why don't you come by tomorrow and see me. How would that be?"

Aaron stood. "It's Saturday. Is that all right?"

Jonas nodded. "Sure, I was going to be in tomorrow anyway. Why don't you stop by—say early afternoon? We can do a few more tests before I give my buddy at Mass General a ring."

Aaron agreed with a slight nod and walked to the door. "Thanks for seeing me this morning, Doc," he said, a hand on the doorknob. "I'm sorry it's been so long."

Dr. Jonas was removing a file from inside a cabinet beside his desk. "No problem, Aaron," he said as he opened the file. "It was good to see you."

Aaron had opened the door and was about to leave when Jonas spoke again to him, bringing him back into the office. The man was standing, looking calm and confident.

"Relax," the psychiatrist said. "We'll work this out, I promise. See you tomorrow."

As he stepped out into the morning sunshine, Aaron could not shake the gnawing feeling that something was suddenly not right with his world.

Something over which he had no control.

* * *

Aaron crossed the street and stepped over the low, dark green, pipe fence that encircled Lynn Common.

He'd arrived early to his former psychiatrist's office, so he had parked on the other side of the common and waited there. He'd always enjoyed this place, with its oak trees and unkept grass. Even though it was a bit rundown, it still had its charms. Besides the beach, it was one of his favorite places to walk Gabriel when the fickle New England weather cooperated.

He walked across the expanse of green trying to clear his head. As he reached the middle of the open area, he remembered an odd bit of Lynn trivia: the common had been built in the shape of a shoe. The voice of his junior high history teacher, Mr. Frost, droned on in his brain about the history of the city.

Settled in 1629, Lynn ultimately became a major producer of shoes. Though the construction of the common was first begun in 1630, the present-day sections were shaped into the approximate proportions of a shoe during the nineteenth century, the larger area being the sole, and the smaller, the heel. At that moment, Aaron was inside the sole.

He'd always wanted to take a helicopter ride over the city to verify that the common was indeed in the shape of a shoe. Mr. Frost had talked about a book at the library that contained an aerial shot of the common. Since he had planned to finish out the day at the library anyway, perhaps he'd take the time to look it up, he thought as he continued on a path to his car.

Aaron suddenly shuddered, as if someone had just slipped an ice cube along his spine. The strange feeling that he was being watched rolled over him in waves, and he stopped to look around.

He glanced at the ancient bandstand squatting in the center of the sole. The shabby structure was once used for summer band concerts, but was now more of a hangout for kids skipping school or people passing time between unemployment checks. Today it was empty.

He continued to look about, and there, just where the heel began, he could make out a figure standing over one of the "Keep Lynn Beautiful" trash barrels. There was a shopping cart parked near the man. *Probably collecting cans for the deposit money,* Aaron thought as he continued on his way, studying the lone figure in the distance. Yes, he was sure of it. The man was staring at him. Aaron could actually feel his gaze upon him.

"Probably deciding whether he should run over and hit me up for change," he muttered beneath his breath as he reached the other side of the common.

Aaron stepped over the low fence. His metallic blue, '02 Toyota Corolla was parked directly across the street, and he waited for an opportunity to cross. As he fished his keys from his pocket he thought about what he would do for the rest of the day. He had skipped school, but it didn't mean that he was going to shirk all his academic responsibilities. He'd spend the afternoon in the library beginning his research for Ms. Mulholland's senior English paper, a paper required for graduation. He hoped a look around the library would help him decide on a topic. Ideas danced around in his head: the duality of good and evil in the works of Edgar Allan Poe, Herman Melville and religious symbolism, Shakespeare's use of—

The hair at the back of his neck suddenly stood on end. His senses screamed. Someone was behind him.

Aaron whirled around and came face to face with the man he'd seen at the barrel far across the common. The old man was dressed in a filthy overcoat, pants worn at the knees, and sneakers. The faint smell of body odor and alcohol wafted off him, and Aaron almost gagged on the unpleasant stench.

He was taken aback, not sure of what to do as the man began to lean toward him. *What the hell is he doing?*

The man appeared to be smelling him. He moved in close to Aaron and sniffed at his face, his hair, his chest, and then he stepped back. He nodded, as if in response to a question to which only he was privy.

"Can . . . can I help you with something?" Aaron stammered.

The man responded, speaking in a language Aaron had

never heard before, a language he somehow sensed had not been uttered by anyone in a very long time.

"Can you understand the tongue of the messenger, boy?" asked the old man in the arcane dialect.

Aaron answered in kind. *"Yes,"* he said, the strange words feeling incredibly odd as they rolled off his tongue. *"I can understand you . . . but I don't understand the question."*

The old man continued to stare, his gaze even more intense. Aaron could have sworn that he saw what appeared to be a single flame dancing in the center of each ancient eye, but knew that it was probably just a trick of the light.

"You answer my question as you speak," the man responded, still using the bizarre-sounding language, *"and what you are becomes obvious to me."*

"What . . . what I am?" Aaron asked. *"I don't understand what . . ."*

The strange old man shuffled closer. *"Nephilim,"* he whispered as he raised a dirty hand to point. *"You are Nephilim."*

The word reverberated through Aaron's skull and a sudden panic gripped him. He had to get away. He had to get away from this strange old man, from that word. He had to get away as fast as he could.

"I really have to be going," he muttered as he slipped his key into the lock and hauled open the car door.

Aaron got inside his car and locked it. He couldn't remember a time when the need to run was so strong. He put the key into the ignition and turned the engine over. As he put the car in drive, he chanced a look at the old man. He was still standing there, staring in at him with those intense eyes.

Aaron turned away and pulled out into traffic. He glanced in the rearview mirror at the old man receding in the distance. He continued to stand there, watching him drive away, mouth moving, repeating a single word. Aaron knew what he was saying.

The old man was saying "Nephilim," over and over again. *Nephilim.*

Aaron splashed cold water on his face and stared at his dripping features in the water-speckled mirror of the Lynn Public Library's restroom.

What the hell is going on? he thought, studying his reflection. *What's happening to me?*

There was fear in the face that looked back from the mirror. *What was that with the old man?* he wondered for the thousandth time. *What did he mean by the language of messengers—and what's a Nephilim?* His thoughts raced feverishly.

He pulled some paper towels from the dispenser on the wall and wiped the water from his face. As he reached to the side of the sink for the restroom key, attached to an unusually large piece of wood, he noticed that his hand was shaking. Aaron snatched up the key and clenched the wood tightly in his grasp.

"Gotta calm down," he told himself in a whisper. "The

old guy was just crazy, probably done the exact same routine to ten other people today. What are you getting so worked up over? You know this city is loaded with kooks."

There was a gentle knock at the bathroom door. He took a deep breath, composed himself, and opened the door. An old man was standing there with a coat slung over his arm.

"You done in there?" he asked with a nervous smile.

Aaron did the best that he could to return the pleasantries as he stepped out of the restroom. "Yeah, sorry I took so long," he said as he handed the old-timer the block of wood with the key attached.

"No problem," the old man said as he took the key and moved into the bathroom. "Just wanted to make sure you didn't fall in."

Aaron turned as the door closed and saw that the man was chuckling. He didn't much feel like it, but found himself laughing at the man's good-natured dig anyway. "Wouldn't that have been the icing on the cake if I had," he said to himself as he climbed the white marble steps from the basement to the first floor.

He found an empty table far in the corner of one of the reading rooms and slung his jacket over the back of a chair. He wasn't sure how much he'd be able to accomplish now, but at least he had to make an attempt. Besides, he needed something to distract him from the bizarreness that seemed to be following him of late. He had brought a notebook in with him and removed a pen from its front pocket.

He settled in and spent hours perusing books on a number of different authors and literary subjects, searching for something that piqued his interest enough for a research paper. He'd pretty much made up his mind to go with the topic of good and evil's duality in the works of Poe, when he realized that he had zoned out, and had been doodling in the border of his notepad, writing something over and over with a variety of spellings.

Nefellum. Nefilem. Nifillim. Nephilem. Nephilim.

Aaron tore out the page and stared at it. *What does it mean? Why can't I just forget about it?* he wondered, reviewing each of the spellings.

He got up from his chair and headed toward the computer room, which was crowded, so he continued into the reference area of the library. The first book that he pulled from the shelves was a *Webster's New World College Dictionary.* He placed the large book down onto a table and began to look for the word, trying all the incarnations he had written. He found nothing.

Maybe it doesn't mean a thing, he thought as he returned the dictionary to where he had found it. *Maybe it's just a nonsense word made up by a crazy person, and I'm equally nuts for giving it this much attention.*

Aaron decided that he had already wasted enough time and energy on the old man's rants, and headed back to his table to begin an outline for his paper. If anything could be salvaged from this train wreck of a day, at least he could get a head start on that.

He crumpled up the piece of paper in his hand and headed back to the reading room.

But the word continued to jump around in his head, as if it had a life of its own and was taunting him. Nephilim.

Aaron casually glanced into the library's computer room again as he passed. This time a computer was free.

Seizing the opportunity to satisfy his curiosity, he walked in and sat down at one of the computers. This would be it, the mystery word's last chance to mean something. If he didn't find it here, he would purge it from his mind forever and never think of it again. He signed in with the library's password and called up a search engine. The screen appeared and, choosing one of the varied spellings, he typed in the mystery word. He hit the Enter key and held his breath. The page cleared and then some information appeared.

"Do you mean Nephilim?" asked the message that appeared on top of the new page.

He maneuvered the mouse and brought the arrow over to the revised spelling, clicked once and waited as the new pages loaded.

Aaron was startled to see how many sites appeared with some kind of connection to the word. *So much for it being nonsense,* he thought as he scrolled down the page, reading a bit about each of the sites. There were multiple sites about a rock group, some about a role-playing game, all using the name Nephilim, but none gave a meaning.

A site that specialized in religious mythologies finally caught his attention. *Is that it?* he wondered, as the page began to upload. *Does it have something to do with religion?* In that case, it was no wonder he had no familiarity with it. He'd never been much of a religious person, and neither had the Stanleys.

The site appeared to be a who's who of people, places, and things from the Bible, and the first thing he saw was a definition that he eagerly read.

> *The biblical term* NEPHILIM, *which in Hebrew means "the fallen ones" or "those who fell," refers to the offspring of angels and mortal women mentioned in Genesis 6: 1–4. A fuller account is preserved in the apocryphal Book of Enoch, which recounts how a group of angels left heaven to mate with women, and taught humanity such heinous skills as the art of war.*

Aaron sat back in his chair, stunned. *Offspring of angels and mortal women,* he read again. "What the hell does that have to do with me?" he muttered, moving closer to the computer screen.

Somebody coughed behind him, and he turned to see four people waiting in the doorway of the computer room. A heavyset kid with a bad case of acne, wearing an *X-Men* T-shirt, tapped the face of his Timex watch and glared at him.

Aaron looked back to the screen and quickly read a bit more before closing the site and signing out. He removed his pen from his pocket and on the wrinkled piece of paper where he had written his various attempts at the mystery word, he crossed out the incorrect spellings leaving only the correct one.

Nephilim.

Sighing heavily, he returned to his seat and his books in the other room. He sat down with every intention of working on his paper, but found that he could not concentrate, his thoughts stalled on the story of human women having babies with angels. A shiver of unease ran up and down his spine as he chillingly recalled the subject of his recurring dream. Again he saw the boy attacked by the winged creatures dressed in golden armor. It was too much of a coincidence to ignore.

He got to his feet and snatched up the notepad from the table. He had to find out more. It was as if something was compelling him to dig deeper. *Maybe there's some way I can maneuver this into a research subject,* he mused.

Aaron used another computer in the lobby of the building to search the library's inventory, and found that most of what he was looking for was kept in a separate room off the reference area.

He wrote the titles down on his notepad and began his search. In a book called *The Lost Books of Eden,* Aaron learned more about the Book of Enoch. It was an apochryphal book of the Old Testament, written in Hebrew about a century before the birth of Christ. The original version was lost near the end of the fourth century, and only fragments remained until Bruce the Traveler brought back a copy from Abyssinia in 1773, probably made from a version known to the early Greek fathers.

What followed were some passages from the ancient text of Enoch, and what Aaron read summed up all that he had learned so far:

> . . . that there were angels who consented to fall from heaven that they might have intercourse with the daughters of the earth. For in those days the sons of men having multiplied, there were born to them daughters of great beauty. And when the angels, or sons of heaven, beheld them, they were filled with desire; wherefore they said to one another: "Come let us choose wives from among the race of man, and let us beget children."

Aaron was amazed. He'd never heard of such a thing. His knowledge of angels was limited to what was often found on holiday cards or at the tops of Christmas trees—beautiful women in flowing, white gowns, or children with tiny wings, and halos perched on their heads.

Fascinated, he was reaching for the list of books he'd yet

to examine when again he was overcome with the feeling of being observed. He quickly turned in his chair, half expecting to see the crazy old man pointing his gnarly finger and calling him Nephilim over and over again—but was shocked to see Vilma Santiago.

The girl gave him the sweetest of smiles and meekly came into the room. "I thought that was you," she said with only the slightest hint of an accent.

"Yep, it's me," he said nervously as he stood up from his chair. *"I'm just doing some, y'know, research and stuff for Ms. Mulholland's research paper and . . ."*

Vilma looked at him strangely and he stopped talking, afraid that his nose had started to run, or something equally gross and embarrassing had happened.

"Is . . . is something wrong?" he asked, tempted to reach up and quickly rub his nose.

The girl shook her head and grinned from ear to ear. "No, nothing is wrong," she said happily. "I just didn't know that you could speak Portuguese."

He was confused at first, wondering how she could have known about his sudden power, when he realized what he had done.

"Was I . . . was I just speaking to you in Portuguese?"

She giggled and covered her mouth with a delicate hand. "Yes, yes, you were, and quite well, I might add. Where did you learn it?"

He had no idea how to answer. Aaron shrugged his shoulders. "Just picked it up, I guess. I'm pretty good with languages."

Vilma nodded. "Yes, you are."

There was a moment of uncomfortable silence, and then she looked down at the table and the books he was reading.

"That's just some stuff I'm looking through to get ideas. I haven't decided yet, but I might . . ."

She picked up a book called *Angels: From A to Z* and began to thumb through it. "I love this one," she said as she flipped the pages. "Everything you could want to know about angels and even a section at the back of the book that lists movies about angels." She looked up from the open book in her hands and squinted her eyes in deep thought. "I really think this one might be my favorite."

Vilma placed the book back onto the table and began to rummage through the other volumes. "I love anything to do with angels." She reached into her shirt and removed something delicate on the end of a gold chain. "Look at this."

Aaron looked closer to see that it was an angel. "That's really pretty," he said, looking from the golden angel to her. At the moment, the necklace wasn't the only thing he found pretty.

"Thanks," she said, putting the jewelry back inside her shirt. "I just love them, they make me feel safe—y'know?"

Aaron could have been knocked over with a feather—

angel or otherwise. He just stood there and smiled as he watched the girl go through the books he had pulled from the shelves. It must have been some weird form of synchronicity, he imagined. *What are the odds?* It boggled his already addled brain.

"Is this what you are planning to do your paper on?" Vilma asked excitedly, interrupting his thoughts.

"I don't know . . . yeah, maybe," he stammered, unsure of his answer. "Yeah, maybe I will. Seems like it might be really interesting."

She beamed as she began to talk about the topic. "It's fascinating. When I was little and lived in Brazil, my auntie would tell me stories of how the angels would visit the villages in the jungles disguised as travelers and . . ."

Vilma suddenly stopped her story and looked away from him. "I'm sorry for babbling, it's just that I find it so very interesting, and to get a chance to talk about it with somebody else, well, I really enjoy it is all."

She seemed embarrassed, going suddenly quiet as she pulled at the sleeves of her denim jacket.

"It's all right, really," Aaron said with a smile that he hoped wasn't too goofy. He snatched his notepad off the table. "Maybe, if you're not too busy, you could help me with my research."

Her eyes grew wide in excitement.

"The stories from Brazil, the ones your aunt told you?

They would probably be really cool to talk about in the paper, if you didn't mind helping me."

He couldn't believe what he was doing. Vilma Santiago, the hottest girl in the Lynn public schools, and he was asking her to help him with his research paper. *What an absolute idiot,* he berated himself.

"That would be really fun," she said, nodding her head in agreement. "I even have some other books you could use."

Aaron was in complete and utter shock. The girl of his dreams had agreed to help him with his paper, and actually seemed to be excited about doing it. He had no idea what to say next, afraid that if he opened his mouth to speak, something completely stupid would spill out and he'd ruin everything.

Vilma was silent also, nervously looking at the books on the table then back to him. She glanced at her watch.

"Well, I have to catch the bus," the girl said, walking toward the doorway. "Maybe we can talk some more about your paper in school Monday—you *will* be in school Monday, won't you?" She smirked.

He couldn't believe it. She actually noticed that he was absent today. Maybe there was something to what she had said to her friends yesterday. Maybe she actually did think he was cute.

"I'll be there," he said. "All day in fact."

She laughed and gave him a small wave as she stepped

out of the room. "I'll see you Monday, Aaron. Have a good weekend."

He could do nothing but stand there, numbed with disbelief. It was almost enough to make him forget all about the disturbing dreams, his strange new linguistic skills, and the cryptic ramblings of a crazy old man.

Almost.

CHAPTER FOUR

Samuel Chia lay upon his bed, twisted in sheets of the finest silk, and dreamed of flying. Of all that was lost to him, he missed that the most.

It was not true sleep by human standards, but it was a way for him to remember a time precious to him, the time before his fall.

Sam rolled onto his back and opened his eyes to the new day. He did not need to check a clock to tell him the hour; he knew it to be precisely eight A.M., for that was when he wished to rise.

He lay quietly and listened to the sounds of Hong Kong outside and far below his penthouse apartment. If he so wished, he could listen in on the conversations of the city's inhabitants as they lived out their drastically short existences. But today he had little interest.

Sam rose from his bed and padded naked across the mahogany floor to stand in front of the enormous floor-to-ceiling windows that looked out over the city. A Chinese junk, its sails unfurled, caught his attention as it cruised gracefully across the emerald green water of Victoria Bay. He had lived in many places in his long life on this planet, but none brought him as much solace as this place. China spoke to him. It told him that everything would be all right, and on most days, he believed that to be true.

He pressed his forehead against the thick glass and allowed himself to feel the cold of its surface. His naked skin responded with prickled gooseflesh, and although he reveled in the human experience, everyday he longed for what he once had, for what was lost when he refused to take a side in the Great War.

His head still pressed against the window, Sam opened his eyes and gazed at the panorama before him.

Yes, he longed for the glory that was once his, but each day this place—this wondrous sight sought to seduce him with its vitality. A distraction that sometimes made it easier to accept his fate.

Sometimes.

Sam was slipping into his black silk robe, enjoying the sensation upon his pale, sculpted flesh, when the phone began to chirp.

He knew who was calling. Not from any innate psychic

ability, but because she called each morning at this very time.

Joyce Woo was the human woman he allowed to manage his various business affairs, including his nightclubs, casinos, and restaurants.

Sam strolled from the bedroom to the chrome-and-tile kitchen and let the machine pick up. He decided to play a little game—to see if he could guess the problems she was calling to report. What trivial piece of nonsense would she choose to annoy him with this time? he wondered: an unexpected shortage of truffles at his French restaurant perhaps, or the local constabulary requiring increased compensation for their lack of interest in certain illicit activities performed at his clubs, or maybe she was finally calling to confess that she'd been skimming off the top of his earnings for the last nine months.

Sam popped a cork on a bottle of Dom Perignon and drank from it as he listened to the message.

"Good morning, Mr. Chia. This is Joyce," said a woman's voice in Cantonese.

He toasted the incoming call with the bottle.

"There was an incident at the Pearl Club last night that may require you to speak with the chief of police. I can give you more details when you come into the office this morning, but I wanted you to be aware."

He could hear her turn the page of a pad of paper where she had written her notes.

"And be reminded that you have a two o'clock conference with the zoning committee about the Pier Road project."

Believing that she had finished, he walked through the kitchen, bottle in hand, toward the bathroom. But she began to speak again. He paused in the hall to listen.

"Oh yes," she said, "an old friend of yours—a Mr. Verchiel, stopped by the office this morning. He said he will only be in town for a short time and hoped the two of you could get together."

"Verchiel," he whispered. The bottle dropped from his hand to the floor, shattering and spilling the expensive contents onto the black and white tiles.

"He said that he will be in touch," Joyce said from the machine. "There are a few other items, but we can discuss them when you get here. Good morning, sir."

The line disconnected and still he didn't move.

Verchiel.

Sam Chia bounded to his bedroom and threw open the doors of the heavy wooden armoire. He shed his robe and pulled out clothes. There would be no time for a shower today and he would not be going into the office.

He had to leave Hong Kong. It was as simple as that. If Verchiel had found him, then there was no doubt that the Powers had come to China. And if that were the case, then none of his ilk was safe.

Sam finished buttoning his white cotton shirt and began

to tuck its tails inside his pants. He cinched the brown leather belt around his waist.

He thought briefly about contacting the others, to warn them of the Powers' presence, but decided against it for it was likely already too late.

He slipped his bare, delicate feet into a pair of Italian loafers and donned a navy blue sports jacket.

He would go to Europe; France would suffice. He would stay in Paris until Verchiel and his dogs left China. Joyce could manage his affairs until he returned.

Sam placed his billfold inside his coat pocket and picked up the phone to summon his driver. He would go to the airport, charter a plane, and contact Joyce once in flight.

"Are you going out, Samchia?" asked a voice from somewhere in the room.

Startled, Sam dropped the phone and spun around to face the voice.

"How disappointing," said the man in the gray trench coat standing in the living room in front of the sixty-inch flat-screen television. "After we've spent all this time searching for you."

There was a small, dirty child with him who pressed its unwashed face against the smoothness of the television screen and licked eagerly at his reflection.

"I'm sorry, do you prefer being called by your monkey name—Samuel Chia?" Verchiel asked as he slid his hands inside his coat pockets and began to slowly advance toward him. The child followed, heeling obediently at his side.

"What do you want?" Sam asked as the man approached.

Verchiel's dark eyes roamed about the luxurious living quarters taking in every extravagant detail.

"Did you think that these would hide you from me?" he asked, pointing to a series of arcane symbols painted on the penthouse walls. To the human eye they appeared as decoration, but in actuality, they were much more than that.

The feral child had hopped up onto Sam's leather coach, jumping from foot to foot, as he muttered happily to himself in a singsong voice.

"The spell of concealment must have gone stale with all the recent changes here," Verchiel said, making reference to the recent shift in Chinese government. "My hound caught scent of you as soon as we arrived." He patted the child's head affectionately as he passed the sofa. "You live like a king amongst the animals," the pale-skinned man said as he fixed his bottomless black gaze upon Sam. "For this you abandoned Paradise?"

Verchiel's words stung like the barbed end of a whip's lash.

"You know that's untrue, Verchiel. I left because I did not want to choose sides. I loved the Morningstar, as I loved all my brethren, but to question the Almighty—I could think of no other solution but to flee." Sam lowered his head, disgraced by his admission. Even after all this time, his actions shamed him.

"A coward by your own admission," Verchiel said with a snarl as he moved closer. "If only the others could be so honest."

The phone began to ring again, and Sam watched Verchiel's attention turn to the device as the recorded message played out and Joyce began to speak.

"Joyce again, sir. Mr. Dalton from the licensing board just called and asked if you could reschedule Monday's meeting to—"

A blast of searing white light erupted from Verchiel's hand and melted the phone into nothing more than sputtering, black plastic slag. Startled, the child leaped from the sofa and ran to hide, as if sensing the violence that was sure to follow.

"The sound of their voices," Verchiel said, his right hand gesturing toward his ear, "like the chattering of animals. It annoys me to no end." Verchiel glided closer. "How do you stand it?"

Sam clenched his fists. Anger unlike any he had ever experienced coursed through his body. Perhaps he *had* spent too much time among the humans, he thought. Their rabid emotions had obviously begun to rub off on him.

"I'll ask you again, why have you come here?"

Verchiel cocked his head to one side. "Is it not obvious,

brother?" he asked. "Have you not been awaiting me since your fall?"

"Yes," he hissed, "but it's been years—thousands of years."

Verchiel shook his head as he replied. "A second, an hour, a millennium; increments of time that mean nothing to the Powers," he said with a cold indifference. "You have sinned against the Allfather, and time does not change that fact."

Sam began to back away. "Haven't I suffered enough?" he asked. "My self-imposed exile on this world has taught me that—"

Verchiel's hand shot up into the air in a gesture to silence him. "Cease your mewling; I do not wish to hear it." The leader of the Powers pointed toward the windows behind him. "You sound like one of them." There was revulsion in his voice.

Sam knew it was probably for naught, but if there was anything he learned from living among humans, it was that it didn't hurt to try. "But isn't it enough that I have been denied the voice of my Father, that my true aspect is but a shadow of my former glory? Does this not count for anything?" He touched his chest as he continued his plea. "You may not believe it, but I have suffered."

Verchiel again looked about the opulent living space. A cruel grin began to form on his pale white features as he fixed Sam with his icy stare.

"Suffered, have you?" he asked as he began to spread his arms. "Your suffering hasn't even begun."

Sam experienced a strange sense of elation mixed with sheer terror as he watched the enormous wings erupt from Verchiel's back.

I once had wings as mighty, he remembered with overwhelming sadness. Wings that could have taken him away from this place, allowed him to flee the judgment of Verchiel. But that was long, long ago, and what were once mighty, were now nothing more than an atrophied shadow of their former glory.

Verchiel began to rhythmically move his wings and the penthouse was suddenly filled with winds as strong as tropical storms.

"Verchiel, please," Sam pleaded, just before a crystal ashtray hit him in the face. It opened a bleeding gash above his right eye.

Sam's body went limp and he ceased to struggle against the currents for a brief moment. He was picked up by the powerful gale and hurled backward, pinned against the picture windows. As he slammed against the glass, the sound of something cracking filled his ears, and he wondered if it was the window behind him or his bones.

Verchiel's wings beat the air with ferocious abandon, their furious movement a ghostly blur.

"There is no mercy for what you have done, Samchia!" Verchiel shrieked over the pounding of the air. "Your time has come, as it will come for all the others who have fallen from His grace!"

Sam tried to pull himself away from the window, but the strength of the wind was too great. He wanted to speak, to scream out that he was truly sorry for his sins, but the blood from his head wound streamed down his face into his mouth, silencing him. He had never even seen his own blood, but now it was filling his mouth with its foul taste.

The inch-thick pane of window glass behind him began to crack and spiderweb across its surface. Windows that had been built to withstand powerful storms from the Pacific Ocean were no match for the power of Verchiel.

Again Sam struggled to speak. "Verchiel . . . ," he managed to bellow above the sounds of his brother's merciless wings.

Verchiel continued his advance, wings flapping faster and faster still. "I can't hear you!" he screamed in response.

Sam yelled all the louder. "Tell Him—tell Him that I'm sorry." He could see the look of revulsion on Verchiel's face, and knew his words of repentance were heard.

A heavy chrome kitchen chair tumbled away from the table, and as if made of tin, was propelled through the air toward him.

Sam closed his eyes on the horrible visage of Verchiel, his wings unmercifully assaulting the air. His time was at an end, of this he was certain. What he had feared most since falling to Earth was finally to claim him.

Samuel Chia, formerly Samchia of the Heavenly Host,

willed his mind elsewhere, to a time before the war, before impossible choices, before the fall.

The chrome projectile did not strike him directly, but smashed into the window to the left of him, shattering the glass, allowing it to give way beneath the turbulent force of Verchiel's wings.

Within a twinkling shower of razor-sharp glass and debris, Sam fell yet again.

And as he descended to his end, he dreamed.

He dreamed of flying.

Gabriel trotted happily into the living room where the Stanleys had assembled for Chinese takeout and the weekly Friday night movie rental. He was proudly holding a purple stuffed toy in his mouth.

Aaron sat on the floor with Stevie building a multicolored tower with Duplo blocks. Occasionally he looked up at the television to see what Mr. Schwarzenegger was blowing up. The fact that this was at least the third time his foster dad had rented the movie in the last six months didn't bother him. The night was all about distraction, anything to keep from thinking about the strange incidents of the last two days. Except for the conversation with Vilma Santiago, he wished he could forget them completely.

The dog dropped the purple toy before Aaron and it rolled to topple the Duplo tower.

"Gabriel," Aaron said, annoyed, as he batted the toy aside and attempted to right the structure.

"Play with Goofy Grape now," Gabriel demanded with a wag of his thick, muscular tail.

Aaron ignored him and helped the child select some more blocks to fortify the tower.

Gabriel lunged forward and snatched up the toy with his mouth. He gave it a ferocious shake and let it fly. The stuffed toy bounced off young Stevie's head and landed among the piles of unused blocks.

"Goofy Grape now," the dog said even louder.

Aaron glared at the animal. "No Goofy Grape," he said sternly, referring to the toy that he had nicknamed because it resembled an enormous grape with a face. "I'm playing with Stevie now. Go lie down."

He could feel the dog's intense stare upon him, as if he were attempting to use mind powers to sway his decision. Aaron didn't bother to look up, hoping the dog would eventually grow tired and go away.

Gabriel abruptly turned and quickly strolled from the room.

Good, Aaron thought, connecting a blue block to a yellow. He didn't want to hear the dog talking tonight. To anyone else it was typical dog noise, a series of whines, growls, and barks, but to Aaron it was a language—a language he could easily understand. Tonight he wanted it to be like it used to be. A bark, an excited wag of the tail—that was all the conversation he really needed from his four-legged friend.

From the couch Tommy Stanley let out a happy guffaw in response to one of the movie hero's patented catch phrases.

"No one says 'em like Arnold," his foster father said aloud, a critical observation about the art of action films. "Your Van Dammes, Seagals—they're all well and good with the fightin' and blowin' up crap, but nobody delivers the goods like *Ahnold*." He said the name with a mock Austrian accent and then went back to watching the film, sucked into the cinematic world of a one-man army out to rescue his little girl from the bad guys.

Aaron heard the sound of toenails clicking across the kitchen linoleum toward the living room, and then a strange grunting sound. He didn't even have to see what the dog was bringing from his toy box; he knew just from the sound. Squeaky Pig was on its way.

Gabriel came around the corner, a pink stuffed pig clutched in his maw. With his muscular jaws he squeezed the body of the pig repeatedly, and it emitted a sound very much like that of a pig grunting.

As before, the dog approached and let the toy fall to the floor.

"Squeaky Pig better," he said with a hint of excitement in his gruff-sounding language. *"Play with Squeaky Pig."*

Aaron felt his temper rising. He was angry with the day and all the stuff that had happened, angry with the dog for reminding him that things are not how they used to be, angry with himself for being angry.

"He's pretty vocal tonight," Lori said from the recliner, looking up from her book. When she had seen what movie her husband brought back from the video store, she had gone upstairs to get out her latest romance novel. "Does he need to go out or something?"

The dog is being "vocal," he thought. *If you only knew the half of it.*

"No," he said, giving Gabriel the evil eye. "He doesn't need to go out, he's just being a pain in the butt."

Gabriel flinched as if he'd been struck. He blinked his soulful, brown eyes repeatedly and lowered his ears flat against his skull.

"Not pain in the butt," the dog grumbled as he began to back from the room, his tail lowered and partially stuck between his legs. *"Just wanted to play with Aaron. Bad dog. Go lie down. Bad dog."*

He turned and sadly slunk from the room.

Gabriel's words stung. *How could I be so cruel?* Aaron thought disgustedly. Here he was with the unique ability to understand exactly what the dog wanted—to be played with, to be shown some attention—and he was so caught up in his own problems that he couldn't be bothered to give in to the dog's simple request. *I ought'a be ashamed.*

"Gabriel," he called out. Aaron had to call for him two

more times before the dog finally responded, peeking around the doorframe.

"C'mere," he said, patting the floor with his hand and smiling. "Come over here."

Gabriel bounded into the room tail wagging, and began to lick Aaron's face excitedly.

"Gabriel not pain in butt, yes?" he asked between licks.

"No," Aaron answered, taking the dog's blockhead in his two hands and looking directly into his brown eyes. "You're not a pain in the butt; you're a good boy."

"I'm a good boy," the dog happily repeated, and began to lick his face again.

Gabriel plopped his large body down beside Aaron and was having his tummy rubbed when Stevie looked up from his blocks. Aaron noticed the child's stare and smiled.

"Hey there, little man, what's up?" he asked the autistic child.

The child's change of expression could be described like the sun burning through a thick haze of storm clouds. His usually blank face became animated as his eyes twinkled with the light of awareness. A smile so bright and wide spread across Stevie's face that Aaron was genuinely warmed by its intensity.

"Bootiful," Stevie said, holding out his hand.

"Stevie?" Lori questioned, her paperback falling to the floor. "Tommy, look at Stevie."

But the sound of his son's voice had already pulled Tom away from the movie. They both slid from their seats to the floor and watched as their child gently touched Aaron's cheek with a tiny hand, a smile still radiating from his usually expressionless face.

"Bootiful," the child repeated. "Bootiful."

Then, as quickly as awareness had appeared, it was gone, the clouds again covering up the sun.

Stevie showed no sign that he even remembered what he had just done. He simply returned his attention to his blocks.

"He spoke to you," his mother said, grabbing Aaron by the shoulders and squeezing excitedly. "He actually spoke to you."

Tommy kneeled by his son, grinning from ear to ear. "What do you think it means?" the big man asked, his voice filled with emotion. "He hasn't said a word in two years." He touched the boy's head lovingly. "That would be something, wouldn't it?" he wondered aloud, his eyes never leaving Stevie. "If he started to talk again."

Both parents began to play with the child and his blocks, hoping to elicit another verbal response. Something, anything to prove that the boy's sudden reaction wasn't just a fluke.

Stevie remained in his world of silence.

Aaron got up. "Do you want an apple?" he asked Gabriel.

The dog sprang to his feet and wagged his tail. *"Apple, oh yes,"* he said. *"Hungry, yes. Apple."*

As they left the room Aaron couldn't shake the uncom-

fortable feeling that Stevie's behavior was somehow connected to the bizarreness that had been affecting his life since
his birthday. *So much for distraction,* he thought as he took an
apple from the small wicker basket atop the microwave and
brought it to the cutting board on the counter.

"Did you see the way he looked at me?" Aaron asked the
dog as he took a knife from the dish strainer by the sink and
split the fruit in half. "It was like he was seeing something—
something other than me."

"Bootiful," Gabriel responded, gazing up by his side. *"He
said bootiful."*

Aaron cut the core out, then cut half of the apple into
strips.

"The way he looked at me, it was like the old man at the
common."

He fed the dog a slice of apple, which Gabriel eagerly
devoured.

Aaron saw the old man in his mind pointing at him. *"You
are Nephilim,"* he had said.

"First I'm Nephilim and now I'm bootiful," he said to
himself as he leaned against the counter.

"More apple?" Gabriel asked, a tendril of thick drool
streaming from his jowls to the floor.

Aaron gave him a slice and took one for himself. Something weird was happening to him. And he realized that he
had no other choice than to find out exactly what that was.

He took another bite of the apple, then gave the rest to Gabriel.

It was a crazy idea, but he was desperate to know what was happening to him. He would have to take a chance. Before his appointment with Dr. Jonas the next day, he would try to find the old man from the common.

"Hey, Gabriel," he asked the dog, who was still chewing, "do you want to go to the common with me tomorrow?"

The dog swallowed and gazed up at him. *"More apple?"* he asked.

Aaron shook his head. "No. Apple's gone."

The dog seemed to think for a moment and then gave his answer.

"No apple. Then go to common."

What was I thinking? Aaron scowled to himself. He pulled back and let the tennis ball fly.

Gabriel bounded across the common in hot pursuit of the bouncing ball. *"Get ball,"* he heard the dog say in an excited, breathless voice as he grew closer to capturing the fluorescent yellow prize.

It was a beautiful spring morning, with just the hint of winter's cold that had only begrudgingly begun to recede a few short weeks ago. The wind still had a sharpness to it and he zipped his brown leather jacket a little higher.

Gabriel cavorted with the ball clenched tightly in his mouth.

Since his strange ability to communicate with the dog manifested, Aaron was amazed at how little it took to make Gabriel truly happy: a scratch above his tail, a piece of cheese, calling him a good boy. Simplicity. *It must be pretty awesome to get so much from so little,* he mused as he watched the dog gallop toward him.

"Give me that ball," Aaron demanded, playfully lowering himself into a menacing crouch.

Gabriel growled; the muscles in his back legs twitched with anticipation.

Aaron lunged and the dog bolted to avoid capture.

"C'mere, you crazy dog," he said with a laugh, and began to chase the animal.

There was a part of him that really wasn't too disappointed they hadn't seen the old-timer. It meant a reprieve from serious thoughts of recent events, the weird questions with probably equally weird answers that he wasn't quite sure he was ready to hear.

He snagged Gabriel by the choke chain around his neck and pulled the growling beast toward him. "Gotcha," he said as he leaned close to the dog's face. "Now I'm gonna take that ball!"

Gabriel's growl grew louder, higher, more excited as he struggled to free himself. Aaron grabbed the spit-covered ball and pried it free from the dog's mouth.

"The prize is mine!" Aaron proclaimed as he held the dripping ball aloft.

"Not prize," Gabriel said, able to talk again now that the ball had been removed. *"Just ball."*

Aaron wrinkled his nose in revulsion as he studied the slime-covered ball in his hand. "And what a ball it is," he said.

He watched the dog's head move from side to side as he tossed the tennis ball from one hand to the other. "Bet you want this bad," he teased.

"Want ball bad," Gabriel responded, mesmerized by its movement.

Aaron made a move to throw it, hiding the ball beneath his arm, and the dog shot off in hot pursuit of nothing.

He laughed as he watched Gabriel searching the ground, even looking up into the air just in case it hadn't fallen to earth yet.

"Yoohoo!" he called to the dog. And as Gabriel looked in his direction, he held the ball up. "Looking for this?"

Surprised, the dog charged back toward him. *"How you get ball back?"* he asked with amazement.

Aaron smiled. "Magic," he said and chuckled.

"Magic," Gabriel repeated in a soft, canine whisper of wonderment, his eyes still stuck to the ball.

The dog suddenly became distracted by something beyond Aaron. *"Who that?"* he asked.

"Who's who?" Aaron turned around.

At first he didn't recognize the man sitting on the bench across the common, soaking up the sunshine. But then the man waved, and he suddenly knew. Aaron felt his heart beat faster, questions turning through his mind, questions he wasn't entirely certain he wanted answered.

"What wrong?" Gabriel asked, concern in his voice.

"Nothing," Aaron said, not taking his eyes from the man on the bench.

"Then why afraid?"

Aaron looked down at the dog, startled by the question. "I'm not afraid," he said, insulted by the dog's insinuation.

The dog looked at him and then across the common. *"Afraid of stranger?"*

"I told you I am not afraid," Aaron said anxiously, and began to head toward the man.

"Smell afraid," the dog stressed as he followed by his side.

They were about six feet away when Gabriel moved ahead of him, his head tilted back as he sniffed the air. *"Man smell old,"* he said. *"Old and different,"* he added between drafts of air.

Aaron could see that the man was smiling, his long wispy, white hair moving around his head in the cool, spring breeze.

"Beautiful day," the old man said in English, rather than the ancient language he'd been speaking when they first met.

Gabriel ran at the man, tail wagging.

"Gabriel, no!" Aaron ordered, speeding up to catch the dog. "Get over here."

The dog leaped up, putting his two front paws on the

bench, and began to lick the stranger's face as if they were old friends.

"Hello, I Gabriel," he said as he licked and sniffed at the man's face, neck, and ears. *"Who you?"*

"My name is Ezekiel, but you can call me Zeke," the man answered as he patted the dog's soft yellow head.

"Are you telling me or the dog?" Aaron asked as he took Gabriel by the collar and gently pulled him away. "Get down, Gabriel," he said sharply. "Behave."

The dog went silent, bowing his head, embarrassed that he had been scolded.

"He asked me what my name was and I told him," Zeke said as he sat back on the bench and smiled at the dog. "He's a beautiful animal. You're very lucky to have him."

Aaron stroked Gabriel's head in an attempt to keep the excitable animal calm. He laughed at the old man and smiled slyly. "So the dog spoke to you?"

Zeke smiled back. "You spoke the language of the messenger to me yesterday," he said, folding his arms across his chest. "Don't tell me you can't understand the dog."

Aaron felt as if he had been slapped; a hot, tingling sweat erupted at the base of his neck and shoulder blades. "Who . . . who are you?" he asked—not the best of questions, but the only one he could dredge up at the moment.

"Zeke," Gabriel answered helpfully, pulling away from Aaron to lick at the man's hands. *"Zeke, Aaron. He Zeke."*

Zeke smiled and reached out to rub beneath the dog's chin. "He's right, aren't you?" he asked the panting animal. "I'm Zeke and you are—what did he call you? Aaron?"

The old man wiped the dog's slobber on his pant leg and extended his hand toward Aaron. He hesitated at first, but then took Zeke's hand in his and they shook.

"I'm very pleased to meet you, Aaron. Sorry about yesterday. Did I scare you?"

Their hands came apart and Aaron shrugged. "Wasn't so much scaring as confusing the hell out of me."

Zeke nodded in understanding and continued to pet Gabriel. "I bet it's been pretty strange for you the last couple a' days."

Questions screamed to be asked, but Aaron kept them at bay, choosing to let the old man reveal what he knew at a natural pace. He didn't want to appear too eager.

"And how do you know that?"

The old man tilted his head back, closed his eyes, and sniffed the air.

"How do I know that summer's right around the corner?" he asked, letting the morning sunshine bathe his grizzled, unshaven features.

The man didn't appear as old as Aaron originally had thought, probably in his early sixties, but there was something about him—in his eyes, in the way he carried himself—that made Aaron think he was much older.

"It's in the air, boy," Zeke said. "I can smell it."

"Okay," Aaron said. "You could smell that I was having a bad time. That makes sense."

Zeke nodded. "Kinda, sorta. I could smell that you were changing, and just assumed that you were probably having some problems with it."

Aaron had put the tennis ball inside his jacket pocket and now slowly removed it. Gabriel's eyes bugged like something out of a Warner Brothers cartoon. "I can't believe I'm having this conversation," he said as he showed the ball to Gabriel and threw it across the common. "Go play."

Gabriel ran off in pursuit. They watched the dog in silence. Aaron wanted to leave—but something kept him there. Perhaps it was the chance of an explanation.

"What happened first?" Zeke asked, breaking the silence. "Was it the language thing? Did the dog start talking and you thought you'd lost all your marbles?"

Aaron didn't want to answer but found it was impossible to hold back. "Kids at school were speaking Portuguese. I don't know how to speak Portuguese, but suddenly I could understand them perfectly fine, like they were speaking English."

Zeke nodded with understanding. "Doesn't matter anymore what language somebody is talking," he said. "You'll be able to understand and speak it as if it were your native tongue. It's one of the perks."

Gabriel was running in a circle. *"I got the ball!"* he yelled,

diving at the tennis ball lying in the grass and sending it rolling. He pounced on it with tireless vigor.

"The language doesn't even have to be human, as you've
probably guessed by now." The old man looked at him. "Wait
until you hear what a tree sloth has to say."

"It's insane," Aaron muttered.

"Not really," Zeke responded. "They just have a unique
way of looking at things."

Aaron was confused. "What? Who has a unique way of
looking at things?" he asked.

"Tree sloths," Zeke answered.

"I wasn't talking about sloths," Aaron said, growing agitated.

"Oh, you were talking about all this with the languages
and stuff?" Zeke asked. "Well, you'd better get used to it
'cause it's what you are," the old man said matter of factly.

Aaron turned from watching his dog play and faced the
man. "Get used to being insane? I don't think—"

Zeke shook his head and held up his hands. "Not insane,"
he said. "Nephilim. It's what you are; you don't have a choice."

There was that word again. The word that had disobedi-
ently bounced around inside Aaron's skull since he first heard
it, impossible to forget—like it didn't want to be lost.

"Why do you keep calling me that?" he asked, tension
coiling in his voice as he readied himself for the answer.

The old man ran both hands through his wild, white hair.

Then he leaned forward and rested his elbows on his knees. "The Nephilim are the children of angels and—"

"Angels and human women," Aaron interrupted. He didn't want to waste any time hearing things he already knew. "I know that; I looked it up in the library. Now tell me what the hell it has to do with *me*."

"It's kind of complicated," Zeke said. "If you give me half a second and let me speak, I might be able to clear some things up."

He stared at Aaron, a stare both intense and calming, a stare that suggested this was not a typical, crazy old man, but someone who was once a figure of authority.

Gabriel had wandered over to a newly planted tree and was sniffing the spring mulch spread at its base.

"I'm sorry," Aaron said. "Go on."

Zeke stroked his unshaven chin, mentally found his place, and began again. "Okay, the Nephilim are the children of angels and mortal women. Not too common really, the mothers have a real difficult time bringing the babies to term—never mind surviving the delivery. But every once in a while, a Nephilim child survives."

Gabriel had returned and dropped the ball, now covered in the fragrant mulch, at Zeke's feet. *"Look, Zeke, ball."*

Zeke reached down and picked it up, turning it over in his hands as Gabriel stared attentively.

"They're something all right, part heavenly host, part

human, a blending of the Almighty's most impressive creations."

The old man bounced the ball once, and then again. The dog's head bobbed up and down as he watched it.

"Nephilim usually have a normal childhood, but once they reach a certain level of maturity, the angelic nature starts to assert itself. That's when the problems begin, almost as if the two halves no longer get along." Zeke threw the ball and Gabriel was off. "Seems to happen around eighteen or nineteen."

Aaron felt the color drain from his face, and he turned to the old man on the bench. "You're trying to tell me that . . . that my mother . . . my mother slept with an angel? For Christ's sake!"

Gabriel returned with the ball and stopped at Aaron, sensing his master's growing unease. The dog sniffed at his leg, determined that things were fine and went to Zeke.

"Did you know your father?" Zeke asked, idly picking up the ball.

"It doesn't matter," Aaron barked, and turned his back on the old man and his dog.

He could see his car parked across the street and wanted to run for it. He could feel himself begin to slip—teetering on the brink of an emotional roller coaster. Zeke's question had hit him with the force of a sledgehammer. His mother had died giving birth to him, and the identity of his father went with her.

"That's where you're wrong, Aaron," Zeke said from behind him. "It does matter."

Aaron faced him. He suddenly felt weak, drained of energy.

"There is a choir of angels called the Powers. They are the oldest of the angels, the first created by God."

Gabriel had caught sight of some seagulls. *"Big birds,"* he grumbled, and began to creep stealthily toward them like some fearsome predator.

Zeke stood up and moved toward Aaron. "I want you to listen to me very carefully," he said, holding him in that powerful stare. "The Powers are kinda like—" He stopped to think a moment. "The Powers are like secret police, like God's storm troopers. It's their job to destroy what they believe is offensive to the Creator."

Aaron was confused. "I don't understand," he said, shaking his head.

"The Powers decided long ago that Nephilim are offensive. A blight before the eyes of God."

"The Powers kill them?" Aaron asked, already knowing the answer.

Zeke nodded slowly, his expression dire. "In the beginning it was a slaughter; most of the ones killed were still just children. They didn't even know why they had to die." The old man reached out and grabbed Aaron's arm in a powerful grip. "I want you to listen very carefully because your life might depend on it."

Zeke's grip was firm and it had begun to hurt. Aaron tried to pull away, but the man's strength held him tight.

"It's still going on today, Aaron. Do you understand what I'm saying to you? Nephilim are still being born, and when they begin to show signs of their true nature, the Powers find them."

Aaron finally yanked his arm free. "Let go of me," he snarled.

"The Powers find them and *kill* them. They have no mercy. In their eyes, you're a freak of nature, something that should never have been allowed to happen."

Aaron was suddenly very afraid. "I have to go," he told the man, scanning the common for his dog. He whistled and saw Gabriel in the distance lifting his leg against a trash barrel. The dog began to trot in their direction.

"You have to listen to me, Aaron," Zeke warned. "Your abilities are blossoming. If you're not careful—"

Aaron whirled and stepped toward the old man, fists clenched in suppressed fury. He couldn't hold it back anymore. He was scared—scared and very angry for he was starting to believe Zeke's wild story. He wanted answers, but not these—these were a ticket to a locked ward.

"What?" he screamed. "If I'm not careful these storm trooper angels are going to fly down out of the sky and kill me?" Aaron suddenly thought of his dream, the recurring nightmare, and wanted to vomit. It made him all the angrier.

"I know it sounds insane," Zeke said, "but you've got to understand. This has been going on for thousands of years and—"

"Shut up!" Aaron exploded in the old man's face. "Just shut your stupid mouth!" He began to walk away, then stopped and turned back. "And how do you know all this, Zeke?" he asked, sticking his finger in the man's face. "How do you know about Nephilim and Powers and the killing?"

The old man looked perfectly calm as he spoke. "I think you already know the answer to that, and if you don't—think a bit harder."

Aaron laughed out loud, a cruel sound and it surprised him. "Let me guess. You're a Nephilim too?"

Zeke smiled sadly and shook his head. "Not a Nephilim," he said, and began to unbutton his threadbare raincoat. He was wearing a loose-fitting green sweater beneath and some faded jeans. "I'm a fallen angel, a Grigori, if you want to be specific," he said as he moved closer.

He yanked on the collar of his sweater, pulling it down over his right shoulder to expose unusually pale flesh—and something more. A strange, fleshy protrusion, about six inches long, jutted from the old man's shoulder blade. It was covered in what appeared to be a fine coat of white hairs—no, on closer examination it wasn't hair at all—it was covered in downy, white feathers. Aaron jumped back as the protrusion began to move up and down in a flapping motion. Something similar on the other shoulder moved in unison beneath the sweater.

"What the hell is it?" Aaron asked, both fascinated and disgusted by the wagging, vestigial appendage.

"It's all I've got left of them," Zeke said softly, an almost palpable sadness emanating from him in waves. "It's all that's left of my wings."

CHAPTER FIVE

K now what, I've had enough," Aaron said as he threw up his hands and backed away from Zeke. "I'm done."

He felt as though he were falling farther and farther into the depths of insanity, only with Zeke's addition, he had a buddy for the trip. Even the voice of reason inside his head was beginning to come undone. *Maybe it is all true,* he thought. *What else could those things be on his back but the stumps of wings . . .* He wanted to slap himself for thinking it. *No way. It would be better if it were a brain tumor making me understand these languages—making me think that my dog is talking to me. That would make it easier,* he reasoned. Then he could brush off the old man as just another lunatic.

Aaron called again for his dog. "C'mon, Gabriel," he said, clapping his hands together. "Let's go for a ride."

He continued to walk away from the crazy old man, and his equally crazy delusions.

"Aaron, please," Zeke pleaded. "I have more to tell you—to show you. Aaron?"

He didn't turn around. He couldn't allow himself to be ensnared in this madness. Yes, Zeke was pretty convincing and knew all the right buttons to push, but angels? It was just too much for Aaron to swallow. Space aliens, maybe—angels, not a chance. He would see Dr. Jonas later today and then set up an appointment with the doctor's friend at Mass General. Between the two of them, a rational explanation for his condition—*could it actually be called a condition?* he wondered—a rational explanation for his current situation would be found. At this stage of the game a tumor might not even be so bad. At least it was some kind of concrete explanation that he could accept, understand, and deal with.

Angels. Absolutely friggin' ridiculous.

Aaron looked down to see if Gabriel still had his ball. It was the Lab's favorite toy, and Aaron could see himself here at ten o'clock tonight with a flashlight searching for it.

The dog wasn't with him.

He looked around the common. Had the dog become distracted, as he so often did, by a squirrel or a bird or an interesting smell in the grass?

Aaron caught sight of him on the other side of the common where a section of the pipe fence was missing. The dog was standing with Zeke. He took a few steps toward them and wondered how they could have gotten way over there so fast.

"Hey, Gabriel," he called, cupping his hands around his mouth to amplify his voice. "C'mon, pup, let's go for a ride."

The dog didn't pay him the least bit of attention. He was standing attentively alongside Zeke, staring up at the man with his tail wagging. An uncomfortable feeling began somewhere in the pit of Aaron's stomach. He'd felt like this in the past, usually right before something bad happened. He remembered a time not too long ago when he had experienced a similar feeling and discovered that Stevie had turned on the hot water in the bathtub when nobody was looking. If he hadn't searched out the source of his uneasiness, the child would surely have scalded himself badly. Aaron felt kind of like he did then—only worse.

Aaron began walking toward them. "Gabriel, come here," he said in his sternest voice. "Come."

The dog glanced his way briefly but was distracted as the old man held up the ball for Gabriel to see. Zeke looked in Aaron's direction, ball held aloft.

The awful feeling squirming in his gut got worse and Aaron began to jog toward them—and then to run.

Zeke looked toward the street outside the common, checking it out as if getting ready to cross. It was getting later in the morning and the traffic had begun to pick up. Zeke again showed the ball to Gabriel and Aaron could see the dog's posture tense in anticipation.

"Hey!" Aaron yelled, his voice cracking. He was almost there, no farther than twenty feet away.

The old man looked into the traffic and then to Aaron. "I'm sorry," Zeke said, raising his voice.

Panic gripped him and Aaron began to run faster. "Gabriel!" he yelled at the top of his lungs. "Gabriel, look at me!"

The dog paid him no mind, his dark eyes mesmerized by the power of the ball. Aaron was almost there.

"There's no other way," he heard the old man say as he again studied the flow of oncoming traffic—and threw the ball into the street.

Aaron saw it as though watching a slow-motion scene in a movie. The tennis ball left the old man's hand and sailed through the air. He heard a voice that must have been his screaming "Gabriel, *no!*" as the dog followed the arc of the ball and jumped. The ball bounced once and Gabriel was there, ready to snatch it up in his mouth, when the white Ford Escort struck him broadside and sent him sailing through the air as though weightless.

They were the most sickening sounds Aaron had ever heard, brakes screeching as tires fought for purchase on Tarmac, followed by the dull thud of a thick rubber bumper connecting with fur, flesh, and bone. His slow-motion perception abruptly ended as Gabriel's limp body hit the street in a twisted heap.

"Oh my God—no!" Aaron screamed as he ran to his pet.

He fell to his knees beside the animal. *There's so much blood,* he thought. It stained the Lab's beautiful yellow coat and oozed from the corners of his mouth. It had even begun to seep out along the ground from somewhere beneath his body.

Aaron carefully wrapped his arms around his best friend. "Oh God, oh God, oh God, oh God," he cried as he pressed his face to the dog's side.

He placed an ear against the still-warm fur and listened for a heartbeat. But the sounds of horns from backed-up traffic and the murmur from curious bystanders was all he could discern.

"Will you shut up!" he screamed at the top of his lungs, lifting his head from the dog's side.

Gabriel shuddered violently. *He's still alive.* Tears of joy streamed from Aaron's eyes as he bent down to whisper in his friend's ear. "Don't you worry, boy, I'm here. Everything is going to be fine."

"Aaron?" Gabriel asked, his voice a weak whimper.

"Shhhhh, you be quiet now," he told the dog in a calming tone. "I've got you. You're going to be all right."

He stroked the dog's blood-stained fur, not sure if he believed what he was saying. He wanted to fall apart, to scream, rant, and rave, but knew that he had to keep control. He had to save Gabriel.

"Aaron . . . Aaron, hurt bad," Gabriel croaked, and began to spasm as frothy pink blood bubbled from his mouth.

"Hang on, pal, hang on, boy. I'm going to help you."

Aaron tried to pick him up, and Gabriel let out a heart-rending shriek so filled with pain that it affected him like a physical blow.

"What do I do?" he asked aloud, panic beginning to override a cool head. "He's dying. What do I do?"

The thought of praying strayed into his head, and he was considering doing just that when he realized that he wasn't even sure how.

"If you want Gabriel to live, you must listen to me," said a voice from behind.

Aaron turned to see Zeke standing over him.

"Get away from me, you son of a bitch!" he spat. "You *did* this! You did this to him!"

"Listen to me," Zeke hissed close to his ear. "If you don't want him to die, you'll do as I say."

For the first time Aaron felt as if he couldn't go on. Even after all he had been through, caught up in the merciless current of the foster care system, he never gave up hope that eventually it would turn out for the best. But now, as he gazed at his best friend dying in the street, he wasn't sure.

"Aaron," Zeke shouted for his attention. "Do you want him to bleed to death on this dirty street? Do you?"

He turned to look at the man, tears running down his face. "No," he managed. "I want him to live. Please . . . please, help him. . . ."

"Not me," Zeke said with a shake of his head. "You. You're going to help Gabriel."

The old man knelt beside him. "We don't have a moment to spare," he said, looking upon the dying animal. "Lay your hands on him—quickly now."

Aaron did as he was told, and placed the palms of both hands on the dog's side.

"Now close your eyes," the old man in structed.

"But we can't—" Aaron started to protest.

"Close your eyes, damn it!" Zeke commanded him.

Aaron did as he was told, his hands still upon Gabriel's body. The dog's flesh seemed to have grown colder, and he grew desperate. The noise around them receded.

"Please, Zeke," he begged as Gabriel's life slipped agonizingly away.

"It's not up to me now," the old man said. "It's up to you."

"I don't understand. If we can get him to a vet maybe . . ."

"A vet can't help him. He'll be dead in a couple a' minutes if you don't do something," Zeke said. "You gotta let it out, Aaron."

"Let what out? . . . I don't understand."

"What's to understand? It's there, inside you, waiting. It's been there since you were born—just waiting for its time."

Aaron sobbed, letting his chin drop to his chest. "I . . . I don't know what you're saying."

"No time for crying, boy. Look for it in the darkness. It's there, I can smell it on you. Look closely. Can you see it?"

Gabriel is going to die, Aaron realized as he knelt by the animal, hands laid upon him, feeling him slip away. There was no way around it. The old man was delusional and dangerous. He debated whether he should hold the man for the police—imagine if Gabriel had been a child. It might be best for the old man to be behind bars or at least in a hospital where he could receive the proper care.

Aaron was about to open his eyes when he felt it stir inside his mind, and he saw something. In the darkness it was there, something he'd never seen before.

And it was moving toward him. *Is this what the old man is talking about?* he asked himself near panic. How did he know it would be there? What was it? What was coming at him through the blackness behind his eyes?

"I . . . I see something," he said with disbelief. "What should I do?"

"Call to it, Aaron," Zeke cautioned, "not with your voice, but with your mind. Welcome it, let it know that it's needed."

Aaron did as he was told, and reached out with his mind. He couldn't make out exactly what it was, its shape kept changing—but it seemed to be some kind of animal—and it was moving inexorably closer.

"Hello?" he thought, feeling foolish, yet desperate to try anything. *"Can . . . can you hear me?"* Was it all some bizarre figment of his imagination brought on by the stress of the situation? he wondered.

It was a mouse scrambling through the darkness toward him, a mouse with fur so white that it seemed to glow.

"I have no idea what I'm supposed to do—or what you are—but I'm willing to try anything to help my friend."

The mouse stopped, its beady black eyes seeming to touch him. It reared back on its haunches, as if considering his words, and then began to groom itself.

"Do . . . do you understand me?" he asked the tiny creature with the power of his thoughts.

It was no longer a mouse, and Aaron gasped. The mouse had become an owl, its feathers the color of snow, and before he could wrap his brain around what had just happened, it changed again. From an owl it turned into an albino toad—and from the toad, a white rabbit. The thing inside his head was now morphing its shape at a blinding rate; from mammal to insect, from bird to fish. But though its form continued to alter, its eyes remained the same. There was an awesome intelligence in those deep, black eyes, and something more—recognition. It knew him, and somehow, he knew it.

It had become a snake—a cobra—and it reared back on its

bone-colored muscular shaft of a body, swaying from side to side, its mouth open in a fearsome hiss as it readied to strike.

"I don't like this, Zeke," Aaron said aloud, eyes still tightly closed. "You have to tell me what to do."

"Don't be afraid, Aaron. It's a part of you. It's been a part of you since you were conceived," Zeke counseled. "But you have to hurry. Gabriel doesn't have much time left."

"I don't know what to do!" he cried as a humming-bird fluttered before him.

"Talk to it," Zeke barked. "And do as you're told."

"My dog is dying." Aaron directed his thoughts toward the shape-changing creature floating before him in a sea of pitch. *"In fact he might already be dead, but I can't give up. Please, can you help me? Is there anything you can do to help me save him?"*

It had become a fetus that looked vaguely human. It simply hovered there in its membranous sack, unresponsive, its dark eyes fixed upon him.

Aaron was angry. Time was running out, and here he was talking to some fetal figment of his troubled state of mind.

"I've had enough," his thoughts screamed. *"If you're going to help me, do it. If not, get the hell out of my mind and let me get him to a vet."*

Like a ship changing course, the child-thing slowly turned, shifted its shape to some kind of fish, and began to swim away.

"It's . . . it's leaving, Zeke."

Aaron felt the man's hand roughly upon his shoulder. "You can't allow it to go. Talk to it, Aaron. Beg it to come back. Whether you're ready or not, it's the only way that Gabriel will survive."

"Please," Aaron projected into the sea of black. *"Please don't let him die, I . . . I don't know what I'd do without him."*

The fish, now an iguana, continued on its way. A luminous bat, and then a centipede, the force within his mind receded, growing smaller with distance. Aaron wasn't sure why he did what he did next.

In the ancient language first spoken to him by Zeke, what the old man had called the language of messengers, he called out once more to the thing in his mind.

"Please, help me," he thought in that arcane tongue. *"If it is in your power, please don't let my friend die."*

At first he didn't think his pleas had any effect—but then he saw that a chimpanzee had turned and was slowly returning with a comical gait.

"It's coming back," Aaron said to Zeke, not in English, but in the old tongue.

"Open yourself to it," he responded in kind. *"Take it into yourself. Accept it as part of you."*

Aaron shook his head violently, eyes still clamped shut. *"What does that mean?"* he asked.

The old man dug his nails painfully into his shoulders. *"Accept it, or you both die."*

A jungle cat was almost upon him, and Aaron gazed into the fearsome beast's eyes.

"*I accept you,*" he thought in the ancient speak, unsure of what he should be saying, and the panther lifted its head to become a serpent, but this was unlike any snake he had ever seen before. It had tufts of silky fine hair flowing from parts of its tubular body, and small muscular limbs that clawed at the air as if in anticipation. And the strangest and most disturbing thing of all, it had a face—something not usually associated with the look of a reptile. This serpent wore an expression on its unusual facial features, one of contentment, and spread its malformed arms, beckoning in a gesture that suggested Aaron, too, had been accepted.

The ophidian beast began to glow eerily, and Aaron could discern a fine webwork of veins and capillaries running throughout the creature's body. The light of the snake became blinding and the solid black behind his eyes was burned away like night with the approach of dawn.

A painful surge of energy that felt like thousands of volts of electricity suddenly coursed through Aaron's body. He opened his eyes and looked down on his dog. He knew that Gabriel's life was almost at an end.

"It's time, Aaron," he heard Zeke say.

Aaron looked at him. For some reason the old man was crying. Aaron's hands tingled painfully and he gazed down at them. A white crackling energy, like eruptions of arc lightning, danced from one fingertip to the next.

"What's happening to me?" he asked breathlessly.

"You're whole now, Aaron. You're complete."

Instinctively Aaron knew what had to be done. Gazing at his hands, he turned them palms down and again placed them upon Gabriel. He felt the energy leave his body, leaping from his fingers to the dog, burrowing beneath fur and flesh. And the air around them was filled with the charged scent of ozone.

Gabriel's body twitched and thrashed, but Aaron did not take his hands away. The blood that spattered the dog's fur started to dry, to smolder, evaporating into oily wisps that snaked into the air.

"I think you've done all you can," Zeke said quietly nearby.

Aaron pulled his hands away from the animal. For a brief moment his handprints glowed white upon the dog's fur— and then were gone. The powerful sensation throughout his body was fading, but he still felt different, both mentally and physically.

"What did I do?" he asked, looking from Zeke to the dog.

Gabriel was breathing slow regular breaths, as if he were merely taking a little snooze.

"What needed to be done if Gabriel—and you—are to survive," Zeke answered ominously.

Aaron reached out and touched the dog's head. "Gabriel?" he said softly, not sure if he believed what he was seeing.

Gabriel languidly lifted his head from the street, yawned, and fixed Aaron in his gaze. *"Hello, Aaron,"* he said as he rolled onto his belly.

Aaron could feel his eyes well up with emotion. He leaned forward and hugged the dog. "Are you all right?" he asked, squeezing the animal's neck and planting a kiss on the side of his muzzle.

"I'm fine, Aaron," Gabriel answered. The dog seemed distracted, pulling away from his embrace.

"What's the matter?" Aaron asked the dog as he looked around.

"Have you seen my ball?" Gabriel asked in a voice filled with surprising intelligence.

And Aaron came to the frightening realization that he may not have been the only one to change.

Too late, the angel Camael thought, perched like a gargoyle at the edge of the building. He sadly gazed down at a restaurant consumed in flames. *Too late to save another.*

Thick gray smoke billowed from the broken front windows of Eddy's Breakfast and Lunch; tongues of orange flame, like things alive, reached out from the heart of the conflagration, hoping to ensnare something, anything to fuel its ravenous hunger.

From his roost across the street, Camael watched as firefighters aimed their hoses and tried to suffocate the inferno with water before it had a chance to spread to neighboring structures. They would need to be persistent, the angel thought, for it was a most unnatural fire they battled this morn.

He had planned to make contact with the girl this very morning, to guide her through the change her body was undergoing, and warn her of the dangers it presented—dangers that came far sooner than even he had imagined.

Camael had been watching the girl—*What was her name? Susan.*

He had been observing Susan since he first caught scent of her imminent transformation. It was so much harder to track them these days; the world was a much larger and more complex place than it had been in the beginning. The enemy used trackers, human hounds, but he could not bear to use the oft-pathetic creatures in that way. Camael found it far too cruel.

Susan was a loner, as was often the nature of the breed, living alone without close friends or family. But she did have a job as a waitress, a job that seemed to be the center of her reality. That was where she came alive: surrounded by the chattering masses of the popular eating establishment. She would serve them, converse with them, and send them on their way back into the world with a kind word and a wave. At Eddy's she was accepted, loved even; but outside its doors was a cold, harsh, unfriendly place.

Camael had watched and waited for the signs of change

in her. He had even started to frequent the restaurant just so that he might observe her more closely. He didn't have long to wait. Her appearance became disheveled, dark circles forming beneath her eyes, an obvious sign that she was not sleeping. The dreams were usually first, the collective memories of an entire race from thousands of years attempting to assert themselves. That alone was enough to drive some of them mad, never mind the changes that were still to come.

The firefighters below seemed to have the blaze under control and were entering the building, most likely to retrieve the bodies of those who had been trapped within.

Camael sighed heavily. At this early hour Eddy's would have been crowded with customers—those coming off the late shift and those just beginning their workday. *Verchiel certainly outdid himself this time,* the angel thought as the first of the victims was carried from the smoldering building.

The girl must have been much further along than Camael had realized if they were able to find her with such ease. If only he had acted earlier this might have been avoided. He might have been able to convince the young woman to run before the Powers had a chance to lock on to her scent.

He would need to move faster with the next.

The firefighters were laying the smoking bodies down behind a hastily constructed screen on the sidewalk in front of the burnt-out shell that had once been Eddy's. Camael counted sixteen so far. The girl's had yet to be recovered.

There was a ferocity to the Powers' latest attacks, a complete lack of concern for innocent lives, a certain desperation to their actions. He thought of Samchia's murder in Hong Kong. There had always been killing, it was what the Powers did—it was their reason for existence. But of late . . . Why this sudden escalation of violence? It disturbed him. What had stirred the hornet's nest, so to speak?

A frightening thought invaded his consciousness. What if she had been the One? What if Susan was the One foretold of in a prophecy thousands of years old?

Camael recalled the moment that had altered his chosen path as if it had happened only moments before. They had descended from the heavens on the ancient city of Urkish, the overpowering desire to eradicate evil spurring them on. It was rumored that the city was a haven for the unclean, a place where those who offended God could thrive in secret. The Powers were on a holy mission, and all who stood against them fell before their righteousness.

In a hovel made of mud and straw they found him, an old man, a seer, one of his eyes covered by a milky caul. He was surrounded by clay tablets upon which something had been written—a prophecy. It was Camael's former captain, Verchiel, who first read the seer's scrawl. His words foretold of the melding of human and angel, and how that joining would sire an offspring—an offspring more than human, more than angel, who would be the key to reuniting those who had fallen from Heaven with their most holy Father.

"Blasphemy!" the captain of the Powers had screamed as he shattered the tablets beneath his heel.

And on that day, all trace of the city of Urkish was wiped from the planet and from history.

But not the words—try as he might, Camael could not forget the seer's words. They spoke of a promise, of a more peaceful time when his existence would not be one filled with the passing of judgment and the meting out of death. The words were what made him abandon his brethren and their holy mission so very long ago. Words that still haunted him today.

But what if Susan had been the One? It was a question he struggled with every time he was too late to save one of them. What if she had been the key to reuniting the fallen with Heaven? What if Verchiel had taken it all away in a self-righteous burst of purifying fire?

Camael finally saw Susan's body among the last to be carried from the fire-ravaged building. Her blackened limbs reached up to the heavens, as if pleading to be saved.

It pained him that he had not been there for her.

What if she . . . a tiny voice in the back of his mind began to ask and he promptly silenced it. He couldn't think that way. He had to keep going or all his past sacrifices would be for naught.

Camael turned from the carnage and strode across the

rooftop. The angel tipped his head back to the early morning sun and sniffed the air.

There were others, others who needed him.

With the Powers' attacks on the rise, he would need to move quickly if any were to be saved.

Zeke motioned for Aaron to sit. There was one chair in the tiny room, a black leather office chair that had probably been rescued from the garbage. A large swath of gray electrical tape ran down the middle of the seat and Aaron touched it to see if it was sticky before he sat.

After the business at the common, the three had quickly left the scene to avoid unwanted questions. The driver of the white Escort seemed genuinely pleased that she hadn't killed Gabriel, and had even petted the dog before driving off. As the crowd rapidly dispersed Zeke suggested they head for his place.

It was a fifteen-minute walk to the Osmond Hotel, a boardinghouse on Washington Street, not too far from downtown Lynn. Because Gabriel was with them, and pets were not allowed in the Osmond, they went around back and entered through the emergency exit held open with a cinder block for cross ventilation.

Zeke lived on the fourth floor, room 416, of the dilapidated building. It wasn't the kind of place where one would expect to find an angel.

"A fallen angel," Zeke corrected as he sat down on the single-size bed covered by a green, moth-eaten army blanket. "There's a big difference."

Aaron had bought sodas and a bottle of water for Gabriel in a bodega they had passed on the way to the rooming house. "Do you have something I can put this in?" he asked as he cracked the seal on the water.

Zeke got up and started rummaging through plastic trash bags that littered the floor. "Sorry, I don't," he said. "Can't cook in the room so there's no reason for me to have any dishes."

Aaron poured some water into his cupped hand and offered it to the dog. "It's okay. We'll manage."

"Thank you," Gabriel said in a well-mannered voice. He dropped his ball between his paws and began to lap the liquid from his master's hand.

Zeke lay back on the bed and popped the top on his soda can. "You all right?" he asked Aaron as he fished for something in the pockets of his tattered trench coat.

Gabriel finished his water. *"Thank you again, Aaron,"* he said, and licked his chops. *"I was very thirsty."*

Aaron wiped the slobber on his pant leg. "Yeah, I'm fine," he said to Zeke, popping the top on his own drink. His eyes never left the dog. "Does he seem—I don't know—smarter to you?"

Zeke produced a nip of Seagram's from his pocket and poured the contents into his can of soda. "Not supposed to have booze in here either," he said with a grin as he took a large gulp of the spiked drink. "Been waiting for that first sip all morning," said the fallen angel, smacking his lips.

Aaron sat at the edge of the office chair and began to stroke Gabriel's head.

"Does he seem smarter?" Zeke repeated, and then stifled a belch with his hand. "Yeah, I guess so, but what did you expect? You fixed him, you made him better—probably better than he ever was."

The angel took another drink.

Aaron sat back in his chair, soft-drink can between his legs, and shook his head in disbelief. "It's all a blur; I have no idea what I did."

Gabriel lay down on his side and closed his eyes. The room was silent except for the sound of the dog's rhythmic breathing as he quickly drifted off to sleep.

"What's happened to me, Zeke?" Aaron asked. There was fear in his voice and he struggled to maintain control. "What did that . . . animal thing inside my head do? Talk to me!"

Zeke's can of soda stopped midway to his mouth. "God's menagerie," he said. "Not animal thing. Let's try not to be disrespectful."

Aaron nodded. "Sorry," he said with a smirk.

"Most people see it as some kind of animal; a dove or a lion. All of His creations."

Zeke tipped the can of soda back and drained its contents. He then tossed the empty can into a trash bag beside the bed. "It made you complete," he said, answering Aaron's original question. "For the first time since you were born, you're how you're supposed to be."

"And how am I supposed to be?" Aaron asked, annoyed with the man's cryptic response.

"You're a Nephilim, Aaron, through and through."

Aaron slammed his fists down on the arms of the chair. "Stop calling me that!" he yelled angrily.

Gabriel jumped and lifted his head. *"Is everything okay?"* he asked.

"Sorry," Aaron apologized, and reached down to scratch beneath the dog's chin. "Everything's fine. You go back to sleep."

Gabriel lay back and almost immediately resumed his nap.

"Sorry to be the one to break it to you, but that's what you are," Zeke said. He had found another nip and was drinking the whiskey straight this time.

"So is this what your kind of angel does? What did you call yourself—a Gregory? Do Gregorys go around outing people who are Nephilim?"

Zeke chuckled and leaned his head back against the cracked plaster wall. "Grigori," he corrected. "And no, that's not what we do. Our assignment came directly from the Big Guy upstairs," he said, pointing to the ceiling. "And I don't mean Crazy Al in room five-twenty." He had some more whiskey before he continued. "God Himself told us what to do. Our job was a simple one really; it's amazing how badly we screwed it all up."

The fallen angel spoke slowly, remembering. "It was our job to keep an eye on mankind. They were still very young when we came here, and in need of guidance. We were to be their shepherds, you know, keep 'em out of trouble and all."

Zeke fell silent and a look of sadness darkened his features.

Aaron placed his empty soda can on the floor beside his chair. Someone in a room close by began to cough violently. "What happened?" he finally asked.

Zeke was staring at the small brown bottle in his hand and did not look up as he took a deep breath and continued. "We became a little too enamored with the locals, lost that professional distance." He nervously turned the bottle in his hand. "We began to teach them things, things the Lord felt they didn't need to know: how to make weapons, astrology, how to read the weather."

Zeke laughed harshly. "One of us sick bastards even taught the women about makeup." The angel brought the nip halfway to his mouth. "So if your girlfriend spends two hours putting her face on before you go out for the evening, you can blame us."

"I actually don't have a girlfriend," Aaron said sheepishly, immediately thinking of Vilma.

Zeke finished the last of his liquor, ignoring Aaron's comment. "And they taught us things as well: how to drink, smoke, have sex. We went native," he said as he squinted into the empty bottle. Annoyed that there was nothing left, he tossed it to the floor. "We began to live like humans, act like humans. Some of us even took wives."

"And is that how the first Nephilim were born?" Aaron asked.

The fallen angel nodded. "You catch on quick. Yep, the Grigori are to blame for that whole mess—but not entirely." Zeke stood up and sloughed off his coat, draping it over the foot of the bed. "We weren't the only angels to find the human ladies attractive. There were others, deserters from the Great War in Heaven. They came to Earth to hide."

A Great War in Heaven; Aaron recalled the subject from John Milton's *Paradise Lost*. He'd read it in Mr. O'Leary's sophomore English class. "So that wasn't fiction?" he asked the Grigori. "There really was a war between angels?"

Zeke plopped himself back down on the bed. Aaron noticed a cigarette in one of his hands.

"It was real all right," Zeke answered.

He pinched the end of the cigarette between two fingers and tightly squeezed shut his eyes. Suddenly Aaron saw a flame and smoke. Zeke had lit the cigarette with his fingers. *I'm dreaming,* he thought.

"The Grigori weren't there for it, but from what I hear, it

was pretty awful." The old angel took a drag and held it. He tilted his head back and blew the smoke into the air above him to form a billowing gray cloud.

"Not supposed to smoke in here either," he said, "but I can't help it. A real bitch to quit."

He took another puff and let it flow from his nostrils. "The Morningstar really blew it," Zeke said, returning to times past. "He didn't know how good he had it."

Aaron was confused. "The Morningstar?"

Zeke puffed greedily on the cigarette as if it were the last one he would ever have. "Lucifer. Lucifer Morningstar? Was once the right hand of God then got greedy? He and those who followed his lead screwed up even bigger than we did."

The room stank of smoke and Aaron wished there were a window to open. He waved his hand in front of his face in an attempt to breathe untainted air.

"Compared to what happened to him, we got off easy."

Gabriel started to dream as he lay on the floor; his legs twitched and paddled as if he were chasing something. Aaron grinned, distracted by his dog's antics. He had always been curious about his dreams. He'd have to ask Gabriel about it when he awoke.

He turned his attention back to Zeke. "You were punished?"

Zeke nodded ever so slowly, his eyes gazing off into the past as he remembered. "We were banished to Earth, never to see Heaven again. We wanted to be human so badly, we could live among them forever, they said." He sucked the cigarette down to the filter trying to get every last bit of carcinogen into his body.

"That wasn't so bad—was it?" Aaron asked, caution in his voice.

Zeke rubbed the tip of the cigarette's filter dead against the bedframe and flicked it to the floor. "Nah," he said in a dismissive tone. "Not really. It was what we wanted anyway."

Aaron could sense the angel's growing unrest. Zeke reached behind himself and began to rub the back of his neck and shoulder blades.

"Except they took our wings," he said. There was a tremble in his voice.

"Who . . . who took your wings?" Aaron asked.

"Who do you think?" Zeke answered sharply as he continued to rub his back and shoulders. "The Powers. They cut off our wings and . . . and they killed our children."

Zeke quickly swabbed at his eyes, smearing away any trace of emotion. Aaron wondered how long it had been since the angel had spoken of his past.

"They're ruthless, Aaron," he said. "They can sense when a Nephilim is reaching maturity—sometimes before. They hunt it down and kill it before it can gain full use of its birthright. That's why I did what I did—to give you a fighting chance."

Gabriel came suddenly awake as if sensing the pervasive atmosphere of sadness that now seemed to fill the tiny room with the cigarette smoke.

"What is wrong?" the dog asked, looking from Aaron to Zeke.

"Is that how you get even?" Aaron asked. "When you find us, you do something to turn us completely into Nephilim? Is that how you get back at the Powers for what they took from you?"

Zeke sadly shook his head. "I learned long ago not to interfere."

"And those others you've encountered—the Powers killed them?"

"Probably," Zeke said in a whisper. "Eventually."

"Why me then?" Aaron asked the fallen angel. "Why did you do it for me and not the others?"

Zeke shrugged. "I really don't know," he answered. "Something told me you're special."

CHAPTER SIX

Inside the V.I. Lenin nuclear power plant, twenty-five kilometers upstream from the Ukrainian city of Chernobyl, an angel screamed in rage.

Verchiel flung open two reinforced steel doors in the dilapidated structure that housed the number four reactor, the one that had exploded in 1986 rendering much of the surrounding Ukrainian countryside uninhabitable. In his time stationed upon this world, he had borne witness to the destructive potential of the human animal many times over, and wondered with disgust how long it would be before they destroyed themselves once and for all.

The master of the Powers strode into the reactor room, followed closely by six of his elite soldiers and the wild-eyed feral child held in check with collar and leash. The child coughed and sneezed as clouds of thick radioactive dust, undisturbed since the plant officially closed just a few years before, billowed into the air with their passing.

The explosion here had released forty times the amount of radioactivity unleashed by the atomic bombs dropped on Hiroshima and Nagasaki. Even now radiation levels were still incredibly high and quite dangerous to all forms of life. But that was of little concern to the nuclear power plant's current residents—or its visitors.

Verchiel stopped and stared with displeasure. The vast chamber had been turned into a place of worship, a makeshift church. An altar of sorts was laid out before him. Hundreds of candles of various sizes burned in front of a crude painting depicting an angelic being in the loving embrace of a mortal woman. And hovering in the sky above this coupling was an infant, a child glowing like the sun. Four figures, dressed in heavy woolen robes, knelt before the altar in silent prayer. Priests of the profane beliefs. They showed no sign that they were aware of his presence.

"Sacrilege!" Verchiel bellowed, his booming voice echoing off the concrete-and-metal walls of the high-ceilinged reactor chamber.

One of the figures stirred from his benediction, muttered something beneath his breath, and bowed his head to the shrine before he stood. The others continued their silent worship.

"Welcome to our holy place," he said.

"You disappoint me, Byleth," Verchiel responded as the figure at the crude altar gradually turned to face him. "A deserter and a disgrace to your host, but this . . ." He gestured to the shrine. "It offends the Almighty to the core of His Being."

Byleth smiled piously and strolled closer, hands clasped before him. "Does it really, Verchiel? Does the belief in a prophecy that preaches the reuniting of God with His fallen children really offend Him?" The robed angel stopped before them. "Or does it simply offend *you*?" Again Byleth smiled.

"What happened to you, Byleth?" Verchiel asked. "You were one of my finest soldiers. What made you fall so far from His grace?"

The angel chuckled softly as his hands disappeared inside the sleeves of his robe. "Is this usually what you ask before you kill us?"

Verchiel's lip curled back in a sneer. "It is merely an attempt to understand how you could turn your back upon a sacred duty to the Creator of all things."

"You must know these things before you condemn us to death?" Byleth asked, his gaze unwavering.

"Yes, before you are executed for your crimes," the Powers' commander answered. "A chance to purge yourself of guilt before the inevitable."

"I see," the priest said thoughtfully. "Has Camael answered for his crimes?"

Verchiel was silent, an explosive rage building inside him.

The priest smiled, pleased with the lack of response. "That is good," Byleth said. "As long as he lives, there's a chance that—"

"It is only a matter of time before the traitor meets with his much deserved fate," Verchiel interrupted, his words dripping with malice.

"Did you feel it, Verchiel?" the angel asked, one of his hands leaving the confines of his robe to gently touch his forehead. "Just a few glorious hours ago, did you feel it come into its own?"

"I felt nothing," Verchiel lied. He had been en route to Ukraine when he felt the psychic disturbance. The angel had been tracking half-breeds for hundreds of thousands of years and never had he felt an emergence so strong. It concerned him. "And if I had, what more could it be but the manifestation of another blemish upon the Creator's world? Something to hunt down and eradicate before it has the opportunity to offend any further."

The boy began to cough and Byleth sadly gazed at the human child who struggled against the confines of his leash.

"That poor creature should never have been brought here, Verchiel," the angel priest said. "The poisons in this air will do it irreparable harm."

Verchiel gazed at the creature with complete disinterest and looked back to the priest. "How else was I to find you in a timely manner?" he asked. "If it should die then so be it; I'll find another monkey to help with my hunt."

The others at the altar were standing now and had turned to watch the encounter. They all wore the same idiotic grin and Verchiel could not wait to see it burned from their faces.

"There is desperation in your tone, Verchiel. You felt it as strongly as we," Byleth said as he shared a moment with his fellow worshippers. "And you are afraid—afraid that the prophecy is coming to fruition."

Verchiel snarled and spread his wings, knocking Byleth to the floor by the altar in a cloud of radioactive dust. "What black sorcery did the human seer use to corrupt so many of you? Tell me so I might have any who practice such poisonous villainy scoured from the planet."

"Always so dramatic, Verchiel," Byleth said, struggling to his feet. "There was no magic, no corrupting spell. Nothing but a vision of unification and an end to the violence."

A sword of fire grew in Verchiel's hand. The larger particles of irradiated dust and dirt in the air sparked as they drifted into contact with the divine flame. Following his lead, his soldiers each manifested blazing weapons as well.

"And what has this idyllic vision brought you thus far?" asked the Powers' leader. "You hide yourself away in the poisoned wastelands created by the animals, denying your true place in the order of things. Is this some kind of punishment, Byleth? Do you think that this half-breed prophet you imagine is coming will look upon you fondly because of it?" Verchiel said with disgust. "Pathetic."

"This place and the poisoned land around it reminds us of what we were and what we have become," Byleth explained. "Once, we were filled with His holy virtue, on a mission to wipe away evil—but we were tainted by the violence and a self-righteousness that said we were acting in His name."

"Everything I do, I do for Him," Verchiel replied, his fiery blade burning brighter and radiating an intense heat.

"That is what you believe to be true," Byleth said. "But there is another way—a way without death, a way that brings the end of our exile and the beginning of our redemption." The angel held out his hand, directing Verchiel to look upon the altar. "*This* is the way, Verchiel. *This* is our future."

Verchiel shook his head. "No, it is blasphemy." He raised a hand to his soldiers behind him. "Remove them from the altar," he commanded.

The Powers leaped into the air, their wings stirring choking clouds of fine, radioactive debris.

"We will fight you, Verchiel!" Byleth cried. A weapon of fire grew in his grip, and others blazed up in the hands of his fellow believers, yet they seemed pitiful by comparison to the swords of the Powers. Feeble wings grew from their backs.

"Look at you," Verchiel said as he strode toward them and their sacred shrine. "Belief in this heresy has reduced you to mere shadows of your former glory. How sad."

"Our past sins have made us thus," Byleth bellowed in anger as he leaped at Verchiel, his sword held high.

But he was intercepted by the savagery of Verchiel's elite guard and forced to the ground beneath their weight. Verchiel watched with great amusement as the priests were hauled away from their shrine.

"This is the future, you say?" he asked as he looked from them to the burning candles and crude artwork.

They struggled against their captors, but the Powers' soldiers held them fast. "It won't end with us," Byleth hissed. "That which has been foretold now walks among us."

Verchiel looked to the altar, fiery indignation burning in his breast. "I see no future here," he said as he flapped his powerful wings. The mighty gusts of air extinguished the candles and toppled the offensive painting. "All I see is the end."

Verchiel grinned maliciously as he turned back to the priests, but his triumph quickly turned to confusion when he noted the serene looks upon their faces.

"It's far from over, Verchiel," Byleth said. "Look for yourself," he added with a tilt of his head toward the altar.

The Powers' leader turned and watched with horror as the candles, one by one, began to reignite. In a burst of fury, he spread his wings and launched himself toward the grinning priest, once a soldier in his service. Savagely he thrust the end of his fiery blade into Byleth's chest, reveling in the change of his expression from a grin of the enlightened to one of excruciating pain.

Byleth's fellow priests gasped in unison. "Please," one of his fellow believers plaintively whispered.

Verchiel leaned in close, watching the flesh of the renegade angel's face bubble and blacken as he burned from within. "They beg for mercy, but alas, their words fall upon deaf ears."

Byleth slid to the floor, Verchiel's blade still within him, his heavy robes beginning to ignite. "And . . . and how are *your* words received, Verchiel?" He gasped as he lifted his head, puddles of liquid flesh sizzling upon the dust-covered ground. "What does the Lord of Lords have to say when *you* speak?"

Verchiel pulled his sword from the priest's chest. "The Almighty and I . . . we do not need to converse."

Byleth smiled hideously, his teeth nothing more than charred nubs protruding from oozing black gums. "As I imagined."

Verchiel felt his ire rise. "That amuses you, Byleth? My lack of communication with the Heavenly Father makes you smile in the face of your imminent death?"

His body awash in flames, the priest slowly raised his charred, skeletal hands to the sides of his face—to where his ears used to be. "Deaf . . . ears," Byleth whispered. "Deaf ears." And then he began to laugh.

The sound enraged Verchiel. He pulled back his arm and brought the heavenly blade down upon the burning priest once, twice, three times, reducing his offender to ash. Then he turned from the smoking remains to face his prisoners. "This is what the profanity of your beliefs has brought you," he said, directing their attention to the ruin of their master.

The sword of flame receded to nothing, and Verchiel strode away toward the doors that would take him from the poisonous chamber.

"Kill them," he said, void of emotion, his back to them. "I want to forget they ever existed."

And he left the room, the screams of the dying priests escorting him on his journey, the malignant words of an ancient prophecy feverishly swirling around in his mind.

Michael Jonas glanced at his watch. He set his pen down on top of the insurance forms he was in the process of completing and picked up the phone.

Where is he? the psychiatrist wondered.

The dial tone droned in his ear as he searched for Aaron's phone number in his file. He punched in the numbers and listened as it began to ring.

Aaron Corbet had been nothing but punctual all the years that he'd treated him, and Jonas found it odd that he would simply blow off their appointment, especially after their discussion yesterday morning.

He would have been lying if he had said he wasn't fascinated by the rather unique talent the young man had exhibited; in all his twenty-five years of practicing he'd never seen anything quite so bizarre and yet, exciting. Certainly Aaron could be delusional, and was already fluent in Portuguese, Spanish, and Latin, but his gut told him no. Jonas grew eager with the thought of the papers he might publish on this specific case, and the accolades he would receive from his peers.

"Hello?" answered a woman's voice from the other end of the line.

"Yes, hi," Jonas said in greeting. "Is Aaron there please?"

"No, he's not," the woman replied. "Can I ask who's calling?"

He would need to be cautious; patient-doctor confidentiality was an issue. "This is Michael Jonas," he responded professionally. "Is this Mrs. Stanley?"

"Yes, Dr. Jonas. How are you? Aaron went out with the dog early this morning and he hasn't returned." There was a pause and Jonas knew what was coming next. After being a psychiatrist for so many years he could read people and their reactions. "Is there a problem, Doctor? Is . . . is Aaron going to see you again?"

She was concerned and he wanted to put her mind at ease without sharing Aaron's personal business.

"No need for panic, Mrs. Stanley. I'm just checking in, calling to see how he's doing. Would you have him get in touch with me when he comes in? I should be at the office until well after six."

"Certainly, Doctor," she said, less tension in her tone. "I'll give him the message."

"Thanks so much, Mrs. Stanley. You have a good day."

"Same to you," she responded, and hung up.

Jonas returned the receiver to the cradle and again glanced at his watch. *Interesting,* he thought. *Aaron went out early and no one's seen him since.* Jonas wondered if he had frightened him away. Maybe he shouldn't have mentioned his friend at Mass General.

The cartoon image of a scholarly paper with flapping wings flying out a window danced across his mind and he smiled. Jonas reached for his pen to resume his weekly paperwork and saw that he wasn't alone.

"Jesus Christ!" he gasped as he threw himself back against his chair, startled.

A man stood in front of his desk. He appeared older, but was tall, striking, and although he wore a suit, Jonas could see that he was in good physical condition.

"How did you get in here?" Jonas asked nervously.

The man simply stood staring at the desktop. He seemed to be studying Jonas's paperwork.

"Can I help you with something, Mr. . . . ?"

The stranger said nothing, continuing to gaze at the top of the desk. And then he raised his head and looked at Jonas. He was handsome in a distinguished kind of way. He reminded the psychiatrist of the actor who used to play James Bond, and later starred in that movie about the Russian submarine. But it was his eyes that were strangely different. There was something wrong with them. Jonas thought of the eyes of a stuffed owl that his grandmother had kept on display at her summer cottage in Maine: dark black in the center and encircled with gold.

"Camael," the stranger answered in a powerful timbre. "I am Camael—and I've come in search of the child."

Camael tilted his head back and sniffed the air. "The child was here," he said as he turned in a slow circle, "not long ago—a day perhaps." He moved closer to the desk, the sour smell of the human's fear mixing with the strong essence of the Nephilim. It was a masculine odor, a male scent. "I mean the child no harm, but it is imperative that I find him."

Dr. Jonas stood and slammed his meaty hands down onto the desktop aggressively. "Listen," he said, "I don't have a clue as to what you're talking about."

The psychiatrist was a large man. He might have been powerful once, but the years had been unkind and his body had gone to seed. He pointed a square finger authoritatively to the door. "So I'm going to have to ask you to leave."

As if on cue, the office door swung slowly open and Camael snarled as two of Verchiel's Powers came into the room.

The two took notice of him immediately and emitted a snakelike hiss from their mouths. "The betrayer," spat one with a head of jet-black hair, his body lowering to a readied crouch. It had been millennia since Camael had last commanded them, but he believed this one was called Hadriel.

"What the hell is going on here?" the human blustered. "Leave my office at once or I'm going to . . ."

"Silence, ape!" the other angel warned. Camael knew the name of this one for certain. He was Cassiel, one of Verchiel's crueler operatives.

"I strongly advise you to take cover, Doctor," Camael warned. He did not take his eyes from the Powers, feeling that special calm before battle slowly wash over him.

"This *ape* is going to call the police," the flustered psychiatrist said as he reached for the telephone on his desk.

Cassiel moved as a blur. His hand shot out and from his fingertips a searing white light emanated. "I asked you to be quiet."

The doctor screamed out in agony as his body burst into flame. He fell back against the wall and crumpled to the floor, completely engulfed by fire. He twitched and thrashed in excruciating death and everywhere he touched began to burn as well.

Camael used the distraction to strike. In his mind he saw the weapon he wanted and it formed in his grasp, composed of heavenly fire. He attacked, swinging the burning blade at

Hadriel, who seemed engrossed in the psychiatrist's death throes. But the angel reacted quickly, summoning a weapon of his own, a spear—and blocking the swipe that would have certainly taken his head.

The weapons clashed, sounding like the grumble of thunder.

"The great Camael," Hadriel taunted as he pushed him away and thrust forward with the burning spear. "One of our greatest, reduced to living amongst the human animals."

Camael sidestepped to avoid the spear thrust and brought his blade down, cutting his attacker's weapon explosively in two. "You talk too much, Hadriel," he said as he stepped in close and lashed out, the pommel of the sword connecting with the side of the soldier's head, bringing him to his knees. "A human trait, I believe," Camael said to the stunned angel.

Camael heard the whisper of another weapon cutting through the air. He unfurled his wings and flew upward as Cassiel's sword passed harmlessly beneath him.

"Are you lonely, Camael?" Cassiel asked as he too pushed off from the floor and spread his wings to join him in the air.

Camael parried Cassiel's next thrust and maneuvered in closer. He brought a knee up sharply into the angel's stomach. "My mission is all the company I need," he said as he drove his forehead into the angel's face. "I've grown to enjoy my solitude."

Cassiel plummeted to the floor.

The office was on fire and a thick black smoke filled the air.

"Despised by your brothers, feared by the kind you once destroyed." Cassiel struggled to all fours. He looked up at Camael and smiled. "All for the ramblings of an animal plagued by madness."

"Feel no sadness for me, brother," Camael said as he glided down toward the angel, his sword at the ready. "But ask yourself this: What if the seer was right? What if it all turns out to be true? What then?"

Cassiel shrieked and attacked again. "It will never come to be," he screamed as a dagger appeared in his hand and he slashed at Camael, driving him away. "Lies, all lies!"

Camael recoiled from a swipe of Cassiel's blade, reared back, and drove the heel of his foot into the angel's chest. Cassiel was propelled back by the force of the blow and tumbled over a chair in front of the desk.

The smoke had grown thicker and Camael knew that it wouldn't be long before the office was completely consumed by fire. He had to find out the identity of the boy. *The essence about this Nephilim is strong, perhaps the strongest I have ever felt,* he thought. *So strong, in fact, that the Powers had no need of a tracker to find him.* He tensed, waiting for Cassiel to rise, his mind aflutter. *Could he be the reason why Verchiel has increased the frequency and savagery of his attacks?* He again dared to wonder, *could this actually be the One?*

Camael screamed out in sudden pain and rage as Hadriel's

spear tore through his shoulder from behind. It was sloppy of him. Distracted by his musings, he had failed to notice Verchiel's other henchman emerge from the thick smoke, a new weapon in hand.

"Finish him," Cassiel ordered as he climbed to his feet among the flames.

Hadriel pulled back the spearhead and lunged again, but this time Camael was ready. He sprang from the floor, wings spread. He had summoned new weapons as well—short swords—from the armory of his imagination and held one firmly in each hand.

Hadriel's thrust passed beneath him and before he could react, Camael brought one of his swords viciously down, cleaving the angel's skull like the wood of a rotted tree stump.

"No!" Cassiel shrieked as he soared toward Camael, eager to avenge his fallen comrade.

"Verchiel's soldiers have grown sloppy," Camael taunted as he pulled the weapon from the angel's skull and blocked the enraged Cassiel's attack with it. He thrust upward with the other blade and pierced his attacker's chest.

Cassiel wailed and thrashed, his wings beating frantically, as he fell to the floor clutching at the weeping chest wound.

Camael strode through the smoke and fire toward his fallen foe. "What does Verchiel know about this one—the Nephilim boy?" he questioned. "Tell me and I'll let you live."

Cassiel struggled to his feet using the wall for support.

"You'll let me live? Do you hear yourself, Camael? I thought you deserted the Powers because you tired of the violence, of all the killing." The angel held a trembling hand to his bleeding wound. "I think you've become what you most hate," Cassiel hissed as he reached into the fire by the wall and pulled out the blackened, still-burning skull of the psychiatrist and hurled it at him.

Camael hacked at the flaming projectile, cutting it in two as it neared him. Using the moment, Cassiel spread his wings and leaped toward the burning curtains across the room. The fleeing angel passed through the flaming material, and then the glass of the window beyond, to escape with an explosive crash.

The fire burned brighter, larger, as the sudden blast of oxygen fed the hungry conflagration.

The Nephilim's identity more important than pursuit, Camael rushed to the desk. The papers strewn about its surface had already started to smolder and curl. His eyes scanned the documents, searching for something—anything that would tell him who the boy was.

Beneath a folder charred at the edges, he saw it. A single sentence scrawled upon a piece of notepaper attached to a file. "Patient believes he now has the ability to understand and speak all foreign languages."

Camael snatched up the folder. Something moaned above him and he moved out of the way as a portion of the ceiling collapsed in a shower of flaming debris. In the distance, the mournful howls of fire engines filled the air. He had what he needed and prepared to leave the scene with haste.

Time was of the essence, for as soon as Verchiel learned of his involvement, all Hell would most assuredly break loose.

CHAPTER SEVEN

Within the unused bell tower of the Church of the Blessed Sacrament, Verchiel stared into the familiar face of human mortality. Since the Powers' return from the poisonous wasteland that was Chernobyl, their human tracker had fallen terribly ill. The poor creature lay upon a plastic tarp in a darkened area of the tower where once a bell had hung. It shivered, moaning softly as it slowly died from the radioactive poisons it had been exposed to on their last hunt.

"Is there nothing more you can do for it?" Verchiel asked the human healer who was administering to the wounded Cassiel.

The healer, called Kraus, turned his blind, cataract-covered eyes toward the sound of Verchiel's voice.

"I've done all I can, my master," he said as he nimbly

plucked a golden needle from inside a worn leather satchel and deftly placed a thick thread through its eye. His lack of vision had not affected his skill with a needle. "It won't be long before he succumbs to—"

"Its skill served me well," the Powers' leader interrupted, taking his eyes from the dying boy covered in black oozing sores. "It will be bothersome to find another."

Verchiel moved across the cluttered tower, its space now used for storage, to loom over the healer and his current patient, the boy almost completely forgotten. "And you, Cassiel," he asked smoothly, "have you served me as well?"

"Yes, my lord," Cassiel answered breathlessly as he lay upon the dusty floor while the blind old man sewed closed his wound.

"You say that Camael was there before you?" Verchiel asked as he watched the old man, whose job it was to care for the angels' physical forms, pull shut the wound in his soldier's chest with skillful stitches. Though primitive by angelic standards, the human apes did occasionally surprise even him with their usefulness.

Verchiel squatted beside the healer as he completed the task. "He will heal?" Verchiel asked. "The wound will not kill him?"

Kraus flinched from the power of Verchiel's voice. "It . . . it will not," the man stammered as he turned his blind gaze toward his master. "The injury will need time to mend, but it will heal."

What is it about the defective ones, the blind, the mentally challenged, that makes them such superior servants? Verchiel wondered, thinking of the nonimpaired humans often driven to madness just by being in the angels' presence.

"You are done here," Verchiel proclaimed, and gently brushed the top of the older man's head with the tips of his fingers. "See to the tracker; ease him into death if need be."

The man gasped aloud, his body trembling as if in rapture, as if touched by God—or the next best thing. Kraus folded shut his satchel of healing instruments and scurried away to the darkened corner to help a dying member of his own breed.

Perhaps their imperfections make them more receptive to the extraordinary. It was a hypothesis Verchiel hoped to explore further someday, when their mission was finally complete. He roused himself from his contemplation. There was still much to do.

"The Nephilim I sense so keenly—what information have you brought of him?" Verchiel asked Cassiel, who still lay upon the wooden floor.

"I bring information about Camael," Cassiel said eagerly. "Living amongst the apes has made him frail and weak. It . . . it can only be a matter of time before we destroy the traitor and . . ."

"Frail and weak, you say?" Verchiel asked, a sour smile upon his thin lips. In the church below, Mass was beginning with the sound of a pipe organ. The melodious chords of a hymn drifted up into the bell tower. The music annoyed him. "But not so frail and weak as to prevent him from slaying Hadriel and gravely wounding you?"

Cassiel squirmed, struggling to sit up. "The . . . the space was cramped and there was blinding smoke. Please . . ."

The music from the church below came to an end and the murmuring of prayer began.

"So you bring me nothing of the half-breed?"

Cassiel pushed himself into a sitting position. A dark fluid began to seep from around the wound's stitching as his movements pulled them taut. "The fire . . . it was burning out of control and Camael was already present. There was little we could do . . ."

The piteous words of his soldier enraged Verchiel almost as much as the monkeys' attempts to speak with God drifting up from the ceremony in the church below. Verchiel reached down to Cassiel's wound and dug his fingers beneath the stitching.

Cassiel screamed.

"Silence," Verchiel spat as he tore the thick, black thread away from the angel's flesh.

How dare they think they can speak to Him, he thought, revolted by the worshippers praying in the church below. *If the Lord God will not speak with me, then why do they have the audacity to believe that He would listen to their pathetic chatter?*

Verchiel thought, perturbed. He cast aside the surgical thread and bits of torn skin that dangled from it.

Cassiel lay silently writhing upon the floor, his wound now gaping wide, and weeping.

"You failed me," Verchiel growled as he picked Cassiel up from the floor and held him aloft. "And I do not deal well with failure."

The organ played again and the monkeys were singing. *Why do they insist on doing that?* he wondered. Did they believe that the discordant sounds from their primitive mouths would please the Creator, He who had orchestrated the *symphony* of creation?

Cassiel flapped his wings as he struggled in his leader's grasp. "Master Verchiel . . . mercy," he wheezed.

Verchiel needed to hear something other than the animals' wailing below, something that would calm his frenzied state. Holding Cassiel by the throat, he reached out and grabbed one of his soldier's wings.

"Please . . . no," Cassiel pleaded.

Verchiel took the delicate appendage in his hand and began to bend it, to twist it. The sound was horrible— sharp—as the cartilage gave way beneath his grip. The angel was screaming, begging and crying to be forgiven for his trespasses.

Verchiel let Cassiel drop from his hands. The angel sobbed, his wing twisted at an obscene angle.

"Administer to him," Verchiel barked, knowing that the healer was listening from the shadows, waiting to serve. "Disappoint me again, and I'll tear them both from your body," Verchiel instructed Cassiel as he turned his back upon him.

He had decided to be merciful; it was what the Creator would have done.

Aaron was dreaming again.

An old man with a milky white eye is using a pointed stick to write on a tablet made of red clay.

Aaron looks around at his surroundings. Where the hell am I? he wonders. He is in a single-room structure, a hut, and it appears to be made out of straw and large mud bricks. Primitive oil lamps placed around the room provide the only source of light. It stinks of body odor and urine.

The old man is deathly thin, his hair and beard incredibly long. There are things living in the wild expanse of his hair. He finishes a symbol on the clay tablet and slowly raises his shaggy head to Aaron.

He points the writing instrument and in a guttural tongue he speaks. "It is you I see in the future—you I write of now."

The bad eye rolls obscenely in the right socket, and Aaron cannot help but think of the moon.

The old man reaches down with a skeletal hand covered in a thin, almost translucent layer of spotted skin and turns the tablet so Aaron can see—so he can read.

Gazing down at the primitive script, Aaron knows what the man has written. It is a prediction of some kind, something about the union of angel and mortal woman, creating a bridge for those who have fallen.

What the heck does that mean? he wonders. He starts to speak but stops, interrupted by screams from outside the hovel, and something else.

The old man stares at him and slowly brings a hand up to cover the bad eye. "Go now," he whispers. "You have seen your destiny. Now you must fulfill it."

Cries of fear are moving closer, and there is another sound in the air—a now familiar sound that fills him with dread.

The pounding sound of wings.

Aaron came awake with a choking gasp. His heart raced and his body crawled with nervous perspiration.

He could still hear wings flapping, and then they were silent.

Gabriel, lying beside him atop the covers, had also awakened and was staring at him.

"Did I wake you, boy?" Aaron asked groggily as he reached out from under the bedclothes and stroked the dog's head. "Sorry, bad dreams again."

As he patted the dog he felt himself begin to calm, his pulse rate slow. Gabriel was as good as a tranquilizer.

The dog licked his hand affectionately. *"The old man was scary, wasn't he?"* Gabriel said, nuzzling closer.

"Old man? You mean Zeke, Gabe?" Aaron asked, eyes beginning to close, still patting the velvety fur that covered the dog's hard head.

The dog turned his gaze to him. *"No, not Zeke,"* he answered, *"the old man in the dream. He scared me, too."*

It hit him with the force of a pile driver. Aaron struggled beneath the sheets and blanket into a sitting position. He reached over and turned on the bedside light.

"How do you know about the old man in the dream, Gabriel?" Aaron asked, terrified by what the answer might be.

"I dreamed it," the dog answered proudly. His tail thumped happily. *"I have different dreams now, not just running and jumping and chasing rabbits."*

Aaron leaned back and let his head bounce off the wooden headboard. "I can't believe this. You had the same dream as I did?"

"Yes," Gabriel said. *"Why did his eye look like the moon, Aaron?"*

Aaron felt as though he were on a roller coaster, perpetually plunging farther and farther into darkness, picking up speed, with no sign of the horrific ride's end.

And there was nothing he wanted more than to get off.

"Please make it stop," he whispered.

Gabriel crawled closer and lay his chin upon Aaron's leg. *"It's all right, Aaron,"* the dog said devotedly. *"Don't be sad."*

Aaron opened his eyes and began to pat the dog again.

"It's not all right, Gabe. Everything is spinning out of control. What's happening to me—what's happened to you, it . . . isn't right."

Gabriel pushed himself into a sitting position and pressed his butt against his master. *"I was hurt very badly and you made me better,"* the dog said with a tilt of his head. *"Are you upset that I'm . . . different now?"*

Aaron looked his best friend in the eyes and shook his head. "No, I'm not upset about that. Matter of fact, that's the only thing about this business that I'm willing to get used to." He reached out and stroked the side of the dog's head. "It's everything else—the bizarro dreams, the stuff Zeke's been telling me. . . ."

He leaned back against the headboard again and sighed with exasperation. "I don't want this, Gabriel. I have enough to worry about. I have to finish high school with a decent enough GPA to get into a good college."

"GPA?" the dog questioned. *"What is this GPA?"*

"Grade point average," Aaron explained. "Doing very, very well in my classes at school."

Gabriel nodded in understanding.

"All this crap about angels and Nephilim—I don't care if it's true, I just can't deal with it." At that moment Aaron made a decision. "I'm gonna tell Zeke I'm done. I don't want to know anything else. Everything is going to be just like it was before my birthday."

He glanced at the clock on the nightstand. It was close to four A.M. and he wanted to go back to sleep; he was both mentally and physically exhausted. But he also feared the dreams.

"Well, let's give this another try," he said as he reached over and switched off the light. He lay his head down on the pillow and put his arm around the dog.

"Good night, Aaron," Gabriel said as he moved up to share the pillow. *"Try and dream only good dreams."*

"I'll do my best, pal," Aaron answered, and before long, fell into a deep sleep active with dreams, not of old men, ancient prophecies, and angels, but of running very fast in the sunshine and chasing rabbits.

Verchiel noiselessly descended the winding wooden steps from the bell tower of the Blessed Sacrament Church. The stairway was enshrouded in total darkness, but it meant nothing to a being that had navigated the void before the Almighty brought about the light of Creation.

At the foot of the stairs was a locked door, and Verchiel willed the simple mechanism to open, and it swung wide to admit him to the place of worship. The angel found his way from the back room where the holy men prepared themselves to address their tribe, and went out onto the altar. He gazed above him at the steepled ceiling and the giant cross of gold, the symbol of their faith, hanging there. From his place on the altar, he looked out at the church, the early morning sunrise diluted by colorful stained glass windows. There was a certain peacefulness here that he did not expect from the animals.

Verchiel stepped from the altar and strode down the aisle. When he had traveled half the length of the church, he turned to face the great hanging cross. This was how the primitives did it, he mused, taking in the sight before him. This was how they attempted to communicate with God.

He recalled the countless times that he scoffed at their crude practices, as they built their altars of stone and wood and attempted to speak to the one true God through the act of prayer. It was a thought that filled him with unease, but perhaps this house of worship was where he could re-establish his connection with Heaven and again converse with the Creator of all things.

He recalled how they did it—how they prayed—and moved into one of the wooden pews. Awkwardly Verchiel knelt down and folded his hands before him, his dark eyes upon the altar ahead.

"It is I, Lord," he uttered in the language of animals. "It has been too long since we last spoke, and I am in need of Your guidance."

The angel gazed around the holy place for signs that he was being heard. There was nothing but the fading echo of his own voice.

Perhaps if he were closer. He left the pew and strode back to the altar.

"My mission, my very reason for existence, grows murky these days."

He gazed intently at the golden cross, hanging in the air above.

"There is a prophecy of which I'm certain You are aware. It talks about forgiveness and mercy for those who have fallen from Your grace, oh Heavenly Father."

Verchiel began to pace in front of the altar.

"It says that You will forgive them their most horrid trespasses—and that there will be a prophet of sorts, one who will act as the bringer of absolution."

He was growing agitated, angry. The air around him crackled with suppressed hostility. "And he will be a Nephilim," Verchiel spat, reviled by the word. "A Nephilim, a creature unfit to live beneath Your gaze, a mockery of life that I have done my best to eradicate from Your world with fire and flood."

The angel stopped pacing. "The wicked say that the time for the prophecy is nigh, that soon a bridge between the fallen angels and Heaven will be established." He moved up onto the altar, his gaze never wavering from the golden symbol. "You need to tell me, Lord. Do I follow my instincts and ignore the blasphemous writings of those little better than monkeys? Or do I ignore the purpose bestowed upon me after the Great War in Heaven? I need to know, my Father. Do I continue with my sacred chores and destroy all that offends You, or should I step back and let the prophecy prevail?"

Verchiel waited, expecting some kind of sign, but there was none, his plaintive questions met with silence.

The rage that had served him in war all these many millennia exploded from inside him. His wings came forth from his back and a mighty blade of flame appeared in his grasp. He shook the burning sword at the cross and voiced his anger. "Tell me, my God, for I am lost. Give me some indication of Your will."

There was a sound from somewhere upon the altar, and Verchiel stood mesmerized.

Has the Creator heard my plea? the angel thought. Was the Almighty about to bestow upon him a sign to assuage his doubts?

An old woman came out from the back room, a plastic bucket of water in one hand and a mop in the other. It was obvious that she had heard his supplication and was curious to see who prayed so powerfully.

Her eyes bulged from her ancient skull at the sight of him. The bucket of soapy water slipped from her grasp to spill upon the altar floor.

What an awesome sight he must be to behold, he mused, spreading his wings to their full span, catching the muted, morning sunlight.

She attempted to flee, wild panic in her spastic movements, but stopped cold in her tracks. An ancient hand, skeletal with age, clutched frantically at her chest and her mouth opened in a silent howl. The old woman fell to the ground in a heap, her dying gaze rooted upon the golden symbol of her faith displayed above her.

Verchiel smiled. "So nice to hear from You again," he purred, divining meaning from what he had just borne witness to.

"Thy will be done."

Still in his sweatpants and T-shirt, Aaron slowly descended the stairs. Gabriel waited eagerly at the bottom. Aaron yawned and smacked his lips. The foul taste of sleep still coated the inside of his mouth. Hopefully he could get some juice and then get back upstairs to run a toothbrush around his mouth before he had to speak to anybody.

He'd slept longer than he wanted to, but seeing that he'd had some problems last night, and that it was Sunday, he wasn't all that concerned—just very thirsty.

"Can I eat now?" Gabriel asked from his side as Aaron padded barefoot down the hallway to the kitchen.

"Just as soon as I get some juice," he told the dog.

The linoleum was cold on the soles of his feet, and it helped to clear away the grogginess that came with morning. Lori sat at the table beneath the kitchen window, feeding cereal to Stevie.

"Hey," Aaron said, pulling on the refrigerator door.

"Hey, yourself," his mother answered.

Gabriel momentarily left his side to wish Lori and Stevie a good morning. Aaron almost drank from the carton, but thought better of it and reached to the cabinet for a glass. Filling it halfway, he leaned against the counter and attempted to quench his great thirst.

Lori was staring at him. She had that look on her face, the one that said something was wrong—that she had bad news to tell. Aaron was familiar with the look; it was the same one she'd worn when the family vacation to Disney World was canceled because the travel agency had unexpectedly gone out of business. They never did get to Disney.

"What's wrong?" he asked.

Stevie decided to feed himself and took the spoon from her. He shoveled a mound of Sugar Smacks onto the spoon and then, halfway to his mouth, dumped it on the floor.

Gabriel immediately went to work cleaning up the spillage.

"Stevie, no," Lori said as she took the spoon away from the child and pushed the bowl from his reach. "I have some really bad news for you," she said, placing a soiled, rolled-up napkin on the table.

"What is it?" Aaron asked, moving to join her.

Lynn's Sunday newspaper was on the table, and she turned it around so that he could see the headline.

PSYCHIATRIST KILLED IN BLAZE it read.

Aaron wasn't sure why he should be upset, until he noticed the picture that accompanied the story. The picture was of Lynn firefighters as they fought the blaze in an office building. The caption below read, "Dr. Michael Jonas was killed yesterday when his office at 257 Boston Street was engulfed in flames. Fire officials are still investigating the blaze, but believe that a gas leak may have been responsible for the explosion."

Aaron pried his eyes from the newspaper and looked at his mother. "Oh my God" was all he could manage.

Lori reached across the table and squeezed his hand. "I'm so sorry, hon," she said supportively. "Did you try to reach him last night?"

Aaron heard the question at the periphery of his thoughts. Dr. Jonas was dead. He was supposed to have seen the man yesterday, but after the business with Zeke, he'd completely forgotten. He'd planned on calling Monday to apologize.

His mother's hand was still on his. She gave it a squeeze. "Aaron?" she asked.

"I'm sorry," he said. "I zoned out. What did you say?"

"Dr. Jonas—he called yesterday while you were out," she answered. "Did you try to return his call?"

Aaron slowly shook his head. "He called? I . . . I didn't see the message."

When he'd come in last night he'd been tired. The family was out to supper, and the quiet in the house was so inviting.

He'd fed Gabriel, taken him out, and then gone up to bed to watch some television. He hadn't even thought to check for messages.

"I didn't know he called," he said dreamily, picturing the man just two days ago, full of life and eager to help him. "How could this happen?" he asked, not expecting an answer.

"They said it was probably a gas leak," Lori replied as she picked up the child's cereal bowl and brought it to the sink.

Stevie got down from his chair and toddled off toward the family room, oblivious to anything in his path.

Gabriel hovered around Aaron and he realized that the dog had yet to be fed. "I'm sorry, pal," he said, going to the drainboard at the sink and retrieving the dog's food bowl.

Lori was doing the breakfast dishes. "If it was gas, just one spark would do the trick—"

Aaron filled Gabriel's bowl and placed it on the mat near his water dish. His mother was still talking, but it was her last words that created the disturbing image in his mind.

He saw Zeke lighting his cigarette.

"If it was gas . . ."

His mother's words echoed through his head.

Zeke lit his smoke with the tips of his fingers. Fire from the tips of his fingers.

". . . just one spark would do the trick."

CHAPTER EIGHT

Aaron couldn't wait for Monday to arrive.

Ken Curtis High had become his safe haven. Once behind its walls, the rules were simple—go to class, do the homework, take the test. Not so in the real world lately, a place that was becoming less and less real for him with each passing day.

At school he could push thoughts of talking dogs, Nephilim, Powers, and death to the back of his cluttered mind—at least until the bell rang at two thirty. School was the ultimate distraction, and that was exactly what he craved.

At lunchtime Aaron was at his locker dropping off books from his morning classes. He wasn't feeling hungry, but knowing he had to work at the clinic right after school, he figured he should probably eat something.

His psychology text slipped to the floor, and his thoughts turned to Michael Jonas as he bent to pick it up. The questions flooded forward as if a faucet had been turned on to its maximum. *What really caused the fire?*

He saw Zeke's fingertip flash and his cigarette ignite.

Why am I thinking like this? he wondered, returning the book to the shelf in the locker. He knew that Zeke didn't have anything to do with the fire that took his psychiatrist's life. The newspaper said it had started in the early afternoon, when he and Gabriel had been with the fallen angel in his hotel room.

But what about the others? he thought with a wave of foreboding. *What about the . . . Powers?*

His stomach churned uneasily as he slammed closed his locker. *Maybe I'll just skip lunch and go to the library.*

Head down, he turned and nearly plowed into Vilma Santiago.

Aaron stumbled back. "Hi," he blurted out nervously. "Didn't see you there, sorry."

"Hi."

She seemed unconcerned with his clumsiness, but as nervous around him as he was feeling around her. In the background by her locker, he could see two of her friends playing Secret Weasel, trying not to be noticed.

"How're you doing?" Aaron asked lamely. If he hadn't blown it yet, it was only a matter of time.

"I'm good," she answered. "How're you?"

"I'm good," he said with a nervous nod and an idiot grin. "Real good." His mind was blank, completely void of all electrical activity. He had no idea what to say next, and wondered how she'd react if he started to cry.

The silence was becoming painfully awkward when she spoke. "Are you going to lunch?" she asked, looking quickly away.

And all of a sudden lunch seemed like a wonderful idea.

"Yeah, lunch is great—it's lunchtime—sure, I'm going to lunch." Aaron couldn't believe how he was acting. *What a complete idiot.* He wouldn't blame her in the least if she turned around and walked away. No. *Ran* away.

"Do you want to have lunch with me?" she asked, her voice growing incredibly soft, as if expecting rejection.

He was speechless. No words available, please try again later. He was horrified, he couldn't even think of something *stupid* to say.

Vilma suddenly looked embarrassed. "If you have something else to do, I completely understand and . . ."

"I'd love to," he finally managed. "Sorry . . . it's just that I'm kind of . . . y'know, surprised, that you'd want me to."

She smiled slyly, and it felt as though the temperature in the hallway rose sixty degrees. *Great, now I'm sweating,* he thought. *Real cool.*

"I'm full of surprises, Aaron Corbet," she said with a flip

of her dark hair. "So, do you want to go to the caf or off campus?"

Just then somebody called his name. They both turned to see Mrs. Vistorino, the guidance office secretary, coming down the hallway. She was notorious for her brightly colored pantsuits, and today she was wearing lime green with shoes to match.

"Aaron," Mrs. Vistorino called again. "I'm glad I caught you."

"Is there something wrong?" he asked cautiously, the sickly feeling in the pit of his stomach returning.

"There's an admissions representative from Emerson College in the office, and he wants to see you about your application."

"Emerson?" Aaron muttered to himself. "But I didn't . . ."

The woman turned and started back from whence she came. "He mentioned something about a full scholarship, so I'd get my butt down there if I were you."

Vilma touched his arm. "You'd better get going," she said, looking genuinely excited for him.

He was torn. He really wanted to go to lunch with Vilma, but the potential for a scholarship was something he couldn't pass up. "What about you?" he asked. "I really want to—"

"We can do lunch tomorrow," she said, cutting him off. "Don't worry about me." She turned toward her friends who were still gawking from across the hall. "I'll just grab some lunch with them. No problem, really." Vilma pointed him down the hall. "Maybe you could meet me later—let me know how the interview went?"

"Sure," he responded, stunned by her interest. "I'll meet you at your locker after last period." He was going to turn and wave good-bye, then decided against it. It wouldn't be cool.

But as he turned the corner he lost control, looked back, and waved. Vilma was still watching him and waved back. Her two nosey friends were with her now and they both began to laugh.

As he headed toward the guidance office, he mentally reviewed the college applications he had already sent out. And try as he might, he couldn't remember ever sending one to Emerson.

Mrs. Vistorino was on the phone behind her desk as Aaron entered the office.

"He's in Mr. Cunningham's office," she whispered as she put her hand over the receiver. "Mr. C's gone for the rest of the day."

She removed her hand from the phone to resume her call. "Good luck," she mouthed as he tapped on the office door. Then he turned the knob and entered.

The man's back was to Aaron as he stared out the window on to the school's parking lot. Aaron gently closed the door and cleared his throat. The man turned and fixed him with a stare so intense it was as if he were trying to see through Aaron's skull to the inside of his brain.

"Uh . . . hi," Aaron said, moving away from the door. "I'm Aaron Corbet—Mrs. Vistorino said you wanted to speak with me?"

He held his hand out to the man. It was something his foster dad had stressed. When you meet someone for the first time, always introduce yourself and shake the person's hand. It shows character, he'd say. The man looked at Aaron's outstretched hand, as if deciding whether it was clean enough to touch.

"And you're . . . ?" Aaron asked, to break the uncomfortable silence.

"Call me Messenger," the man said in a powerful voice, and took Aaron's hand in his.

"It's very nice to meet you Mr. . . . Messenger."

Aaron was suddenly overcome with panic. He couldn't remember ever feeling this way before. He wanted to run—to get as far away from this man as he possibly could. *What's wrong with me now?* he wondered, using every ounce of willpower he had to not yank his hand away.

Messenger released him, and Aaron quickly brought his hand to his side. It felt odd, tingling, like it had when he'd brought Gabriel back from the brink of death. He rubbed his palm against his pant leg.

"I'm glad that I have reached you first," Messenger said, studying Aaron with a strange look in his eyes. "You've matured much faster than most, a sign that you are certainly more than you seem."

Aaron was startled by the admissions rep's words, unsure of their meaning and how he should react. "Excuse me?" he began. "I really don't understand what . . ."

"I believe that you do," Messenger's voice boomed, and for a split second, Aaron saw the man for what he was. He was clothed in armor that seemed to be made from sunlight, and in his hand he held a sword of fire. From his back, enormous wings emanated.

"I am Camael," he said in a voice like the rumbling growl of a jungle cat. "And I have come to protect you."

Aaron closed his eyes and then opened them. Camael had returned to his human state. No armor, no wings, no flaming sword; just a distinguished-looking gentleman with spiky, silver-gray hair and a goatee to match.

"Messenger my ass," Aaron grumbled with disgust. "I should have known. Zeke said you'd be coming for me."

Camael looked perplexed. "Zeke?" he asked.

"Ezekiel," Aaron answered. "Zeke—he's a Grigori . . ."

"A Grigori," Camael said, interested, stroking his goatee. "Then you've already made contact with our kind."

"Right, and he told me the Powers would be after me because of what I am—but I won't go easily."

Camael chuckled. "Spirited, that's good. We'll need a bit of fire if we're going to weather what is to come."

Aaron started to back toward the door, at the moment, confused. "Aren't you one of them—the Powers?"

Camael shook his head as he casually sat on the corner of Mr. Cunningham's desk. "Once it was my holy mission to eradicate the likes of you." He pointed at Aaron and then crossed his arms. "But that was long ago. I've come to save, not destroy. If my suspicions are correct, you have a very important destiny to fulfill, Aaron Corbet."

Aaron suddenly remembered his dream from the weekend—the old man and his tablets. "Does this have anything to do with me building some kind of bridge?"

Camael nodded. "Something to that effect."

Aaron could feel it again, that dangerous curiosity that got him into this predicament. If he'd ignored it originally, he would never have gone in search of Zeke and things would have stayed status quo, or so he tried to convince himself. Well, this time he would put an end to it here and now. He didn't want to hear anything more from Camael.

"Sorry to disappoint you, but it isn't going to happen," Aaron said rather brusquely as he turned to the door. "I don't care what or who you think I am, I'm not having anything to do with this prophecy business." He grabbed the doorknob.

"You might not have a choice," Camael said coolly.

Aaron spun to face the angel. "That's where you're wrong,"

he barked, attempting to keep his voice down so that none of the insanity being tossed around the office would spill out into the real world. "I've been told my entire freakin' life that *I'm* in control of my future—*me*, Aaron Corbet." He jabbed his thumb at his chest for effect.

"And I've got it all planned out. I'm gonna finish high school, go to a good college, graduate in the top of my class, and get an amazing job that I love." Aaron had no idea what that job would be, but he was on a roll and couldn't stop himself if he tried. "I'll meet a nice girl, get married, and have a bunch a' kids."

Camael said nothing, staring without emotion, allowing him to rant.

"That's how it's going to be, and note—there was no mention of angels, Nephilim, or ancient prophecies. Sorry, there just isn't enough room."

The angelic being stood and moved toward him. "You're different, Aaron. I can feel it coming off you in waves. Let me help. . . ."

"No," Aaron spat. "I'm through." He pulled open the door. "Go back to Heaven and leave me the hell alone!"

And as he stormed out into the main office, he thought he heard the angel whisper, "That is what we're trying to do."

Camael did not wish to be seen, and so, he wasn't.

He stood on a grassy area in front of the high school

beneath the flagpole and watched as students poured out into the world, finished for the day. The young ones had always fascinated him. So full of life, so sure that they had a complete understanding of everything around them and the universe beyond.

To be so certain of anything, he thought, *it must be bliss.*

He remembered how it had been when he first abandoned the host under his command. Even though he knew what he was doing was right, there was still that nagging uncertainty festering in the dark corners of his mind that could not be dispelled. Yes, deep down he felt what the seer foretold was truth, but if he had known in advance the suffering he would have had to endure these many centuries following the prophecy, would he still have taken up the cause?

How many had he saved? How many had he enlightened with the knowledge of their true nature? How many plucked from the destructive path of the Powers? And where were they now? he wondered. Hiding? Waiting for the time when they would be recognized by the eyes of God? And by that account, how many would never see that day of acceptance? How many were slain before even becoming aware they'd been touched by Heaven?

Was it worth it? he reflected, watching the last of the students trickle from their place of learning, milling about in front of the orange brick building in small chattering packs.

And then the one named Aaron Corbet stepped from the

school and he experienced an elation the likes of which he had not felt since the day he first bore witness to the seer's words of redemption. *Is this truly the One?* he pondered. Was this the one who would make all the loneliness and pain he had endured worthwhile? If the answer was yes, all he need do was protect him—all he need do was keep him alive to fulfill his destiny and it would all be worthwhile.

But am I strong enough? Camael wondered.

The boy was with a female, very attractive by what Camael had come to understand of human standards: dark hair, skin the color of copper, a radiant smile. And by the looks of it, Aaron was smitten.

This will not do, thought the angelic protector. *There are far more important things for this boy than matters of the heart. He has no idea how much is at stake.* Yet, there was something about the girl, the way she moved, the power in her smile—

"Is that the one that has caused so much excitement?" a voice said from behind.

Camael turned to face Verchiel standing just beyond him. He tensed, a weapon of Heaven just beyond his thoughts.

"Of course it is," Verchiel continued. He leaned his head back slightly and sniffed the air catching the scent of the Nephilim that he had followed here. "Doesn't smell much different than any of the others: heavenly power awash in a stink of offal."

Camael chanced a quick glance to see where Aaron and

the girl were. They were talking at the end of the school's main walk.

He looked back to see that Verchiel had moved closer.

"Look at him," Verchiel said, "completely oblivious to the world around him. He doesn't even see us. How powerful can he be?"

"It's not that he can't," Camael explained. "He just doesn't want to."

Verchiel mulled this over for a moment, his hawklike gaze still upon Aaron. "I see . . . he denies his true nature. He clings to his humanity while suppressing the angelic."

The girl laughed at something Aaron said, and Verchiel flinched. "I hate the sounds they make," he said, eyes narrowing with distaste. "Don't you?"

"I have spoken with the boy and he rejects it all," Camael said calmly, with just a touch of disappointment for Verchiel's sake. "He wants nothing to do with his heritage."

Aaron and the girl began to move across the parking lot.

"So he is of no immediate threat to us?" Verchiel asked, his head slowly moving as he followed the pair with his unblinking stare.

"He is content with being human," Camael said, watching Verchiel closely.

"His contentment matters not, not in the least," Verchiel said as he turned his attention to Camael. "He still needs to be put down, for his own sake." The angel smiled, fully aware of the effect of his words. "He's far too dangerous to live."

Camael heard the sounds of car doors slamming shut and suspected the couple had gotten into Aaron's vehicle. A burning blade manifested in his hand and he stood his ground, ready to fight if he had to. "Then you will need to go through me," Camael said, an electrical energy radiating from his body and charging the air around them.

"You draw a weapon against me?" Verchiel asked as similar energy began to leak from his eyes and leap from the top of his head.

From the parking lot, car alarms inexplicably wailed, headlights blazed, and horns blared as if pronouncing the coming of a king. The humans ran about frantically, bewildered, not able to see the battle brewing in their midst.

"We were brothers once, Camael, sharing the same duty to our Heavenly Sire with equal zeal—and this is what it has come to?"

Over the din from the parking lot, Camael located the sound of a single vehicle starting up and driving away. Relieved that Aaron had managed to escape for now, he said nothing.

"I came here to warn you, Camael," Verchiel said, his energy receding. "As former brothers, I believe I owe you at least that."

Camael did not put his weapon away, scanning the area for more of Verchiel's soldiers.

"It's all coming to a resounding close," Verchiel said as he casually slid his hands inside the pockets of his coat and turned away. "After so long, it is finally going to end. A day of reckoning, so to speak."

Camael watched Verchiel begin to walk away. He wanted to call out to him, to make him explain further, but doubted that Verchiel would share any more.

"This moment of truce is over," Verchiel said. "If you should stand in my way, I will not think twice about striking you down," he warned. "Be careful which side you choose, for if you choose wrong—you will share their fate."

The weapon in Camael's hand gradually returned from whence it came. And as he watched his former comrade recede to nothing, he felt a familiar stirring from within. He knew the feeling well. It was something he had attempted to lock away when deciding to follow the words of the ancient prophecy, something he had held at bay, denying it freedom. But Verchiel's words had drawn it from the shadows and fed its growth.

And its name was doubt.

CHAPTER NINE

Aaron drove his '02 Toyota Corolla down Western Avenue and into McDonough Square. He had been in this area of Lynn thousands of times since learning to drive, but had never paid quite as much attention as he did now.

This was Vilma's neighborhood. Febonio's Smoke Shop, Snell's Grocery, Mitchell's Men's Shop—all establishments that he never knew existed until now, all landmarks he would use if he ever had the chance to return.

"It's up here, Aaron. On the left," Vilma said, pointing through the windshield.

Aaron followed her direction and noticed the narrow street just beyond a small store advertising "Everything Brazilian."

"Here?" he asked, snapping on his blinker and slowing down.

"Yep," she answered. "It's a dead end, a real pain to get in and out of."

Aaron waited for the oncoming traffic to slow. A guy in a black van with a crude airbrushed painting of the starship *Enterprise* on its side finally waved him by, and he drove down the dead-end court called Belvidere Place.

"It's the brown house on the end," she said, hefting her bookbag from the floor onto her lap.

The street was very small, only a little wider than his car from nose to backend. A chain link fence across the end of the street separated it from a church and its parking lot beyond. There were eight houses, four on either side, all looking pretty much the same.

Aaron pulled over in front of the last house on the right, put the car in park, and turned to look at Vilma. She was staring straight ahead, her hand starting to move toward the door handle. *She can't wait to get away from me,* he thought. He knew he'd been distracted since leaving school. No matter how hard he tried, he couldn't shake the effects of his meeting with Camael, and he was afraid that his moodiness was a turnoff for Vilma.

"I'm sorry your meeting with the Emerson guy didn't work out," she said, her voice filled with sympathy.

He had told her that the admissions rep had been a jerk and that he had given the man some attitude, probably eliminating himself from the running for a scholarship.

"That's all right," he said with a shrug. "I didn't really want to go there anyway."

He hated to lie to her—it didn't bode well for their future—but what choice did he have? There was no way he could share with Vilma the freak show his life had become over the last week. He had even begun to wonder if it was a good idea to start any kind of relationship with her. The last thing he wanted was for to her to be sucked up into the maelstrom of insanity swirling about him.

The silence in the car was nearly unbearable. Vilma finally opened the door a crack and looked at him. He smiled.

"Thanks for the ride. I really appreciate it," she said, returning his smile. Only, Aaron thought it put his to shame. "I think I had to bring every book in my locker home tonight. My bag's popping at the seams," she said, patting the stuffed nylon bag resting on her lap.

"No problem," he said as he slid the palms of his hands over the smoothness of the steering wheel. "Anytime."

The car door was open but she wasn't leaving. He wondered if there was some gentlemanly thing he was supposed to do like go around to the other side and help her out.

"You know you can call me if you want," she blurted out, as she played with the zipper on her bookbag. "If you wanted to, you know, talk about stuff? Like the Emerson thing—or our paper—I could help you with yours."

Aaron looked at her—really looked at her. Suddenly any

nervousness he had been feeling—any lack of self-confidence—was not an issue. In that instant, he decided that not only was Vilma the most beautiful young woman he had ever seen, but also the most real. There were no games with her. She said exactly what was on her mind and he liked that. A lot.

"Now why would you want me to do that?" he asked, looking back to the steering wheel. "I'm sure you have a lot more interesting things to do with your time than talking to me."

She seemed to think about it for a moment and then began to nod her head slowly. "You're probably right. Cleaning up after my cousins, doing laundry, my homework—yeah, you *are* right—I'd much rather do those things than talk with a cute guy on the phone."

He was a bit taken aback, and reached up to nervously scratch the back of his head. "Are you saying that you think I'm cute, or is there some other guy you're going to call?"

Vilma laughed and rolled her beautiful almond-colored eyes. "I thought you were supposed to be the dark, brooding guy—not the big doofus." She shook her head in mock disbelief.

Vilma was laughing at him, but Aaron didn't care. The sound was one of the coolest things he had ever heard, and he began to laugh as well.

"I've never been called a doofus before," he said. He again looked at her. "Thanks."

She reached out to squeeze his arm. "I like you, Aaron," she said.

He had never wanted to kiss a girl so badly. Yeah, there had been that time with Jennine Surrette in junior high, but that was because he had never done it before. Kissing Vilma now would seem almost like his first time—like all the other kisses since Jennine were just practice leading up to this one.

He started to lean his head toward her, his lips being pulled to hers by some irresistible force that he couldn't negate—that he didn't want to negate. Aaron was relieved to see that she seemed to be having the same difficulty, leaning toward him as well.

There came a sudden knock at the passenger-side window, and the spell that was drawing them inexorably closer was abruptly broken.

A little girl, looking like how he imagined Vilma must have looked when she was around seven or eight, peered into the car, smiling. There was an open gap in her comical grin where her front baby teeth used to be.

Vilma shook her fist at the child and she ran off laughing.

"My cousin," she said, looking a bit embarrassed.

The moment was gone, lightning in a bottle—now free to be captured again some other time. But that was all right. Kissing Vilma could wait—but hopefully, not for too long.

"I like you too," he said, and briefly touched her hand. It felt remarkably warm.

Vilma unzipped the side pocket of her bookbag. She took out a tiny pink pencil and small pad of paper and began to write.

"My aunt and uncle won't let me get a cell phone yet, so here's my home phone number and e-mail address," she said as she tore the paper from the notepad and handed it to him. "Call between six and nine, my aunt and uncle kind of freak when anybody calls too late. You can e-mail me anytime and I'll get back to you soon as I can."

He looked down at the phone number. It was as if he had been given the winning number of a billion-dollar lottery—only better.

"You can give me yours later," she said as she got out of the car, lugging her bag behind her. "I gotta get inside and kill my cousin." She turned and leaned back in. "Maybe you can give it to me when we talk tonight," she suggested with another winning smile.

He was about to tell her that it was a deal when he remembered he had to work. "I can't call tonight—gotta work and probably won't get in until after nine."

"Ahh, blowing me off already," Vilma said in mock disappointment.

"Give me that pencil," he ordered.

She handed it to him, smiling all the time, and watched as he began to write at the bottom of the piece of paper she had given him.

"I'll give it to you now," he said as he finished. He folded the paper and tore away his number. "This way there'll be no mistaking my intentions," he said as he handed her the slip of paper.

"And what exactly are your intentions, Mr. Corbet?" she asked as she slipped the paper into her back pocket.

"In time, Ms. Santiago," he said with a devilish grin. "All in due time."

"Thanks for the ride," he heard her say as she laughed and slammed the door closed.

He watched her walk up to the front porch. She opened the white screen door and turned to wave before she vanished inside.

The clock on the dashboard said that it was close to three o'clock. He had less then five minutes to get across town to work, but it didn't really bother him. As he struggled to back out of the tiny, dead-end street, he realized he wasn't really worried about much of anything right then. Everything was going to work out just fine.

He didn't remember ever before feeling this way.

But it was something he could get used to.

Ezekiel drank from a bottle of cheap whiskey and pondered the question of redemption.

He shifted upon his bed to get comfortable and leaned his head back against the cool plaster wall. He took a long, thoughtful pull off his cigarette.

Redemption. Strangely enough, it was something he thought of quite a bit these days, since meeting the boy.

Zeke reached down to the floor again for the bottle of spirits and brought it to his mouth. Cigarette smoke streamed from his nostrils as the whiskey poured down his throat. It burned, but still he drank.

It was a kind of punishment, he thought as he brought the bottle away from his thirsty mouth and replaced it with the cigarette, a punishment for all that he had wrought.

It's odd thinking about this after so long, he thought, staring at the wall across from him. A cockroach had started to climb the vertical expanse and he silently wished it luck. He could have told the insect directly but the communication skills of a bug were so primitive.

Forgiveness—is it even possible? After the Grigori were exiled, they had tried to make the best of it. Earth became their home. They knew they would never see Heaven again. The idea that they might be forgiven had never even entered his mind—until the day he first saw the boy at the common.

He took another drag from his cigarette and held the smoke in his lungs. There he was, minding his own business, looking through the trash for redeemable cans, when he sensed him—clear across the common he could feel the kid's presence. He'd encountered others over the centuries, but none ever had that kind of effect on him. Aaron was special. He was different.

Zeke released the smoke from his lungs in a billowy cloud.

The cigarette was finished and he threw the filter to the floor. He wanted another and considered asking a neighbor to spot him one until he remembered that he already owed cigarettes to several people in the building. He would need to drown the urge to smoke.

What would I say to Him—to the Creator? he wondered as he picked up the bottle. "I'm sorry for messing things up," he muttered, and had some whiskey.

He let the bottle rest against his stomach and gazed up at the ceiling, concentrating on a water stain that reminded him of Italy.

Was saying he was sorry even enough?

Zeke dug through the thick haze of memory to find what it was like to be in His presence. He closed his eyes and felt the warmth of his recollection flood over him. If only there was a way to feel that again—to stand before the Father of all things and beg His forgiveness.

He opened his eyes and brought his fingers to his face. His cheeks were wet with tears.

"Pathetic," he grumbled, disgusted with his show of emotion. "Tears aren't going to do me a bit of good," he said aloud as he brought his bottle up to drink. He leaned his head back and swallowed with powerful gulps. He belched loudly, a low rippling sound that seemed to shake the rafters. "Should'a thought how sorry I'd be before I started handing out makeup tips," he said sarcastically.

The smell suddenly hit him. Smoke. And not the kind he desperately craved. Something was burning.

He rose from his bed and walked barefoot across the room to the door. If Fat Mary down the hall was using her hotplate again, they'd all be in trouble. The woman could burn water, he mused as he opened the door to the hallway.

A blast of scalding air hit him square and he stumbled back, arms up to protect his face. The hall was on fire and quickly filling with smoke.

Panic gripped him, not for his own safety, for he was almost sure the flames could not kill him, but for the safety of the other poor souls who called the Osmond their home.

He stumbled out into the hallway, his hand over his mouth, a bit of protection from the noxious clouds swirling in the air. There was a fire alarm at the end of the hallway, he remembered. If he could get to it, he might have a chance to save some lives.

Zeke pressed himself to the wall, feeling his way along its length.

He could hear the cries of those trapped inside their rooms by the intense heat.

The smoke was growing thicker. He got down on all fours and began to crawl. The wood floor was becoming hot to the touch, blistering the skin on his hands and knees as he moved steadily forward. He couldn't be far now.

Zeke looked up, his seared and tearing eyes trying to discern the shape of the alarm on the wall—and that was when he saw them. There were two of them, slowly making their way through the smoke and fire.

He tried to yell, but all he could manage was a series of lung-busting coughs.

The smoke seemed to part and they emerged to stand over him, flaming swords at the ready, wings slowly fanning the flames higher.

"Hello, Grigori," said the angel whom Zeke fearfully recognized as one who had helped to sever his wings so long ago.

"We've come to tie up loose ends," said the other.

They both smiled predatorily at him.

And Zeke came to the horrible realization that the fire was the least of his worries.

Aaron pulled his car into the driveway of his home on Baker Street a little after nine o'clock. He switched off the ignition and wondered if he had the strength to pull himself from the car and into the house.

To say that he was exhausted was an understatement. It was the first time he had been back to the veterinary hospital since his language skills had—how had Zeke put it?—blossomed.

It had been insane from the minute he rushed through the door, barely on time. The docs had been running late, and the waiting area was filled with a wide variety of dogs and cats, each with its own problem. There had even been a parrot with a broken wing and a box turtle with some kind of shell fungus.

He had immediately set to work, making sure that everybody had done the proper paperwork and apologizing for the delays.

And it was as if the animals could sense his ability to communicate with them. As he attempted to carry on conversations with their owners, the pets tried everything in their power to get his attention. A beagle puppy named Lily rambled on and on about her favorite ball. Bear, a black Labrador-shepherd mix, sadly told him that he couldn't run very fast anymore because his hips hurt. A white Angora cat called Duchess yowled pathetically from her transport cage that she felt perfectly fine and didn't need to see a doctor. A likely story, Aaron mused, and one probably shared by the majority of waiting animals.

It was constant: Someone or something was yammering at him from the moment he had walked into the place. Aaron wasn't sure if it was scientifically possible, but he was convinced that his head was going to explode. All he could think of was his skull as a balloon filled with too much air. Bang! No more balloon.

Aaron forced himself from the car with a tired grunt. He would have been perfectly happy to have spent the remainder of the night in the car—but he was hungry. He got his backpack from the trunk and began the pained journey to the house.

He smiled as he recalled how he had prevented his brain from detonating at work. The animals had been carrying on, Michelle had him running back and forth to the kennels for pickups and drop-offs, the docs wanted their exam rooms cleaned so they could bring in the next patient. And there he was, on the verge of blowing up, when he thought of her. He thought about Vilma and a kind of calm passed over him. The chattering of the patients became nothing more than droning background noise, and he was able to finish out the evening with a minimum of stress. Just thinking of her smiling face, coupled with what she had said in the car—it was enough to calm him and release the internal pressure.

Maybe I'll e-mail her after I eat, he thought with a grin.

There was a menacing rumble above him and he looked up. Thick gray clouds like liquid metal undulated across the night sky, on the verge of completely blotting out any trace of the moon and stars.

Looks like we're in for a pretty big storm, he thought as he turned his attention to finding the back-door key.

The scream from inside was bloodcurdling.

Aaron hurriedly opened the door and shouldered his way into the house.

"Mom?" he called out. He dropped his bookbag on the floor.

There was another scream, high pitched and filled with terror. It was Stevie, Aaron was sure of it. He tore down the hallway in search of his foster parents and brother.

"Mom!" he called again as he raced through the kitchen. "Dad!"

More screams.

He found his family in the living room, huddled on the floor in front of the television, which showed only static. Lori tightly gripped the thrashing Stevie in her arms, rocking him back and forth, cooing to the child that everything was going to be fine. Gabriel paced beside them, his tail rigid, hackles up.

"What's wrong with him?" Aaron asked. He had never seen Stevie this agitated.

"Theycom!" the child screamed over and over again. "Theycom! Theycom! Theycom!" His eyes rolled to the back of his head, foamy saliva bubbled from the corners of his mouth.

"He's been like this for half an hour," Tom said, panic in his voice. He stroked his son's sweat-dampened hair. "We don't know what he's trying to say!"

"Theycom! Theycom! Theycom!" Stevie bellowed as he struggled to be free of his mother's arms.

"I . . . I think we should call nine-one-one," Lori stammered. There were tears in her eyes when she looked at Aaron and her husband for support.

Tom rubbed a tremulous hand across his face. "I don't know . . . I just don't know. Maybe if we wait a little longer . . ."

Aaron turned from his parents to find Gabriel no longer pacing, but standing perfectly still. The dog looked up at the ceiling and sniffed the air. He began to growl.

"Gabriel? What's wrong, boy? What do you smell?"

A crack of thunder shook the home from roof to foundation. The lights flickered briefly, and then the power quit altogether, plunging the room into darkness.

"Theycom! Theycom!" the child continued to scream inconsolably at the top of his lungs.

"Something bad," Gabriel said with a menacing edge to his bark. *"That's what Stevie is trying to say. Something bad is coming."*

CHAPTER TEN

There was another rumble of thunder and the windows in the living room rattled ominously. Aaron began to experience the same overpowering sense of panic he had felt in the guidance office when coming face-to-face with Camael.

"We need to get out of here," he said, gazing up at the ceiling. "We . . . we should get Stevie to the hospital right away."

Gabriel's words echoed through Aaron's head. *Something bad is coming.*

"I don't know, Aaron," Lori said. "He seems to be calming down." She looked at her child; there was uncertainty and fear in her eyes.

Stevie's struggles were indeed waning. He had screamed himself hoarse but still tried to squeak out his warning.

Tom leaned down and kissed the boy's head. "I've never seen him like this before, maybe Aaron's right. Maybe we should take him—just in case."

"Good, we'll take my car," Aaron said quickly as he and Gabriel moved into the darkened kitchen.

"He doesn't have any socks on," he heard his mother say behind him. "Let me go upstairs and get his sneakers and socks. I should probably bring his coat, too, just in case . . ."

"We don't have time for that, Mom," Aaron barked. His panic was intensifying. "We have to get out of here right now."

Every fiber of his being screamed for him to get away, to leave everything and run as fast as he could into the night. It took every ounce of his self-control not to leave his parents and little brother behind. Nothing would make him do that, in spite of what his senses were telling him. After so many tumultuous years in the foster care system, the Stanleys were the only people, the only *family,* who'd stuck it out with him, showering him with love, and more importantly, acceptance. . . .

His foster dad came up from behind. "Take it easy, pal. He'll be okay. There's no reason to get crazy with your mother. I'll get his shoes and we'll be out of here in no time."

"No time," Gabriel said suddenly, staring at the kitchen door.

Clack!

They all jumped at the sudden sound as the deadbolt on

the kitchen door slid sideways as if moved by some invisible force.

"What the hell is that?" Tom asked, trying to get around his son.

"Go," Aaron said forcefully. "Take Mom and Stevie and go out the front door."

The door began to slowly open with the high-pitched whine that Tom had been threatening to put oil to since the summer, and three men entered on a powerful gust of wind. Aaron's senses were blaring and he winced in pain from their razor-sharp intensity. He knew what these men were. Not men at all.

Angels.

He was enthralled by the way they moved. They didn't so much walk into the house as glide, as though on wheels or a conveyor belt.

"What is *this*?" Tom Stanley hollered, pushing Aaron out of the way. "Get the hell out of my house before I beat the livin'—"

It happened quickly. Tom advanced, fists clenched, intent on defending his home and family. Fire suddenly leaped from an invader's hands and his father stumbled back, covering his eyes as he fell to the linoleum floor.

Aaron couldn't believe what he was seeing. It was just like his dream. The three invaders were holding swords. Swords made of fire.

"Call the police!" his father shouted as he struggled to stand.

Aaron ran to help him. "Get up! You have to get Mom and Stevie out of here."

One of the invaders stalked slowly toward them, his face eerily illuminated by the light of his weapon. There was something unnerving about the way he looked—the way *they* looked. They were deathly pale, almost luminescent in their whiteness, and their features were perfectly symmetrical— too perfect. Aaron felt as though he were looking at mannequins come to life.

"Do we frighten you, monkey?" the invader asked in a voice like nails running down a blackboard. "Does our presence make you tremble?"

"Get away from them!" Lori screamed from the doorway to the living room.

In her arms she held the limp and nearly catatonic Stevie, his eyes large and glassy, like saucers. Gabriel stood by them, tensed, preventing her from entering the kitchen.

Aaron got his father to his feet and pushed him back toward the living room. The stranger raised his flaming sword above his head. Wings dappled with spots of brown dramatically unfolded from his back. Aaron and his father froze, awestruck by the sight of something they once believed to be purely of fiction—of myth.

The angel prepared to strike them down. "We are the

Powers—the harbingers of your doom. Look upon us in awe!"

The blade of fire began its descent, and Aaron stepped in front of his father to take the hit. Suddenly there was a flurry of movement and a yellow-white blur passed over him with an unearthly grace, landing in front of the sword-wielding attacker and snarling ferociously.

Gabriel.

"No!" Aaron screamed as he watched his beloved friend lunge at the supernatural invader.

The dog's jaws clamped down upon the wrist of the angel's sword hand with a wet crunch, like the sound of celery being crushed between eager teeth. The sound made Aaron wince with imagined pain.

The sword of fire tumbled from the angel's grasp to dissipate in a flash before it could touch the floor—and the creature began to scream. The sound was like nothing Aaron had ever heard before, part crow caw, part whale song, part the screech of brakes.

"What is happening?" Lori cried aloud, clutching her moaning child to her.

"We've got to get out of here!" Tom shouted as he lunged toward his family and wrapped his arms protectively about them.

Gabriel dangled from the angel's wrist, growling and thrashing, as if trying to sever the hand from the arm. The angel seemed stunned by the savagery of the animal's attack. The other two, who had remained uninvolved in the background, now stepped forward to assess their comrade's situation.

"It hurts, my brothers!" wailed the Powers soldier as he frantically tried to shake Gabriel loose. "The animal is not as it should be—it has been changed!"

The angel flailed his arm wildly and Gabriel finally released his grip, falling to the floor.

"Gabriel, come! Now!" Aaron yelled.

The Lab stayed where he had landed, in a crouch, baring his fangs and snarling at the angels. A thick black blood, like motor oil, streamed from the injured angel's wounds to form glistening puddles on the yellow-check flooring.

"*No,*" said the dog between snarls. "*Get Mom, Dad, and Stevie out. I will keep these beasts here.*"

Aaron was torn. "I'm not leaving you!" he yelled.

But he knew that every second counted. Aaron quickly gathered up his family and ushered them toward the hallway. He would try to get them out the front door to his car and then come back for his friend.

They stepped through the kitchen door and stopped short. Another angel was crouched in the hall, going through his bookbag, its eyes glistening wetly in the darkness. "Going nowhere, silly monkeys," it hissed.

A powerful gust of wind pummeled the house from outside and it creaked and moaned with the force of the blow. Aaron tensed, sensing that something bad was to follow. The front door explosively blew in, torn from its hinges, practically crushing the squatting angel against the wall, and driving Aaron and his family back toward the kitchen in a shower of debris.

Aaron shielded his eyes from pieces of flying matter, and when he looked up he saw that another of them now stood in the doorway, an angel with long white hair. The way this one stood—the way he carried himself—Aaron was certain he was in the presence of the leader, the one Zeke had called Verchiel.

The newcomer cocked his head strangely and surveyed all that was before him. Others slunk into the home behind their leader: all deathly pale, all wearing the same kind of clothes.

There must have been a sale somewhere, Aaron thought perversely, almost starting to giggle. The angels followed Verchiel closely as he strode down the hallway as if he belonged there, and Aaron forced his family back into the kitchen, out of his destructive path.

"What has happened here?" he heard Verchiel ask, in a low, melodic voice that was almost pleasing to the ear.

The Powers soldier held out his wounded arm to his master and averted his gaze. "The animal—it has been altered."

Verchiel moved toward them—toward the family, his dark gaze on Gabriel, and they retreated to the living room.

"Stay away from my family," the dog growled menacingly, baring his teeth and putting himself between the Stanleys and the angel leader.

"*He* has done this to you," Verchiel said in disbelief, looking from the dog to Aaron. "It is worse than I imagined," he whispered. "The Nephilim has spread its taint to a lowly beast."

"I'm not lowly," Gabriel snarled, and leaped at his newest adversary.

In a flash, powerful wings appeared from Verchiel's back and swatted the dog violently away.

The animal yelped in pain as he hit the far wall, narrowly missing the windows, and crashed to the floor.

"See the damage you have already wrought, monster? *This* is why we act," Verchiel growled, his wings slowly flapping like the twitching of a pensive cat's tail before it strikes. "*This* is why the unclean must be purged from *my* world—" The angel paused, considering what he had just said before he continued. "For if allowed to fester, the consequences would be inconceivable."

Aaron left his family to go to his dog's side. "Are you all right?" he asked.

Gabriel struggled to his feet and shook his body vigorously, shedding the effects of his injury like water. *"I'm fine, Aaron,"* the dog said, fixing his gaze on Verchiel. *"And I won't let him hurt you."*

Aaron stood and patted his dog's head. "That's all right, this is over now."

Gabriel gazed up at his master, a quizzical expression on his canine features.

Aaron addressed Verchiel. "No matter what you think . . . I'm no threat to you or your mission."

Verchiel tilted his head to one side as he listened.

From the corner of his eye Aaron could see that more of the angelic soldiers had moved into the room to encircle him and his family. He didn't react. He didn't want to show any signs of aggression.

"Whatever you've heard—or sensed—about me is a lie. I want nothing to do with Nephilims—or the crazy prophecy that comes with it. I already told Camael, I renounce it. Whatever *it* is, it's not going to be part of my life," Aaron said firmly. "Please, leave my family and me alone."

Verchiel smiled and Aaron was reminded that he was in the presence of something all together inhuman.

"Camael believes you are the One," Verchiel said smugly, moving his head from one side to the other.

"He's wrong," Aaron responded emphatically. "I want nothing more than to have a normal life."

"He believes you to be the one whose coming was foretold in an ancient prophecy, that you are going to reunite the fallen angels with God."

Aaron shook his head vigorously, remembering the old

man with the cataract-covered eye from his dream. "I don't know anything about that and I don't care to know."

"Criminals," Verchiel spat. "Those who fought alongside the Morningstar against the Father during the Great War and fled to this pathetic ball of mud, those who disobeyed His sacred commands—those are the ones of whom the ancient writings speak. If this prophecy were to come to fruition, they would be forgiven."

Aaron said nothing. He glanced at his parents who were huddled with Stevie, Verchiel's soldiers surrounding them with their flaming weapons. They appeared to be in shock. He wanted to tell them how sorry he was for bringing this down upon them. He hoped there would be time for that later.

Verchiel shook his head. "Imagine the Almighty looking favorably upon the by-product of angel and animal. It is an insult to His glory."

"I swear you have nothing to fear from me," Aaron said. "Please, leave us alone."

Verchiel laughed, or at least Aaron believed it was a laugh. It sounded more like the caw of some great, predatory bird.

"Fear you, Nephilim?" Verchiel said with what seemed to be amusement. "We do not fear you or anything like you." An orange flame sparked in the palm of his hand and began to grow. "The Powers' mission is to erase anything that would displease our Lord of Lords. This has been our purpose since Creation, and we have performed it well these many millennia."

Verchiel now held an enormous sword of fire, and Aaron heard Lori gasp. "It's a nightmare," she said softly, "some kind of bad dream."

If only that were true, he thought sadly.

Verchiel watched the weapon blaze in his grasp, his eyes of solid black glistening. "And when our mission is finally complete, He shall give us this world—and all who live upon it will know that *I* sit by His side and *my* word is law." The Powers' leader admired his weapon. "But there is still much to be done."

Verchiel pointed the blade at Aaron. "You must die, and so must everything that has been tainted by your touch." He motioned toward Gabriel and then across the room at Aaron's parents and Stevie.

"Listen to what I'm saying," Aaron pleaded, stepping forward. Two of Verchiel's soldiers grabbed him, driving him roughly to his knees. *"Please,"* he begged as he struggled against his captors.

Verchiel still pointed his sword toward Tom, Lori, and Stevie who had again begun to flail in his mother's arms, moaning and crying at the angel's attentions.

"Beg all you like, Nephilim. It will do you no good. You shall be destroyed." He paused, suddenly interested in the cries of the child. "All except the young one," the angel said thoughtfully.

"I think I'll keep him."

Verchiel garnered a certain measure of perverse satisfaction as he watched the Nephilim squirm. This was the savior? The one who was supposed to bring about a peace between Heaven and Earth the likes of which had not been seen since Genesis? It was laughable—yet, there was something about him.

"Bring me the child," he ordered with a wave of his hand.

If there was ever to be peace, it would not be until the enemies of the one true God were turned to ash drifting in the wind. This belief, of his own devising, was the only one he could ever come to imagine.

"Leave him alone!" the one called Aaron shouted, struggling mightily against his captors.

The accursed dog moved defiantly toward him, the skin of its snout pulled back in a ferocious snarl. The blood of angels stained its muzzle.

"Shall we see who has the worse bite?" Verchiel asked, and brought his sword to bear on the dog.

"No!" the Nephilim cried. "Come, Gabriel. Please, come to me."

Hesitantly the dog returned to his master's side, growling and snarling at the angels who held him. "Good boy," Verchiel heard him say. "It's okay, everything is okay."

Verchiel decided that it was time to show the boy how wrong he was. He motioned toward Uriel, still nursing his wound from the Nephilim's tainted animal.

"The child," he ordered Uriel. "Bring it here."

The angel tore the squalling youth from its mother's arms while Sammael and Tufiel restrained the parents. The cacophony of screams and wails put Verchiel's nerves on edge, but he restrained himself. After all, they were only animals.

Uriel brought the writhing child before Verchiel, holding him by the hair for closer examination. "This one," the wounded angel noted, "seems full of spirit."

Yes, Verchiel thought, staring into the child's unfocused gaze. *He shall serve us well.* He brought the burning sword up beneath the child's eyes and moved the blade back and forth. Its eyes followed the fire attentively.

"A hound perhaps," he said aloud. "You have the eyes of a tracker."

It was then that the Nephilim began to carry on, and Uriel stepped back with the child in his arms.

"Calm yourself, Nephilim," Verchiel said in his most soothing tone. "I told you, I wish the little one no harm."

There is a great power growing within this one, Verchiel observed, studying the Nephilim. He could feel it radiating dangerously from the young man's body.

"The parents, on the other hand," he said slowly as he pointed his blade at the husband and wife. "I have little use for them. And since they have been infected by your presence . . ."

Sammael and Tufiel stepped quickly away from the two as the flame from Verchiel's blade roared to life—and hungrily engulfed the pair in its voracious fire.

Aaron's parents screamed for mere seconds—but it seemed to him an eternity. Their blackened skeletons, burned clean of hair, skin, and muscle, collapsed to the ground in a clumsy embrace.

Verchiel looked to him, seemingly savoring his expression of complete despair. "Now," he said, a hint of a smile on his pale, bloodless lips. "Shall we continue?"

Gabriel tossed his head back and began to howl, and Aaron was certain he had never heard anything quite so sad.

His parents were dead—burned alive before his eyes.

He jarringly recalled the day—his birthday, in fact— when he had stood and stared at his sleeping foster mom in this very room, and thought of her now no longer in his life. His heart raced and he could barely catch his breath.

The pungent aroma of overcooked meat hung sickly in the air, and he did all that he could to keep from vomiting.

Verchiel was saying something, but he wasn't listening. The smoke alarm was blaring from the ceiling above him and he barely heard it. The image of the two people he loved most in the world being consumed by fire kept replaying before his mind's eye as their skeletal remains still smoldered before him.

Disturbingly, Aaron wondered if the fire used by the murderous angels was the same as what he cooked with, or what burned on the head of a match. Maybe it was a special fire, given to those with special identification by high-ranking officials at the pearly gates. Aaron smiled, more like a grimace of sharp and sudden pain. *If I'm so special, maybe I can wield this fire as well.*

He caught movement from the corner of his eye and pulled his gaze from what was left of Lori and Tom Stanley.

Stevie was being taken from the house. The angel—what had he been called? he asked himself. *Uriel?* Uriel was taking his little brother out through the broken front door. But to where? Where were they taking his little brother? He didn't have on any socks or shoes. Aaron thought about trying to follow, but was distracted by the latest nightmare unfolding in the middle of the living room.

They had Gabriel.

Four angels pinned the dog in place while Verchiel stood before them. He still held the sword in his hand—the one he had used to kill Aaron's parents, to burn them to bones.

Gabriel was struggling, foaming at the mouth and snapping his jaws trying to take a chunk out of the creatures that held him. Aaron wanted to cheer his dog on, but found that he just didn't have the strength.

He looked back to his parents. Even the bones were almost gone now and he wondered if his bones would burn as fast. Something called to him. He could hear it echoing far off in the distance, but didn't pay it any attention. He was busy, watching the fire finish the gruesome task it had started.

Again he was called, louder, sharper and Aaron realized that the sound wasn't coming from inside the room, but from somewhere inside his head. He turned to see Verchiel raise the sword above Gabriel. It seemed to be happening in slow motion.

How come everything horrible seems to happen in slow motion? he wondered with building dread.

Again Aaron heard the sound of his name, this time far more forceful. It partially shook him from his stupor, and he came to realize how angry he was. How enraged. They'd killed his parents, taken his little brother. He couldn't let Gabriel die too. But what could he do? It was just too much for him to bear.

Two angels still held him in their grasp. He was on his knees, his arms pinned behind his back. He felt their hands roughly grab his head. They wanted him to watch, to see Verchiel's blade end his best friend's life.

The voice from inside his mind continued to urge him from his complacency, not in words, but in feeling—raw emotion. He knew what it was that called to him. When he had last encountered it, it had resembled the strangest of serpents, and it had held open its arms to him and he had accepted it.

Now it was older, more mature—stronger.

And as much as he hated to admit it, it was part of him.

A surge of strength coursed through his body and Aaron struggled to his feet, throwing off his captors with extraordinary power.

Verchiel stopped his blade's descent and glared. "You only delay the inevitable," he said, advancing toward Aaron. "But if you are so eager, then you may die before the animal."

And they closed in around him. Each of them summoned some weapon of fire, and Aaron braced himself for their attack. He was prepared to go down fighting.

The windows of the living room exploded inward, showering the room with broken glass as two more entered the fray.

The Powers seemed to be as startled as he. Gabriel broke from those who held him and ran, panting nervously, to Aaron's side. The angel called Camael slowly straightened to his full, imposing height before the shattered window, a burning sword of flame in his hand. And beside him, his skin singed a scarlet red and his hand holding what appeared to be an old Louisville Slugger with multiple six-inch nails pounded into it—turning it into a kind of primitive mace—was the Grigori, Zeke.

"Camael here's been telling me some interesting things about you, Aaron," Zeke said with a cagey wink, breaking the palpable silence. He raised the bat as if to swing at a pitch.

"Told ya you were special."

CHAPTER ELEVEN

It was the sound of a thousand fingernails dragged down the length of a blackboard—only earsplittingly louder. The Powers shrieked their shrill cry of battle and surged toward Aaron's would-be rescuers, weapons afire. For the moment, they had forgotten him. On his hands and knees Aaron crawled to the mound that still glowed red, the mound that used to be his parents. Gabriel, silently and sadly, moved with him. Within the pile of ash, Aaron could see Lori and Tom's skulls still burning, their hollow black gazes accusatory.

"I'm so sorry," he whispered, and reached a shaking hand toward the pyre of ash and bone. He quickly pulled it away as his own flesh was singed by the intensity of the heat.

"It's not your fault," Gabriel said consolingly. He tried to lick away the hurt from his master's hand.

The intensity of the screams turned him from his parents' remains to the battle being waged in the living room. Aaron was amazed by its ferocity.

Zeke buried the nails adorning his baseball bat into the side of an attacker's head. The angel fell to its knees, twitching and bleeding as Zeke yanked the bat free with a grunt and hit him again before he could recover. Then, satisfied with the death he'd wrought, the fallen angel turned his savage attention to another.

Camael's movements were a hypnotizing blur. He moved among the Powers, hacking and slashing, his fiery blade passing through their flesh with pernicious ease. It was like watching the beauty of a complex dance, but with deadly results. Aaron could see that he was battling his way toward Verchiel, who simply stood, weapon in hand, waiting patiently as his soldiers fought and died around him.

The grisly scene of violence stirred the presence within Aaron. He could feel it roiling around inside him, so much stronger than before, like having the serpentine bodies of multiple eels beneath his flesh. It was excited by the battle— the sights, sounds, and smells.

And then he saw—no, felt—Verchiel staring at him from across the living room. The angel's nostrils flared, as if smelling something in the air. He snarled and began to move toward Aaron.

"It wants to come out, Aaron," Gabriel said by his side.

He sniffed him up and down. *"It's inside you and wants to get out."*

Aaron couldn't take his eyes from the angel stalking methodically across the room.

Gabriel suddenly licked his face and, startled, Aaron glared at the dog.

"What's inside of you is inside of me," Gabriel explained. *"I can sense your struggle, but you can't keep it locked up."*

Verchiel was almost upon them.

Slowly Aaron got to his feet, eyes locked on the ominous form of the angel moving inexorably closer. *Maybe I should just let him finish me,* Aaron thought. It was an option he should have considered before his parents were turned to ash. Perhaps if he had offered his life, sacrificed himself, the Powers' leader would have spared them.

"Gotta set it free before it's too late," he heard Gabriel say from his side, an edge of panic in his voice.

Verchiel stopped before Aaron. "It all comes to an end when you are dead," he growled. He raised his weapon and as Aaron stared into his lifeless black eyes, he knew that even if he had offered himself up, his family's gruesome fate would not have changed.

He could feel the heat of Verchiel's sword upon his face as it came at him. A Louisville Slugger blocked its descent. The fire of the blade flared wildly as it cut through the wooden bat, shaking Aaron from his paralysis.

"Get the hell outta here, kid," Zeke yelled as he brought the still-smoking half of the bat up and smashed it as hard as he could into Verchiel's snarling face.

Verchiel was stunned by the fallen angel's blow, but only for an instant. A line of shiny black blood dribbled from his aquiline nose to stain his lips and perfect teeth.

Aaron and Gabriel threw themselves at Verchiel, the intensity of their anger fooling them into thinking that they could help their friend. But Verchiel's wings lashed out from his back again, and the sudden torrent of air threw them back.

Verchiel grabbed Zeke by the back of his scrawny neck and hefted him off the ground with inhuman strength. "It wasn't enough that I took your wings and the lives of your filthy children? Now you want me to end your life as well?"

"Don't!" Aaron shrieked.

Zeke struggled, the piece of broken bat falling from his hand as he writhed. "You have to live, Aaron," he croaked, his voice strained with pain.

"So be it," Verchiel snapped as he ran his blade of fire through Zeke's back in a sizzling explosion of boiling blood and steam.

Zeke screamed, his head tossed back in a moan of agony and sorrow.

Aaron lunged at Verchiel and grabbed his arm in a powerful grip. "You son of a bitch," he screamed. "You killed him! You killed my parents, you vicious son of a . . ."

"Unhand me, filth," Verchiel said, lashing out with a vicious slap that sent Aaron hurtling across the room.

He landed atop the recliner in the corner of the living room, tipping it over and tumbling to the floor. He fought to remain conscious.

Through eyes blurred with tears, Aaron saw Zeke's twitching body slide off of Verchiel's blade and fall to his knees. A cry like the wail of eagles filled the air, and Camael charged across the room swinging his sword with abandon as he cut his way toward Verchiel. The look upon his face was wild—untamed.

Gabriel was suddenly at Aaron's side, pulling at his clothes. *"Get up,"* he said between tugs. *"You have to set it free. If you don't, you're going to die. We're all going to die."*

Aaron got to his feet and stumbled toward Zeke as Camael and Verchiel battled savagely, their blades blazing hotter, whiter as they clashed. He got to his knees beside the old Grigori and took his hand in his.

"You'll be all right," Aaron told him, his eyes locked on the smoldering black hole in the center of the fallen angel's chest. "I'll . . . I'll help you. Hang on and . . ."

Zeke squeezed his hand and Aaron pulled his gaze from the wound to look into his old eyes.

"Don't worry about me, kid," Zeke said in a whisper. "Nothing you can do except . . ."

"Except what?" Aaron asked, moving closer to the angel's mouth. "What can I do? Tell me."

An explosion sounded from overhead and Aaron instinctively threw his body over Zeke's to protect him. As he gazed up through a cloud of plaster dust and falling debris he saw that Camael and Verchiel had taken their fight outside—up through the ceiling, through the roof—to battle in the sky. He could hear their shrill cries echoing through the stormy night.

"You have to make it true, Aaron," Zeke said, pulling the boy's attention back from the yawning hole above them. "For the sake of all who have fallen . . ."

Zeke's grip upon his hand was intense, and Aaron was overcome with an enormous sadness. He could feel it inside him again, the power churning about at the center of his being. But he didn't want to set it free, for he knew to release it would mean that all he was and all he ever dreamed of becoming would be forever changed.

"You gotta make it happen," the old-timer pleaded.

The presence flipped and rolled inside Aaron, fighting against the restraints that he'd imposed upon it. And he knew that, no matter how hard he tried to deny it, he could not avoid his destiny any longer.

Slowly, gradually, he let his guard down, and the power surged forward just as it had the day he saved Gabriel. An energy coursed through him, a supernatural force that seemed to charge every cell of his body with throbbing vigor.

Aaron opened his eyes and looked down upon his friend—and the fallen angel was smiling.

"It's true," the Grigori whispered. "It's all true."

Aaron felt as if he too were on fire, burning from within. The presence radiated from his body in snaking arcs and he was unsure if mere flesh would be able to contain its power— and still it continued to grow.

His skin felt as though it were melting away. He tore at his clothing, ripping away his shirt to gaze at his naked flesh that was most assuredly afire. Strange black marks were bleeding across his exposed skin from deep within him. With a mixture of fascination and horror, he watched them appear all over his body. They looked like tribal markings, tattoos worn by some fearsome, primitive warrior hundreds and thousands of years ago.

"What's . . . what's happening to me?" he fearfully asked.

Gabriel lay down on the floor nearby and stared, eyes filled with awe. *"Let it happen, Aaron,"* he said consolingly. *"Everything is going to be just fine."*

There was sharp, excruciating pain in Aaron's upper back. "Oh God," he said breathlessly as the agony continued to intensify. Red spots of impending unconsciousness bloomed before his eyes.

He reached over his shoulders, clawing wildly at his back. His fingers touched two tender spots on either side of his shoulder blades: two large, bulblike growths that pulsed with every frantic beat of his heart. The pressure within them was growing. *Gotta let it out!* He raked his nails across the fleshy protuberances, and his hands were suddenly wet as the skin of the growths split and tore open with a sound very much like the ripping of fabric.

Aaron screamed long and hard in a mélange of pain and relief as feathered appendages emerged from his back, languidly unfurling to their full and glorious span.

Breathless, he looked over his shoulder in utter amazement.

Wings.

The wings were of solid black, like those of a crow, and glistened wetly. Muscles that he'd never felt before clenched powerfully and relaxed, and the wings began to flap, stirring the air. He glanced down at the strange markings that covered the flesh of his body, and an eerie calm seemed to pass over him then, a sense that he had finally achieved a serenity he had strived for most of his life.

For the first time, Aaron Corbet felt whole—he was complete.

Gabriel sat watching and waiting. He could barely contain his enthusiasm, his tail furiously sweeping the floor. *"Are you all right?"* the dog asked.

"I've never felt better," Aaron replied, and gazed up through the hole in the ceiling. He could see the shapes of the Powers as they darted and weaved like bats through the night sky in aerial combat with Camael.

The sudden urge to join the fray was intoxicating.

He held out his hand. Images of weapons scrolled through his mind until he saw the one that struck his fancy.

Aaron thought of that weapon and that weapon alone. He thought hard and felt the fire spark in the palm of his hand. The weapon was growing, the fire taking the shape of a mighty battle sword. He held the burning blade aloft, imagining the damage it could do to his enemies.

Again he gazed at the sky above and flexed his newly born appendages.

"Be careful, Aaron," Gabriel said, getting to his feet. *"I'll stay with Zeke. He shouldn't be alone."*

"Knock 'em dead, kid," Zeke said, and gave him the thumbs-up.

And Aaron leaped into the air, the virginal wings lifting him from the ground with ease.

As if it were something he was born to do.

The doubt was gone, driven away by the faith of one who had fallen.

No matter how he tried, Camael could not wipe the memory of Ezekiel's face from his mind. In the open sky above Aaron's home, swords of fire locked in combat, he fruitlessly attempted to push the recollection aside and pressed the attack.

Camael bellowed to the storm-filled night sky and came at Verchiel with his blade of heavenly fire. The Powers' leader dove beneath the swipe of the sword and dropped below, allowing two of his elite to take his place in battle. It seemed as though Camael's former captain did not wish to waste his prowess on a traitor to the cause.

The angel Sabriel swung his weapon, a scimitar that hissed as it cut into the arm of Camael's jacket and the soft flesh beneath. He grimaced in pain and closed his wings tight against his body. Then he let himself quickly drop like a stone, to fall away from his two attackers. And as he descended, the air whipping around him, he again remembered the Grigori.

He had sought out this Zeke that Aaron had spoken of, hoping that somehow the fallen angel would help him to convince Aaron to embrace his destiny. He had tracked the boy's rather powerful residual scent to a dilapidated hotel, where he found the building in flames and the old Grigori about to be murdered by two of Verchiel's soldiers.

Not wanting to fall too far from the current battle, Camael spread his wings to slow his descent and arced heavenward with three powerful thrusts. The Powers' eager cries filled the night. The sky was filled with them, each waiting for a chance to exact revenge on the one who had abandoned their sacred mission to side with the fallen.

He had helped the Grigori against the murderous Powers, impressed by the way the fallen angel had handled himself in battle. He could not recall the Grigori being all that adept at combat, but then again, Earth was a harsh and often brutally violent place and even heavenly beings had to adapt to survive. After escaping from the burning building, Ezekiel had wanted to know why Aaron was so important, why Verchiel was willing to sacrifice so much in order to see him destroyed.

And that was when Camael shared with him the prophecy and Zeke's hard, world-weary features took on a new expression altogether.

It was an expression of hope—hope for forgiveness, hope for redemption, hope for them all. And even though he knew that Zeke was most likely dead, he could not wipe the memory of that moment from his mind. He would use the Grigori's faith as a kind of banner, to chase away the doubt that had plagued him of late and spur him to victory against his enemies.

Exhilarated by Ezekiel's hope, Camael spun unexpectedly, catching one of the four soldiers on his tail unawares. He swung his sword with all his God-given might and severed the angel's head with a single swipe. He watched it spiral to the yard below, bursting into flame as it hit the perfectly manicured suburban lawn.

He imagined the humans in their homes blissfully unaware of the bloody warfare transpiring outside their windows in the skies above. The angelic magic used this night to mask the assault upon Aaron's home must have been great indeed, he mused, still occupied with the thrill of battle.

Seeing their comrade slain, the other three fled, flying off in different directions, and Camael searched the skies for his true enemy, Verchiel. If he were to fall, the Powers would be leaderless and the fight would certainly leave the others—at least until they chose another to command them. This would give him time to take Aaron away, to hide him until he could come to terms with the turn his life had taken.

Rediscovering their courage, two of the three assailants descended from the cover of clouds, their bloodthirsty squeals of excitement giving them away. Camael surged up toward them, meeting their attack head-on with a savagery he had not felt since the Great War. They seemed surprised, as if believing his years among the humans had made him weak.

That wasn't the case at all. He wielded his sword as if it were an extension of his body, swinging in a wide arc, cutting through one's wings, and disemboweling the other. There was a part of him that despised this, for these were soldiers he had once commanded, soldiers who would have followed him into the most hopeless of battles if he had asked. But there was another part that realized that was a long time ago, and he was no longer the same being that had led them—and they were no longer his soldiers. There was cruelty in their eyes, a cruelty that came from the wanton taking of life. If he had stayed on as their leader, he too would have worn the cold stare of superiority—just as Verchiel now did.

A sound from below distracted him. He hovered, riding the currents of wind, and listened carefully. It had come from

Aaron's house, and the horrible thought that Verchiel might have slain the Nephilim entered his mind.

Again came the sound and he recognized it for what it was. It was a cry of battle—a war cry.

From the hole in the structure's roof something emerged. It moved with incredible speed, on wings as black as a moonless sky. It wielded a weapon of fire and its exposed flesh was covered in markings that Camael recognized as angelic sigils, markings worn only by the greatest of Heaven's warriors.

Camael suddenly understood what he was seeing—who he was seeing. It was the bearer of hope for the future made flesh. Aaron Corbet had completed the transformation. He stared in awe as Aaron soared closer. Never had Camael seen one like this—so full of power—and he couldn't help but wonder who of the heavenly host could have sired one so magnificent.

The angels of the Powers were drawn to this new creature like sharks to blood-filled water. They circled their prey, briefly assessing its weaknesses, then attacked. And Camael watched in wonder as Aaron defended himself.

The Nephilim was awesome to behold, his bony wings spread wide as he darted about the sky, laying waste his attackers with uninhibited zeal.

"That is what you believe will save us all?" came a voice from behind, startling him.

Camael whirled, sword at the ready. This was the second

time in a day that he had let Verchiel sneak up on him. The Powers' leader was close. Dangerously so.

"I will see it dead and burning." Verchiel scowled as he thrust a dagger of fire into Camael.

And he could do nothing but accept the blade, feeling the heat of the weapon break the surface of his flesh and begin to cook the meat of him from the inside. The pain was sudden and blinding, and he didn't even have a chance to cry out as he fell from the sky, surrendering to the black embrace of unconsciousness before striking the ground below.

Verchiel watched the traitor fall toward the embrace of Earth.

"It did not have to end this way," he said regretfully. "This world could have been *ours* if your mind had not been so poisoned by the delusions of inferiors."

One of his soldiers cried out pitifully, and Verchiel returned his attention to the aerial battle at hand.

"The Nephilim," he cursed, watching another of his elite soldiers fall to the prowess of the creature's blade.

How is it this monster fights so fiercely? he asked himself, watching with perverse fascination as it moved through the air on wings of black as if by second nature. It was hard for him to imagine that this nightmarish joining of Earth and Heaven believed itself merely human only a few short days ago.

Another of his soldiers cried out in defeat and fell from the sky afire. The Nephilim's style was crude, erratic, lacking in discipline—yet it fought with an unbridled savagery effective against those who knew not what to expect. The Powers had grown soft over the centuries, untested against a true adversary, but Verchiel knew this foe. Here was the personification of all he'd been fighting against, all that he despised, and he yearned to see it finally vanquished.

To destroy this creature, this symbol of a perverted future too horrible for him to imagine, would be the greatest victory of all. Kill the Nephilim and the prophecy would die with it.

Verchiel still held the dagger he had used to kill his former commander. With a thought, he willed the blade away and summoned another weapon, one he considered sacred. It had not been used since his battle against the armies of the Morningstar. He called this broadsword Bringer of Sorrow, and it was for only the most profound and important of battles.

This was to be such a battle.

The sword materialized in his hand and he pointed it up toward the kingdom of Heaven. And with arcane words used by his kind to bend the elements to their will, he called down a storm upon the world of God's man, a storm to aid him in the defeat of the most horrible of evils.

A storm to wash away the malignant blight of prophecy.

CHAPTER TWELVE

The storm cover above his neighborhood had grown dense with dark steely clouds that appeared substantial enough to touch. Aaron maneuvered through them, water vapor lightly dampening his bare skin, invigorating him for the next wave of attack. The Powers had suddenly retreated, using the concealing clouds to hide and most likely regroup. Aaron imagined them lying in wait to take him by surprise, and he was ready.

He gazed about the expanse of sky over Baker Street, trying to understand the events of the last several minutes. He had wings. He was flying. And he was involved in a fight for his life, hundreds of feet above his home. It was insane—a thing of bad dreams. Yet he knew it was real.

The Powers had been relentless, coming at him from all sides. And he had fought them well. With his sword of fire he battled as though it were something he had done every day of his life, as if it were something he was meant to do.

Once he had accepted the transformation, the other-worldly presence had filled his mind with incredible knowledge. He remembered things that he had never known. Aaron suddenly knew the Powers, not just as heavenly beings bent on punishment and destruction, but as warriors who once served a noble cause.

Thunder rumbled and the gray skies were eerily illuminated by a flash of lightning. His eyes scanned the rolling clouds. *More Powers tricks?* he wondered as he looked for signs of imminent attack.

The winds were increasing in strength, and he was buffeted by their force as he continued to search the sky for his enemies. A crack of thunder that he felt from the top of his head to his toes shook the air, and lightning lit the sky. It was a full-fledged storm now, powerful winds, lightning, rain, and thunder. And still the Powers were nowhere to be found.

Aaron gazed with curiosity at the ceiling of churning weather above him and soared up ward with powerful thrusts of his ebony wings. He broke through the storm cover and looked beyond his neighborhood. He was not at all surprised to see a calm, star-filled night above the city of Lynn—everywhere except over Baker Street.

He gasped in sudden pain as something hidden in the clouds below grabbed his ankle and viciously yanked him downward. He lashed out blindly with his sword and the hold upon him was relinquished, but not before he found himself back within the raging storm.

The wind howled and the rain fell in sheets. *Heaven is crying,* Aaron thought distractedly, not sure where such an idea would have come from. And before he had the chance to think about it further, above the wail of the winds and the hiss of torrential rain, he heard a powerful voice call out to him.

"Nephilim!"

Aaron twirled in the air, searching for the source, but knowing full well who it would be.

Verchiel emerged from the storm, an awesome sight to behold, white wings carrying him through the turbulent air with ease. He held aloft an enormous sword of fire that sizzled and spat as the rain fell upon it.

Aaron looked nervously at his own weapon and wondered if it would be wise to summon something larger.

"Your time is at an end," the Powers' leader bellowed.

The storm raged harder and Aaron found it difficult to stay aloft.

"I will sweep away your existence like so much dust in the wind," Verchiel said as he turned his pale features toward Heaven and spread his arms wide.

Lightning zigzagged from the sky, a fracture of luminescence that struck the side of Aaron's home while he looked on in horror.

"No!" Aaron screamed as he fought the raging winds to descend. *Gabriel, Zeke*—his mind raced.

It sounded like the crack of an enormous whip as another bolt descended, and the roof exploded in a flash of white and began to burn. So overwhelmed was he that he became careless. New instincts warned him not to turn his back on Verchiel, but he paid them no mind. He had to get to his friends; if there was anything he could do it had to be now.

Aaron was grabbed from behind, his arms and wings pinned against his body. He watched helplessly as his sword tumbled from his grip to evaporate in the air below.

"This is but the beginning," the angel whispered maliciously in his ear.

Verchiel's breath smelled of spice and decay, and it made Aaron want to gag. He strained his every muscle, to no avail. The Powers' leader was remarkably strong. The mighty storm winds buffeted them, blowing their bodies about like corks caught in a river current. And still he struggled.

Aaron screamed in rage, tapping into the primal emotion that now coursed through him. He thrashed violently and rammed his head back in a brutal blow to the unsuspecting Verchiel's face.

It was just enough to loosen the angel's grip upon him, and Aaron was able to twist his body around. He looked into his attacker's sneering face, into the eyes of solid black—and in their limitless depths he saw the deaths of thousands.

They were just like him, still children, unaware of the heritage that had marked them for death. Aaron could feel their pain, their desperation, their fear of what they were becoming.

And how was their terror addressed? How were these beings of Heaven and Earth helped to understand their true origins? Only with more horror, as Verchiel and his soldiers came for them. And they were killed, cruelly, methodically, all in the name of God.

Thunder boomed and Aaron freed one of his arms and raked his nails down the angel's face, snagging one of those horrible, bottomless black eyes. Verchiel shrieked above the wail of the storm, his cry like that of a mournful seabird. He recoiled and grabbed at his injured face.

Aaron pushed himself away from his attacker, pure adrenaline pumping through his body—and something more. He chanced a glance below and saw that his house was on fire and part of the roof had collapsed. His anger intensified and he began to scream, a frightening sound incapable of being produced by human vocal cords.

Verchiel continued his taunts. "And when you are dead, we shall move through this city like a firestorm and everywhere you've been, everyone you've had even the slightest contact with—all will be washed away in torrents of fire."

Aaron flew at Verchiel, flaming sword forming in his hand, poised to strike. "You killed them," he shrieked, remembering the faces of those the angel had slain through-out the ages—as well as his own loved ones.

Verchiel blocked his blows with blinding speed, an evil grin slowly spreading across his pale features. The four bloody furrows Aaron had dug into the angel's face had already begun to heal.

"Yes, I did, and it is just the beginning," Verchiel said with an emotionless smile as he fought back with equal sav-agery. "You are a disease, Aaron Corbet." Verchiel spat his name as if it were poison on his tongue. "And I will cut from the body of this world all you have infected."

Aaron dove beneath the angel and went at him from behind. "All this death—," he began.

Verchiel spun with incredible swiftness. Aaron just man-aged to duck as the angel's blade passed over his head. He could feel its heat on his soaking scalp.

"—you do it in the name of God?" Aaron asked incredu-lously.

"Everything I do," Verchiel said with a hiss, fury etched into his scarred features, "I do for Him."

"What kind of god do you serve?" Aaron questioned, struggling to avoid the angel's thrusts, hoping Verchiel's anger would make him careless. "What kind of god would allow you to murder innocents in his name?"

Aaron delivered a blow to the angel's face, rocking his head back and to the side. A wicked thrill went through his body as he watched the angel recoil from the force of his strike. Before the transformation, he wouldn't have lasted two seconds against this berserk force from Heaven, but now Aaron believed that he could at least give Verchiel something to remember him by.

Verchiel spat blood from his wounded mouth and lunged forward, swinging his blade. His attack was relentless, driving Aaron back and away. Aaron blocked the pitiless descent of the broadsword, the blows so forceful that they began to fragment his own blade, finally causing it to disintegrate in his hand.

"Surrender, monster," Verchiel said in a voice as smooth as velvet. "It is God's will." The angel prepared to cut him in half.

Aaron flexed his wings and propelled himself toward Verchiel, driving his shoulder into the angel's stomach.

He grabbed Verchiel's wrist, preventing the sword of fire from descending.

"Is it His wishes you're following, Verchiel—or yours?" he asked as they struggled within the grip of the storm.

Verchiel brought a knee up and slammed it into Aaron's side. He felt the air from his lungs explode and his hold upon the angel's wrist falter.

"I am the leader of the Powers," he heard Verchiel say over the intensifying weather. "The first of all the hosts to be created by the Allfather."

Aaron wanted to call up another weapon to defend himself, but the burning pain in his side and lungs barely made it possible for him to stay aloft. He didn't want to die, to become yet another of the poor souls to fall beneath Verchiel's sword.

Verchiel came at him, sword in hand. He raised the great blade above his head. "His wishes—my wishes," he said, eyes wild with bloodlust.

The winds raged, blowing Verchiel back as he prepared to bring the sword down upon Aaron. "They are all one and the same," he said, straining against the exhalation of nature in turmoil that he had turned loose.

Aaron feebly managed the beginnings of a weapon to continue the struggle, when there was an explosion of sound that seemed to encompass all the heavens. It was a sound Aaron imagined might have been heard at the dawn of creation.

A bolt of lightning arced down from the sky, and he shielded his eyes from the intensity of its resplendence. Like the skeletal finger of some elemental deity composed entirely of crackling blue energy, it roughly tapped the top of Verchiel's head, as if to show its displeasure.

The angel screeched in pain as the lightning invaded his body, to explode free from the sole of a foot. His body seemed to glow from within, his mouth agape in a scream drowned out by the ruckus of the storm. Verchiel exploded into flames, his body no longer able to contain the raging power coursing through it. And, like Icarus, who had flown too close to the sun, he fell from the sky.

"One and the same—are you sure about that?" Aaron asked Verchiel, watching the blazing form of the Power as it spiraled earthward. Then he turned his attentions to the heavens above.

"Are you really sure?"

Verchiel lay upon his side on the cold, damp ground, wracked by a pain the likes of which he'd never felt before. His body, charred black by the power of the lightning strike, smoldered as it cooled in the evening air.

He rolled onto his back to gaze up at the heavens where his Master resided.

The storm clouds were breaking apart, the angelic magic used to manipulate the weather in all its fury dissipating like wisps of smoke carried away by the wind.

"Why?" he croaked, slowly raising his charred arm, reaching a beckoning hand out to the star-filled night.

But the Creator was silent.

And then they were there, the faithful of his host—those who had survived, looking down upon him, their faces void of emotion. They bent to lift him from the ground, laying the burden of his weight upon their shoulders. And they bore him up into the sky away from the battleground, away from the scene of his most heinous defeat.

"Why?" he asked again, carried closer to the place where his Father dwelled, but still so far that He did not answer.

"Why have you forsaken me?"

The ground grew steadily closer, and Aaron flexed the newly developed muscles in his back. His wings flapped once, and then again to slow his descent.

He touched down on a small patch of lawn in front of the house, falling forward in a scramble to reach the smoking wreckage that had once been his home.

"Stevie?" he screamed, running up the walk that was littered with pieces of burning shingles and wood. Maybe they left him. Maybe they decided they didn't want the little boy after all. "Stevie? . . . Gabriel?" he called frantically into the ruins.

"Gabriel," Aaron called again as he cupped his hands to his mouth, desperate for something of his family to have survived. "Gabriel, Zeke—are you there?"

He sensed an angel's presence behind him and spun around, a new weapon sparking to life in his waiting hand. He had already slain many heavenly beings today, and had no problem adding another to the tally.

"Stay away from me," he warned.

Camael limped closer, paying no heed to his threat. "The child is gone," he said.

The angel looked like hell, his face and clothing spattered

with drying gore. He was pressing a hand against a wound in his chest, trying to stem the flow of blood.

"Where is he?" Aaron asked as a combination of emotions washed over him. He was truly glad that his foster brother was still alive, but an awful dread filled him when he thought of who had taken him.

Camael stumbled closer. "The Powers . . . took him. I tried to stop them but—" He removed his hand from the wound and carefully examined it. "I was having some difficulty of my own." From his back pocket he produced a white handkerchief and placed it beneath his coat against the injury. "And no, I do not know where they have taken him."

The angel seemed to fall forward. Aaron reached for him but Camael caught himself on the twisted remains of the wrought-iron porch railing.

"Are you okay?" Aaron asked.

Camael nodded slowly, his eyes studying him. "You're certainly a sight to behold," he said with a dreamy smile. "One that I've yearned to witness since . . ."

Aaron held up his hand to quiet the angel. He didn't want to hear anymore, especially now.

Gabriel bounded out from behind the house calling his name excitedly. Aaron's face lit up at the sight of his canine friend and he knelt to embrace the dog.

"You're okay," he said as he stroked the animal's head and kissed the side of his face. "Good boy, good dog."

"I'm glad to see you, too," Gabriel said, *"but you have to come quick."*

Gabriel pulled away and trotted to the corner of the house.

"Gabe?" Aaron said, following.

"He doesn't have much time left," the dog said as he disappeared around the house into the backyard.

Zeke was lying very still in the middle of the yard beside the swing set, Gabriel sitting attentively by his side.

"I got him out of the house after the lightning hit—but I think he's going to die." The dog looked at Aaron, sadness in his rich, caramel eyes. *"Is he going to die, Aaron?"*

Aaron knelt down in the grass beside the fallen angel and gently took his hand. "I don't know, Gabe," he said. Zeke's hand was cold, like a stone pulled from a mountain stream. "I . . . I think he might."

"Oh," the dog said sadly, lying down beside the Grigori. *"I thought maybe you could do something for him."*

Zeke's eyes slowly opened. "Look at you," he said, a hint of a smile on his weathered features. Zeke gave Aaron's hand a weak squeeze. "All grown up and everything." He began to cough violently and dark blood frothed at his lips. "Damn," he said as he reached up to feebly wipe away the blood. "That don't feel so hot."

Aaron was in a panic. "What should I do?" he asked Zeke, squeezing his hand. "Should I call for an ambulance or . . ."

Zeke shook his head and the blood ran down the sides of his mouth. He didn't seem to notice—or maybe he just didn't care. "Naw," he said with a wave of his hand, his voice starting to sound more like a gurgle. "Too late for that."

Camael had joined them, and Aaron looked to him for guidance. "Is there anything . . . anything we . . . I can do to help him?"

The angel shook his head of silvery hair and closed his eyes. "The Grigori is dying. Verchiel's blade must have struck something vital."

Zeke gasped and began to convulse violently.

Aaron clutched his hand tighter and leaned in closer. "Zeke?" he asked. "Does . . . does it hurt you?"

"It's okay, kid," he said. His voice was weak, practically a whisper. "Pretty much had my fill of this place anyway."

The fallen angel went silent for a moment, his eyes gazing unblinkingly up at the star-filled sky.

"But I do got something to say," he said, turning his gaze from the heavens to Aaron.

"What's that?" he asked.

Zeke swallowed with difficulty and took a long, tremulous breath. It sounded full of fluid. "I want to say I'm sorry . . . ," he said, his voice trailing off in a gurgling wheeze.

Aaron didn't understand. "For what? What are you sorry for?"

The Grigori seemed to be gathering his strength to

answer. "For everything," he said, straining to be heard. "I want to tell you that I'm sorry for *everything* I've done."

At first Aaron wasn't at all sure what he was supposed to do—but suddenly, like the lightning that knocked Verchiel from the sky, it became excruciatingly clear.

Aaron knew exactly what needed to be done. In all his life, he had never been so certain of anything.

His body began to tingle, the hairs on his arms standing at attention as if he were about to receive the world's largest static shock. He held Zeke's hand and felt the energy begin to move, flowing from the swirling force that seemed to have settled in his chest, down his arm and into the fallen angel.

Zeke went suddenly rigid, but still Aaron held him. He watched in amazement as cracks began to appear in the facade of the Grigori's flesh, from which a brilliant white light shone.

Gabriel leaped to his feet and backed away. *"What's happening to his skin?"* he barked. *"What's happening?"*

But Aaron did not answer.

What had once been flesh fell away from Zeke's body like flecks of peeling paint, and what lay beneath pulsed with a radiance amazing to behold.

This is what it's all about, Aaron thought as he squinted through the white light, still holding tight to his friend's hand.

No longer did Aaron gaze upon a fallen angel, banished to Earth, dying of injuries sustained while trying to protect him. Now he beheld a being of awesome beauty, its body composed entirely of light.

This is what he must have looked like before his fall, Aaron thought, almost moved to tears by the glorious sight.

Bootiful, Aaron thought, remembering his little brother's praise.

The angel Ezekiel gazed up through the milky haze of light, his eyes wide with expectation. And Aaron realized what had yet to be said—what needed to be said in order to set his friend free.

"You're forgiven," he whispered in the language of messengers, and felt warm tears of even warmer emotion trail from his eyes to run down his face.

He released his friend's hand and the aura of energy surrounding him grew in intensity, brighter, warmer. Aaron got to his feet, moving away from the spectacle of rebirth unfolding before him.

Ezekiel rose up from the ground on delicate wings of sunlight. And he turned his beatific face up to the heavens and smiled.

"Thank you," said a voice in Aaron's mind like the opening notes of the most beautiful symphony imaginable. He was overwhelmed in its flow of unbridled emotion.

Then, in a flash of white, like the birth of a star, Ezekiel was gone, restored to a place long denied him.

Forgiven.

CHAPTER THIRTEEN

Drained, Aaron fell to his knees upon the lawn. His eyes were closed but still he saw the beautiful image of Ezekiel burned upon his retinas. He started to relax and felt the wings on his back begin to recede, the appendages of cartilage and feathers disappearing beneath the flesh of his shoulder blades. His skin began to prickle and he opened his eyes to see that the black markings on his arms and chest had begun to fade as well.

Gabriel came to him, tail wagging so furiously that it looked as though the dog had no control over his back end. He dug his head beneath Aaron's arm and flipped it with his snout, demanding to be petted. *"That was nice, Aaron,"* the dog said happily. *"You let him go home."*

Aaron looked to Camael. "What the hell just happened?" he asked, struggling to stand on shaking legs. "What did I do?"

The angel was looking up into the sky with longing on his soiled, yet still-distinguished features. "There is no more doubt, Aaron Corbet," Camael said, shaking his head, looking from the sky to him. "You are the One whose coming was foretold so long ago. Finally you have come to—"

"What did I do?" Aaron demanded to know.

The angel pulled at his silvery goatee as he spoke. "You have the power to grant absolution," Camael explained, a hint of a smile playing on his features. "Any who have fallen from the grace of God will be granted forgiveness in your presence, as long as they have seen the error of their ways."

"That's nice, Aaron," Gabriel said, looking up at his master, tail still happily wagging. *"Isn't it nice?"*

"Yeah, it's nice. So they're forgiven, what does that mean?" Aaron asked the angel. "Where did Zeke go?"

Camael again gazed upward. "He has returned home."

Aaron, too, looked into the sky. There was no longer any sign of the storm that had battered his neighborhood. "You're telling me that Zeke went back to Heaven."

"Your people have many colorful names for where he has gone: Paradise, Elysium, Nirvana, the happy hunting ground—Heaven is but one of them," Camael explained.

Aaron mulled this over. "And I sent him there?"

Camael pointed at Aaron with a long, well-manicured finger. "You are the bridge between the fallen and God."

"God, huh?" Aaron slipped his hands casually into the

back pockets of his jeans. He gazed toward what was left of his home, painfully remembering what had been done to it, to his parents—all in the name of God. He scowled and stormed away. "Y'know what?" he said, walking around the house to the front. "I don't think so."

Camael followed. "You can't run away from this, Aaron," he said, catching up to him. "It is your destiny. It was written of—"

Aaron spun around, stopping the angel cold. "Thousands of years ago," he finished. "I know all about it and I'm not too sure how happy I am serving a God who would allow *this* to happen." He gestured to the still-smoldering remains of his home. "Not to mention the hundreds—maybe thousands—of others He's allowed Verchiel to kill in His name." Aaron was furious, ready to take on the Creator Himself if necessary. "You tell me how I'm supposed to do this."

The Stanleys' neighbors had begun to emerge, cautiously making their way from their homes to view the devastation that they believed was caused by a storm.

Aaron gazed at what remained of the only home he'd ever known, both he and the angel watching as the last of the fire burned down to glowing embers.

"I understand your anger," Camael said.

Climbing the crumbled brick steps to where the front door once stood, Aaron stepped over what was left of the entryway into the rubble of his home. "Do you, Camael? Do you really understand?" He stood where the living room once was—where his parents had died. "Up until a few days ago I didn't believe in Heaven, angels, or flaming swords—never mind God." He kicked at a piece of wood that still glowed red. "And now I find out I'm part of some elaborate plan to reunify Heaven, to reunite all of God's children so they can be one big happy family again."

He remembered the boring simplicity of movie night with his foster family, and almost began to cry. But he was too angry for tears.

"How am I supposed to do this for Him when He couldn't even bother to save my family? Can you tell me that, Camael, because I'm really curious."

The sad wail of sirens could be heard in the distance.

"The Almighty," Camael began, "the Almighty and His actions or lack thereof . . . they are part of a much larger scheme. We may not understand it but—"

"The Lord works in mysterious ways," Aaron interrupted sarcastically. "Is that how you're going to try and explain this? That it's all part of some big picture that we're not privy to?"

There were neighbors in the street in front of the demolished home. There was fear in their eyes. Aaron could practically hear the thoughts running through their minds. *How could this have happened without me knowing? I didn't even know it was raining. Was there an explosion? I live right next door. This could have happened to me. I hope everyone is all right.*

"I know how hard this must be to grasp in a moment of tragedy. It is a quandary I, too, have come to ponder in my time upon this world." The angel walked to an area of collapsed wall and squatted before it. "The Father is aware of everything," he said, reaching beneath the plaster. "No matter how harsh or random things may appear, He does have a plan."

Camael pulled something from the rubble and brought it to Aaron. It was a broken frame and undamaged within it was a picture of his entire family. They were all wearing Santa hats, even Gabriel. Aaron took it and gazed at the happy image. He remembered when it was taken two years ago— how appalled he had been to have to wear the stupid hat. He had been even more mortified when the Stanleys had used the picture for their Christmas card that year.

Aaron carefully took the picture from the frame, a remembrance of a life now horribly altered by an ancient destiny.

"Sometimes the bad must precede the good," Camael said in another attempt to make him comprehend the machinations of the Creator. "Do you understand what I'm trying to say?" he asked.

Gabriel sniffed about the burned remains of what had been the recliner, sticking his nose beneath its twisted metal skeleton in search of something. Aaron was about to tell the dog to be careful when Gabriel pulled a filthy tennis ball from beneath the chair.

"*Look, Aaron!*" he said excitedly, his speech distorted

by the ball rolling around in his maw. *"I've found my ball. I thought I'd lost it forever!"* The dog eagerly let the ball fall from his mouth. For a brief moment his friend was happy, all the sadness of the past few hours pushed aside.

Aaron didn't like Camael's explanation of how things worked, but guessed he had no choice but to accept it. There was method to God's madness, so to speak.

He looked at the picture of his family one more time, then folded it and slid it into his back pocket.

"I have to find my little brother," Aaron said, looking to the angel that stood at his side. "Will you help me get him back?"

The fire engines screamed onto Baker Street, lights flashing, sirens howling as if mourning all the sadness they'd borne witness to.

"I will do that," Camael said with little emotion. Aaron might as well have asked him if he wanted milk or cream in his coffee.

Gabriel brought the ball to Aaron and let it drop at his feet. He wagged his tail as he leaned his head forward and lovingly licked his hand. *"Don't worry,"* he said. *"We'll find Stevie. You'll see, Aaron, everything will be fine."*

And as he gazed around at the smoldering ruins of his home, reflecting upon the shambles his life had become, thinking about the unknown that was the future ahead, Aaron wasn't so sure that anything would ever be fine again.

EPILOGUE

Are you sure about this, Aaron?" Principal Costan asked from behind the desk in his office at Kenneth Curtis High.

It had been two days since the supposedly freak lightning storm took the lives of his foster mother, father, and little brother, and Aaron felt it would be best that he leave school, and the city, as soon as possible.

Aaron nodded as he handed the man the papers he had signed officially withdrawing from Ken Curtis. "I'm sure, sir. I just can't stay around here anymore. It's for the best."

It had been the same at the animal hospital, people asking him if he was certain that this was what he really wanted to do. Of course it wasn't, but the threat of the Powers had left him little choice.

Mr. Costan took the papers and frowned. "Y'know, it's

none of my business, but running away from something isn't going to make it any—"

"I'm not running away," Aaron cut in, perturbed at his principal's suggestion.

The disturbing image of Verchiel and his soldiers descending from the sky, fire in their hands, laying waste to the school and everyone inside it, played out in his mind.

"There are just too many memories here," he said. "I think I'd seriously benefit from a change of scenery." And the quicker he got on the road, the quicker he could find Stevie, he thought as he watched the man behind the desk across from him.

Camael had explained why the Powers had taken his little brother. It had something to do with the handicapped—"the imperfect" as Camael had coldly referred to them—having some kind of sensitivity to the angelic, making them perfect servants. The thought of his little brother acting as a slave to the monster Verchiel both chilled him to the bone, and made him seethe with anger. He had to find Stevie before any harm could come to him.

The principal scrutinized the completed documents and placed them in an open folder on his desk. "Very well then. It doesn't appear that I can change your mind. And since you're now of legal age . . ." Mr. Costan closed the folder and stood, extending his hand.

Aaron stood as well and took the principal's offered hand.

"Good luck, Aaron," Costan said, "and if you ever want to come back to finish your senior year, I'm sure we could work something out."

Aaron shook the man's hand briefly and then let it go. "Thanks for everything," he said as he turned and quickly left the office, desperate to escape before the principal tried yet again to make him reconsider his decision.

The clock in the reception area said that it was a little after nine. If he hurried, he could clean out his locker, drop off his books, and be out of the school before first period ended.

The halls were empty as he made his way to his locker for what would be the last time. Memories flooded through his mind. He remembered the first day of freshman year as if it were only a few months ago. The place had seemed so huge then; he thought he'd never learn his way around. Aaron smiled sadly—if only his problems had remained so inconsequential.

At his locker he removed the textbooks and gathered his belongings, double-checking to be sure he hadn't left anything behind. He slammed the metal door closed for the final time, and was overcome with an intense sadness and anger.

It isn't fair, he thought. He was supposed to leave this place just like everybody else: finish up senior year, attend graduation wearing that brightly colored gown and the seriously goofy mortarboard, and then go off to college.

But fate had dealt him a cruel hand, and his destiny lay down a different path altogether.

Aaron lashed out and kicked the locker to release some of his pent-up frustration. The sound was thunderous in the empty halls. He lost his grip on the books beneath his arm and they tumbled to the floor in disarray. Aaron felt like screaming, but somehow managed to control himself. He bent down to retrieve his belongings with a heavy sigh, feeling like a complete moron. An angry, complete moron.

"Do you want some help?"

Aaron quickly looked up, feeling the sudden weight of sadness press him even further into depression. This was why he'd wanted to get out before the first period ended. He hadn't wanted to see her.

Vilma Santiago knelt down beside him and helped him gather his books.

"Thanks," he said, trying as hard as he could not to make eye contact.

"You were leaving without saying good-bye, weren't you?" she said softly as she handed him his history book.

He looked at her then and saw that her eyes were moist and red. She had been crying.

"I don't know how, but I knew you were out here." She showed him a piece of pink paper, a hall pass. "I said I had to go to the bathroom."

She smiled and laughed a bit. Though filled with sadness, it still was a disturbingly beautiful sound, and his heart ached. Nervously he straightened the stack of books, unsure of how he should address her accusation.

"I didn't want to go through the whole good-bye thing," he said, wishing with all his heart that he could tell her he was only trying to keep her safe. "I just can't deal with anything else that's sad."

He was dying inside. Of all the things he was leaving behind, Vilma was the thing that pained him the most. There was no one else here to say good-bye to. Aaron stood, holding the stack of books beneath his arm.

"For what it's worth," she said with a sniffle, "in Brazil . . . when my mother died, I didn't think I would ever be happy again."

A tear began to fall from her left eye and Aaron almost dropped the armful of books to wipe it away.

"I'm sorry." She looked embarrassed and quickly reached up to wipe away the moisture from her face. "I know you've been through a lot; I don't want to make you feel any worse."

The nine-fifteen bell began to ring and the empty hallway was filled with its jarring, metallic peal.

"What I'm trying to say, Aaron, is that it won't hurt like this forever. Right now you probably don't think so, but trust me on this, okay?"

He nodded and tried to smile. "Thanks," he said as the

corridor crowded with students going from one class to the next. "I really appreciate it."

He started to move away from his locker, from her. He had to go now or there was a good chance that he would never leave.

"I have . . . I have to go," he stammered, backing away.

She started to follow. "Where will you go?"

"I don't know," he answered truthfully. "I . . . I just have to get away." He had to find his brother and something inside was urging him to travel north. Camael said that it would be in their best interest to trust these urges.

Aaron started to turn away from her.

"Will you be back?" she asked hopefully, now at his side.

He shook his head. "No. I doubt it," he said, and looked away from her with feigned indifference. This was killing him. He hated to be so mean, but it was for her own good.

Aaron again heard Verchiel's cold words threatening to kill everyone close to him.

"I really have to go," he said, and quickened his pace, leaving her behind.

She moved in front of him, blocking his path, leaned in close, and took him in her arms. She smelled incredible, clean, like bath powder and fresh-cut flowers. She gave him a hug and a warm, gentle peck on the cheek that made his legs begin to tremble.

"You take care, Aaron Corbet," she said softly in his ear. "I'll miss you very much."

And he felt his heart shatter into a million, razor-sharp pieces that tore his insides to ribbons.

He didn't say anything more, forcing himself down the hall. After turning in his books at the main office, he practically ran from the building.

Outside on the steps, the wind blew and Aaron pulled the collar of his leather jacket up around his neck. Although it was officially spring, there was still a cruel bite of winter in the air. He was parked in the school's horseshoe-shaped driveway, and could see Camael and Gabriel waiting for him by the car.

This is it, he thought, and put his hands inside his pockets for warmth as he began to descend the steps.

Something was in one of his pockets, something that hadn't been there before.

He removed the piece of folded paper and opened it. It was from Vilma and it was her e-mail address and telephone number. She must have put it there when she hugged him. At the bottom of the paper, in delicate handwriting, it said, "Just in case you want to talk."

Aaron thought about throwing the paper away, but couldn't bring himself to do it. He placed it safely back inside his pocket and continued on his way to the car. For some reason, he felt strangely warmer.

He could hear Camael and Gabriel talking as he approached.

"For the last time, no," he heard the angel say, a touch of petulance in his tone.

"What's the problem?" Aaron asked as he came around the side of the car.

Gabriel had dropped the tennis ball at Camael's feet, and Aaron knew immediately what the problem was.

"He won't throw the ball for me, Aaron. I asked him nicely and he still refused. I think he's mean."

The angel seethed. "I have never thrown a ball and have no desire to ever do so. It has nothing to do with my temperament."

Aaron squatted down to the dog's level. "What did I tell you about trying to force people to play with you?"

The dog playfully swatted the ball with his paw and caught it in his mouth before it could roll away.

"Gabriel?" he cautioned.

The dog lowered his head, shamed by his master's disapproval. *"He wasn't doing anything, and I got bored."*

"He said he didn't want to play and you should respect that."

"I'm sorry, Aaron," Gabriel said, ears flat against his head.

Aaron lovingly ruffled the dog's floppy ears. "That's all right. Let's just try and be a little more considerate." Then he shot a withering look at the angel. "Though it probably wouldn't have killed you to toss the ball a couple of times."

"I still think he's mean," the dog muttered beneath his breath before he defiantly snatched up the ball in his mouth.

"Did you accomplish your task?" Camael asked, ignoring the animal, hands clasped behind his back.

Aaron turned and looked back at the school, taking in every detail of the brick and concrete structure. "Yeah," he said, saving the image of his high school to memory. "I'm ready to go."

He was opening the driver-side door of the car when Gabriel let out a cry.

"Shotgun!" he bellowed, startling them as he scrambled to the front, passenger-side door.

Camael looked at him, an expression of confusion on his goateed face. "What did you say?" he asked the dog.

"I said shotgun," Gabriel explained. *"It's what you're supposed to say when you want to ride in the front seat."*

Aaron could not help but laugh. No matter how many conversations he had with the animal, Gabriel's increased intelligence still managed to surprise him.

"That's what I thought you said," Aaron said. He then looked to Camael. "Do you mind riding in the back?"

"Front or back," Camael growled with an air of distaste. "It doesn't matter. I despise the confines of these hellish contraptions no matter where I ride."

"Great," Aaron said as he pulled open his door and pushed the driver's seat forward so that the angel could crawl into the back. Then he went around to the front passenger door to let his best friend in. "Shotgun is all yours," he told Gabriel, and let the dog hop up into the copilot seat.

"Awesome," said the dog, bright pink tongue lolling happily from his mouth as he panted with anticipation.

Aaron started to close the door. "Watch your tail," he said, and slammed the door closed.

He plopped himself down behind the wheel and started the car up, but did not put it into drive.

Aaron was staring at the school again—his school—and thought about all the things lost to him over the past few days: the closest thing to mother and father he had ever known, his home, his job, his school—and even his humanity.

He thought about Vilma, her eyes red from crying. If only he could have explained; yet another thing taken away from him.

"Are we ready, Aaron?" Camael asked impatiently from the back.

Aaron used the rearview mirror to look into the backseat and the angel seated there.

"To be perfectly honest, no, I'm not," he said, putting the car into drive. "But, from what you've told me about the prophecy and all, I don't think I really have much of a choice."

He pulled the car away from the curb and proceeded down the driveway. At the end of the drive he waited for his chance to go, and pulled out into the flow of traffic, pointing the car to the north and the uncertainty of the future, the still-tender memories of things loved and lost left sadly behind.

"Where are we going, Aaron?" Gabriel asked, his head moving excitedly from side to side as he watched the other cars on the road with them.

"I'm not sure," he answered, changing lanes to pass a minivan in need of a new exhaust system.

"Then how will we know when we get there?" the dog asked, concerned.

Aaron could feel the animal staring at him, waiting for an answer. He reached over and scratched beneath the dog's neck. "Don't worry, pally," he said, keeping his eyes on the road. "I have a feeling we'll know."

It's supposed to be like this, he thought with disdain as he took the exit that would lead them onto the highway going north.

Predestined, whether he liked it or not.

The Saint Athanasius Church and Orphanage, vacant since 1959, squatted dark and brooding at the end of a seldom used road in western Massachusetts.

It was supposed to have been turned into elderly housing sometime in the mid-eighties, but the cost of refurbishing and renovating the buildings far exceeded their value.

There was an air of disquiet about the place, as if the old, ramshackle structures had gained sentience, and were bitter about being abandoned. It was this atmosphere that gave the grounds its reputation of being haunted.

So there it sat for the last forty-some years, its structure slowly wasting away at the mercy of the elements, absent of life except for the wild creatures of the fields that had gradually found their way inside the buildings, to live within the walls and nest in the belfry.

Mournfully vacant—until a few days ago.

From a wooden seat upon the altar within the Church of Saint Athanasius, Verchiel gazed up at the rounded, water-stained ceiling and examined the depiction of Heaven painted there.

The angel shifted uncomfortably in his chair as he studied the artwork. Pieces of burned flesh painfully flaked away from his body and fell to the altar floor.

"You haven't the slightest idea," he mused aloud as he gazed at the castle of gold floating among the clouds, and the harp-wielding angels that blissfully circled above it.

Kraus, the healer, crept carefully toward him, his worn leather satchel of medical tools wedged beneath his arm. Though blind, he stopped before Verchiel's chair, sensing his presence—his divinity—as only the imperfect could.

"I am here to minister to your needs, Great Verchiel," Kraus said, bowing his head in reverence.

Verchiel had been in perpetual agony since the lightning strike, the entire surface of his body charred black. "Proceed," he said with a wave of his blackened hand, his nerve endings vibrating in blinding pain with even the slightest movement.

The healer knelt down before Verchiel. He placed the satchel upon the ground, undid the tie, and rolled it open to expose the instruments contained within. His hands hovered over the wide variety of scalpels, blades, and saws—tools of healing used by his predecessor and hundreds of others before him.

By touch he found what was needed, a twelve-inch blade that glinted sharply in the beams of sunlight that streamed in through openings in the boarded-up windows.

"Shall we proceed?" the human monkey asked, the sourness of his breath offensive to Verchiel's heightened senses.

The quicker he was treated, the quicker he could be away from the offensive animal. "Do as you must," Verchiel responded. He lifted one of his arms and presented it to the healer, a sound like dry leaves rustling in the wind filled the air.

The healer leaned forward, and with great skill, began to cut away the burned, dead flesh.

The pain was unbearable, but Verchiel did not cry out, for it was part of the price he must pay. What was it when the monkeys begged forgiveness for their indiscretions?

Doing penance, he believed it was called.

It was obvious that he had disappointed his Holy Master, for why else would he have been punished so? The pain was his penance. For failing to slay the false prophet he had to suffer, to show that he was truly sorry.

Kraus carefully peeled away a swath of dead skin to expose the raw, moist flesh beneath. If he was to eventually heal, this would need to be done to his entire body; all the burned, dead skin would need to be removed. It would be a long, painful process, but it was something Verchiel was willing to endure—the penance he would pay to receive the Creator's forgiveness.

The sound of a child's moan distracted him from his agony.

The Nephilim's brother, the imperfect one called Stevie, sat on the far side of the altar and rocked from side to side, staring wide-eyed at what had been placed before him.

It was a helmet the rich color of blood, cast in the forges of Heaven—a gift to the child from his new master.

The child groaned again, his eyes transfixed upon it, almost as if he were somehow cognizant of the fate he, and it, would eventually share.

"I shall change you, my pet," Verchiel said with a hiss, his body trembling with torment as more of his skin was cut away. A pile of dead flesh grew at his feet as the healer continued his gruesome task.

"Transforming you into my hunter of false prophets—"

The child rocked from side to side, his repetitive cries of "no" echoing through the once holy place.

"A tool of absolution," Verchiel said as he leaned his head back against the chair and again looked to the church ceiling and the all too human images of Paradise. A place that, if he were to have his way, only the truly worthy would ever be allowed to enter.

"My instrument of redemption."

LEVIATHAN

For Tobi and all the other special friends lost to us.
You will always be missed and never be far
from our hearts; best friends forever.

As always, this book could not have been possible without the loving support of my wife, LeeAnne, and the daily inspiration provided to me by Mulder, the King of the Labs (or so he believes).

A special tip of the hat to my partner in crime, Christopher Golden, and to Lisa Clancy and her assistant to die for, Lisa Gribbin.

And special thanks are also due to Mom and Dad, Eric "the Goon" Powell, Dave Kraus, David Carroll, Dr. Kris, Tom and Lorie Stanley, Paul Griffin, Tim Cole and the usual cast of characters, Jon and Flo, Bob and Pat, Don Kramer, Pete Donaldson, Kristy Bratton, and Ken Curtis for the use of his name. Thank you one and all, good night, and drive carefully.

PROLOGUE

Amidst the south Serbian Mountains, nestled within the gorge of the Black River, sat the Crna Reka Monastery. The wind howled piteously, like the sad wails of a mother mourning the loss of her child, as it blew across the high rocks and sparse vegetation surrounding the holy hermitage.

It was a lonely place, a place for reflection and absolution. The church itself was constructed within a large cave during the thirteenth century—a homage to the Archangel Michael. The hermit monks soon built their cells around the church, and a small drawbridge was erected over the Black River. By a great blessing of God, the river disappeared underground just before the monastery, and then reappeared several hundred meters later, sparing the monastery the deafening roar of the water's noise.

The repenter knelt upon a worn, wicker mat in a cold,

empty room of the monastery in the rocks, and listened to the prayers of the world. No matter the time, be it day or night, someone, somewhere, searched for the aid or guidance of the Divine. A woman in Prague prayed for the soul of her recently departed mother, a man in Glasgow for the continued health of his wife stricken with cancer. A farmer in Fort Wayne asked for relief from a fearsome drought, and a truck driver parked alongside a road in Scottsdale begged for the strength to live his life another day. So many voices, a cacophony of cries for help—it made his head spin.

He tried to lend them all a slight bit of his own strength, and asked the Creator to listen to their pleas. *Does the Lord of Lords hear me?* he wondered. The penitent hoped so. Though others would have him believe that the Holy Father had stopped listening to him a long time ago, it did not prevent him from speaking on behalf of those who prayed—a conduit to Heaven.

Eyes tightly closed, ears filled with the sounds of benediction, the kneeling man smiled. A six-year-old named Kiley prayed with the passion of a saint for a brand-new bike on her birthday. Had he ever prayed with such fervor for anything? The answer was obvious—it was the reason he continued to wander the planet, searching out the most sacred places, hoping to quell the burning turmoil at the core of his being.

The sinner sought forgiveness—forgiveness for the evil he had wrought.

The sound of tiny claws scrabbling across the stone floor

wrested him from his concentration, and he opened his eyes. A mouse stood on its hindquarters, nose twitching eagerly toward him.

"Well, hello there," the penitent said softly, his voice filled with affection for the gray-furred rodent. He and the mouse had become good friends since his arrival at the monastery six months before. And in exchange for bits of bread and cheese, the little animal kept him abreast of events outside the hermitage.

From within the long sleeves of his robe, the repenter produced a crust of bread from the previous night's supper and offered it to the small creature. *"And how are you today?"* he asked in a language only it would understand.

"Others here," the mouse replied in a high-pitched squeak as it took the bread in its front paws.

For the last two months he had sensed something growing in the ether, building steadily over the past few days. Something with the potential for great danger—and yet also wondrous. He had his suspicions, but did not want to get his hopes up only to have them dashed to pieces again.

"Others like you," the mouse finished, nervously gnawing on the piece of bread.

Suddenly the repenter was glad that he had sent the Crna Reka brothers to town for supplies this day. If what the mouse was telling him was true, he did not wish to risk the well-being of anyone else. The brothers had been quite gracious in allowing him into their place of quiet solitude, and he did not want to see any of them suffer for their charity.

He listened, focusing on the sounds of the monastery around him: the muffled roar of the Black River flowing beneath the structure; the creak of the bridge outside, jostled by the winds blowing into the gorge from the mountains above; the rumble of thunder.

No, not thunder at all, something far more ominous.

The penitent picked the mouse up from the floor and placed it in his palm as he stood. *"And where exactly did you see these others?"* he asked.

"Outside," it answered, continuing its nibbling. *"In sky. Outside in sky."*

It was then that the repenter began to feel their presence. They were all around him. The floor of the monastery began to shake, as if in the clutches of an angry giant. Rock, dust, and wood fell from the ceiling, and the walls began to crumble. He clutched the tiny life-form to his breast to protect it from the falling debris. An explosion, filled with sound and fury, rocked the monastery, and the walls before him fell away, sliding into the Black River Gorge to reveal the Serbian Mountains, and those who awaited him.

They hovered there, at least twenty in number, their mighty wings beating the air—the sound like the racing heartbeat of the wilderness valley surrounding them—and in their hands they held weapons of fire.

The repenter stepped back from the jagged edge of a yawning precipice and held the trembling mouse closer. He did not
take his eyes from them. He was not afraid. Some bowed their
heads as his gaze fell upon them, remembering a bygone time
when he had commanded their respect—but that was long,
long ago.

"Lift your heads," ordered an angry voice in the language
of messengers. Their numbers began to part, and he who led
them moved forward. *The time for this one to be shown reverence passed when the first seeds of the Great War were sown.*

The penitent was familiar with he who spoke: a wrathful
angel in the Choir called Powers. His name was Verchiel, and
he bore the scars of one who had recently fought a fierce battle.
The repenter wondered why they had not healed, and almost
asked the angel—but decided this was not the time.

"We have come for you, son of the morning," Verchiel said,
pointing his sword that burned like the heart of an inferno.

With those words, the angels of the Powers glided closer,
their weapons raised for conflict.

"Your corrupting time upon God's world has ended," Verchiel
said with a gleam in his deep, dark eyes of solid night.

"You'll receive no fight from me," the repenter replied, looking from the fearsome Powers drawing inexorably closer to the
mouse still held in his hand against his chest. *"Just keep your voices
dawn,"* he continued as he ran a finger along the soft, downy fur
of the trembling rodent's head. *"You're scaring the mouse."*

"Take him!" Verchiel cried in a voice that hinted of madness, scars hot and red against his pale flesh.

And they flew at him.

The repenter did as he imagined he must. No weapons of fire sprang from his palms, no powerful wings unfurled to carry him away. He slipped the fragile creature that had become his friend inside the folds of his simple robes, and let himself be taken.

Shackles of a golden metal not found on this world, their surface etched in an angelic spell of suppression, were slapped roughly upon his wrists, and he felt himself immediately sapped of strength by their inherent magick. Some of the Powers, but not all, clawed at him, striking him, beating him with their wings—even though he offered no resistance. The penitent could understand their resentment and did nothing to halt their abuse.

"Enough!" Verchiel bellowed, and the angelic soldiers stepped away from the repenter's prone form on what remained of the room's floor.

The leader of the Powers approached, and the prisoner looked up into his cold, merciless gaze. *"So angry,"* he whispered as he studied the expression of cruelty burned upon the angelic commander's face. *"So filled with blind hatred. I've seen that look before. It's very familiar to me."*

Verchiel motioned for his men to lift the repenter from the ground, and they did just that—but he continued to examine the leader's troubling features.

"I used to see it every time I saw my reflection," he said as he was borne aloft by the angels of the Powers.

His words struck a sensitive chord. Verchiel's expression changed to one of unbridled fury, and he lunged toward the repenter, a new weapon of flame taking shape. *Will it be a sword to cleave my skull in two—or maybe a battle-ax to separate my head from my shoulders?* he wondered. The weapon became a mace, and the angel swung with a force that would shatter mountains. It connected with the side of the prisoner's head, and an explosion, very much like the birth of a galaxy, blossomed behind his eyes.

As he slipped into the void, he was accompanied by the fading sounds of the world he was leaving behind, the murmurs of prayer, the moan of the mountain winds, the pounding wings of vengeful angels, and the rapid-fire beating of a frightened mouse's heart.

Then, for a time, all was blissfully silent.

CHAPTER ONE

Aaron Corbet accelerated to seventy mph on 1-95 heading north. He turned up the volume of the speakers and casually glanced to the right to see the angel Camael wincing as if in pain.

"What's wrong?" Aaron asked. "Do you sense something? What is it?"

The angel shook his head, his expression wrinkling with distaste. "The noise," he said, pointing a slender finger at the car's stereo. "It brings tears to my eyes."

Aaron smiled. "Oh, you like it?"

"No," the angel grumbled as he shook his head. "It pains me."

"It's the Dave Matthews Band!" Aaron exclaimed, genuinely stunned.

"I don't care whose band it is," the angel growled, moving agitatedly about in the passenger seat. "It makes my eyes water."

Annoyed, Aaron hit the eject button, and the CD slowly emerged with a soft, mechanical whir. "There," he said; gripping the steering wheel with both hands. "Is that better?"

The radio had come on, and the sound of Top 40 pop filled the vehicle. One of the popular boy bands—he could never tell them apart—was singing about lost love. He glanced again at Camael to see that the angel was still making a face.

"What's wrong now? I turned off my music."

"And I am appreciative," the angel warrior said as he gazed out the window at the scenery whipping past. "But I find all of your so-called music to be extremely discordant. It offends my senses."

Gabriel reared up in the back and stuck his yellow-white snout between the front seats. *"I like the song about Tasty Chow,"* the dog said.

Happy to be talking about anything that can end up in his stomach, Aaron thought as he squeezed the steering wheel in both hands.

"How does that song go, Aaron?" the Labrador retriever asked. *"I've forgotten."*

"I don't know, Gabriel," he said, becoming more irritated. "That's not even a real song—it's a dog food jingle, a commercial."

"I don't care," the dog said indignantly. *"I like that song a lot—and the commercial is good too. It's got kids and puppies, and they play on swings and run and jump and then the puppies eat Tasty Chow. . . ."*

Gabriel stopped mid-sentence as Aaron reached out to shut off the radio, plunging the car into silence. *Great,* he thought as he drove, *just what I need.* Without the distraction of music, his wandering mind had another opportunity to examine how completely insane his life had become.

Just over two weeks ago, on his eighteenth birthday, Aaron learned he was something called a Nephilim—the child of a human mother and an angel. Aaron never knew his biological parents, having been in foster care all his life. So when he began to exhibit rather unique abilities, like being able to speak and understand foreign languages—human and animal—he thought that maybe he was losing his mind.

Which was exactly what he was going to do if he didn't stop thinking about this stuff. He glanced over at the powerfully built man—*no, angel*—sitting in the passenger seat beside him. "So what kind of music do you like?" he asked to break the silence.

Camael had once been the leader of an army—a Choir of angels, the Powers, whose purpose it was to eliminate all things offensive to God. After Lucifer's defeat in the Great War in Heaven, many of his followers fled to Earth. Barred from Heaven, these angels began a life upon the world of man, some even taking wives and having children. It was the job of the Powers to destroy these defectors and their abominable offspring, the Nephilim.

"You are speaking to one who has heard the symphony of

Creation," the angel said in a condescending tone. "How can the sounds produced by the likes of your primitive species even compare?"

As Aaron knew, on one of his many missions to eradicate the enemies of Heaven, Camael had been made privy to a prophecy—a prophecy that described a creature, both human and angel, that would reestablish a bond between the fallen angels on Earth and God. This being—a Nephilim—would forgive these angels their sins and allow their return to Heaven. After so much violence and death, Camael thought this was truly a great thing, but his opinion was not shared by his second-in-command, a nasty piece of work that went by the name of Verchiel.

"So you don't like any of it?" Aaron asked, dumbfounded by the angel's broad dismissal of the entire musical spectrum. "You don't like classical or jazz—or rock or country? None of it? Everything gives you a headache?"

The angel looked at him, eyes burning with intensity. "I haven't had the time to sample all forms of your music," he said. "As you are aware, I have been rather busy."

Camael left the Powers to follow the prophecy. For thousands of years he wandered the planet, attempting to save the lives of Nephilim—hoping that each might be the one of which the prophecy foretold. Now led by Verchiel, the Powers would do anything to eliminate the blight of half-breeds from God's world, making the prophecy but an ancient memory.

"But you've been here forever," Aaron said with a disbelieving grin. "I don't mean to be a pain in the ass, but . . ."

"That's exactly what you are, boy," Camael said, looking back out the side window. "You are the One—as well as a pain in the ass."

So besides being a Nephilim, which was bad enough, Aaron Corbet was also the subject of the prophecy. It wasn't something he had even been aware of—until the Powers, under Verchiel's command, attempted to kill him. The attacks resulted in the deaths of his psychiatrist, his foster parents and a fallen angel by the name of Zeke—who had helped him finally tap into his angelic abilities and save himself.

"I'm sorry," Aaron said, slowing down as a red sports car pulled up alongside him on the two-lane road, then sped up to pass. "It's just that you come off all holier-than-thou because you're an angel and everything—when in fact you really don't know what you're talking about."

"Though I no longer associate with their Choir, I am of the Powers," Camael said, "one of the first created by God, and it is my right to have an opinion that disagrees with yours."

The abilities called to life with Zeke's urgings saved not only Aaron's life, but also the life of his dog, Gabriel. When the Labrador was struck by a car and mortally injured, Aaron called upon his latent powers and healed the dog, as a result changing Gabriel into something more than just a dog.

"You can't have a real opinion unless you've actually

listened to the stuff. It's like saying you don't hike broccoli when you've never even tasted it," he said, frustrated by the angel's attitude.

"I like broccoli," Gabriel said suddenly. *"I wish I had some right now. All that talk about Tasty Chow has made me very hungry."*

Aaron glanced at the digital clock on the dashboard. It was a little before noon. They had been on the road since the crack of dawn, and it had been a long time since breakfast. *Maybe we should pull over and get something to eat,* he thought. Then he remembered Stevie and immediately felt guilty. Who knew what was happening to his foster brother?

When the Powers attacked his home, the angels took his seven-year-old foster brother. Stevie was autistic, and according to Camael, angelic beings often used the handicapped as servants because of their unique sensitivity to the supernatural. This was the main reason they were on the road, to rescue Stevie—that and to prevent the Powers from hurting anyone else Aaron might care about.

Aaron was distracted by the sound of something spattering and looked down near the emergency break to see saliva pooling from Gabriel's mouth. "Gabriel," he scolded, reaching back to push the dog into his seat, "you're drooling!"

"I told you I was hungry," the Lab said, leaning back. *"I can't stop thinking about that Tasty Chow commercial."*

Aaron looked over at Camael, who was silent as he gazed

stoically out the window. "So what do you think?" he asked. "I'm getting kind of hungry myself. Should we stop and get some lunch?"

"It makes no difference to me," the angel said, not looking at him. "I have no need of food."

Aaron chuckled. "You know, that's right," he said, the realization sinking home. "I've never seen you eat."

"I love to eat," said Gabriel from the back.

"How is that possible?" Aaron asked, finding himself interested in yet another aspect of the alien life-form known as angel. "Everything has to eat to survive—or is this some bizarre kind of supernatural nonsense that I won't understand?"

"We feed off the energies of life," Camael explained. "Everything that is alive radiates energy—we are like plants to the sun, absorbing this energy to maintain life."

Aaron thought about that for a moment. "So, since you're sitting here with me and Gabe—you could say you're eating right now?"

The angel nodded. "You could say that."

"I'm not eating right now, although I wish I was," the dog said irritably.

"Okay, okay," Aaron replied, preparing to take the next exit. "We'll find someplace for a quick bite, but then we have to get back on the road. I don't want Stevie with those murdering sons of bitches any longer than he has to be."

As he took the exit and merged right, onto a smaller,

more secluded stretch of road, Aaron thought about all he had left behind. Every stretch of highway, every exit, every back road took him farther and farther away from the life he was used to. He already found himself missing school, something he hadn't thought possible. It was senior year, after all, and in some perverse way he had been looking forward to all of the final papers and tests, the acceptances and rejections from colleges. But that was not to be; being born a Nephilim had seen to that.

Aaron caught sight of a roadside stand advertising fried clams, hamburgers, and hot dogs. There were picnic tables set up in a shaded area nearby—perfect for Gabriel.

As he pulled into the dirt lot, an image of Vilma came to mind. Before his life collapsed, he had almost believed that he was going to go out with one of the prettiest girls he had ever seen. They never did have an opportunity for that lunch date, and now probably never would. Suddenly Aaron wasn't quite as hungry as he had been.

Vilma Santiago sat at the far end of the cafeteria at Kenneth Curtis High School and was glad to be alone. It was a beautiful spring day, and most of the student body had taken their lunches outside, so she'd had no difficulty finding an empty table.

The elusive memory of the previous night's dream—*or was it a nightmare?*—teased her with its slippery evasiveness. She hadn't slept well for days, and it was finally beginning to affect her. The girl felt tired, irritable, with the hint of a headache, its pulsing pain just behind her eyes.

But most of all, she felt sad.

Vilma opened the paper sack that contained her lunch and removed a yogurt and a sandwich wrapped in plastic. She had been in such a state that morning, she couldn't even remember what kind of sandwich she'd made. She hoped the lunches she'd prepared for her niece and nephew were at least edible, or she would be hearing from her aunt when she got home.

Without bothering to check the contents of the sandwich, she placed it back inside the bag. *The yogurt'll be plenty,* she thought as she removed the plastic lid and then realized that she didn't have a spoon.

It was no big deal, there were plenty of plastic spoons at the condiment table—but the intense, irrational disappointment of the moment made her want to cry.

Vilma had been feeling a bit emotional since Aaron Corbet left school—left the state, for all she knew—a couple of weeks ago. She had no idea why she missed him so much. She had just barely gotten to know him.

She placed the lid back on the yogurt and pushed that away as well. She really didn't feel like eating, anyway.

There was something about Aaron, something she couldn't quite understand, but a kind of comfort and calmness seemed to envelop her whenever he was around. Though they had never been on a date—or even held hands, for that matter—Vilma felt as though a very important part of her had been surgically removed with Aaron's departure. She felt incomplete. She wanted to believe that it was a silly crush, a teenage infatuation that would eventually fade, but something inside her said it wasn't, and that just made her all the more miserable.

Vilma sat back in her chair, looked out over the cafeteria, and unconsciously played with the angel that hung on a gold chain around her neck.

According to the news reports, Aaron's foster parents and little brother had died in a fire when their house had been hit by lightning during a freak thunderstorm. He'd said he was leaving because there were too many sad memories. But she'd known he was holding something back—although she didn't know how or why she knew this. Not for the first time she felt her eyes begin to burn with emotion.

There had been talk at school, silly hurtful whispers, that Aaron had been responsible for the fire that took the lives of his family, but Vilma didn't believe it for a second. Sure, he was a foster kid who'd been shifted around a lot. He was entitled to be angry. But, she knew in the depths of her soul that he wasn't capable of harming anyone. Still, the mystery of his abrupt departure continued to gnaw at her.

Vilma jumped as a voice suddenly addressed her. She had

been so lost in her thoughts that she'd failed to notice the approach of one of the cafeteria staff.

"I'm sorry, hon," said the large woman with a smile. She was dressed in a light blue uniform, her bleached blond hair tucked beneath a hairnet. "I didn't mean to scare you."

"That's all right," Vilma answered with an embarrassed laugh. "Just not paying attention, I guess."

"You done here?" the woman asked, gesturing to Vilma's discarded lunch.

"Yes, thank you," she replied as the woman swiped a damp cloth across the table and carried away her trash.

Vilma continued to sit, gently stroking the golden angel at her throat. Maybe that was why she hadn't been sleeping. Since Aaron left, her nights had been plagued with dim nightmares. She'd awaken in the early morning hours, panicked and covered in sweat, the recollection of what had caused such a reaction a nagging unknown.

That had to be it. Not only had Aaron made her sad by leaving, he was now keeping her awake with bad dreams. She wished he were here so she could give him a piece of her mind. And when she was done, she'd hold him tightly and they would kiss.

Vilma imagined what that would be like and felt her heart begin to race and her eyes well with tears.

"Vilma!" somebody called, the voice echoing around the low-ceilinged lunchroom.

She rubbed at her eyes quickly and looked around. From a door in the back corner, she saw her friend Tina heading toward her. The girl was wearing dark sunglasses and walked as if she were on the runway at a Paris fashion show. Vilma smiled and waved.

"What are you doing in here?" Tina asked in their native Portuguese.

Vilma shrugged. "I don't know," she answered sadly. "Just didn't feel like going out."

Tina pushed the sunglasses back onto her head and crossed her arms. "I bet you didn't even eat lunch," she said, a look of disgust on her pretty face.

Vilma was about to tell her otherwise but didn't have the strength. "No," she said, her fingers again going to the golden cherub. "I wasn't hungry."

Tina stared at her, saying nothing, and Vilma began to feel self-conscious. She wondered if her eyes showed that she'd been crying.

"What?" Vilma asked with a strained smile, switching to English. "Why are you looking at me like that?"

Tina reached down, grabbed her by the arm, and pulled her out of the chair. "C'mon," she ordered in a no-nonsense manner. "You're coming with me and Beatrice, and we're going to Pete's for a slice."

Vilma tried to pull away, but her friend held her arm fast. "Look, Tina," she began. "I really don't feel like . . ." But then she noticed the expression on her friend's face. There was concern, genuine worry.

"C'mon, Vilma," Tina said, letting go of her arm. "We haven't talked in days. It'll do you good. It's gorgeous outside, and Beatrice has promised not to talk about how fat she's getting."

Vilma chuckled. It felt kind of good to laugh with someone, she realized.

"Let's go," Tina said, holding out her hand.

Tina was right, Vilma knew, and with a heavy sigh she took her friend's hand and followed her outside to catch up with Beatrice. It would be nice to get out with her friends. She needed a distraction.

The three girls headed down the driveway toward Pete's. Tina regaled them with tales about how her mother had threatened to throw her out of the house if she even thought about getting a belly button ring, and Beatrice, true to form, talked about her expanding bottom.

But Vilma was lost in thoughts of her own. She thought about how nice the weather was, now that spring had finally decided to show, and wondered if the sun was shining as brightly wherever Aaron Corbet was—and if it wasn't, she wished him sunshine.

Inside the cave, Mufgar of the Orisha clan squatted on bony legs and removed four pumice rocks from a leather pouch at his side. The diminutive creature with leathery skin the color of a dirty penny stacked the stones and, with the help of his three brethren, coaxed the remembrance of fire from the rocks.

The volcanic stones began to smolder, then glow an angry red as the four murmured a spell used by their kind for more than a millennia. Mufgar laid a handful of dried grass atop the rocks, and it immediately burst into flame. Shokad added some twigs to feed the hungry fire as Zawar and Tehom gathered their weapons and placed them against the cave wall until they were needed again.

The fire blazed warmly, and Mufgar adjusted his chieftain's headdress, which was made from the skull of a beaver and the pelts of two red foxes, upon his overly large, misshapen head. Sitting down before the roaring campfire, he raised his long, spindly arms to the cave ceiling.

"Mufgar of the Orisha clan has called this council, and you have answered," he growled in the guttural tongue of his people. He leaned toward the fire and spit into the flames. The viscous saliva popped and sputtered as it landed on the burning twigs. "Blessed be they who are the Powers, those who allow us to experience the joys of living even though we have no right to this gift."

The three others cleared their throats and, one after the other, spewed into the blaze. "Praise be for the mercy of the Powers," the Orishas said in unison.

"We are as one," Mufgar said as he brought his arms down. "The council is seated. It has begun."

Mufgar gazed at the three who had gathered for this calling, saddened by how their numbers had dwindled over the centuries. He remembered a time when a cave of this size wouldn't have begun to hold the clan's numbers. Now, that was but a distant memory.

"I have called this council, for our merciful masters have bestowed upon us a perilous task," Mufgar said, addressing his followers. "A task with a most generous reward, if we should succeed." He looked at what remained of his tribe and saw the fear in their eyes—the same fear he felt deep within his own heart.

Shokad, the shaman, shook his head. His long, braided hair, adorned with the small bones of many a woodling creature, rattled like chimes touched by the wind. He murmured something inaudible beneath his breath.

"Does something trouble you, wise Shokad?" Mufgar asked.

The old Orisha ran a bony hand across his wide mouth and gazed into the crackling fire. "I have been having troubling dreams of late," he replied, the small, dark wings on his back fluttering to life. "Dreams that show a place of great beauty, a place where all our kind have gathered and we live not under the yoke of the Powers," he whispered, making cautious reference to the host of angels that were their masters.

Mufgar nodded his skull-adorned head. "Your dreams show a future most interesting," he observed, stroking the long braid hanging from his chin. "If we succeed in our new task, our masters say they will reward us with blessed freedom. Our independence we will have earned."

"But . . . but to achieve this we must hunt the Nephilim," Tehom stammered. "Capture it and bring it to Verchiel." The great hunter looked as though he would break into tears, he was so filled with fright.

"If we wish to be free of the Powers," Mufgar said to them all, "we must complete this sacred chore. Then, and only then, will we be allowed to search for the Safe Place."

With the mention of the Orishas' most sacred destination, all four blessed themselves by touching the center of their foreheads, the tips of their pointed noses, their mouths, and then their chests.

Zawar climbed to his feet, frantically dancing from one bare foot to the other. His wings fluttered nervously. "But our task is impossible," he said, pulling at the long, stringy hair on his head. "The Nephilim will destroy us with ease—look at how he bested the great Verchiel in combat. You saw the scars—we all saw the scars."

Mufgar remembered the burns covering Verchiel's body. The scars were severe, showing great anger and strength in the one who inflicted them. If that could be done to the one who was the leader of the Powers, what chance did they have? "It is the task bestowed upon us," he said with the authority that made him chief. "There is no other way."

"No," Shokad interjected, slowly shaking his head from side to side. "That is not true. The dreams show me a world where our masters have been destroyed by the Nephilim."

Mufgar felt himself grow more fearful. The shaman's dreams were seldom wrong, but what he was speaking—it went against the ways of the Orishas. Since their creation, they had served the Powers.

"You speak blasphemy," the leader hissed as he pointed a long, gnarled finger at the shaman. "It would not surprise me if Lord Verchiel himself appeared in this very cave and turned you to ash."

Tehom and Zawar huddled closer together, their large eyes scanning the darkness for signs of the terrifying angel's sudden arrival.

Shokad fed the fire with another handful of sticks. "I speak only of what I see in the ether," he said, moving his hand around in the air. "There is a new time coming, the dreams tell me. We need only pay attention."

It's tempting to embrace these new ideas, Mufgar thought, *to push aside the old ways and think of only the new.* But during his long life on this planet, he had seen the wrath of the Powers firsthand, and did not care to risk having it directed toward him.

"I will hear no more of this madness," Mufgar declared,

his voice booming with power. "Our service to the masters is what has kept us alive."

Zawar climbed to his feet and went to their belongings stashed across the cave against the wall. "We live only as long as the Powers allow us to," he said, searching for something amongst their supplies. Finding it, he returned to the fire, where he sat down and opened the small bundle. Inside were the shriveled remains of dried field mice and moles. "When they no longer have need of our skills, they will destroy us, as they did our creators," Zawar said as he picked up a mouse and bit off its head for emphasis. He offered the snacks to the others.

Mufgar could not believe his ears. Had they all been stricken with madness? *How can they speak such treason?* he wondered. But deep down he knew. The Powers had no love for them, thinking they were no better than animals. "Our creators broke the laws of God by making us," Mufgar explained in an attempt to restore their sanity with a reminder of their people's history. "We are blemishes upon the one God's world. The Powers have allowed us to live—to prove ourselves worthy of the life bestowed upon us by their fallen brethren. When we have done this, then and only then will we be given our freedom and allowed to search for the Safe Place."

Again, the Orishas blessed themselves.

"But what of the others of our clan?" Tehom asked, taking a stiffened mole from their rations. "What of those who defied our masters and went to find our most prized paradise?"

Mufgar did not want to hear this. No matter how he himself felt, to question the old ways would certainly bring about their doom. He remembered how he had tried to convince the others to stay, all the time wishing that he had had the courage to go with them. But he was chief, and was slave to the traditions of old.

Mufgar crossed his arms and puffed out his chest. "They are dead," he said definitely. "They have disobeyed our laws."

The shaman looked to Zawar and Tehom, who were both chewing their meal of dried vermin, then back to Mufgar. "But what if they aren't dead?" he asked in a clandestine whisper. "What if they succeeded in finding the paradise for which we so yearn? Think of it, Mufgar—think of it."

The chief stared into the fire, pondering the words of the shaman. *Could it have always been this simple? To steal away unnoticed and find their own Heaven.* "Lord Verchiel has said that any who defy his wishes would be expunged from existence."

Shokad slid closer. "But times are changing, Great Mufgar," he said. "Verchiel and his Powers are distracted by the prophecy."

"The Nephilim," Tehom said in a whisper, spitting fragments of dried mole into the fire.

Zawar, sitting next to him, nodded and flapped his wings. "It is said that he will bring forgiveness to the fallen." He picked a piece of tail from between his two front teeth. "And our masters do not want this, I think."

It had been hours since he'd last fed, and Mufgar snatched up a dried carcass from the open pouch. "So you suggest we disobey the Powers, ignore our orders—forsake our chance at true freedom." He took a bite of the mouse's head and waited for an answer. The dried meat had very little flavor, and he yearned for his favorite meal. It had been quite some time since he had feasted upon the delectable flesh of canine. Mouse and mole were fine for a time—but the meat of dog was something that he often dreamed of when his empty belly howled to be filled.

"A great conflict is coming between our masters and the Nephilim," the holy man proclaimed, "and only one will survive. The Nephilim's power is great. To attack him would invite our downfall."

Zawar and Tehom nodded in agreement. "Let the Nephilim destroy the Powers," Zewar said.

"And then we will be free," Tehom added.

Mufgar swallowed the last of his snack and climbed to his feet. He had heard enough. It was time to pass judgment. He raised his arms above his head again, gazing at the fire and his followers around it. "I, Mufgar, chief of the Deheboryn Orisha, have listened to the words of my clan and have applied my great wisdom to their concerns."

In his mind's eye he saw an image of those who had left

the clan in search of the Safe Place. He saw them living in the beauty of Paradise—but then a dark cloud passed over, and from the sky, fire rained down upon them. The Nephilim had not defeated the Powers, and for their betrayal of the old ways, the Orishas were destroyed forever.

"We will continue to hunt the Nephilim," Mufgar said, avoiding the disappointed looks in his followers' eyes. "It is the only way I can guarantee the continued existence of our kind. We will track the enemy of our masters and capture him—when we succeed, then we shall be set free." Mufgar lowered his arms. "I have spoken," he said with finality. "This council is ended." He turned from the fire and headed for a darkened part of the cave where he would rest before resuming the hunt.

"You doom us all," he heard Shokad say to his back.

Mufgar reached for the dagger of bone tied to his leg and leaped into the air, his wings carrying him over the fire. He landed upon the shaman, knocking him back to the floor. Zawar squealed with fear as Mufgar placed the knife against the old Orisha's throat.

"I will hear no more of your blasphemous talk," Mufgar said, gazing into Shokad's fear-filled eyes. He pricked the leathery skin of the oldster's throat with the tip of the dagger, drawing a bead of blood. "And if I do, the Nephilim will not have his chance at you—for you will have already doomed yourself."

Mufgar sheathed his blade and left the shaman and the others cowering by the dwindling fire. Alone, curled into a tight ball on the floor of the cave, the chief chased elusive sleep. Finally he found it as the fire burned down, the stones forgetting their past, leaving the cave in darkness.

CHAPTER TWO

Gabriel's tail wagged crazily as Aaron approached the picnic table at the back of the roadside restaurant.

"That's our lunch, isn't it, Aaron!" the dog said happily, his back end swaying from side to side with the force of his muscular tail. *"It sure smells good,"* he said with a heavy pant, sniffing at the bottom of the bags Aaron carried. *"I'm so hungry, I could eat cat food."*

Aaron laughed as he set the bags down on the wooden table. "Was that a joke, Gabe?" he asked the excited dog.

"No," the dog replied, his eyes never leaving the white bags. *"I really would eat cat food."*

Aaron laughed again and began to remove the food from the bags. Camael was sitting on one of the wooden benches gazing off into space, as if he was watching something a thousand miles away. For all Aaron knew, that very well could have been what he was doing.

"Did he give you a hard time while I was gone?" Aaron asked Camael. For some reason, Gabriel had not taken to the angel and was prone to being difficult when Aaron was not around.

"He chattered, but I ignored him," Camael said without turning. "And he did eat something off the ground, a filthy habit."

Aaron glanced down at the dog sitting obediently at his feet. "You know you're not supposed to do that," he said sternly.

Gabriel wagged his tail some more. *It was gum,* he said, as if that would make it all right.

"I don't care," Aaron said, picking up one of the wrapped sandwiches. "You could get sick."

"But I like gum."

Aaron squatted down in front of the dog and began to unwrap the burger. "Gum isn't for dogs. No gum. Get it?"

The Lab ignored him, instead sticking his snout inside the sandwich wrapper to see what Aaron held. *Is this for me? Is this my lunch?*

"Yep, it is," Aaron answered as he removed the meat from the bun. "You don't need any bread, though." He discarded the roll into one of the now empty bags.

"Hey, what are you doing that for?" Gabriel panicked. *"That's my lunch, you said. Why are you throwing it away?"*

Aaron held out the hamburger. "Here, this is what you want. I just threw away the bread. It'll make you fat."

Gabriel couldn't stop looking at the bag. *"But I want the bread, too,"* he whined pathetically.

Aaron sighed and shook his head. At first it had been fun being able to communicate with his best friend, but now he found it more and more like dealing with a small child. "Look, are you going to eat this or not?" he asked. "Usually you don't even have lunch, so this should be a treat."

The dog reluctantly pried his gaze from the bag and gently snatched the burger from Aaron's hand. He chewed once and then swallowed with a loud gulp.

Aaron patted the dog's side. "That was pretty good, huh?"

Gabriel licked his lips and gazed into his master's eyes. *"Any more?"*

"No," Aaron said. "I bought one for me and one for you. That's it."

"Are you going to eat your bread?" Gabriel asked.

"Yes, I'm going to eat my bread."

"It will make you fat."

"You're too much, Gabriel." Aaron laughed. He took a bottle of water and poured some into a paper cup. "Here's some water to wash down your burger," he said as he set the cup on the ground in front of the dog.

Gabriel began to lap at the cup, careful not to tip it over. *"I'm still hungry,"* he grumbled between laps.

"Sorry," Aaron said, picking up his own burger and sitting down beside Camael. "Think of how good your supper will taste."

The dog grunted and strolled off to sniff at an overgrown patch of grass near the edge of the parking lot.

Aaron watched him go. He hated to be mean, but if he allowed Gabriel to eat every time he said he was hungry, the dog would weigh three hundred pounds. He couldn't begin to count all the overweight Labs he'd seen while working at the veterinary clinic back in Lynn, Massachusetts. It was the Labrador retriever curse—they loved to eat.

He sighed as he picked up his burger and took a bite. It was good, cooked just the way he liked it, medium rare, with lettuce, tomato, and a little mayo. He chewed for a moment, swallowed, and turned to Camael, still sitting silently and staring off into space. "What exactly are you looking at?"

"I see a great deal," the angel replied, his voice like a far-off rumble of thunder. "A father and son fishing by a stream, an old woman hanging laundry in her yard, a female fox teaching her litter how to hunt frogs." He paused, tilting his head as if to examine something at another angle. "It is what I do not see that interests me."

Aaron opened another bottle of water and took a sip. "Okay, what don't you see?"

"As of now, I see no sign of pursuit."

"And that's a good thing—right?" Aaron took another bite of his burger and reached for a cardboard container of French fries. He dumped half on the wrapper with the remains of his burger and placed the container with the rest in front of Camael.

The action broke the angel's steely stare, and he looked down on the container before him. "I told you, I do not need to eat," he said with a hint of a scowl.

Aaron bit half of a large fry and chewed. "You don't *need* to," he said. "Doesn't mean that you *can't.* Try one."

Camael slowly placed his hands on either side of the container. "As I was saying," he said, studying the French fries as if they were new forms of life, "I have seen no trace of the Powers since leaving your city of Lynn, so it would appear that the magickal wards I left to mask our passing have proven beneficial."

"Is that what you've been doing?" Aaron asked with surprise. He consumed the last bite of his burger. "I was a little worried by how slow we've been moving. I thought you were getting a little wrapped up in the whole sight-seeing thing."

Camael removed a French fry from the container and glared at it. "I have been on this planet for thousands of years, boy. The urge to 'sight-see' was purged long ago."

And then the angel did something that Aaron imagined he'd never see. Camael popped the French fry into his mouth and began to chew. He chewed for what seemed an insane amount of time and then swallowed. "Adequate," he said, tilting the container toward him and reaching for another.

Aaron took a sip of his water and smacked his lips. "Do you think these wards will be enough?" he asked. "I mean, will it keep them off our backs until we can find where they're keeping Stevie?"

The angel was eating fries like a pro, three and four at a time. *For someone who doesn't need to eat, he certainly seems to be enjoying himself,* Aaron thought as he waited for an answer.

"The wards are merely a distraction. My magickal skills are nowhere near Verchiel's and the Archons in his service—"

"Archons?" Aaron interrupted.

"Angels of the Powers who have mastered the complexities of angelic magick. They will see through our ruse sooner rather than later, but let us hope the wards will buy us enough time to find that to which you are being drawn."

Aaron had felt the strange sensation since leaving Lynn behind. He still didn't understand what it was—it seemed to be an urge, a need to travel north. Through New Hampshire, Vermont, and now Maine, he was being drawn inexorably northward. Even as he sat, finishing his lunch, he could feel it pulsing in his mind, urging him onward. "Do you think what I'm feeling will take us to Stevie?" he asked with hope.

Camael had finished the last of the fries, tipping over the container to be sure it was empty. "Your abilities are still young, Aaron. They are as much a mystery to me as they are to you."

"But it's possible, right?" he persisted. "Like maybe I'm somehow connected to Stevie—and I'm being drawn to him."

The angel nodded slowly. "It is possible," he said, his large hand stroking his silvery gray goatee. "But it may be that you are being pulled to something else—something of greater importance."

"I don't understand." Aaron stared intently at the angel. "What could I be drawn to if not Stevie? What can be more important than him?"

The angel remained silent, continuing to stroke his bearded chin, seemingly lost within his own thoughts.

"Camael?" Aaron prompted, raising his voice slightly.

"It is a most elusive place," Camael finally answered, his eyes glazed. Then he turned to Aaron and fixed him in an intense glare. *"Aerie,"* he whispered. "You could be taking us to Aerie."

Faces flashed before Camael's eyes; images of those he'd saved from the destructive wrath of the Powers throughout the innumerable centuries since he'd left the angelic Host. *Where had they gone?* It was a question he often asked himself. Some were eliminated later, the Powers eventually tracking them and succeeding in their malevolent goals. But there were others, others who had managed to find a very special place, a place that still eluded him.

"Aerie?" Aaron was asking. "Isn't that a bird's nest or something?"

"It is a place unlike any other on this world, Aaron, a special place—a secret place, where those who have fallen await their reunion with Heaven." Camael folded his hands before him, remembering the times when he thought he had found it—only to be sadly disappointed.

"Have you ever been to this place?" the Nephilim asked.

"No. Aerie is hidden from me, for I am not fully trusted,"

he replied. "Remember, I was once the leader of the Powers, and they would like nothing more than to burn away Aerie and all it stands for."

"Are you sure there really is such a place?" Aaron asked.

Camael tried to imagine what his existence would have been like without the idea of Aerie's presence to comfort him. He doubted he would have been able to continue his mission without the promise of something better awaiting those he struggled to save—something better for himself. "It exists," he said quietly. "I'm sure of it—just as I know that you are of whom the prophecy speaks. And Aaron, those who live there, in this secret place, *they* believe in the prophecy that you personify." He paused. "They're waiting for you, boy."

Aaron seemed taken aback by this latest revelation. In a way, Camael felt pity for the youth and his human perceptions of the world. The idea of what he actually was, and what his true purpose was to be, must have been quite overwhelming for his primitive mind. Although he did have to admit that, at this moment, the youth wasn't doing too badly.

"All the people in Aerie—they're waiting for me to do for them what I did for Zeke?"

Camael nodded, remembering the valiant Grigori, who had helped him rescue Aaron during the Powers' attack on the boy's home. Zeke had been mortally wounded and the Nephilim had used his prophetic gift to forgive his trespasses and allow his return to Heaven. "It is your destiny to release *all* who repent," he said,

Aaron seemed to be digesting his words, the importance of his destiny sinking in even deeper. "Before I do any more forgiving, we're going to find Stevie," he said. "Wherever this urge is taking us, whether it's to my brother, or to Aerie, or to a place that makes really great tacos, finding Stevie and getting him away from that bastard Verchiel is the number one priority—agreed?" Aaron demanded, an intense seriousness in his look.

Camael thought about arguing with the youth, but he sensed that it would be for naught. No matter how different Aaron Corbet had become since awakening the angelic power that resided within him, he still thought of himself as human. "Agreed," he answered.

There was still much Aaron had to learn—but that would come over time.

"That wasn't very nice," Gabriel grumbled as he sniffed along the grounds of the picnic area. *"Not very nice at all."*

He was following a scent, something that made his stomach growl and his mouth salivate. Gabriel was hungry—although there was seldom a time that he wasn't feeling the pangs of hunger. At a green trash barrel, he found the crumpled remains of an ice-cream sandwich wrapper. There were other pieces of trash that had missed the receptacle as well, but he would investigate those later, after he'd given the wrapper his full attention.

The dog was hurt that Aaron could be so insensitive to his needs. He was hungry, and Aaron still would not let him have the bread that he was going to throw away, anyway. It was frustrating and only served to make him hungrier.

Gabriel nudged the wrapper with his nose, pulling the delicious scents of dried vanilla ice cream and chocolate cookie up into his sensitive nostrils. His tongue shot out to lap at the wrapper, the moisture making the scents clinging to the refuse all the more pungent.

You don't eat things off the ground, he remembered Aaron scolding him. And he knew that he shouldn't, but he was angry, and so very hungry. Gabriel took the ice-cream sandwich wrapper into his mouth and began to chew. It didn't taste like much, but then, dogs don't have taste buds. The deliciousness of something was based entirely on its smell. If it smelled like something to eat, that was good enough for a dog, especially a Labrador. Very few things required more than a chew or two, and the paper wrapper was soon sliding down Gabriel's throat and into his stomach.

Unsatisfied and a little guilty, Gabriel turned his attention away from the barrel and toward a family of three who were having lunch at another of the picnic tables. The dog approached them, tail wagging in happy greeting. There were two adults, a mother and a father, and a little girl who was about the same age as Stevie.

A wave of sadness passed over the animal as he viewed the

family. He missed the other members of his own pack; Tom and Lori were dead, and the Powers had taken Stevie away. But at least he still had Aaron. It wasn't how it used to be, but it would do for now. He still wasn't sure about the one called Camael. There was something about him that he didn't quite trust. He smelled too much like that nasty Verchiel to be accepted by him into the pack.

"Hello, doggie!" the little girl squealed as she turned on the bench and caught sight of him.

Gabriel could smell the caution seep from her parents' pores as he approached. He took no offense; after all, he was a strange dog and there were many that he himself would have been cautious of. He sat down, as Aaron had taught him, brought one of his paws up in greeting, barked softly once, and wagged his tail.

The little girl laughed happily, and he noticed the adults smile as well.

"May I pet him?" the child asked, already sliding off the bench.

"Let him smell you first, Lily," the father said cautiously. "You don't want to scare him."

The child held out her hand, and Gabriel sniffed the pink skin of her palm. Fragments of scents clung to her flesh: soap that smelled like bubble gum; cheese crackers; sugary fruit juice; her mother's perfume. Gently, he lapped the child's hand.

Lily squealed with delight and began to pat his head. "You're a good dog, aren't you," she cooed, "and your ears are so soft."

Gabriel already knew that, but it didn't prevent him from

enjoying the child's attentions, until he caught the delicious aroma of food. He lifted his snout and pulled in the olfactory delights as he watched Lily's mother place a hot dog on the table where the child had been sitting.

"C'mon, Lily. Let the doggie go back to his family and you eat your lunch."

Lily patted his head again and leaned in very close. "Good-bye, doggie," she said, kissing his nose as his stomach gurgled loudly. "Was that your belly?" She giggled.

Gabriel looked deeply into her eyes. *"Yes,"* he answered with a short, grumbling bark.

She couldn't understand him as Aaron did, but still, she seemed to grasp his answer—as if he were somehow able to touch her mind.

"Are you hungry?" she asked.

Gabriel could not lie to the child and barked affirmatively while he used his mind to tell her that he would love a bite of her lunch.

The child suddenly turned and walked toward the picnic table. She snatched up her hot dog, tore off a hunk—bread and all—and brought it back to Gabriel.

"I don't know if you should do that, honey," her father cautioned.

Lily presented the food to the Lab, and he gently plucked it from her hand, swallowing it in one gulp. *Thank you, Lily,* he thought, looking into her eyes.

"You're welcome," she responded with a pretty smile.

Lily's father walked over, carrying his own sandwich in one hand. "Okay," he said, trying to steer the child back toward the table. "I think the doggie's had enough. Say good-bye now."

Gabriel stared intently at the man. *"Before I go,"* he directed his thoughts toward Lily's father, *"can I have a bite of your sandwich?"*

Without a moment's hesitation, the man tore off a piece of his hamburger and tossed it to the Lab.

Gabriel was satisfied. The painful pangs of his empty belly had been temporarily assuaged with the help of Lily and her parents—it had been awfully generous of them to share their lunch—and he was heading back to join Aaron, exploring as he went.

The tinkling of a chain was the first thing to capture his attention, and then he became aware of her scent.

Gabriel stopped at the beginning of an overgrown path that led to a small area designated for children. He noticed some swings, a tiny slide, and a wooden playhouse shaped like a train. Again came the jangle of a chain, and from behind the playhouse appeared another dog, her nose pressed to the sand as she followed a scent that had caught her fancy.

Gabriel's tail began to wag furiously as he padded down the path and barked a friendly greeting. *How good is this?* he thought. *A full belly and now somebody to play with.*

The female flinched, startled by his approach. Her tail

wagged cautiously. She, too, was a yellow Labrador retriever and she wore a pretty, red bandanna around her neck, as well as the chain.

He moved closer. *"I'm Gabriel."*

The female continued to stare, and he noticed that the hackles of fur at the back of her neck had begun to rise.

"Don't be afraid," he said soothingly. *"I just want to play."* He lay down on the ground to show her that he meant no harm. *"What's your name?"*

The female moved slowly toward him, sniffing at the air, searching for signs of a threat. *How odd,* thought Gabriel. *Maybe her family doesn't let her play with other dogs. "I'm Gabriel,"* he said again.

"Tobi," she replied, hackles still raised.

"Hello, Tobi. Do you want to chase me?" he asked pleasantly, rising to all fours.

Tobi sniffed at him again and growled nervously. Slowly, she began to back away, her tail bending between her legs.

Gabriel was confused. *"What's the matter?"* he asked, advancing toward her. *"You don't have to chase me if you don't want to—I could chase you instead."*

Tobi snapped at him with a bark, her lips peeled back in a fierce snarl as she continued to back toward the playhouse.

Gabriel stopped. *"What's wrong?"* he asked, genuinely concerned and quite disappointed. *"Why won't you play with me?"*

"Not dog," Tobi growled as she sniffed the air around him.

"Different," she spat, and fled around the playhouse in the direction she'd come.

Gabriel was stunned. At first, he had no idea what Tobi meant, but then he thought of that day when he had almost died. He flinched, remembering the intensity of the pain he had felt when the car struck him. Aaron had done something to him that day, had laid his hands upon him and made the pain go away. That was the day everything became clearer.

The day he became different?

He left the play area, his mind considering the idea that he might not be a dog anymore, when he heard Aaron call. Gabriel quickened his pace and joined his friend and Camael. They were cleaning up their trash and getting ready to resume their journey.

"Where've you been?" Aaron asked as they headed toward the parking lot.

"Around," Gabriel replied, not feeling much like talking.

A car on its way out of the lot passed them as they waited to cross to their own vehicle. In the back, he saw Tobi staring intently at him. It wasn't only the window glass that separated him from her, he thought sadly as he watched the car head down the road.

"Are you all right?" Aaron asked as he bent to scratch under the dog's chin.

"I'm fine," Gabriel answered, unsure of his own words—recalling the truth revealed in another's.

"Not dog. Different."

INTERLUDE ONE

This will sting, my liege."

Verchiel hissed with displeasure as the healer laid a dripping cloth on the mottled skin of his bare arm. "Why do I not heal, Kraus?" the leader of the Powers asked.

The blind man patted down the saturated material and reached for another patch of cloth soaking in a wooden bowl of healing oil, made from plants extinct since Cain took the life of his brother, Abel. "It is not my place to say, my lord," he said, his unseeing eyes glistening white in the faint light streaming through the skylight of the old classroom.

The abandoned school on the grounds of the Saint Athanasius Church, in western Massachusetts, had been the Powers' home since the battle with the Nephilim. This was where they plotted—awaiting the opportunity to continue their war against those who would question their authority upon the world of God's man.

Verchiel shifted uncomfortably in the high-backed wooden chair, stolen from the church next door, as the healer laid yet another cloth upon his burn-scarred flesh. "Then answer me this: Do these wounds resemble injuries sustained in a freak act of nature, or do they bear the signature of a more divine influence?"

He was trying to isolate the cause of the intense agony that had been his constant companion since he was struck by lightning during his battle with Aaron Corbet. The angel wanted to push the pain aside, to box it up and place it far away. But the pain would not leave him. It stayed, a reminder that he might have offended his Creator—and was being punished for his insolence.

"It is my job to heal, Great Verchiel," Kraus said. "I would not presume to—"

Verchiel suddenly sprang up from his seat, the heavy wooden chair flipping backward as his wings unfurled to their awesome span. Kraus stumbled as winds stirred by the angel's wings pushed against him.

"I grant you permission, ape," the angel growled over the pounding clamor caused by the flapping of his wings. "Tell me what you feel in your primitive heart." His hands touched the scars upon his chest as he spoke. "Tell me if you believe it was the hand of God that touched me in this way!"

"Mercy, my master!" Kraus cried, cowering upon the floor. "I am but a lowly servant. Please do not make me think of such things!"

"I will tell you, Verchiel," said a voice from across the room.

Verchiel slowly turned his attention to a dark corner of the classroom, where a large cage of iron was hanging from the ceiling, its bars etched with arcane markings. It swayed in the turbulence caused by his anger. The stranger taken from the monastery in the Serbian Mountains peered out from between the iron bars, the expression on his gaunt face intense.

"Do you care to hear what I have to say?" he asked, his voice a dry whisper.

"Ah, our prisoner is awake," Verchiel said. "I thought the injuries inflicted by my soldiers would have kept you down for far longer than this."

The prisoner clutched the bars of his cage with dirty hands. "I've endured worse," he said. "Sometimes it is the price one must pay."

Verchiel's wings closed, retracting beneath the flesh of his bare back. "Indeed," the angel snarled.

Kraus still cowered upon the floor, head bowed. "You will leave me now," Verchiel said, dismissing the human healer. "Take your things and go."

"Yes, my lord," the blind man said, gathering up the satchel containing his tools of healing and carefully feeling his way to the exit.

"Why do they do it?" the prisoner asked as he watched the healer depart. "What perverse need is satisfied by the degradation we heap upon them? It's a question I've gone round and round with for years."

"Perhaps we give their mundane lives purpose," Verchiel responded, advancing toward the cage. "Providing them with something that was lacking when they lived among their own kind." Verchiel stopped before the hanging cage and gazed into the eyes of his prisoner. "Or . . . maybe they are just not as intelligent as we think," he said with perverse amusement.

"And that's reason enough to exploit and abuse them?" the prisoner asked.

"So be it, if it serves a greater good. They are aiding us in carrying out God's will. They are serving their Creator—as well as ours. Can you not think of a more fulfilling purpose?"

Still dressed in the tattered brown robes of the Serbian monastery, the prisoner sat down with a smile, leaning back against the bars of the cage. "And you seriously have to wonder what it was that struck you down?" He chuckled, making reference to Verchiel's scars. "Wouldn't think you were that dense, but then again . . ."

Verchiel loomed closer, peering through the black iron bars. "Please share with me your thoughts," he whispered. "I'm eager to hear the perceptions of one such as you—the most renowned of the fallen. Yes, please, what is the Lord God thinking these days?"

The prisoner casually reached within his robes and withdrew the mouse. Gently, he touched the top of its pointed head with the tip of his finger as it crawled about on his open palm. "That I couldn't tell you, Verchiel," he said, looking up as the tiny creature scuttled up the front of his robe to his shoulder. "It's been quite some time since the Creator and I last spoke. But looking at your current condition, I'd have to guess that He's none too happy with you either."

And then the prisoner smiled—a smile filled with warmth and love, and so stunningly beautiful. How could he not have once been the most favored of God's children?

Verchiel felt his rage grow, and it took all the self-control he could muster to not reach into the cage and rend his captive limb from limb. "And I am to believe the likes of you"—the Powers' leader growled reaching out to clutch the bars of the cage—"the Prince of Lies?"

"Touché," the prisoner said, as the mouse explored the top of his head. "But remember," he said with a grin, "I *have* had some experience in these matters."

CHAPTER THREE

Trudging through the wood, in search of his prey, Mufgar, chieftain of the Deheboryn Orisha, knew that his decision the previous night had been the right one.

With his primitive elemental magicks, Mufgar had coerced the dirt, rock, and stone of the tunnel system in which they traveled to alter its labyrinthian course and open a passageway to the surface. "We will never catch a scent down here," he had said to his party as the dirt face of a nearby wall became like a thing of liquid, swirling and falling away to reveal a newly fashioned tunnel that ascended to the surface. "It is on the land above where our destiny awaits us."

Mufgar had thanked the elements for their assistance, leaving an offering of dried fruit before beginning his ascension into the new morning sun. It had been eight hours since he and his tribe had emerged from below, eight hours since any had spoken a word to him.

He sensed their anger, their fear, and their disappointment over the judgment he had passed upon them. He was truly sorry that they questioned his decision, but he knew they would not abandon their duty to their masters. They would hunt the Nephilim as the Powers had ordered, capture him, and earn their freedom. *That is how it will be,* he thought, remembering the strange vision he'd had while sleeping. A vision of success.

Mufgar raised his hand to stop their progress through the dense wood. He listened carefully to sounds around him, the chirping of various birds, the rustling of the wind through trees heavy with leaves—and something else.

"Is it the Nephilim, Mufgar?" Tehom hissed at his side, raising his spear and looking nervously about the forest.

"No," the Orisha chieftain said. He listened again to the sounds way off in the distance, the sounds of machines. *What are they called?* He searched his brain for the strange-sounding word. *Automobiles,* he remembered with great satisfaction. "Not the Nephilim," he whispered "but vehicles that will bring him to us."

Mufgar pointed through the woods to somewhere off in the distance. "I saw it in a vision of my own," he said, deciding to share his experience with his subjects, to give them faith in his leadership. He turned and glared at Shokad. "As I slept, I, too, had a vision. A vision that the Nephilim would come to us—"

The shaman quickly looked away with a scowl upon his ancient features.

"—and he would fall against our might." Mufgar raised his spear in an attempt to rally his hunters. "And for our bravery, Lord Verchiel bestowed upon us our freedom, and we found the location of the blessed Safe Place."

The Orishas all bowed their malformed heads, blessing themselves furiously.

It had been the strangest dream, as clear as the day they hunted in now. It was all there for him, all the answers he had sought. The doubts he had been experiencing since the last council all dispelled like smoke in the wind. A holy vision had been bestowed upon him, maybe from the spirits of the great creators themselves, a vision that told him they would be victorious. He could ask for nothing better.

Mufgar turned to the shaman, who lagged behind. The old Orisha squatted down and took a handful of bones and smooth, shiny rocks from a purse at his side.

"You do not trust your chieftain's sleeping visions, Shokad?" he asked the shaman.

The old creature said nothing as he tossed the bones and stones onto the ground before him. His wings unfurled and fluttered nervously as he began to read the results of his throw.

"Hmmmm," he grumbled, rubbing his chin as he discerned the signs.

"What do you say, Shokad?" Mufgar asked. "Do the bones and stones speak of victory and freedom?"

The old Orisha was silent as he gathered up his tools of divination and returned them to his purse.

"Speak, shaman," Mufgar ordered. "Your chief commands you to reveal what you have seen."

"The bones and stones speak of death," Shokad said gravely.

Zawar and Tehom gasped beside him. "Death?" Tehom asked in a voice filled with dread.

"Death . . . but for whom?" Zawar wanted to know.

Shokad shook his head, the bones in his hair rattling as they sruck one another. "They were not specific, but I can imagine no less for those who would go up against the might of the Nephilim." He glared at Mufgar, challenging his word as chief.

"But what of those who abandon the wishes of their masters?" Mufgar asked in return. "What is the fate of those who defy the Powers? Is the edict of that not death as well?"

The shaman scowled. "Possibly," he answered, "but it does not change the fact that death is our companion. We must choose our path wisely, or we may never have the opportunity to seek out the paradise that has long eluded us."

Zawar and Tehom glanced at each other, the conflicting messages of chief and shaman bringing the curse of dissension to their ranks.

"Great Mufgar," Zawar whispered as he looked about the woods, searching for any telltale signs of imminent death, "how do we choose?"

Mufgar looked back toward the sounds of the road in the distance. "There is only one choice," he said, moving away from them toward the road. "The hunt—and from that shall spring our freedom." He didn't even turn to see if they were following. Mufgar did not need to, for he knew that they were behind him. He had seen it in his dream.

Aaron kept his speed at forty-five and continued down the winding, back road. He tightened his grip on the steering wheel as the excitement continued to build within him. They were getting closer to their destination, he could feel it thrumming in his body. "Is it just me, or do you feel this too?" he asked.

Camael grunted, staring at the twisting road before them.

"What?" Aaron said. "Do you see something?"

The angel remained silent, squinting as if trying to see more clearly ahead. Aaron couldn't take it anymore. The sensation he felt was akin to a guy with an orange flag at the finishing line. He was close—to what, he wasn't exactly sure, but his body was telling him that this is where they were supposed to be. "What do you see, for Christ's sake!" he yelled.

Camael slowly turned his attention from the windshield to the boy. His gaze was steely, cold.

"Sorry," Aaron said, attempting to squelch the feeling

of unbridled excitement that coursed through his body. "It's just that I think we've found where they've taken Stevie—I'm excited. I didn't mean to yell at you."

The angel turned back to the road before them and pointed. "In the distance, not too far from here, I see a town."

Aaron waited a minute, but Camael offered no more. "That's it?" he asked impatiently. "That's all you see, a town?"

Gabriel, who had been in a deep, snoring sleep in the backseat, began to stir. In the rearview mirror, Aaron could see the Lab sit up, languidly licking his chops as he surveyed his surroundings.

"Where's the town?" the dog asked. *"All I see is woods."*

"Camael sees it in the distance," Aaron answered. "I've got a feeling that it might be where Verchiel has taken Stevie."

"There is something about this town," Camael said slowly, his eyes closed in concentration, his hand slowly stroking his silver goatee. "But I cannot discern what it is. It perplexes me."

Aaron reached over to the glove compartment and popped it open. The angel recoiled, but Aaron paid him little mind as he rummaged through the compartment while trying to keep his eyes on the road and the car in its lane. "What's it called? Maybe I can find it on the map," he said, slamming the glove compartment closed and shaking the map out in his lap.

"It is called Blithe," Camael said. "I believe the settlement would be considered quite old, by human standards."

"Is it even on here?" Aaron asked, dividing his attention

between the map and the road. "I want to see how much farther we have to go—"

"Let's stop now," Gabriel suddenly said from the back.

"Let's see how far away Blithe is first," Aaron said as he glanced at the dog in the rearview mirror.

Gabriel seemed genuinely uncomfortable, climbing to all fours and pacing around the seat. *"I don't think I can wait,"* he said, a touch of panic in his voice.

Aaron was about to reply when the smell wafted up from the back. "Oh, my God," he said, and frantically rolled down his window.

"What are you doing?" Camael asked with his usual touch of petulance as the wind from the open window whipped at his hair. And then Aaron watched as the angel's expression turned from one of annoyance to one of absolute repulsion. "What is that smell?" he asked with a furious snarl.

With one hand over his nose and mouth, Aaron motioned over his shoulder to the sole inhabitant of the backseat.

The angel turned to face the dog. "What have you done?"

Gabriel simply stared out the back window.

"He's got gas," Aaron explained, his voice muffled by the hand still over his face. "It happens when he eats stuff he's not supposed to."

"It's vile," Camael said, glaring at the dog. "Something should be done so that it never happens again."

Aaron gazed into the rearview mirror. "What did you eat

at that rest stop, Gabe?" he scolded, already knowing full well that the dog would have eaten anything.

Gabriel did not respond. Aaron didn't really expect him to. He pulled the car to the side of the road.

"What now?" Camael asked.

"There's only one way to deal with this problem," he said as he parked the car and got out. He opened the back door to let his friend out. "Maybe one of these days you'll learn not to eat everything in sight," he scolded the dog.

Gabriel jumped to the ground. *"I didn't eat everything—they still had plenty when I left."*

"Wait a minute," Aaron said, watching as the dog strolled away, snout firmly planted to the forest floor. "Who still had plenty? Did somebody give you food?"

"I have to do my business," Gabriel said, eluding his master's question and moving deeper into the woods.

"What's the matter with right here?" Aaron asked, exasperated. "Gabriel, we have to get going."

"I can't go if you're watching me," he heard the dog say before disappearing around a cluster of birch trees.

"When did you become so freakin' modest?" Aaron muttered beneath his breath. "Probably happened when I brought you back from the dead." He walked to the front of the car where Camael stood looking up the road. "So what do you think?" he asked the angel. "What are we going to find in Blithe?"

Camael shook his head slowly. "I honestly do not know."

Aaron crossed his arms and gazed at the road ahead. "The way I'm feeling right now, I'd have to say it's definitely something interesting."

"I will certainly agree with that," Camael said. He tilted back his head and sniffed at the air.

Aaron watched him grow suddenly tense and look about them cautiously. "What's wrong?"

"Do you not smell it?" he asked.

Aaron sniffed the air. He could smell nothing except the spring forest in full bloom. "I can't smell anything but the woods . . . ," he began, and then he caught a whiff of it. It was a musky scent, an animal smell, but one he did not recognize. "What is it?"

Camael held out his hand, and Aaron watched as a spark of orange flame appeared and grew into a sword of fire.

"Orishas," the angel growled.

Aaron was about to ask what an Orisha was, when Gabriel's barks of fear ripped through the quiet stillness of the woods beyond, like a staccato burst of gunfire. "Gabriel," he cried, a fire sword of his own sparking to life in his hand.

Aaron charged into the woods, his blade decimating saplings and low-hanging branches in his path. Camael was at his side when the two stopped abruptly at the edge of a clearing.

"What the hell are those things?" Aaron whispered in fearful wonder.

There were four in all; ugly creatures no more than three feet tall, with skin the color of tarnished copper. They appeared primitive, dressed in strips of leather and fur, their long, stringy hair adorned with bones. One wore a fancy headdress made from what looked like animal pelts. From their backs sprang small, black-feathered wings that fluttered noisily, like flapping window shades. They had thrown a makeshift net over Gabriel, and were attempting to subdue the struggling dog.

"Those are Orishas," Camael answered. "Crude attempts by my fallen brethren to create life."

"Not very successful, I'd gather?"

"Miserable failures that would have been eradicated long ago if it weren't for the Powers. They use the Orishas as slaves, as hunter trackers."

"So they're not that dangerous—right?" Aaron asked as he watched the Orishas forced back by Gabriel's wild thrashing.

"On the contrary," Camael said. "They have proven quite ferocious in battle, despite their diminutive size."

Gabriel's blocky head emerged from beneath the netting, and he snapped at his attackers. *"Aaron, I could use some help!"* he hollered, catching sight of his friend.

The Orishas turned and began to stalk toward Aaron and Camael, snarling menacingly. Three snatched up crude spears from the forest floor, and the one with the headdress removed a dagger from a sheath on its bony leg.

Aaron tensed, holding his flaming weapon before him. "What do we do?" he asked the angel standing calmly beside him.

"The Powers have probably put a bounty on our heads," Camael said casually as if talking about the weather. "The Orishas will try to capture us, and if that is not possible, they will surely attempt to kill us."

The primitive creatures were closer, and Aaron could hear them growling, a high-pitched sound like an air conditioner in need of repair—only much more horrible. "What do we do?" he repeated frantically.

"I thought it obvious, boy," the angel said as enormous wings of white languidly unfurled from his back. "We kill them."

"Something told me you were going to say that," Aaron said, just as the Orishas shrieked a cry of war and launched themselves at their chosen prey.

The power that resided within Aaron wanted out in the worst way. He could feel it pacing about inside, like a bored jungle cat in its cage at the zoo. It had started when Camael first mentioned the Orishas. Like asking Gabriel if he wanted to go for a ride, the power of the Nephilim had perked right up, pushing at the restraints he had imposed upon it.

The Orishas were taking flight, their small, ebony wings flapping with blurring speed, and the angelic power struggled harder to be free, but Aaron wouldn't allow it. In fact, just the thought of undergoing the transformation, as he had that horrible night in Lynn, made him tremble with fear. "You're lucky I'm even using one of these damned swords," he muttered to himself as he raised his burning weapon and swatted the first of his attackers from the air.

The creature shrieked in agony as it plummeted to the ground, one of its wings aflame. It began digging up clumps of cool dirt and rubbing it on its smoldering feathers as Aaron turned his attention to Camael.

Another Orisha was moving with blinding speed toward the angel—spear aimed at his face. At the last second, the creature suddenly changed direction and thrust its shaft down into Camael's chest. With a great bellow of pain, the angel raised his sword and sliced the warrior creature in two.

"Aaron, look out!" Gabriel called from behind him.

Aaron quickly turned, just in time to block the attack of another of the horrible beasts. It was the one with the elaborate headdress.

"You will fall before our might," the chieftain shrieked in its savage tongue. *"I have foreseen it."*

Aaron swung his mighty sword, and the Orisha fluttered backward as the burning blade nearly severed his overly large head from its diminutive body. The power within Aaron was wild now, straining for release. The chief again pressed the attack, and this time his knife found its mark, sinking into the soft flesh of Aaron's shoulder. He cried out in pain as the creature hovered just out of reach.

"Aaron, are you all right?"

"I'm fine, Gabriel," he said as he watched the dog try to pin the fighting Orisha with the burned wing to the forest floor. "Just pay attention. These things are dangerous."

The wound pulsed painfully, and a strange, burning sensation began to spread down his arm, making it difficult to hold his weapon. *Poison?* he wondered. He turned to Camael, just in time to watch the angel warrior fall to his knees.

"Did I mention that the Orishas dip their blades in a narcotic that immobilizes their prey?" Camael asked, his speech slightly slurred.

"You don't say," Aaron replied with sarcasm, as the sword fell from his numbed hand, imploding to nothing before it could hit the forest floor.

No longer concerned with them, now that the drug was coursing through their veins, the surviving Orishas turned their attention to Gabriel. Aaron watched helplessly as his friend lost his grip on the creature with the burned wing and it scuttled over to join its comrades.

"Get out of there, Gabriel!"

The chief had retrieved the net, and the three warriors slowly advanced on the snarling dog.

"You should know by now that I won't leave you," the Lab growled, standing his ground.

"Loyal to a fault," Camael said as he swayed upon his knees and fell to his side, the Orishas' poison taking hold.

The Orishas threw themselves at Gabriel. Two grabbed hold of the snarling dog while the chieftain tossed the net over his head. Quickly, they staked the net to the ground, trapping the Labrador.

"We will eat hardy tonight, my brothers," the chief said excitedly as he leaned in to sniff at the still snarling animal. *"A meal befitting warriors—warriors who are about to receive their freedom and safe passage to paradise."*

The Orishas began to cheer, their poison-dipped weapons raised to the heavens in a dance of victory.

"They're going to eat Gabriel?" Aaron asked with horror. His entire body had gone numb, and he slumped to the ground near Camael.

"It appears that way," the angel managed. "And then they will bring us to Verchiel at first light."

"What are we going to do?" Aaron asked while keeping his eyes on the jubilant Orishas, who seemed to be getting quite a kick out of tormenting poor Gabriel.

"It is up to you," Camael calmly replied.

"What the hell is that supposed to mean?" Aaron angrily barked.

"You have the power. All you need to do is use it."

As if on cue, Aaron felt the presence surge within him once again. "I don't know what you mean," he lied, using all his might to hold it at bay.

"Don't play games with me, Aaron," the angel snapped.

"I can sense how it struggles to exert itself. Set it free."

"I . . . I can't do that," Aaron replied, gripped by fear. "I don't know if I can control it."

"I thought we were beyond this." The angel sounded exasperated. "The power is part of you—it is what you are now."

Deep down, Aaron knew the angel was right—but it didn't make it any less scary. The force was wild, its potential for destruction great. He remembered how he had felt the night Verchiel killed his foster parents. Such strength, such power, it had been exhilarating—at first. *Am I strong enough?* he wondered. *Or will it drive me crazy as it has others before me?*

"I . . . I can't," he stammered. It was becoming more difficult to speak.

"You must," Camael declared. "If you do not, Gabriel will die and we will share a fate at the hands of Verchiel."

Aaron was silent. He watched the Orisha chief step away from the celebration and remove two sets of restraints from a satchel hidden in the thick underbrush. *"When the Orishas' poison wears off, you will go nowhere,"* the ugly little creature cackled as he moved toward Aaron.

"Do something!" Camael bellowed.

For a moment, Aaron thought about letting the power loose, feeling the electric surge of his true supernatural nature course through his body. He remembered the excruciating pain as his newly developed wings tore through the flesh of his back, unfurling to their full and glorious span. He winced, recalling the severe, burning sensation as ancient angelic symbols appeared upon his skin—signaling his transformation into something far more than human.

He thought about it, but he did nothing—and the Orisha's restraints snapped coldly closed around his wrists.

Camael sighed. He'd had such great hopes for the boy, but now he was beginning to have doubts.

"And now you, great angel," the Orisha chieftain said happily as he headed for Camael with the second set of manacles.

"And now me," Camael growled, and began to climb to his feet.

"More poison! More poison!" the leader screamed in panic, pulling his knife from the sheath around his leg. The other two warriors made a frantic dive for their weapons.

Camael was both bored and immensely annoyed. The angel knew that Aaron had been holding back, fearful of his newly emerged nature, and he had seen this as the perfect opportunity for the boy to tame the power, to wrestle it beneath his control. But as he gazed at the youth, lying upon the ground, having succumbed to the effects of the Orishas' poison—he realized how wrong he was. He wasn't ready at all, and Camael began to fear for the fulfillment of the angelic prophecy.

The old shaman was fluttering in the air before Camael, muttering, arms spread wide. The ground beneath the angel's feet began to churn, and he felt himself pulled into the earth as suddenly as liquid. The other two Orishas charged, their weapons glinting with paralyzing poison. *This will not do at all,* the angel thought as a new sword of fire ignited in his hand. Camael swung the fiery blade driving back the warriors and with one great flap of his mighty wings, he lifted himself from the ground's sucking embrace.

With a howl of fury, the chieftain launched himself toward Camael, moving with supernatural speed. But Camael was faster, swinging his sword of fire and cleaving the leader in two.

"Your dream was just that," he said as the two pieces of the once living thing fell away in flames. "A dream."

Without his leader, the Orisha with the burned wings seemed to lose his urge to fight. The fluttering beast drew back his arm, threw his spear, and turned to run. Camael slapped the projectile away, then pointed the tip of his sword at the fleeing primitive. A tongue of flame snaked from the end of the burning blade, and in an instant the Orisha warrior was engulfed in heavenly fire. The creature squealed: words of prayer to some long-dead fallen angel that was its creator upon its lips as it was incinerated.

There is one more, Camael thought as he returned to the ground, wings folding upon his back. Sword ready, his birdlike eyes scanned the trees and underbrush for signs of the older Orisha, but the creature was nowhere to be found.

Aaron moaned in the grip of the poison-induced fever, and

Camael turned his attention to the Nephilim. His sword dissipated as he moved toward the youth and squatted beside him. He touched the locking mechanism on Aaron's manacles and watched as the restraints fell smoldering to the ground. "Get up, boy," he said sternly.

Aaron's eyes fluttered open. "Camael?" he whispered. "How . . . ?"

"I purged the poison from my system," he said, grabbing the teen by the front of his shirt and hauling him to his feet. "It's something you could have done as well, if you'd bothered."

He swayed drunkenly. "Why . . . why did you wait so long?"

Camael strode toward Gabriel still trapped beneath the net. "I was waiting for you to act," the angel answered as he pulled the stakes from the ground.

Gabriel surged up and shook himself free of the net. *"Thank you, Camael."* He sniffed at one of the still burning corpses of the Orisha warriors.

"So this . . . this was some kind of test?" Aaron asked, stumbling toward them on legs still numb with toxin.

Gabriel nuzzled his friend's hand. *"Are you all right? I was very worried about you."*

Aaron absently patted the dog's head as he waited for Camael's answer.

"You handled yourself quite bravely against the Powers— but now comes the difficult part," the angel said. "I wanted to see what you would do."

"Don't you worry about me. I'll be ready to deal with Verchiel when the time comes."

Camael scowled and motioned to the Orisha bodies littering the ground. "These are merely pests in the grand scheme of things, bothersome insects that should have been swatted away easily."

"I'm still new to this," Aaron defended himself. *"I have a hard time killing. There's a lot I need to learn before—"*

"You do not have time," Camael interrupted. "Verchiel is like a wounded animal now—he will do everything and anything in his power to see you destroyed."

"What's this?" the angel heard Gabriel mutter. He glanced over to see the Lab sniffing at a patch of overturned dirt, his pink nose pressed to the ground, his furry brow wrinkled in concentration.

"I'll be ready," Aaron said bravely, distracting Camael from the dog's curiosity. "Don't worry about me."

"I hope you are right, Aaron Corbet," Camael said with caution. "For there is far more at stake here than just your life."

He was about to suggest that they continue on to Blithe when the Orisha shaman exploded from the earth in front of the dog, eyes bulging with madness, jagged teeth bared in a grin of savagery.

"You will not keep me from the Safe Place!" it screamed as it lunged at the startled animal.

The shaman grabbed hold of Gabriel's flank and bit down into the fur-covered flesh of his thigh. The dog yelped in agony, snapping at the creature as it scurried off into the protection of the forest, wiping the dog's blood from its mouth.

Camael and Aaron ran to their injured comrade.

"He bit me, Aaron," Gabriel whined pathetically. *"That wasn't very nice. I didn't even bite him first."*

"He's got a pretty good bite here," Aaron said as he examined the bloody puncture wounds near the dog's hip. "What am I going to do?" Aaron asked, looking to Camael for help.

"That's an excellent question," the angel answered, folding his arms across his broad chest. "What *are* you going to do?"

"Nothing's happening," Aaron said as he laid his hands on the dog's bleeding leg.

"Perhaps you're not trying hard enough," Camael responded in that condescending tone of voice that made Aaron want to tell him to stick it up his angelic butt.

He was still angry with the angel for putting their lives at risk just to test him—although part of him did understand why Camael had done it. After all, there was quite a bit riding on this whole angelic prophecy thing. If he was in fact the one the prophecy spoke of, and they were both pretty sure that he was, then he had a major responsibility to fulfill for the fallen angels living upon the planet.

"Yeah," Gabriel added, interrupting his thoughts. *"Try harder."*

"That's enough out of you," Aaron said, pressing his hands against the bite. If only he could remember what he did that awful morning in Lynn when Gabriel had been hit by the car.

After all, if he could return him from the brink of death then, he could certainly heal a simple bite now.

"It hurts, Aaron."

"I know, pal, I'm going to fix you up, just as soon as . . ."

Camael bent closer. "Let go of your humanity and embrace the angelic," he boomed. "To fear it is to fear yourself."

Aaron was reminded of similar words spoken by Zeke that fateful Saturday—*had it really only been two weeks ago? So much had changed in such a short time.* He closed his eyes and willed the power forward.

He could sense it there, somewhere in the pitch black behind his eyes. He beckoned to it, but it ignored his call, perhaps perturbed at him for not allowing it to manifest during the battle with the Orishas. He concentrated all the more, his body trembling with exertion.

"That's it, rein it in," he heard Camael say quietly from beside him. "Take control and make it your own."

Aaron commanded the power to come forward, and it slowly turned its attention to him. He pushed again with his mind, and suddenly, with the speed of thought, it moved, shifting its form—-mammal, insect, reptile, all shapes of life, the menagerie of God. The force surged through him, and Aaron gasped with the rush of it. His eyes flew open, and he gazed up into the late afternoon sky, at the clouds above and the universe beyond his own. "It's here," he whispered, feeling his body throb with the ancient power.

"Excellent," Camael hissed in his ear. "Now wrestle it, take control—show it you are the master."

And Aaron did as he was told. The power fought him, trying to overwhelm him with the sheer force of its might, but Aaron held on, corralling it, moving its strength to where it was needed. He felt the power flood into his upper body, moving down the length of his arms and into his hands.

"*I . . . I feel something happening, Aaron,*" Gabriel said, fear in his guttural voice.

"It's going to be all right," Aaron soothed as he felt the raw energy flow from the tips of his fingers into the dog's injured leg. He willed the power to heal his best friend, and he stared at the gaping wound, waiting for it to close—but nothing happened. Again, he willed it, and the power danced about the injury—but it did nothing.

Aaron pulled away, exhausted, hands tingling painfully. "I don't understand," he said in a breathless whisper. He looked up at Camael looming above him. "I did what you said—I took control and I commanded it to heal Gabriel's wound—but it didn't do a thing."

Camael stared thoughtfully at the Lab, absently reaching up to run his fingers through his goatee. "Interesting," he observed. "Perhaps your animal has become more complex than even you understand."

Aaron shook his head, confused. "I don't . . ."

"When the animal was healed before—"

"*This animal has a name,*" Gabriel interrupted with annoyance.

"It's okay, boy," Aaron said, patting the dog's head, comforting him.

"As I was saying," Camael said, glaring at the dog, "when the animal was healed before, the power you wielded was raw, in its purest form—its most potent state. You commanded it to repair Gabriel, and it did just that—only I think it may have altered him as well."

"*I don't feel altered,*" the dog said. "*My legs just hurts.*"

"Are you saying that Gabriel is too complicated a life-form for me to fix now?"

The angel nodded.

"But how could I have done that?" Aaron asked as he gently stroked his dog's side.

"You didn't," Camael corrected. "You just gave the command, and the presence within you took it from there."

If he hadn't been afraid of the power that lived within him before, he certainly would be now, but that didn't change the fact that Gabriel was still hurt. "Gabriel needs medical attention," Aaron said, staring down at his best friend. "He may be a complex life-form, but he still needs to have that bite cleaned up."

"Then I suggest we continue on with our journey," the angel said, "and hopefully we'll be able to find medical help for him in Blithe."

"Sounds like a plan," Aaron said after a moment's thought. He reached out and hefted the eighty-pound canine over his shoulder. "Don't worry," he said sarcastically to the angel, grunting with exertion, "I got him."

"Yes, you do," Camael said as he strode into the woods toward the direction of the car.

"Sometimes he bugs the crap out of me," Aaron muttered, following the angel, careful not to stumble with his burden.

"That's just how they are," Gabriel said matter-of-factly.

"How *who* are?"

"Angels."

"What, you're an expert on angels now?"

"Well, I am *a complex being,"* the dog replied haughtily.

CHAPTER FOUR

I am the shaman. They should have listened to me, Shokad of the Orishas thought as he feverishly wove his ancient elemental magicks and tunneled deep beneath the earth. They never should have tried to capture the Nephilim—the bones and stones had told him as much. But did they listen? No. They let their fear counsel them, the fear that spoke to their chief during the night, promising sweet victory. *They should have listened to me,* he thought bitterly.

His throat as dry as dust from spell casting, Shokad stopped speaking, and the earth stilled around him. He leaned close to the curved tunnel wall, looking for signs of life. Careful not to break it, he pulled a thick, squirming earthworm from the dirt and popped it into his maw. He chewed vigorously, the juice from the worm's muscular body filling his mouth and coating his throat. He ate his fill, then squatted in the tunnel to rest.

Where do I go from here? the shaman pondered. He closed his eyes, and his mind immediately was filled with blissful images of what could only have been the Safe Place. He saw his people, the ones who had abandoned the Deheboryn many seasons ago, living in harmony with nature, no longer fearing the wrath of the Powers. "They were not killed," he muttered, completely enthralled with the vision. They had managed to evade the wrath of Verchiel and his soldiers, and had found Paradise.

Shokad blessed himself repeatedly, basking in the glory that was the vision of his people thriving within the confines of the Safe Place. It filled him with such joy—and a newfound purpose.

The shaman opened his eyes to the cool darkness of the tunnel and climbed to his feet. He could feel it calling to him now. He could hear it whispering in his ears, drawing him to its secret location. The Safe Place was calling, and all he need do was follow.

He faced the solid wall of dirt before him and recited the ancient words taught by his angelic creators. With these words he could commune with the elements, making them bend to his requests. Shokad asked the dirt wall to allow him passage, and it did as it was asked, flowing around the shaman as he moved toward the promise of Paradise. The wings upon his back flapped eagerly as he trudged through the earth, the Safe Place whispering in his ear, closer—and closer still.

Again he saw them in his mind, those that had left the

tribe long ago. *So happy,* he thought. If only Mufgar had had the courage to abandon the old ways, he and Zawar and Tehom could all have experienced the joy that was soon to be his.

The Safe Place was singing now, urging him forward with even greater speed. *You are so close,* it said in a voice filled with promise. *So close to realizing your dream.*

Shokad spoke the words of the spell faster, and the earth in front of him melted away like water. Partly running, partly flying, he burrowed his way toward Paradise, images of those who had come before him in his mind. Suria, Tutrechial, Adririon, Tandal, Savlial: They were all there—some he could have sworn were slain in service to the Powers. It was curious indeed, but he was not about to argue with Paradise.

"Oh, Shokad, you are almost here."

The Orisha began to giggle and angled his tunnel toward the surface. The earth grew thick with rock, making it harder to push forward—but it did not stop him.

"So close, Shokad. So very, very close."

The shaman broke through to the surface. His hands were cracked and bleeding, and the air upon them was cold and damp. *Where is the warm sunshine?* he at first wondered.

Shokad squirmed from the hole in the ground and peered through the eerie greenish light. He found himself in a vast, underground cavern. Somewhere in the distance, beyond the walls of rock, he could hear the rush of water.

"I am here," he said aloud, expecting his people to come

forward and welcome him. They did not—but something else moved amongst the rocks at the far end of the cave.

"Greetings," Shokad said as he scrambled toward the noise. It was an odd sound, like something large and heavy being dragged across the rocks. "I am Shokad."

Perhaps they are afraid, he thought as he climbed over the rocky ground, deeper into the cavern. "I mean you no harm," he said aloud. "I, too, have come seeking Paradise."

As he drew closer, he could just barely discern objects in the shadows—fleshy, egglike sacks that hung upon a large, muscular mass, blacker than the cave's deepest shadows. It writhed and pulsed, a thing alive.

"What are you?" Shokad whispered. Cautiously, he stepped forward. "Where are my people?" He stood on tiptoe to peer inside some of the opaque, membranous growths—and his questions were answered.

The Orisha shaman wanted to scream, to ask the divine power that had brought him here why it had shown him this horror, but he didn't have a chance. Something slithered with lightning speed from the shadows behind him and grasped him in its heavy, wet embrace.

Yes, Shokad wanted to scream—for neither he nor his people had found Paradise.

So this is Blithe, Aaron thought as he drove into the center of town. He expected more, but it was much like every other small town they'd driven through in the last two weeks. Quaint old shops, their windows displaying dusty souvenirs, surrounded a grassy common with a fancy white bandstand in its center. It was a beautiful, sunny afternoon, and people strolled in and out of the shops while children played ball in the common.

"How you doing, Gabe?" Aaron asked the dog lying quietly in the backseat.

"I'm okay," Gabriel answered, but Aaron could tell that the dog wasn't feeling all that great.

The Orisha's bite was bad, and it already looked infected. They needed to find a veterinarian soon.

"Hang in there, pal," Aaron said, drawing closer to the town's center. "See any sign of a veterinarian's office?" he asked the angel sitting in the passenger seat beside him.

Camael remained silent, staring out the window with furious intensity, as he had the entire ride to Blithe.

"Hello?" Aaron asked. "What's the story? You see something?"

The angel glanced at him, scowling. "It's nothing," he said, but Aaron knew that something was ruffling his feathers— *pardon the pun.*

"Well, I'm going to ask one of the locals, then," Aaron said as he pulled over in front of a small hardware store.

An older man wearing a soiled Red Sox cap, plaid shirt, and overalls came out of the store with a paper bag and stopped to put his change inside a rubber coin purse.

Aaron reached across Camael, rolled down the passenger window, and called out, "Excuse me!"

The man, his face deeply tanned and crisscrossed with the mileage of age, slipped the change purse into the back pocket of his overalls and stooped slightly to look through the window. His eyes quickly passed suspiciously over everyone in the car.

"Hi," Aaron said in his most friendly voice. He even waved. "I'm hoping you can help us."

The man said nothing, continuing to watch him stoically. Aaron had heard that people in Maine were cautious of strangers, but this was really taking things a bit too far.

Camael meanwhile remained perfectly still, and Aaron wondered if he was willing himself invisible again. Aaron had discovered that he did this from time to time, when he didn't feel like dealing with humans. The last time was two days ago, when they had stopped to walk the dog and were accosted by four elderly sisters who wanted to know everything about Gabriel and Labrador retrievers. Afterward, Aaron told Camael that he was being rude, and the angel responded by saying that it was only because Aaron couldn't yet do it himself.

"My dog was bitten by something in the woods, and I need to get him to a vet."

The old man looked at the dog, his gaze zeroing in on the bite. "What got 'im?" he asked in a raspy voice with a distinctly Maine accent.

"Raccoon," Aaron said quickly. "Sure hope it wasn't rabid."

"Don't look like any 'coon bite I ever seen," the old-timer growled, studying the wound through the open window. "Too wide."

"Well, I only saw it from the back as it ran away. I guess it could have been something else."

The old man glared at Aaron, adjusting the rim of his Red Sox cap. "It wasn't a raccoon—so I guess it *had* to be somethin' else."

Aaron smiled tightly, feeling his patience begin to slip. "Yeah, I guess you're right." He paused and counted to ten. "So I was wondering if there's a vet around here?"

The man seemed to think about it for a minute or two, then slowly nodded his head. "Yep, there is." He fell silent, continuing to stare.

Feeling his blood begin to boil, Aaron wondered how long it would be before Camael summoned a sword and dispatched the annoying old man. "Do you think you could give me directions?" he asked, the strained smile on his face beginning to ache.

Again, the old man thought for a minute, nodded his head slowly, and gave them complex directions to an office just a few miles away.

"That was a rather odd fellow," Camael said as Aaron pulled away from the curb, reviewing the convoluted directions in his mind.

"First meeting with a Mainiac?" Aaron asked, taking a left onto Portland Street, just before a large white church. *"You go beyond that and you've gone too far,"* the old man had stressed.

"I've encountered many madmen in my long years on this planet."

"No, not maniac—*Mainiac,"* Aaron explained as he slowly drove down Portland. "People from Maine, that's what they're called."

"Whatever the case, he certainly was odd."

"And you didn't even have to talk to him," Aaron said, on the lookout for a dirt road on the right. "Did you will yourself invisible again?"

"I have no idea what you're talking about," the angel replied, refusing to look at him.

"I'm sure you don't," Aaron said with sarcasm, taking the turn onto a rutted stretch of winding road.

After half a mile, the dirt road opened up into a large, unpaved parking lot. A building to the left of the lot looked as if it had once been a country store with an apartment above. The apartment seemed to still serve that function, but the storefront had been converted into a veterinarian's office. Two sports utility vehicles were parked in the lot, one with Maine plates, the other from Illinois.

"This is it," Aaron said. He parked as close to the building as he could. "Let's get you fixed up, Gabriel."

The dog lifted his head and looked around. His nose

twitched and dribbled moisture as he scented the air. *"Where are we?"* he asked.

"The vet," Aaron answered as he got out of the car and opened the back passenger door.

"No we're not," Gabriel said, continuing to sniff at the air. *"We're not in Lynn."*

"This is another office," Aaron explained, leaning into the backseat to check out the wound.

"There's more than one?" Gabriel asked incredulously.

"Lots more than one," Aaron answered as he helped his friend to the ground.

"I never knew that," the dog muttered. He leaned against Aaron for support, holding up his injured leg.

Aaron looked over the top of the car at Camael, who had gotten out and was also sniffing the air. "Are you coming with me?" he asked, squatting down and lifting up the dog.

"No," the angel said succinctly, and turned back toward the dirt road.

"Well, I'm going to be in here for a while if you need me," Aaron said to the angel's back. Camael continued on without responding. "All right then, Aaron," he muttered to himself as he carefully made his way up the four steps to the front door. A metal placard announced KEVIN WESSELL, DVM. "You take care of Gabriel, and I'll be out here looking around."

Aaron struggled to shift his burden so he could grab the doorknob and turn it. "Thanks for the help, Camael," he said with mock cheeriness. "You certainly are one considerate angelic being."

"Camael's gone," Gabriel reported.

"I know he's gone," Aaron grunted. He turned the knob and pushed the door open with his foot.

"Then why are you still talking to him?"

"I don't know, Gabe," Aaron grumbled as he maneuvered into the small lobby. "These days I do a lot of crazy things."

The place was old, not like the state-of-the art clinic where he had worked in Lynn. The room was done in dark wood paneling, with framed pictures of hunting dogs hung sporadically on the walls. A few plastic seats placed against the wall and an old coffee table covered with magazines and children's books served as the waiting area. The reception desk was straight ahead.

The lobby was deserted, but Aaron could hear the sounds of paper shuffling and a sigh of exasperation corning from behind the desk. He approached and saw a girl surrounded by stacks of paper and medical folders. Her hair was an unusually dark shade of red, and she wore it pulled back in a tight ponytail. Obviously she hadn't heard his entrance, so he cleared his throat and watched as she jumped, startled by his sudden appearance.

"You scared me," she said with a nervous laugh. She moved a stray red hair from her forehead.

"Sorry," Aaron said with a grunt, trying to shift Gabriel's

weight in his arms. "Do you think we could see the vet?" he asked.

"Sure," she answered, moving one stack of folders to an even larger one that teetered dangerously. "Just give me a second here and we'll see what we can do."

"I'm . . . I'm not feeling so good, Aaron," Gabriel whined in his arms.

The dog shivered and Aaron guessed that a fever was brewing. He felt his temper spike. He'd already wasted enough time with the Mainiac in the Red Sox cap; he wasn't about to let his dog suffer anymore. "Look," he said rather forcefully, "I'll fill out all the forms you have, but could you please get the doctor out here? I think he's got a pretty nasty infection and I want to get some antibiotics into him as soon as possible. . . ."

"All right, all right," the redhead said as she stood and moved around the counter. "Let's take him in back and I'll give him a look." She motioned for them to follow.

"You're not Dr. Wessell," Aaron said, taken aback.

"No," she responded. "But I almost was. I'm just plain Katie McGovern right now." She laughed. "But not to worry, I'm also a licensed veterinarian."

Aaron laughed self-consciously as he carried Gabriel toward the examination room. "I'm sorry, I didn't mean to come off like a jerk, it's just that it's been a really long day and I thought you were—"

"The receptionist?" she asked. She opened the door to the exam room and stepped back for him to enter.

"Yeah," he answered. "You don't look old enough to—"

"I'm twenty-seven," she said, closing the door. "The product of fine Irish genes. I can show you my diploma from the University of Illinois College of Veterinary Medicine," she added as she helped him lay Gabriel on the metal table. "How you doing, buddy?" she asked the dog, stroking his head and rubbing his ears.

"My name's not Buddy," Gabriel growled. *"It's Gabriel."*

"His name is Gabriel," Aaron told her.

"Hello there, Gabriel," Katie said as she slipped on a pair of rubber gloves. "Let's take a look and see what we can do about fixing you up." She examined the wound in his leg, gently prodding the seeping injury. "What did you say bit him?" she asked.

"I think it was a raccoon," Aaron answered lamely.

"A raccoon?" she questioned, looking up from the oozing bite. "If that's a raccoon bite, I'm a teenage receptionist."

Camael could feel it on the breeze—one of many strange things he could sense ever since he finally arrived in the town of Blithe.

He walked slowly down Portland Street, taking a right as he left the stretch of dirt road. Something in the atmosphere told him that he belonged here, that he was welcome—but there was also something else, something he couldn't identify. It was an odd sensation hidden beneath layers of other, far more pleasant impulses.

The angel widened his perceptions as he turned onto Acadia Street. It was as quiet as death here, void of life, the only sounds the gentle hiss of the warm presummer breeze and the pounding of the surf far off in the distance. Offices lined both sides of the short street: Johnson's Realtors, McNulty Certified Public Accountants, Dr. Charles Speegal, Optometrist, and the largest building belonging to the Carroll Funeral Home, which took up almost one whole side of the street.

Everything about this town said that he was supposed to be here. It disarmed him, made him think about and feel things he had not experienced in thousands of years. There was an unwarranted contentment here, and the angel wondered if he and Aaron had indeed stumbled across the haven that was Acrie. He crossed the street to stand before the white, two-story building that was the Carroll Funeral Home, and looked around carefully. *But then, where are the others?*

Again came that wave of sensation he could not immediately identify, like a great beast of the sea breaking the surface for air before diving again beneath the dark, murky depths. But this time there was something in it that he finally recognized: the scent of an ethereal presence trying very hard to hide beneath sensations of serenity. Now that he had the scent, he had to be careful not to lose it. It was old, very, very old—a whiff of chaos that had not been breathed since the days of creation.

Camael heard the sound of a door opening and turned back to face the funeral home, willing himself invisible. An old man, dressed in a dark suit and tie, was standing on the top step, looking down at him. Camael was perplexed; it was as if he were able to see the angel—but of course, that was impossible.

The feelings of tranquility tripled, bombarding Camael with sensations meant to keep him complacent, but he held on to the ancient scent. No matter how hard it tried to hide beneath the oceans of serenity radiating from the town, he knew that at the core of Blithe there was chaos.

The man continued to stare at him with eyes black and deep, and Camael knew that the man in the suit could see him. "How is this possible?" Camael asked.

The old man's head cocked to one side strangely, and he smiled. Then he blinked slowly, and Camael noticed a milky, membranous covering over his eyes. Not something that he had ever perceived on the human anatomy before. Sensing that he might be in danger, Camael was about to summon a weapon of fire when the old man leaned forward, his bones creaking painfully, and coughed. Tiny projectiles, about the size of a cherry, and barbed, were expelled from his mouth to stick in Camael's face and neck.

The angel scowled angrily, reaching up to pluck the offensive matter from his flesh, when he felt his body growing numb. "Poison," he grumbled, tearing one of the barbed projectiles from his face and staring at it. It was brown and pulsed with an organic life of its own. It was the second time that day that some primitive form of life had attempted to vanquish him using toxins.

Camael closed his eyes and willed the poison from his body. Shockingly, it did little good, and he found that he did not have the strength to open his eyes again. The world seemed to tilt beneath his feet, and he fell to the ground.

Through the darkness behind his eyes, he heard the sound of the old man's feet as he shuffled down the stairs toward him. Pulled deeper and deeper into the clutches of unconsciousness, Camael was consoled by the town of Blithe.

"You were meant to be here," it said, easing the angel on his way into oblivion. *"For without you, I would die."*

Aaron petted Gabriel as he watched Dr. McGovern shave away the fur on the dog's leg, then squirt some saline solution into the wound. She dabbed at it with a cotton swab and leaned in to examine it more closely.

"Mouths are filthy, so I just assume that all bites are infected," she said, squirting more saline into the wound. "This one is particularly nasty, though—especially for a raccoon bite." She looked up to catch Aaron's eye.

"I said I thought it was a raccoon," he responded, flustered. No way was he going to explain that Gabriel had been bitten by a nasty little creature created by fallen angels. "I didn't get that good of a look at it—I guess it could have been just about anything."

"It was an Orisha, Aaron," Gabriel grumbled.

"I know, I know," Aaron said reassuringly.

"He's pretty vocal, isn't he?" The vet threw the soiled cotton swabs into a barrel, then rubbed Gabriel's head affectionately.

"You don't know the half of it," Aaron replied with a sly smile and a chuckle. "Say, is he going to need a rabies booster?"

"A shot?" Gabriel grunted, lifting his head from the table.

"When did he get his last vaccination?" Dr. McGovern asked.

"I just got a shot," the Lab whined.

"About six months ago," Aaron said, ignoring his best friend.

"Yeah, why don't we do a booster, then. Better to be safe than sorry," she said, pulling a syringe from a drawer and getting a vial of vaccine from a tiny fridge beneath the counter.

"Better no shot than sorry," Gabriel growled.

"He doesn't sound too happy," the vet said, filling the needle.

"He's not, but he doesn't have a choice. He has to get a shot or else *he'll get sick."* Aaron emphasized the last of the sentence specifically to the dog.

"Do you think he understands you?"

"I know he does," Aaron answered, rubbing the thick fur around Gabriel's neck. "This guy is pretty special."

"Aren't they all," she said, and with one quick move, administered the injection with not so much as a yelp from the dog.

"See," she cooed, leaning into Gabriel's face and rubbing his ears. "That wasn't so bad, was it?"

"She smells good, Aaron," the dog woofed, his large, muscular tail thumping happily on the metal table.

Aaron laughed. "Don't worry, Gabriel doesn't hold many grudges. Give 'im some affection and a cookie and he'll forget all about the trauma."

The doctor disposed of the syringe in a red plastic container on the counter. "All right," she said, looking over her notes. "Let's see, keep the wound uncovered so it can dry out and . . ."

"Warm compresses three times a day and two weeks of amoxicillin twice daily to kill the infection," Aaron continued as he watched Gabriel sit up carefully on the table.

Dr. McGovern smiled, setting her pen down. "Pretty good." She nodded. "Do we have an interest in the veterinary sciences?"

"I used to work in a vet's office," Aaron explained, the recollection of the life he had left behind washing over him in a wave of melancholy. He quickly turned back to Gabriel. "Do you want to get down?"

"Let me help you," the vet said, and together they lowered Gabriel to the floor.

"You know," she said, "I'm only here temporarily—but I could use a hand around the office. I can't pay great money, but I could pay you something, and I could look after Gabriel's bite—what do you say?"

It certainly was a tempting offer. There was something about this little town that had really gotten into Aaron's system. It seemed to be saying that *this* was the place where he wanted to be. The fact that he could earn some money to bolster his dwindling savings account wasn't a bad idea either. "Shouldn't you check with Dr. Wessell first?" he asked.

Dr. McGovern nodded slowly. "I imagine so, but since my former fiancé is nowhere to be found, I'd say that gives me leeway to bend the rules a bit. You interested?"

"Let's stay, Aaron," Gabriel whined. *"I'm tired of the car."*

"I'd have to check with my traveling companion," Aaron said with a shrug. "But sure, if it's okay with him I'd love to hang around for a couple days."

"Great," she said, extending her hand, "I'm Katie, and I know this is Gabriel, but it might bet nice to know your name, too, especially if we'll be working together."

"Sorry." He took her hand in his and gave it a shake. "Aaron," he said. "Aaron Corbet."

"Great to meet you, Aaron." She released his hand. "Why don't you go check with your friend and let me know what you'll be doing."

Aaron and Gabriel stepped from the building into the warm, spring afternoon and headed for the car. Gabriel was able to walk on his own with a minimum of discomfort, thanks to Katie's ministrations.

"Where's Camael?" Gabriel asked as Aaron opened the door and helped him into the backseat. He immediately lay down to check out the wound on his leg, sniffing and licking at the antiseptic goo that covered it.

"I don't know," Aaron answered. "And leave your leg alone," he added, looking around for signs of the angel.

Since the battle at his home, he and the former Powers' commander had formed a strange kind of bond. Aaron was always aware of the angel's presence, and although he could feel something unusual about Blithe, right now he felt no sense at all of Camael. That alone was troubling. *Looks like we* will *be staying a while,* he thought.

At that moment, Katie came outside to get supplies from the back of her truck.

"Stay here a minute," Aaron told Gabriel, jogging over to the vet, who was trying to balance three large boxes in her arms and close the back of her SUV.

"Katie, looks like I'll be taking you up on your offer," he said as she peeked out from behind the teetering boxes.

"Great," she replied. "And your first assignment?"

Aaron snapped to attention. "Sure, what's that?"

"Give your boss a hand with these boxes," she said. "Damn things are heavy."

CHAPTER FIVE

Where do you think he went?" Gabriel asked from the backseat as Aaron continued his patrol of Blithe.

"I have no idea," he said, scanning the streets for signs of the wayward Camael. "Maybe he found another Nephilim he likes better and skipped town."

"Do you think he would do that?" Gabriel asked, aghast.

"I'm just kidding." Aaron chuckled as he eyed a coffee shop.

An elderly couple came out of the shop, and Aaron tried to see inside as the door slowly closed—but no luck. *Besides, why would he be in a coffee shop—he doesn't even have to eat,* Aaron thought as he brought his car to a stop at a crosswalk, allowing an older woman with a shopping cart to cross. *But then again, they might have had French fries.*

In the rearview mirror he watched the Labrador tilt his

head back and sniff the air. *"Do you want me to get out and see if I can find him?"* Gabriel asked. *"I might be able to pick up his scent. He does smell kind of funny, you know."*

"No, that's all right, Gabe," Aaron replied. "He'll turn up. Why don't we just find someplace to stay that'll take pets."

"I'm much more than a pet," the dog said with pride.

"So you've told me," Aaron responded, taking a left onto Berkely Street. "Katie said there's a place that rents rooms down here."

At the end of the dead-end street stood a large, white house surrounded by a jungle of colorful wildflowers. A wooden ROOMS FOR RENT sign moved in the breeze.

"There it is," he said, pulling to the curb in front of the house and turning off the engine. "You stay here. I'll go find out how much they charge and if they allow pets."

"You tell them I am not just a pet," Gabriel called through the open window as Aaron headed up the walk beneath a wooden arch bedecked with snaking purple flowers.

"Can I help you?" asked an aged voice from somewhere amongst the lush vegetation.

"Yeah," he responded, startled, not sure where to direct his answer. "I'm looking for a room."

An old woman emerged from behind a thick forsythia bush, sharp-looking pruning sheers in her hand. She glared at him through thick, dark-framed sunglasses that made her look like one of the X-Men, and wiped some sweat from her brow with a glove-covered hand. "I have a few—ain't that a coincidence."

Aaron laughed nervously. "Cool," he said with what he hoped was a charming smile.

"You alone, or with somebody?" She craned her neck to get a look at the car parked on the street. "Thought I heard you talkin' to somebody."

"I was talking to my dog," he said, studying her face for a response.

The woman scowled. "You got a dog?"

Aaron nodded slowly.

"You want me to rent you a room—with a dog?" she asked incredulously.

He sighed. "Sorry to have wasted your time," he said with a polite wave as he hastily turned and headed back toward the car.

He was just beneath the flowered archway when he heard the woman's voice very close behind him. "What kind of dog is it?"

"He's a yellow Labrador," Aaron answered, not quite sure what difference it made.

"Yellow?" she repeated, eyeing his vehicle.

Aaron nodded. "Yellow Lab, yes."

She followed him as he continued to the car. "My father used to raise Labs," she said as she pulled off her work gloves and stuck them in the back pockets of her worn blue jeans. "Sometimes I have a soft spot for them."

Aaron opened the back door of the car, exposing Gabriel. "Hey Gabe," he said, "somebody wants to meet you."

The old woman kept her distance, but crouched to peer into the car. Gabriel panted happily and wagged his tail against the back of the seat. It sounded like a drumbeat.

"What did you call him?" she asked, removing her funky shades, giving him a lesser version of the scowl from the yard.

"Gabriel."

"That's a good name." She stared into the car. "What happened to his leg?" she asked, pointing at the nasty wound.

"Oh, he got bit by a—a possum, I think," Aaron said. "That's one of the reasons why we're looking for a place to stay. The leg needs to heal a bit before we move on."

"That ain't no possum bite," the old woman said with a shake of her head. She leaned into the car and let Gabriel sniff her bony, callused hands. "What bit you, boy?" she asked, petting his head.

"I think it was called an Orisha," Gabriel woofed.

"Would you look at that," she said with a genuine smile. "You'd think he was trying to answer me."

"He's very talkative," Aaron said, giving Gabriel a thumbs-up behind the woman's back.

"He housebroke?" she asked, still rubbing the dog's velvety soft ears and stroking the side of his face.

"Of course he is," Aaron answered, holding his indignation

in check. "And he doesn't bark or chew. Gabriel's just an all-around good dog."

She emerged from the car and gave Aaron the once-over. "Well, you don't look like a Rockefeller, so it'll be a hundred dollars a week, with meals—but you have to eat with me. This ain't no restaurant."

"That's great," he answered cheerily. "It'll be nice to have something other than fast food for a change."

The old woman studied him for a minute then turned and began to walk up the path into her yard. "Don't go thanking me yet," she said, placing her sunglasses back on her face and removing the work gloves from her pockets. "Never told you if I was a good cook or not."

She stopped suddenly and turned back to him. "Since you're gonna be living underneath my roof for a bit, you might as well tell me your name."

"It's Aaron," he said with a smile. "Aaron Corbet."

"Aaron," she said a few times, committing it to memory. "I'm Mrs. Provost—used to be Orville, but after my husband died in seventy-two, I figured I'd go back to my maiden name. Never cared for much he gave me, especially the name."

She continued on her way up the path, tugging the gloves on her hands as she walked.

"Well, are you?" he suddenly asked her.

She stopped and turned around with that nasty scowl decorating her face. "Am I what?" she asked, annoyed.

"Are you a good cook?" he asked with a grin.

Try as she might to hold it back, Mrs. Provost cracked a smile, but quickly turned around so Aaron could not see it for long. "Depends on who you ask," she said, picking up the pruning sheers from the steps leading to the front porch. "My husband thought I was pretty good—but look how he ended up."

"It's nice," Aaron said as he walked into the room and looked around.

The theme was grapes. There were grape lamp shades, a vase with grapevines painted on its side; even the bedspread had grapes on it. It was kind of funky, but he thought it was cool. Gabriel hobbled in and immediately found a place to lie down beside the queen-size bed where the warm sunlight streamed through the window.

"Is that where he'll sleep?" Mrs. Provost asked.

"The floor is good, but sometimes I like to sleep with Aaron," Gabriel barked.

"Is that where you'd like him to sleep?" Aaron asked with a sly smile.

"He can sleep wherever the hell he wants," she said, moving toward the closet. She opened the door and pulled out a white comforter adorned with grapes. "Just thought if he was going to sleep on the floor, he might be more comfortable lying on this."

As she approached, Gabriel got up and let her place the downy bedspread in the patch of sunlight. "There you go, boy," she said, smoothing out the material. "Give this a try."

And the dog did just that, lying back on the comforter with a heavy sigh of exhaustion.

"I think your dog's tired," she said, reading into her blue jeans pocket. She handed Aaron a key on an I-LOVE-MAINE chain. "Here's your key. It works on the front door, too, which I lock promptly at nine o'clock every night." Mrs. Provost moved toward the door. "I eat supper at six," she said as she walked out into the hall. "If you like meat loaf, I'll see you in the kitchen. If not, you're on your own."

"I like meat loaf," Gabriel yipped from his bed as the old woman closed the door behind her.

"Is there any food you *don't* like?" Aaron asked, kneeling down to check the injured leg.

"Never really thought about it," Gabriel replied thoughtfully.

"Tell you what," Aaron said, patting his head. "Why don't you give that question some serious thought while I go see if I can find Camael."

"Will you be all right?"

"I'll be fine." Aaron climbed to his feet and walked to the door. He was just about to leave when Gabriel called.

"Aaron, do you think we'll find Stevie here?"

Aaron thought for a moment, trying to make sense of the

odd feelings that were still with him. "I don't know. Let me poke around a little and we'll talk later." Then he left, leaving his best friend alone to rest and heal.

Aaron strolled casually up Berkely Street, taking in his surroundings. He turned left onto a street with no sign, committing landmarks to memory so he wouldn't get lost. Lots of quaint homes, nicely kept up, many with beautiful flower gardens more tame than Mrs. Provost's version of the Amazon rain forest.

At the end of the nameless street he stopped to assess his whereabouts. There was still no sign of Camael, and the bizarre sensation he'd been feeling since arriving in Blithe continued to trouble him. It felt as though he'd had too much caffeine after a late night of studying. He knew he had the ability to interpret this strange feeling, but he didn't know how to go about it. There was still so much he had to learn about this whole Nephilim thing.

"You will need to master these abilities," Camael had said during their ride to Blithe. *"Sooner rather than later."*

Aaron found the angel's words somewhat annoying. Mastering these so-called abilities was like reading a book without knowing the alphabet. He just didn't have the basics.

He recalled a moment not long after they'd first left Lynn. Camael had been describing how an angel experiences the five senses—not as individual sensations, but as one overpowering perception of everything around it. *"Do as I do,"* the angel had said to him, dosing his eyes, *"Feel the world and everything that makes it a whole, as only beings of our stature can."* Aaron had tried, but only ended up with a nasty headache. Camael had clearly been disappointed—apparently Aaron just wasn't turning out to be the Nephilim that the former leader of the Powers thought he should be. *Maybe it's not me the seer wrote about in the prophecy,* he thought. *Maybe Camael's finally realized this, and took off to find the fallen angels' real savior.*

Something rustled in a patch of wood behind him, and Aaron turned toward the noise. He noticed a glint of red in a patch of shadow and then, as if knowing that it had been discovered, a raccoon slowly emerged from its hiding place. *This is odd,* Aaron thought, watching the animal. *I thought raccoons are nocturnal.* He recalled how he'd hear them late at night through his bedroom window as they tried to get into the sealed trash barrels.

The raccoon moved closer, its large dark eye unwavering. It was moving strangely, and he wondered if it was rabid. *"Is that it?"* he asked aloud, knowing instinctively that the animal would understand him. *"Are you rabid?"*

The raccoon did not respond. It just continued to stare, and pad steadily closer.

As Aaron gazed into its eyes, an overwhelming sense of euphoria washed over him. It was all he could do to keep from bursting out in laughter and then breaking down in tears of sheer joy. He closed his eyes and swayed with the waves of emotion.

Stevie. His little brother was *here*—in Blithe, he was sure of it. Aaron could feel him, waiting to be picked up—embraced, played with. Stevie was unharmed, and that brought Aaron the greatest pleasure he had ever felt. Nothing would ever come between them again.

"Excuse me," a voice suddenly interrupted his reverie.

Aaron opened his eyes and saw that the odd raccoon was gone, replaced by a police officer who was eyeing him strangely. "Is there a problem sir?" the policeman asked him, moving closer, his hand clutching his gun belt.

Aaron swayed, feeling as though he'd been on a roller coaster. "I'm fine," he managed. *What just happened?*

"You don't seem fine," the officer barked. "You been drinking?" he asked, stepping closer to sniff Aaron's breath.

Aaron shook his head, feeling his strength and wits slowly returning. "No sir, I'm fine. I think I might have sunstroke or something."

"Can I ask you what you're doing here?"

"Actually, I'm looking for a friend of mine," Aaron said, bringing a hand up to his brow to wipe away beads of sweat. "Tall, silvery white hair and goatee, dressed in a dark suit?"

The policeman continued to watch him through his mirrored glasses. "I'd like to see some identification," he finally said, holding out his hand.

Aaron was getting nervous. First Camael disappears, then the strange raccoon—and now an evil sheriff. As he handed the police officer his license, he couldn't help but wonder what other surprises the town of Blithe had in store for him.

"Just passing through Blithe, Mr. Corbet?" the policeman asked, handing back his identification.

Aaron returned the license to his wallet. "I'll probably be here for a couple of days," he said, sliding his wallet into his back pocket. Sudden Aaron couldn't help himself; the attitude he had worked so hard to keep in check was rearing its ugly head. It had been the bane of his existence—he just couldn't learn to keep his mouth shut. "Is there a problem, Officer . . . ?" he asked, an edge to his tone.

"Dexter," the policeman said, touching the rim of his hat. *"Chief of Police* Dexter. And no, there isn't any problem—now." He smiled, but Aaron saw little emotion in it. If anything, it appeared more like a snarl than a smile. "Blithe is a quiet town, Mr. Corbet, and it's my job to make sure it stays that way, if you catch my meaning."

Aaron nodded, biting his tongue. After all, he was a stranger, and evidently that made him immediately suspect.

Chief Dexter began to walk toward a cruiser parked by the side of the road nearby. Aaron had been so caught up in the bizarre spell of raw emotion that he hadn't even heard the policeman pull up. He looked back to the wooded area. "Chief Dexter?" he called.

The policeman stopped, his hand on the door handle of his cruiser.

"You didn't happen to see a raccoon when you pulled up here, did you?" Aaron asked.

Dexter pulled open the door, and the squawk from his radio drifted out to fill the still air of the neighborhood. He smiled that nasty, snarling smile again before easing himself into the driver's seat. "No raccoons around this time of day, Mr. Corbet. They're nocturnal."

"Thought so." Aaron nodded. He stared at the police officer. There was something about him . . .

"Enjoy your visit, Mr. Corbet," Chief Dexter said. "Hope you find your friend," he added, before slamming closed the door of his car, banging a U-turn, and driving away.

From a woman who brought her dog in for its annual heartworm check, Katie McGovern learned that her former fiancé had been missing for at least four days. Apparently, the dog—an eight-year-old poodle named Tatty—had had an appointment for Monday morning, but no one had been in the office until Katie arrived that Wednesday afternoon. *It's very unlike Dr. Wessell to miss an appointment. I hope everything is all right,* the dog's middle-aged owner had said, her voice touched with concern.

Katie had made up a story about a family emergency that Kevin would have to deal with when he finally got back—*if he does,* said a nasty little voice at the back of her mind. She had tried to ignore the voice by cleaning up the office and catching up with Kevin's appointments. *From organization comes order,* her mother had always said. *And from order comes answers.* But the creeping unease she'd been feeling in the pit of her stomach since receiving that first e-mail from her former lover a little over two weeks ago continued to grow.

Think I've found something here that might interest you— care for a visit? Katie had thought it nothing more than another attempt by Kevin to get her back into his life, and she'd ignored the message—until she received another a few days later.

Not sure if I can handle this. Really need to see you. Please come.

There was a certain urgency in the communication that had piqued her curiosity. She had called him the next day, but there was no answer at the clinic. And when Kevin had failed to return the multiple messages she'd left on his home phone over several days, she'd decided to take some vacation time and head to Maine. They may have broken up nearly two years earlier, but it didn't mean they weren't still friends.

The office had been in complete disarray—Kevin did have a tendency to become easily distracted. In fact it was a *distraction* with another woman that had brought an end to their relationship. But this was different.

Katie glanced at her watch; it was nearly six, and she felt as though she hadn't stopped to breathe all afternoon—between appointments, trying to bring order to the place, and figure out where Kevin had gone. She thought of Aaron Corbet. He seemed just the person to help her keep the practice afloat during Kevin's absence.

She snatched up his dog's file from the corner of the desk and casually began to review it. The words "raccoon bite" stuck out like a sore thumb. Katie had seen many bites in her years as a vet—and Gabriel's hadn't been caused by any raccoon. She wasn't even sure if the bite had come from anything that walked on four legs. In fact, the wound looked as though it might have been made by a small child. *Something else to add to the strangeness of Blithe,* she thought.

The veterinarian sighed and closed the folder. She moved to the file cabinet next to the desk and pulled open the drawer. Katie added Gabriel's file to the others she had organized and tried to slide it closed. But something was blocking it. She reached in and felt behind the drawer. Sometimes a file slipped out of place and became wedged in the sliding track. Her hand closed on what felt like a book. She tugged it free and slammed the drawer shut.

Probably some veterinary journal, she mused, bringing it to the desk to take a look. It was a journal, all right, but one of a far more personal nature: Kevin's journal. She remembered him writing in it each night before bed. It was something he had started in college. *Helps me get my thoughts in order,* he had told her one night when she'd asked him about the habit.

She flipped through the entries and stopped at the one dated June 1:

> Saw another one today on my hike. I'd swear they
> were watching me. Gives me the creeps. Wonder
> what Katie would think.

That was right about the time she had received his first e-mail. With a churning sensation in the pit of her stomach, Katie turned to the date closest to the last message he had sent:

> June 8: Found another one and put it in the freezer
> with the rest. Don't know what the cause is. Don't
> want to alarm the locals YET. Never in all my years
> have I seen anything like it. I wonder if it has anything
> to do with how strangely the local fauna's been
> acting lately. I still swear they're watching me. I need
> somebody else to see this—somebody I trust.
> I'm going to ask Katie to come. I'm feeling a little
> spooked right now, and it'll be good to see her.

"What the hell are you talking about?" Katie said to the journal, her frustration on the rise. It was the last entry and, like the others, it told her very little.

Katie tossed the journal onto the desktop and thought about what she had read. "You found something and put it in the freezer," she said to herself, chewing at the end of her fingernail. Her eyes scanned the reception area, and she bolted to her feet. "All right, let's take a look, then." She hadn't seen a freezer, although most veterinarians kept large units to store deceased animals, tissue samples, and other specimens. *There must be one around here somewhere,* she thought.

She moved away from the desk and strolled down the hallway past the examination room. At the end of the hall was a door that she had originally thought was to a maintenance closet. Katie grabbed hold of the doorknob, turned it, and found herself looking down a flight of wooden steps that disappeared into the darkness of a cellar.

She felt for a light switch along the wall and, finding none, used the cool stone for a guide as she carefully descended. At the foot of the stairs she could just make out the iridescent shape of a lightbulb that seemed to be suspended in the darkness. She reached out, fumbled for the chain, and gave it a good yank.

The bulb came to life, illuminating the cool storage area dug out from the rock and dirt beneath the building's foundation. She recognized Kevin's mountain bike, ski equipment, and even a canoe, but it was the freezer in the far corner that attracted her interest. Plugged into a heavy-duty socket beneath a gray metal electrical box, the white unit sat atop some wooden pallets, humming quietly.

Maneuvering around winter coats hanging from pipes,

Katie approached the freezer. She stood in front of the oblong unit, feeling a faint aura of cold radiating from the white box. Her fingers began to tingle in anticipation as she slowly reached for the cover.

"Let's see what spooked you, Kev," she said in a whisper, lifting up the lid. A cloud of freezing air billowed up, and she breathed the cold gas into her lungs, coughing. The distinctive aroma of frozen dead things filled the air, and she took note of the red biohazard symbols on the bags lying along the freezer bottom. She leaned into the chest, reaching down to pick up one of the bags. It was covered in a fine frost, masking its contents, and Katie brushed away the icy coating so she could see within the thick biohazard container. The thing inside the bag stared back with eyes frozen wide in death.

"Holy crap," Katie McGovern said as she studied the specimen through the plastic bag. A creeping unease ran up and down the length of her spine, making her shudder. "No wonder you were freaked out."

INTERLUDE TWO

Stevie Stanley huddled in a dark corner of his mind, trying with all his might to hold on to the things that made him who he was—those pockets of recollection, moments that had left their indelible marks on his fragile psyche. But the excruciating pain was systematically ripping those memories away. One after another they disappeared: the blue, blue sky filled with birds; the black-and-gray static on the television screen; the yellow dog running in the yard with a red ball in his mouth; Mom and Dad holding him, kissing him. And Aaron—his protector, his playmate—so beautiful.

So beautiful.

Seven Archons surrounded the child's writhing body and continued the ritual that so often ended with the death of the subject. Stevie fought wildly against his restraints as Archon Jaldabaoth painted the symbols of transfiguration upon his pale, naked skin, muttering sounds and words that a human mouth could never manage. Archon Oraios stabbed a long, gold needle into the child's stomach and depressed the plunger to implant the magickal seeds of change.

The sigils on Stevie's flesh then began to rise, to smolder—to burn. The boy screamed wildly as his body was racked with the painful changes. Archon Jao placed a delicate hand over the child's mouth to silence his irksome cries. Things were proceeding nicely, and the Archons waited patiently as the transformation progressed.

Soon there would be nothing left of Stevie. His memory of Aaron burned the brightest, its loving warmth providing some insulation against the agony his tiny, seven-year-old body was forced to endure. Aaron would come for him. Aaron would rescue him from the pain; he need only hold on to what little he still had.

Archon Sabaoth was the first to notice. He tilted his head and listened. Sounds were coming from the child's body—other than the muffled screams of his discomfort. Cracking, grinding, ripping, and tearing sounds: the boy's body had begun to change—to grow—to mature beyond his seven years. This was the most dangerous part of the ritual, and the Archons studied their subject with unblinking eyes, searching for signs that the magicks might have gone awry.

Archon Katspiel remembered a subject whose bone structure had grown disproportionately, leaving the poor creature hideously deformed. Its mind had been so psychologically damaged by the pain that they'd had no choice but to order Archon Domiel to put it out of its misery. It had been a shame, really, for that subject had shown great potential—almost as much as this latest effort.

Stevie held on as long as he could, clutching at the final memory of his brother, friend, and protector—but it was slipping away, piece by jagged piece. He wanted to hold on to it, to remember the beautiful face of the boy who had promised never to leave him, but the pain—there was so much of it. *What was the boy's name?* he wondered as he curled up within himself, no longer knowing the question, no longer caring. It didn't matter. Now there was only pain. He was the pain—and the pain was he.

Archon Erathaol unlocked the manacles around the subject's chafed wrists and ankles while the others watched. *The ritual appears to have been successful,* he mused as they watched the subject curl into a fetal position on the floor of the solarium. What had once been a frail child was now a mature adult, his body altered to physical perfection, and his sensitivity to the preternatural greatly augmented. The Archons had succeeded in their task.

Verchiel would be pleased.

CHAPTER SIX

I t was quite possibly the best meat loaf Aaron had ever had. He shoveled the last bit of mashed potatoes and peas into his mouth, leaving a good bite of meat loaf uneaten. Gabriel lay beside his chair looking up pathetically, a puddle of drool between his paws.

Aaron looked at Mrs. Provost across the kitchen table. She was sipping a cup of instant coffee—*made with the coffee bags, not that granule crap,* she had informed him.

"Do you mind?" he asked, pointing at the piece of meat covered in dark brown gravy and motioning toward the dog.

"I don't care," she said, taking a sip of her coffee. "Would have given him his own plate if you'd'a let me."

Aaron picked up the meat and gave it to Gabriel. "He had his supper, and besides, too much people-food isn't good for him," he said as the dog greedily gobbled the meat from his fingers, making certain to lick every ounce of grease and gravy from the digits. "Makes him gassy."

"Are you trying to embarrass me?" Gabriel grunted licking his chops.

Aaron laughed and ruffled the yellow dog's velvety soft ears.

"That's something I can relate to," the old woman said, hauling herself up from her seat. "Some days I feel like that blimp for the tires, I'm so full a' gas."

Aaron stifled a laugh.

She reached across the table for his plate and stacked it atop hers. "Meal couldn't a' been too bad," she said, staring at his empty plate. "I don't even have to wash this one," she said with a wise smirk.

"Didn't mean to be a pig," Aaron said as Mrs. Provost took the dirty dishes to the sink. "It was really good. Thanks again."

She turned on the water and started washing the dishes. Aaron thought about asking if he could do that for her, but something told him she would probably just say something nasty, so he kept his offer to himself. When she wanted him to do something, he was certain she wouldn't be shy in asking.

"I was cooking for myself, anyway," Mrs. Provost said, wiping one of the dinner plates with a sponge shaped like an apple. "And besides, it's kinda nice to have company to supper every once in a while."

Aaron wondered if the old woman was lonely since the

death of her husband. He hadn't seen any evidence of children or grandchildren.

"Then again, cooking for somebody else can be a real pain in the ass after a while . . . makes you remember why you was eatin' by yourself in the first place."

Well, maybe she was just fine after all. . . .

She left the dishes in the strainer and hung the damp towel over the metal rack attached to the front of the cabinet below the sink. Then she returned to the table to finish her coffee. Aaron wasn't sure if he should thank her and go to his room, or stay and chat. The kitchen was quiet except for the hum of the refrigerator in the corner and Gabriel's rhythmic breathing as he drifted off to sleep.

"Where you from, Aaron?" Mrs. Provost abruptly asked as she brought her coffee mug to her mouth.

"I'm from Lynn—Lynn, Massachusetts," he clarified.

"Didn't think it was Lynn, North Dakota," the old woman replied, setting her mug down on the gray speckled tabletop. "The city of sin, huh? Family there?"

His expression must have changed dramatically, because he saw a look of uncertainty in her eyes. He didn't want her to feel bad, so he responded the best way he knew how. "I did," he said as he looked at his hands lying flat on the table. "They died in a fire a few weeks back."

"I'm sorry," Mrs. Provost said, gripping her coffee cup in both hands.

Aaron smiled at her. "It's all right," he said. "Really. It's why I'm in Maine right now. You know, change of scenery to try to clear my head."

She nodded. "Thought about leaving here once myself— about the time I met my husband," she said, a faraway look in her eye. "Never did, though. Ended up getting married instead."

Mrs. Provost abruptly stood and brought her coffee mug to the sink. Gabriel awoke with a start and lifted his head from the floor, wanting to be sure he wasn't missing anything. Aaron reached down and stroked the top of his head. "So you never left Blithe?" he asked her as she rinsed the cup.

"Nope." She put the cup in the drainer with the other dishes. "But I often think about what might've happened if I had—if my life woulda been different."

It was becoming uncomfortable in the kitchen, and Aaron found himself blurting out a question before he could think about it. "Do you have any children?"

Mrs. Provost wiped her hands on the dish towel and began to straighten up her countertop. "I have a son—Jack. He lives with his wife and daughter in San Diego." She had retrieved the apple sponge from the sink and was wiping down the tops of her canister set. "We were never that close, my son and I," she said. "After Luke died—that was my husband—we just grew further and further apart."

"Have you ever gone to visit them?" Aaron asked, suspecting he already knew the answer.

"Nope," she said, wiping the countertop for a second time. "They bought me one of those computers last year for Christmas so we could keep in touch with e-mail and all, but I think that Internet is up to something. That and the Home Shopping Network."

"You have a computer?" Aaron was suddenly excited. It had been days since he'd last had an opportunity to check his e-mail and communicate with Vilma.

"It's what I said, isn't it?" Mrs. Provost pointed toward the parlor. "It's in the office off the parlor," she said. "My son insists on paying for Internet service even though I never touch the thing. You can use it if you want."

"Thanks," he said.

"But don't go looking up no porno," she warned, placing the apple sponge back where it belonged beside the sink. "I don't tolerate no porno in this house—that and the Home Shopping Network."

Camael knew that he wasn't in Aerie, but a voice in his mind tried to convince him it was so.

"Calm yourself, angel," said the hissing presence nestled within his fervid thoughts. *"This is what you have sought."*

He wanted so much to believe it, to succumb to the wishes of the comforting tongue and finally let down his defenses.

"Welcome to Aerie, Camael," it cooed. *"We've been waiting so long for you to arrive."*

An image of Aaron—the Nephilim—flickered in his mind. *If this is indeed Aerie, he'll need to be brought here,* Camael thought as he attempted to move within the thick, viscous fluid surrounding him. Muscular tendrils tightened around his body, holding him firm.

"*There is no need for concern,*" the voice spoke soothingly. "*The boy will come in time. This is* your *moment, warrior. Let yourself go, and allow Aerie to be everything you have desired.*"

The membranous sack around him began to thrum, a rhythmic pulsing meant to lull him deeper into complacency. The heartbeat of asylum.

"*Let your guard down, angel,*" the voice ordered. "*You cannot possibly experience all you have yearned for—until you give yourself completely to me.*"

Deep down, Camael knew this was wrong. He wanted to fight it, to summon a sword of fire and burn away the insensate cloud that seemed to envelop his mind—but he just didn't have the strength.

"*Your doubts are an obstacle, warrior. Lay them aside—know the serenity you have striven to achieve.*"

No longer able to fight, Camael did as he was told—and the great beast that pretended to be the voice of sanctuary—

It began to feed.

After a few more hours of small talk, Aaron was finally able to get to the computer when Mrs. Provost announced that she was going to bed. He slid the mouse smoothly across the surface of the bright blue pad and clicked on Send. "There," he said, as his e-mail disappeared into cyberspace on its way to Vilma.

"What did you say?" asked Gabriel, who rested on the floor of the cramped office.

"Nothing, really," Aaron shrugged. He began to shut the computer down. "I told her I was thinking about her and that I hope she's doing okay. Small talk—that's all."

"You like this female, don't you, Aaron?"

"I don't like to think about that stuff, Gabriel," he said, turning off the computer and leaning back in the office chair. He ran his fingers through his dark hair. "Verchiel and his goons would like nothing more than to get even with me by going after Vilma. For her own good, e-mail's the closest I'm getting for a real long time." He paused, wishing he could change things. Then he shook his head. "It's the best way."

"At least you can talk on the computer," Gabriel said, trying to be positive.

Aaron stood and switched off the light. "Yeah, I guess that's something," he said, and the two quietly left the office, making their way up to their room.

Once inside, Aaron undressed and prepared for bed. "Are you going to sleep with me or are you staying on the floor?" he asked the dog.

Gabriel padded toward the comforter on the floor and gave it a sniff, *"I think I'll sleep here tonight,"* he said as he walked in a circle before plopping himself down in the comforter's center.

Aaron pulled back the covers on the bed and crawled beneath them. "Well, if you want to come up, wake me and I'll help you."

"I'll be fine down here. This way I can stretch out and I don't have to worry about kicking you and hurting my leg."

Aaron switched off the light by the bed and said good night to his best friend. He hadn't realized how tired he was. His eyes quickly grew heavy, and he felt himself drifting away on the sea of sleep.

"What if he doesn't come back?" Gabriel suddenly asked, his words startling Aaron back to consciousness.

"What was that, Gabe?" Aaron asked sleepily.

"Camael," the dog said. *"What if Camael doesn't come back? What are we going to do then?"*

It was a good question, and one that Aaron had been avoiding since the angel came up missing that afternoon. What would he do without Camael's guidance? He thought of the alien power that existed within him, and his heart began to race. "I wouldn't worry about it, pally," he said, taking his turn to be positive. "He's probably doing angel stuff somewhere. That's all. He'll be back before we know it."

"Angel stuff," Gabriel repeated once, and then again. *"You're probably right,"* he said, temporarily satisfied. *"We'll see him tomorrow."*

"That's it," Aaron said, again closing his eyes, which felt as though they'd been turned to lead. "We'll see him tomorrow."

And before he was even aware, Aaron was pulled beneath the sea of sleep, sinking deeper and deeper into the black abyss of unconsciousness, with nary a sign of struggle.

But something was waiting.

Aaron couldn't breathe.

The grip of nightmare held him fast, and no matter how he fought to awaken, he could not pull himself free of the clinging miasma of terror.

He was encased in a fleshy sack—a cocoon of some kind, and from its veined walls was secreted a foul-smelling fluid. Aaron struggled within the pouch, the milky substance rising steadily to lap against his chin. Soon it would cover his face, filling his mouth and nostrils—and he began to panic. Then he felt something in the sack with him, something that wrapped around his arms and legs, trying to keep his flailing to a minimum. Aaron knew it wanted to hold him in its constricting embrace so the fluid could immerse him completely in its foulness. His body grew numb.

"No," he cried out as some of the thick, gelatinous substance splashed into his mouth. It tasted of death, and left his flesh dulled.

He'd had similar dreams when his angelic abilities had first started to manifest. He didn't care for them then—and cared even less for them now. He intensified his battle to be free of it, but the nightmare did not relent, continuing to hold him fast in its grip.

Aaron was completely submerged now, the warm fluid engulfing him, lulling him to a place where he could quit all struggle. And it almost succeeded.

Almost.

Suddenly, in his mind, he saw a sword of light. It was the most magnificent weapon he had ever seen. Never in all his imaginings could he have built a sword so mighty and large. It was as if the weapon had been forged from one of the rays of the sun.

And as he reached for it, its unearthly radiance shone brighter, and brighter still—burning away the liquid-filled cocoon that held him and the nightmare-realm it inhabited.

He awoke with a start, his body drenched with sweat. Gabriel had joined him on the bed, and his dark brown eyes glistened eerily in a strange light that danced around the room.

"Gabriel, what . . . ?" he began breathlessly.

"Nice sword," the dog said simply.

Fully awake now, Aaron realized that he held something in his left hand. Slowly he turned his gaze toward it—toward what he had brought back from the realm of nightmare.

A blade of the sun.

CHAPTER SEVEN

What do you think it means?" Gabriel asked from the foot of the bed as Aaron stepped from the shower and grabbed a fresh shirt.

He pushed his arms through the sleeves and pulled the red T-shirt down over his stomach. "It was kind of like the dreams I had before this whole Nephilim thing blew up," he said, fingering his hair in the mirror and deciding that he looked fine. "Where I was experiencing old memories that didn't belong to me."

"*Like the sword?*" the dog asked.

Aaron shuddered as he remembered the amazing sight of the sword that he seemed to have brought over from the dream. He knew he was not responsible for the creation of the blade. He was certain that it belonged to someone of great importance, but the question was who—and why had the weapon been given to him. It had only stayed with him for a short time. As if sensing it was no longer needed, it had dispersed in an explosion of blinding light. "Just like the sword," Aaron finally replied. "And like the dreams, I think it was given to help me."

"I thought it was all very scary," Gabriel said, and sighed as he rested his snout between his paws.

"I agree," Aaron said, sitting beside the dog to put on his sneakers, "but it all has something to do with this town."

"Is this a mystery?" Gabriel asked, his floppy ears suddenly perky.

Aaron laughed and gave the dog's head a rub. "It certainly is. Listen, I've got to go to the clinic this morning, but you need to stay here and give that leg a chance to heal. Why don't you think about all our clues and see if you can come up with some answers."

"I've always wanted to solve a mystery," Gabriel said happily.

"All right there, Scooby." Aaron gave the dog another pet and headed for the door.

"Scooby?" the dog said, his head tilted at a quirky angle.

"He's a dog on television, very good at solving mysteries." Gabriel's head tilted the other way.

"Never mind," Aaron said as he stepped out into the hall. "It's not important. I'll see you this afternoon."

"Have a good day, Shaggy," he heard the dog say as he closed

the door. And he began to laugh, marveling again at how smart his friend had actually become.

Aaron was busy at the veterinary clinic from the moment he stepped through the door. He didn't think it possible for a town so small to have that many animals in need of care. Stitches, rabies shots, heartworm tests, a broken forepaw—you name it, he and Katie dealt with it that morning and well into the afternoon.

It feels good to be working with animals again, Aaron thought as he restrained a particularly feisty Scottish terrier, by the name of Mike, who was having some blood drawn.

"No hurt! No hurt!" the little dog yelped as his owner looked on, concern in her eyes.

"It's okay," Aaron said to the dog. "When the doctor is done, you can have a cookie and go home. All right?"

The dog immediately stopped its struggling.

"That's it," Katie said, placing the vial on the counter and turning to the owner. "I'll send this out to the lab this afternoon and give you a call as soon as I know something."

Aaron handed Mike back to his owner and escorted them into the lobby to settle the bill. "And don't forget this," he said, holding out a treat as the woman turned to leave.

The woman smiled, and Mike greedily devoured the cookie.

"I never lie," Aaron said to the dog with a wink and bid them both good-bye.

"Next victim," Katie said wearily, coining out of the examination room.

For the first time that day, the waiting room was empty.

"We're good right now," Aaron told her. "Next one's"—he glanced at the appointment book—"a rabies shot at four. Gives us two hours to catch up."

"You know, you're really good with them," Katie said, leaning against the desk.

"Why, thank you, doctor," Aaron said, smiling. "I enjoy the work."

"No really, they seem to trust you. It's a talent you don't see so often."

"Well, let's just say I speak their language," he said with a grin.

Katie shook her head and looked at her watch. "You say we've got two hours before the next appointment?"

Aaron nodded.

She moved toward the door, took a ring of keys from her pocket, and locked the front door. "What's up?" he asked, a little surprised.

"Being a fellow stranger in this burg, I've got something I want to show you," she said, moving past him and down the hall. "It's in the basement."

Aaron followed her to the door at the end of the hall. There was a sudden tension in the air that hadn't been there before, and it concerned him. "Does this have anything to do with your old boyfriend?" he asked.

"Yeah," she said with a slight nod. "I think it might." She opened the door and started down the creaking wooden steps into the darkness. "Kevin contacted me, asking me to come to Blithe to help him with something, but he wasn't exactly clear as to what the problem was."

At the foot of the stairs she reached out into the inky darkness and pulled the chain for the light, dispelling the darkness to the far corners of the underground room. "So I show up and I find him missing," she continued, as she waited for Aaron to join her. "The office is in disarray. He hasn't been here for appointments for at least four days." Katie ran a trembling hand across her forehead.

Aaron's curiosity was piqued, but something was clearly upsetting Katie, and that was cause for concern.

"Yes, he was a bit of a flake, and that's part of the reason we're no longer together, but he took his job very seriously. I even went to the police to file a missing person's report, but Chief Dexter said I should give it some time—how did he put it? 'Just in case he's out sowing his wild oats.'" The vet laughed with little humor.

"What did you find, Katie?" Aaron asked quietly.

She glanced at him, then turned toward an old freezer in the corner. "First I found his journal, and it mentioned—*things* he had found in town."

"What kinds of things?"

Taking a deep breath, Katie crossed the cellar to the freezer. Aaron followed close behind her.

"Wrong things," she said, pulling open the lid on the unit. "See for yourself."

Katie reached inside the frosty innards of the freezer and withdrew a plastic bag. She let the lid slam shut, then placed the bag on top and opened it, spilling out the frozen contents. The corpse of an animal fell onto the hood with a heavy thud, and Aaron recoiled, startled and a bit repulsed. "What is it?" he whispered as he studied the frost-covered body.

It was the size of an average house cat and bore some resemblance to—of all things—a raccoon, but it wasn't either. Not really. The body was covered in long, gray fur, but the limbs were scaled, like a fish. Curved talons like that of some bird of prey grew from three of its feet—the fourth ended in a stunted tentacle.

"What is it?" Aaron asked again, unable to pull his eyes from the freakish sight.

"Your guess is as good as mine," Katie replied. She pulled a pen from her lab coat pocket and began to poke at the corpse. "This wouldn't happen to be what bit your dog, would it?"

Aaron shook his head. It was as ugly as an Orisha, but it had no connection to Gabriel's injury.

"Looks to be a little bit of everything—a real evolutionary blend." Katie shrugged and continued. "We've got some bird and rodent attributes, as well as fish—and there's also a little bit of cephalopod thrown in for good measure." She pulled the pen away and wiped it against her pants leg. "And that's just *this* one."

He looked at her hard. "There's more?" he asked uneasily.

She nodded, gesturing at the freezer. "There are at least seven others in there—each more grotesque than the last. One, *maybe* two, could pass as a random Mother Nature having a bad day—but this many?"

"What do you think it means?" Aaron asked, gazing at the monstrosity atop the freezer and imagining with disgust how the ones inside looked.

"What do I think it means?" Katie repeated. She started to put the pen back in her pocket, then seemed to think better of it and tossed it into an old barrel beside the furnace. "I think something in this town is making monsters."

Aaron and Katie hurried up the cellar steps, as if the disturbing creatures in the freezer had suddenly come to life and were chasing them. Quietly, lost in their own thoughts, they returned to the lobby, where Katie unlocked the front door.

"So you can see why I'm a little freaked," she said, rubbing her arms with the palms of her hands as if to eliminate a winter's chill.

"Do you have any idea what's causing it?" Aaron asked, leaning against the reception desk. The memory of the previous night's dream and his run-in with the strange raccoon yesterday suddenly flooded his mind and made him flinch. *Could this somehow be connected?*

"It appears to be some kind of mutation," Katie was saying. She had walked around the desk and was pulling open the bottom drawer. She fished around inside for a moment, then removed an unopened package of Oreos. She tore open the bag and stuffed one in her mouth. "Sorry," she said, her mouth full. She offered him the bag. "I have an incredible craving for these when I'm stressed."

Aaron took a few cookies as Katie continued with her theory.

"Maybe some kind of illegal chemical dumping or drug manufacturing." Katie nibbled like a squirrel on an Oreo, eyes gazing off into space. "Something that could change an animal on a genetic level . . ."

"Here?" Aaron asked, surprised. "Is there even any industry around here big enough to cause that kind of damage?"

Katie finished her cookie and grabbed another one. "Not anymore, but there used to be a business in town that made boats. It was Blithe's major employer until it closed about fifteen years ago. The abandoned factory is still standing out by the water. Evidently the owners wanted to expand, but the land there is unstable because of underwater caves that honeycomb the coast. So they took the company to California."

"What, are you an expert on Blithe? I thought you were from Illinois." Aaron laughed, licking the crumbs from his fingertips.

Katie shrugged. "I was going to move here with Kevin before the split, so I did some research."

"You think some kind of toxic waste from the boat factory seeped into the soil?" Aaron reached for another Oreo.

"When I first came into town the other night, I got a little lost and found myself on the road that leads to the old factory." She closed up the bag and returned it to the drawer. "There was an awful lot of activity around there, especially for a place that's supposedly abandoned. I think there's something going on in Blithe, and I think my ex figured that out and that's why he's disappeared."

Aaron recalled his run-in with chief of police. *Is it paranoia talking now, or does this tiny, seaside town really have a deep, dark secret?* he wondered. But there was something—something that seemed to speak to the inhuman side of his nature. It had spoken to Camael as well, and now, like Katie's former boyfriend, he, too, was missing. "Maybe you should go to the state police," he suggested. "That would probably be the smartest thing to do, especially if you think that Kevin might have—"

Katie shook her head emphatically. "No, not yet. I've got to be sure of the details before I start making crazy accusations."

Aaron felt a knot begin to form in the pit of his stomach. "And those details are . . . ?"

"I want to check out the factory—tonight."

The knot in his gut grew uncomfortably tighter. "I'm not sure that's a good idea, Katie."

"It's the only way I can think of to prove that something's up here. Don't worry," she added with a nervous grin. "I'll be fine. I'll just poke around a little, get the evidence I need, and be back here in no time."

Alarm bells were ringing in Aaron's head, but he doubted there was anything he could say to sway the woman's resolve. The voice of reason told him he was going to seriously regret what he was about to say, but he hated the idea of Katie going alone even more. "I'll go with you," he said quickly, before he could change his mind.

Katie approached him, a look of genuine gratitude in her eyes. "You don't have to," she said, and reached out to touch his shoulder. "This is something *I* have to do, just in case Kevin—"

"No, I'm going with you," Aaron interrupted. He shrugged. "After all we out-of-towners have to stick together."

Before they could say any more, the door opened and a mother and two children entered with a pet carrier containing a yowling cat.

"The four o'clock, I'd guess," Aaron said, looking at his watch. "A little early."

"Thank you, Aaron." Katie looked hard into his eyes before stepping out from behind the counter to escort the family into the examination room. "What would I do without you?"

CHAPTER EIGHT

Gabriel awoke with a start.

He'd been dreaming about chasing a rabbit through a dense forest, weaving and ducking beneath thick bushes and low-hanging branches, when his drowsing reverie turned unexpectedly to nightmare. The rabbit had stopped and spun around to glare at him with eyes that did not seem right. They were unusually dark, almost liquid in their shininess, and when they blinked, a milky coating seemed to briefly cover them. Gabriel had seen many rabbits in his years—but never one that looked like this. It was wrong—the bunny was wrong.

Its body had begun to writhe—to undulate as if something inside of it were trying to get out. Slowly, cautiously, Gabriel had backed away, growling in his most menacing tone. The animal lay flat on the ground. Its body had continued to pulse and vibrate, its scary eyes never leaving the dog. Gabriel barked: a succession of sharp staccato bursts and snarls, hoping to scare the rabbit away. He had wanted to run, but didn't want to turn his back on the creature. *How embarrassing,* he had thought in the grip of his nightmare, *to be chased by a rabbit.*

The rabbit had suddenly stopped moving, although its unwavering gaze never left Gabriel. Slowly its mouth began to open—wider—and wider still. The dog heard a disturbing wet crack as the animal's jaw popped from its socket. He wanted to run—but he was afraid. The rabbit's lower jaw dangled awfully, its mouth a gaping chasm of darkness. From within, the sound of movement came. Gabriel had whined with fear and was turning to flee, when something exploded from the rabbit's body. . . .

Still shaken from the disturbing dream, Gabriel glanced about the room from his post atop the bed, nose twitching—searching the air for anything out of the ordinary. Everything seemed to be fine, but then he caught a whiff of something that made his mouth begin to water. Food, and if his senses could be trusted, it was meat loaf. He'd had his breakfast and half an apple before Aaron left for work, but the thought of a snack was quite alluring.

Gabriel turned to sniff at the wound on his leg. Aaron had wanted him to stay off of it, but it was feeling much better. The dog jumped to the floor and stretched the hours of inactivity from his limbs. It felt good, and he barely noticed any discomfort. He walked around the room in a circle, just to be certain. There was a little tightness in the muscles of his thigh, but nothing that could prevent him from heading downstairs for a handout.

He stood at the door and hopped up on his back legs to take the doorknob tightly in his mouth. Slowly, he turned his head, pulling ever so slightly until the door came open. Gabriel made his way down the hallway and carefully descended the stairs. At the foot of the steps, he again sniffed, pinpointed the kitchen as the source of his treat, and made a beeline for the doorway.

Mrs. Provost was sitting at the kitchen table and was about to take a bite from a meat loaf sandwich when Gabriel appeared.

"Well, look who it is," she said with a hint of a smile. She took a large bite and began to chew.

Gabriel padded into the kitchen, tail wagging, nails clicking on the linoleum floor. His eyes were fixed on the plate of food, and he licked his chops hungrily.

"Now don't go giving me the hungry horrors routine," Mrs. Provost said as she wiped her mouth with a paper napkin and looked away. "Aaron said I wasn't to give you anything, even if you came begging."

He watched closely as she took another bite of the delicious-looking meat-and-bread combination. *How can Aaron do this to me again?* he wondered, remembering the incident at the rest stop. He felt the saliva begin to drip from his mouth and land upon the floor beneath him.

"Don't stare at me," Mrs. Provost said, finishing the last of the first half. "He was very serious, made me promise and everything, so you might as well just go on back to your room." She picked up the other half.

Gabriel was sure he'd never been so hungry, and couldn't believe the woman wouldn't share even a small piece of her sandwich. It was very selfish. Remembering his success with the little girl and her family, he reached out with his mind to reassure the woman that Aaron wouldn't be mad if he was given only a bite.

I'm sure it would be fine if you gave me a bite of that sandwich.

Mrs. Provost convulsed violently as his mind gently brushed against hers. The table shook, spilling the cup of coffee next to her plate. Gabriel stepped back, startled.

She had set her sandwich down for a moment, but picked it up again, opening her mouth to take a bite. Again, Gabriel lightly prodded, suggesting that it would be very nice of her to share. She froze and gradually turned in her chair. His tail wagged in anticipation as he came closer. But the old woman stared at him, a strange expression on her face, as if she had never seen him before. She was still holding the sandwich in her hand, and he continued to hope that he would get some of it, but a primitive instinct told him that something was wrong.

He felt the hackles of fur on his back begin to rise. Quickly the dog looked about the kitchen for signs of danger, his nose twitching eagerly as he searched for a scent that was out of the ordinary. There was a hint of something, but he did not know what it was.

Mrs. Provost made a strange noise at the back of her throat, and the skin around her neck seemed to expand, like a bullfrog. And then she blinked, a slow, languid movement, and Gabriel saw that same milky covering over her eyes that he'd seen on the rabbit in his dream.

Suddenly he didn't care whether he got a bite of the meat loaf sandwich. He backed toward the doorway, never taking his eyes from the strange old woman. Her scent had changed. It was like the ocean—but older. He had to get to Aaron.

Gabriel spun around and bolted for the front door. Again, he jumped up and grabbed the knob with his teeth. He could hear sounds of the woman's approach behind him. The knob turned, and he heard the click of the latch—and another sound. The woman was coughing loudly, hard. Gabriel had just pulled the door open when he felt the first of the projectiles hit his left leg. He chanced a quick glance and saw a circular object, smaller than a tennis ball, covered in wet, glistening spines, sticking in his thigh. He wanted to pluck it out with his teeth, but feared the spines would hurt his mouth. *Aaron will get it out,* Gabriel thought as he turned back to the open door.

But Mrs. Provost was coughing again, and he felt the pricks of more barbs as they struck him. Suddenly the door seemed so very far away. *How can this be?* Gabriel wondered. He was running as fast as he could, yet he didn't seem to be going anywhere. It was all so confusing. A horrible numbness was spreading through his body, and he slumped to the floor in the doorway, his nose just catching a hint of the smells of the Maine town outside.

But there was something else that he smelled, and it came from the woman. Gabriel felt her hands roughly grab at him and drag his body back into the hallway. *It smells wrong,* he thought as he slowly drifted down into oblivion, *like something from the ocean.*

Like something bad *from the ocean.*

Aaron couldn't believe what he had committed himself to.

His thoughts raced as he let himself into Mrs. Provost's home. *I've got to be out of my mind.* But it was too late now; he had agreed to help Katie search the abandoned factory, and that was what he was going to do. *Who knows,* he thought, *maybe I'll be able to figure out why I've been feeling so strangely, or where Camael's gone, for that matter.*

"Mrs. Provost?" he called out, walking toward the kitchen. He was hoping for something to eat before his *Mission: Impossible* began. It would be just as easy to make a sandwich, but he wanted to be sure his host wasn't planning for something else.

He didn't want to annoy her; something told him that would be a bad thing.

The kitchen was empty, but he noticed a plate with a half-eaten meat loaf sandwich on the table. Aaron returned to the hallway and called again. "Mrs. Provost? Are you home?"

Getting no response, he decided to go upstairs and check on Gabriel. He would need to clean the dog's wound, then feed him, and most likely make himself something to eat before embarking on his nighttime maneuvers with Katie.

"Hey, Gabriel, how you feeling, boy . . . ," Aaron said as he pushed open the door and stepped into the room. His eyes fell upon the empty bed, then went to the comforter on the floor, and he saw with a growing unease that it, too, was missing his best friend. Aaron stepped farther into the room, leaving the door open wide behind him.

"Gabriel," he called again as he peered around the bed, finding nothing. He began to panic. Maybe the dog had injured himself so badly that he'd had to be taken to the veterinarian, which would also explain the half-eaten sandwich and Mrs. Provost's absence. Aaron decided to give Katie a call, just to be sure. He turned to the doorway and stopped.

Mrs. Provost stood in the hall, just outside the door.

"You scared me," Aaron said with a surprised smile. Almost immediately he knew something wasn't right. "What's wrong?" he asked, advancing toward her. "Where's Gabriel—is he all right?"

The woman did not respond. She simply stared at him oddly with eyes that seemed much darker than they had before.

"Mrs. Provost?" he asked, stopping in his tracks. Instincts that could only be connected to the inhuman part of his identity began to scream in warning. "Is there something . . ."

The old woman's neck suddenly swelled. She bent forward, coughed violently, and expelled something toward him.

The sword from his nightmare was suddenly in Aaron's hand, and instinctively he swatted aside the projectiles. Most exploded into dust upon contact with the blade of light, but pieces of some fell to the hardwood floor, and he tried to make sense of what he saw. They looked like fat grapes, fat grapes with sharp-looking quills sticking out of them.

The old woman grunted with displeasure, a wet gurgling sound like a stopped-up drainpipe, and he saw that her throat again had begun to expand. Aaron swung the blade of white light, directing its powerful radiance toward what he had been fooled into believing was a pretty cool old woman.

"No more," he heard himself say in a voice that did not sound at all like his.

The blade's luminescence bathed Mrs. Provost in its unearthly light, and her throat immediately deflated, expelling a noxious cloud of gas. Her callused hands rose to shield her eyes against the searing light, and he saw something that chilled the blood in his veins—a second eyelid.

Aaron advanced toward her. "What are you?" he asked,

his voice booming. "And where is my dog? Where is Gabriel?"

The woman crouched on the floor. His mind raced with the strangeness of it all, and he thought of the things frozen in the basement of the veterinary clinic. Is *it all connected?* he wondered, and a voice deep down inside him said that it was.

Mrs. Provost sprang from the floor, an inhuman hiss escaping her mouth as she lashed out at him, attempting to swat the blade away. The strangely sweet scent of burning flesh perfumed the air, and Aaron stumbled back, startled by the attack. The old woman screamed, but it sounded more like the squeal of an animal in pain. She threw herself from the room, clutching at her injured hand, where she had touched his weapon.

Aaron wished the awkward sword away and ran after her. Mrs. Provost was running erratically toward the stairs, as if she was no longer in control of her motor functions. He could only watch in horror as her feet became entangled and she tripped, tumbling down the stairs in a shrieking heap.

Aaron ran down the steps as the woman's body spilled limply into the foyer. He knelt beside her and reached to touch her neck for a pulse. Her heart rate was erratic, and her hand had begun to blister, but other than that, she seemed relatively unscathed. A low, murmuring gurgle escaped from her throat, and she began to writhe upon the floor.

Aaron reached down and pried open her mouth, keeping an eye on her throat for swelling. He tilted her head slightly so that he could see into her mouth. Something in the shadows at the back of her mouth scuttled away, escaping down her throat. Disturbingly enough, based on the quick glimpse, whatever it was reminded him of a hermit crab he'd once had as a pet. He quickly took his hands away.

Something was living inside Mrs. Provost. Again, he thought of the frozen animals in the freezer back at the clinic, their bodies changed—twisted into some new and monstrous form of life. He wondered if they, too, had something hiding away inside them.

He touched the woman's chin again, pulling open her mouth slightly. *"What are you?"* he asked, hoping that by using his preternatural gift of languages he could speak to the thing hiding away inside Mrs. Provost. If it worked on dogs and other animals, why not on this?

Her body shuddered, the flesh beneath her clothes beginning to writhe.

"What are you?" he asked again, more forcefully.

It started as a grumbling rumble in what seemed to be the old woman's stomach, and he watched with increasing horror as the bulge that formed in her abdomen traveled upward, toward her chest—and then her throat. The skin of her neck expanded, and Aaron immediately backed away. He was about to summon his weapon of light when Mrs. Provost's mouth snapped open and a horrible gurgling laugh filled the air, followed by an equally chilling voice.

"What am I?" it asked in a language composed of buzzes and clicks. *"I am Leviathan. And we are legion."*

INTERLUDE THREE

"C ome," a voice boomed in the darkness, echoing through the endless void that had become his being. *"Hear my voice and come to me."*

Stevie knew not why, but he found himself responding, drawn to the powerful sound that invaded his solitude. It reverberated through his cocoon of shadow, touching him, comforting him in ways that the darkness could not.

"Oblivion shall claim you no longer."

And then there was a light, burning through the ebony pitch—and he winced, turning his face away, blinded by its awesome intensity.

"Fear not the light of my righteousness," the voice said. *"There is a powerful purpose awaiting you beyond the stygian twilight—work to be done."*

And the radiance continued to grow, consuming the

darkness, pulling him from the embrace of shadow and into the heart of illumination.

"Come to me," said the voice, so very close. *"And be reborn."*

Reborn.

Verchiel knelt before he who mere moments before had been a child. Silently the Archons watched as the angel held the face of the magickally augmented boy in both hands and gazed into eyes vacant of awareness.

"Do you hear me?" he asked. "Your lord and master has need of you."

The angel examined the magnificently muscled body of the boy-turned-man, pleased with the work of his magicians. The arcane symbols that had been painted, then burned into his naked flesh, had formed permanent scars decorating the perfect physique. These were marks that would set him apart from all others; symbols that proved he had been touched by the divine, transformed into something that transcended simple humanity.

Again, Verchiel looked into the eyes of the man. "I call upon you to come forth. There is so much to be done," he whispered. Lovingly he touched the man's expressionless face, running his long, delicate fingers through the blond, sweat-dampened hair. "I have need of you," he hissed, leaning his mouth close to the man's own. "The Lord God has need of you."

Verchiel brought a hand to the man's chin, pulled open

his mouth, and blew lightly into the open maw, an icy blue flame briefly illuminating the cavern of the open mouth. The body of the man, who had once been Stevie, twitched once and then was still. Verchiel continued to stare, willing the man to consciousness, a vacant shell ready to be shaped into a tool of surgical precision.

An instrument of redemption.

The man's body began to thrash, flopping about on the floor of the sunroom, and a smile languidly spread across Verchiel's pale, scarred features. "That's it," he cooed. "I'm waiting—we're all waiting."

Awareness suddenly flooded into the man's eyes, and his body went rigid with the shock of it. He began to scream, a high-pitched wail of rebirth that tapered off to a wheezing gasp as he rolled from side to side on the cold solarium floor.

Verchiel gestured toward the door, and several of his soldiers entered the room. They lifted the man, mewling and trembling, from the ground and held him aloft.

"Look at you," Verchiel said, a cold, emotionless smile on his face. "The potential for greatness emanates from you in waves." He held up a single, long, and pointed finger to the man who was crying pathetically. "But there is something missing. Something that will make you complete." He turned to the Archons, who held pieces of an armor the rich red color of spilt blood. "Dress him," the Powers' leader ordered.

And the magicians did as they were told, covering the

man's body in crimson metal forged in the fires of Heaven. When they completed their task, they stepped away, and Verchiel approached. Every inch of the man's transformed flesh was encased in bloodred metal—all except his head. He was a fearsome sight in his crimson suit of war, but he gazed pathetically at Verchiel, eyes streaming tears of fear and confusion.

"It's all so new to you now," Verchiel said, holding out his hands to the man. "But I will make it right." Fire appeared between the angel's outstretched hands, at first no bigger than the flame on the head of a match, then growing into a swirling fireball of orange. "I will teach you," the angel said as the fire grew darker, taking shape, solidifying into a helmet the matching color of lifeblood. "You shall be my tool of absolution." He placed the helmet over the man's head. "My implement of absolution."

Verchiel stepped back, admiring the fearful visage standing before him, clad in the color of pulsing rage. "Malak—," he said, extending his hand, introducing those around him to the newest weapon in their arsenal. "Hunter of false prophets."

CHAPTER NINE

In the apartment above the clinic, Katie was lost in her thoughts; in a place dark and dank, loaded with hundreds of metal barrels, corroded with age, their toxic contents seeping into the groundwater, invading the ecosystem of the Maine town.

The microwave oven began to beep, and she pulled herself from the disturbing reverie to answer its insistent toll. She took the steaming mug of chicken soup from inside and sat at the little kitchenette. Her stomach felt queasy with nerves, but she knew she should eat something before her late night maneuvers.

In between spoonfuls, Katie pulled a yellow legal pad over and reviewed the list of things she would need to gather before tonight. She tapped the first item on the pad with her finger. "Flashlight," she said thoughtfully. "I saw one around here somewhere."

She got up from the chair and approached some boxes that had been neatly stacked by the doorway to Kevin's bedroom. *How long had he been here and still hadn't completely unpacked?* Katie moved some of the boxes and found the flashlight, pointed it into the room, and turned it on. Its beam cut through the encroaching shadows that accumulated with the coming of dusk.

"Guess that's a check," she said, returning to the table and setting the flashlight beside the pad. She was just about to sit, when she heard a faint knock on the door. She glanced at the clock. She was expecting Aaron, but it was only just seven. Maybe he'd come early to try to talk her out of her planned adventure. "A little early, aren't you . . . ," she began, stopping when she saw that it wasn't Aaron on the doorstep.

Blithe's chief of police stood stiffly in the doorway and stared.

"Can I help you with something, Chief?" Katie asked.

It was almost as if she'd woken him up. He kind of twitched, then politely removed his hat. "Sorry to disturb you, ma'am," he said, "but I've got some news about Dr. Wessell."

Katie felt her heart sink, as though the floor beneath her suddenly gave way and she was falling into a bottomless chasm. "What is it?" she asked in a breathless whisper, stepping aside to invite the sheriff inside.

He stepped in, and she closed the door behind him. The silence in the room became almost deafening, and Chief Dexter nervously coughed into his hand.

"Can I get you something?" she asked as she walked farther into the kitchen, trying to delay the inevitable.

"A glass of water would be fine," he answered.

She took a glass from a cabinet and began to run the water. "You have to run it for a minute," she said offhandedly, putting her hand beneath the stream. "Takes a while to get cold."

He nodded, self-consciously turning his hat in his hands.

She handed him the glass, then leaned back against the sink and folded her arms across her chest. "Is it bad?" she finally asked.

Chief Dexter was taking a drink from his glass when he shuddered violently, as if wracked by an Arctic chill. The glass tumbled from his hand and smashed upon the floor.

"Chief?" Katie asked, moving toward him.

His eyes were closed, but he raised a hand to reassure her. "Dr. Wessell," he began, his voice sounding strange . . . raspy, "he discovered some things about our town—things that should have remained secret."

Katie was kneeling on the kitchen floor, carefully picking up the pieces of broken glass, when the implications of the police officer's words began to sink in. "What exactly are you suggesting, Chief?" she asked, slowly climbing to her feet, the palm of one of her hands piled with shards of glass. "Did someone do something to Kevin?"

She was startled by the man's response. Chief Dexter chuckled, and it was one of the most unpleasant sounds she'd ever heard—like his throat was clogged with fluid—and it must have been a trick of the light, but something seemed to be wrong with his eyes. "He serves the whole—as do we all," he said dreamily, and began to sway from side to side.

Katie was suddenly afraid—very, very afraid. Something wasn't right with the man; something wasn't right with the whole damn town. "I think you had better leave now," she said in her calmest voice. *He serves the whole,* she thought. *What the hell is that supposed to mean?*

"Get out," she said, turning her back on him defiantly and walking to the trash can beside the sink to dispose of the glass in her hand. She didn't want him to know that he'd spooked her. Never show fear; it was something she'd learned in her work with animals. Even still, she kept an especially large shard of glass in her hand—just in case she needed to defend herself, but as she turned she saw that he was walking toward the door.

"Can't have people poking around," he said in that wet, gravelly voice as he reached the door and opened it. "Not when we're so close to being free."

Katie had no idea what the man was talking about and was ready to rush the door and lock it behind him. But the chief just opened the door and stepped back inside, as if waiting for somebody to join him.

This is it, she thought, and dove across the room for the phone. She would try the state police. Their number was on the yellow legal pad she left on the kitchen table. Katie squeezed the razor sharp piece of glass in her hand as she moved in what seemed like slow motion across the kitchen, the pain of the shard digging into her flesh keeping her focused.

From the corner of her eye she saw the policeman begin to crouch. Was he going for his gun? Katie reached out for the handset. *Just a bit farther.*

She collided with the circular kitchen table, almost dislocating her hip, and was reaching for the phone when she heard the noise. Not the sound of a gunshot—but the sound of a cough, a violent hacking sound.

Her hand was on the receiver when she felt it hit her neck, something that made her skin burn as if splashed with acid. Reflexively her hand went to her neck, and she pulled the object from her flesh. It reminded her of a sea urchin, black and glistening, its circular shape covered in sharp spines—but where did it come from? She could feel the numbness spreading from her neck to her body with incredible speed.

Katie looked toward the sheriff by the open door just as he let loose with another of the powerful coughs. A spray of projectiles spewed from his mouth to decorate her body, and she realized with increasing horror that she could not feel a thing. She held up her hand, the one holding the piece of shattered glass, and watched, almost amused as the blood continued to flow from the cuts, running down her arm to spatter upon the floor.

She felt as though she were in a dream, the world around

her suddenly not making sense. Katie glanced down at the urchins attached to her flesh. *They must be coated in some kind of poison,* she gathered as she toppled to the floor, banging her head on the edge of the table.

Katie lay facing the open door. The sheriff still stood beside it. She wanted to scream, but all she could do was lie there and watch him as he stood, like a doorman, waiting for someone to arrive.

She heard the sounds of claws scrabbling on the wooden steps outside. It didn't sound like a person at all, she mused, but like an animal having some difficulty making it up the steps.

"We're so very close," Chief Dexter said, looking toward the door with anticipation. "Nothing must prevent the *whole* from being free."

Again there was the comment about the whole, and she wrestled with the meaning as she fought to keep the numbed lids over her eyes from sliding closed. She had to see what was coming up the steps, had to see what the sheriff so eagerly awaited.

It made its appearance, lurching across the doorframe and into the apartment with great difficulty. Katie knew that she had lost the ability to scream some time ago, but it didn't prevent her from trying, as a monstrosity very similar to the ones dead in the basement freezer came toward her. It was the most horrible thing she'd seen in her life, a thing of nightmare; its body made up of attributes of many other animals, but having no identity of its own. A beaver, a snake, an octopus, a crane, and even a fish; all were represented in the horrific mass that shambled across the kitchen floor. The monster had a great deal of difficulty with the tile floor; one of its back limbs, a clawed flipper, sliding across the smooth surface not allowing it purchase. It smelled of low tide, and she silently wished that her sense of smell had been numbed as well.

Blithe's chief of police knelt beside the abomination. "To keep the secret," he said in a soft gurgle, "you must serve the whole." He reached down and began to stroke the fur, scales, and feathers that grew from the body of the grunting beast. "You must be made part of the whole."

Katie was suddenly filled with an overwhelming sense of dread as her eyes grew unbearably heavy and began to close. She saw the animal begin to shiver, its twisted mouth opening as if it was having trouble breathing. Then, mercifully, her eyes shut upon the nightmarish visage before her. Katie listened to the wheezing and grunting beast, the smell of the tide washing over her as it gasped for breath.

And then she heard a sound that at first she could not identify. It was a sharp sound, one that would have made her flinch if she hadn't been under the effects of a toxin—a ripping sound—followed by the sound of something spilling, something splashing onto the floor.

"Part of the whole," she heard Dexter say softly in the

darkness, as the sound of something on many legs skittered across the tiled floor toward her.

As she slipped further, deeper into oblivion, she felt it touch her.

"Dear God," echoed her last thought as she surrendered to the poisons coursing through her veins. *"It's crawling into my mouth."*

Aaron had no idea what he would find, as he cautiously climbed the wooden steps that led to Kevin Wessell's apartment. He'd called both the clinic and the apartment, but Katie hadn't answered at either place. That awful feeling of dread, which he had become a little too familiar with of late, churned in the pit of his stomach.

The thing living inside Mrs. Provost had continued to rant about something called Leviathan and how the *whole* would soon be free. He had no idea what it was talking about, and finally locked the woman in the basement. There really wasn't much of a choice, he had to find Gabriel and Camael, and make sure that Katie was all right.

The apartment door was unlocked, and he opened it into the kitchen, knocking lightly as he stuck his head inside. "Katie?" he called out. The lights were on, and everything seemed normal until he noticed the splatters of blood on the floor near the kitchen table. There was another puddle of something on the floor near the bloodstains, and he knelt down beside it. It was clear, gelatinous, and he touched it with the tips of his fingers, bringing it to his nose. It smelled strong, reminding him of Lynn Beach during low tide: a kind of nasty, rotten-egg stink.

Aaron wiped the slimy substance on his pant leg and explored the kitchen further. He found the legal pad with Katie's list and the flashlight on the table. She must have been getting ready to go to the abandoned boat factory.

The factory.

He took the flashlight from the table and tested it. The factory seemed as good a place as any to continue the search for his missing friends. He doubted it was anything as simple as a toxic spill cover-up—the thing living inside Mrs. Provost had told him that much. Of course, that's just the way things were lately; nothing was normal—or easy.

Aaron headed into the night, taking the flashlight with him. He and Katie had discussed how to get to the factory earlier in the day, and he thought he could find his way. Keeping mostly to the shadows, he proceeded through the winding side street to the docks. The going was creepy. There wasn't a sign of life anywhere; every house he passed was shrouded in darkness. He began to wonder how many citizens of Blithe had one of those things, like the one in Mrs. Provost, living inside of them. He shuddered, an uncomfortable tightness forming in his throat.

It wasn't long before he could hear the sound of the ocean

and smell the tang of the salt air. Aaron crept from the wooded area and down a sandy embankment to a lonely stretch of road ending in a high, chain-link fence. He could just about make out the shape of the factory beyond it.

A light approached from the opposite direction, and Aaron ducked for cover, watching the road from behind a sprawling patch of wildflowers and tall grass. The Ford pickup truck slowed as it approached the fence, and Aaron watched the driver slowly climb out. With a key from his pocket, he unlocked a padlock and chain, pushing open the fence to allow the vehicle entrance. Though it was dark, Aaron could see that the back of the truck was filled with people: young and old; men, women, and children; some even dressed in their pajamas and bathrobes. With a chilling resonance, his questions about the townsfolk became horribly clear.

The driver locked the chain again after driving through, then continued on toward the factory. Its headlights illuminated the parking area, and Aaron noticed that the lot was nearly full.

Must be the night shift, he thought as he emerged from hiding, hugged the shadows, and squeezed himself between the gates and onto the property. Using the parked cars as cover, Aaron made his way closer to the factory. Some cars had been parked at the front of the sprawling building, their lights on and pointed toward the structure for illumination. He ducked lower as a police patrol car slowly came around the corner.

Peeking out over the hood of a powder blue Volvo, Aaron saw that the car was driven by Chief Dexter, and waited until the policeman had driven around the building before attempting to get any closer.

Aaron watched the group that had been in the back of the pickup stiffly walk from the parking lot toward the factory. A small town with a secret, mysterious disappearances, the locals acting strangely; if he wasn't currently living it, he'd think he had become trapped in a bad sci-fi movie. They entered the building through a large, rust-stained metal door, and Aaron could hear the staccato rattle of what could only be a jackhammer.

He didn't want to chance being noticed, so he avoided the main entrance and sought another, less obvious way into the factory. He stayed close to the building's side, the shadows thrown by the rundown structure serving well to hide him. He was exceptionally cautious of Chief Dexter's patrol, remaining perfectly still in the darkness and holding his breath whenever the squad car passed.

He found what seemed to be an old emergency exit and tried to open it. No good; it was locked from the other side. "Damnit," he hissed. He looked around for something he could use to force the door, but there was nothing. Besides, he didn't want to attract any attention. He needed to get inside. *C'mon, Aaron. Think.*

And then it dawned on him. It was a wild idea, but the

more he thought about it, the more he was convinced that it just might work. Aaron closed his eyes and thought of a weapon—a weapon of fire. It was a different experience than the other times that he had summoned a fiery blade; he was not being attacked in any way, so he wondered if it would even work. The blade of light, brought forth from his recent nightmare, immediately surged into his head, as if eager to be used yet again, but he deemed it too large and unwieldy for the more delicate task he had in mind. Aaron pictured a dagger with a long, thin blade, and he opened his eyes to see it begin to form in his hand.

"Would you look at that," he whispered as the knife took shape. Maybe he wasn't such a lost cause after all, he mused as he brought the glowing manifestation of his power to the door and ran the orange blade between the jamb and the door itself. There was the slightest bit of resistance as the knife dissolved the locking mechanism, the pungent aroma of melting metal wafting up into the air on tufts of oily smoke.

He gave the door a sharp tug, and it opened enough for him to slip inside. It was cool, damp, and completely void of light. Aaron wished the tool of fire away and turned on the flashlight he had stuck in his back pocket. He was in a cinderblock hallway that appeared to be used for storage; every piece of old equipment, desks, chairs, and just general crap were piled inside. Silently, he scrambled over the piles of junk, heading for a doorway on the other side, listening intently for sounds of activity outside.

Aaron got to the other side and proceeded down a shorter hallway. The sounds of machinery were louder now; the whine of gas-powered generators, the roar of heavy machinery, the *beep-beep-beep* of vehicles backing up. He quickened his pace, then stopped in the shadows of another doorway, staring in awe. If this had once been a factory, a place where people had come to work, to make things—sailboats, in fact—it certainly wasn't anymore. Inside the factory, in the middle of the sprawling structure, was an enormous hole.

Aaron skulked closer, using piles of dirt and rock that had been stacked in huge mounds around the dig as cover, and peered over the lip of the hole. The citizens of Blithe were working deep inside, using all kinds of construction equipment to make the opening even bigger. He actually recognized people from the town: the Mainiac with his dirty Red Sox cap, and an older woman who had been in the veterinarian's office with a sick parakeet. The people down below moved around like ants, using picks, shovels, and jackhammers, chopping and digging in areas too small for the bigger machinery, while others carted away wheelbarrows loaded with the rubble of their labors.

This is way too much, he thought. He wanted nothing more than to find Gabriel and Camael and get the hell outta Dodge, but he couldn't do that; he couldn't leave Katie, and he couldn't leave the town in the thrall of Leviathan—whatever the heck that was. He wished his mentor was there; he could have used a little guidance from the angel warrior.

He recalled something that Katie had mentioned about underground caves and tunnels beneath the factory and wondered if they were the reason for this frantic activity. As if compelled, he moved cautiously closer, descending some makeshift stairs that took him deeper into the hole. There were lights strung along the walls, about every five feet or so, and the shadows cast by the workers, as they tirelessly toiled, were eerily disturbing—the distorted versions of themselves upon the tunnel wall more a reflection of the twisted horrors that lived inside them.

At the foot of the stairs he found an entrance to a tunnel, whose edges were not jagged and rough like those hewn with the tools and machines. Flashlight in hand, and making sure that he was not being watched, Aaron darted through the opening and began a descent farther beneath the earth. The walls of the winding passage were strangely smooth, as if polished— *maybe by the flow of the ocean at one time,* he thought as he placed his hand against the cool rock. It still felt wet, cold, as if the sea had left the essence of itself behind. There was a, downward pitch to the tunnel floor, and Aaron nervously wondered how many feet beneath the surface he had traveled. This thought was quickly discarded when the angry sound of something squealing wafted up from the passage ahead.

It was an animal frantically calling for help, and Aaron slowly, carefully, made his way down the declining passageway. He came to a sudden, sharp bend and warily peered around it. The tunnel split, one path veering off to the left, winding down even farther into the darkness, the other ending in a chamber from where he was sure the sounds of distress had come. The animal's squeals of protest became even more frantic and Aaron was drawn closer to its plight.

He cautiously peeked into the chamber and found a makeshift veterinary office. A table, probably from the factory's cafeteria, had been set up as an examination table in the center of the room, and a man, his clothing caked with dirt, was in the process of pulling a large cat from one of many pet carriers stacked around the cave. The carriers held all manner of four-legged creatures—cats, dogs, rabbits—and Aaron checked them all for a sign of Gabriel. But his best friend was not among those imprisoned.

The filthy man had the yowling, long-haired cat by the scruff of its neck and brought it to the table. The other animals had begun to yelp and whine, knowing something bad was about to happen. The man strapped the squirming feline to the table and began to examine it, roughly checking its ears, eyes, and then inside its hissing mouth. *Could this be the missing Kevin Wessell?* Aaron wondered as the man left the cat and moved out of his line of vision.

A strange mewling cry, the likes of which Aaron had

never heard before, filled the cave. The man returned to the examination table, his arms full, and Aaron had to blink twice before his mind could adjust to what he saw. It was one of the . . . *things* that Katie had shown him in the basement freezer—only this one was alive, cradled gently in the man's arms. The animals in the chamber howled and clawed at the walls of their cages. The cat thrashed against its restraints and spat as the man set the abomination down next to it. The twisted animal looked as though it might have, at one time, been a dog—a terrier of some kind, maybe—but now it was horribly more than that.

The man had begun to pet the awful beast, his filth-encrusted hand stroking the beast repeatedly from the top of its misshapen head to the patch of bare, pink flesh in the small of its back. His attention to the animal was growing rougher, more frantic, when Aaron noticed the bulbous growth forming within the barren swath of skin.

The cacophony of animal wails was almost deafening, and Aaron wanted to look away. The poor beasts knew what was about to happen, and it brought them to the brink of madness. The angelic nature residing within him suddenly began to stir; it, too, sensed the potential for danger here, and was attempting to assert itself.

The swollen mass on the creature's back had more than doubled in size and was pulsing with a life all its own. The monstrous animal panted with exertion as the tumor continued to grow, and the man looked on with a dull expression of disinterest, as if he saw things like this every day.

Suddenly the flesh of the beast's back exploded with a faint pop, and a geyser of fluid shot into the air. What Aaron saw next chilled him to the bone. As the fluid drained from the ruptured growth, something emerged from the hollow of the wound. It was spiderlike, crablike. He'd never seen anything quite like it, but was certain that this was what had been lurking in the back of Mrs. Provost's throat. It was black and glistening, the chitinous shell that covered its body catching the light of the Coleman lanterns placed around the cavern. The creature crawled from the open wound of the animal's back and scrambled onto the tabletop.

The caged animals barked, howled, and screeched in protest as the spidery thing approached the restrained feline. Aaron could understand their intensifying terror, but had to ignore their frantic cries, for there was nothing he could do. The cat didn't have a chance. In what seemed like the blink of an eye, he watched the multilimbed life-form throw itself at the cat's face and force its way into the panicked animal's mouth, disappearing down its throat. The cat thrashed and coughed, but in a matter of seconds the panic halted, and the cat relaxed, lying perfectly still, its large, bushy tail languidly waving in the air. He could have sworn he heard it purring.

His mind raced as he wrestled with what he should do, but

the decision was put on hold when he heard the sound of his name being whispered.

"Aaron," the voice hissed in the tunnel behind him, and he backed away from the cavern and turned the corner to see Katie coming closer. His finger immediately went to his lips, urging her to be silent.

She smiled at him strangely, and he felt the hair at the back of his neck suddenly stand on end. Something wasn't right, and he found the sword of light suddenly in his hands—just as her throat bulged and a spray of the grapelike objects spewed from her open mouth. He swatted them away and watched with unease as Katie recoiled violently from the blade's light. The idea of one of those spidery things crawling inside her mouth made him feel sick to his stomach, but he stood his ground, sword aloft, waiting for the next attack.

There was movement in the tunnel behind her, and the people of Blithe moved through in a wave, pushing past Katie to get at him. The angelic essence inside him roared to be free, but he could not unleash that kind of power against these people—they weren't responsible for their actions.

Aaron waved the blade in front of them, hoping to drive them back, hoping to buy himself enough time to flee deeper into the tunnel system—but there were too many, and they were much too fast. The citizens of Blithe were upon him. He had no room to maneuver, no room to block the spiny objects that erupted from their mouths. And the power that resided at his core bellowed its frustration as a rain of projectiles pierced his flesh, clinging to his cheek, his neck, and the backs of his hands—and the numbing effects of the toxin began to course through his blood.

"I will not hurt them," he said stubbornly to the angry power, and the residents of Blithe swarmed upon him, bringing him down to the tunnel floor.

And the power that was his birthright resigned itself to its fate, and allowed the darkness of unconsciousness to enfold them in its welcoming embrace.

CHAPTER TEN

The tide rolled in with a soothing rumble, rushing up to greet him, flowing around his bare legs like eager lapdogs excited to make his acquaintance. Aaron gazed out over the vast expanse of the Atlantic Ocean, watching the seabirds ride the gentle breeze, and felt a peace that he had not known in quite some time.

"It's beautiful here, isn't it, Aaron?" asked a young voice.

Aaron looked down to see Stevie sitting in the sand beside him. The boy had a plastic pail and shovel and was busily digging a hole in the wet ground.

Aaron glanced into the hole and saw that it was far deeper and larger than he had first imagined. *I'll bet there are tunnels under here,* he thought for some reason. *Miles and miles of tunnels.*

"Did you hear me, Aaron?" Stevie asked, drawing his attention away from the hole.

Aaron looked into the boy's expectant face. "I'm sorry, Stevie," he said. "I guess I zoned out for a minute there."

The little boy was only wearing a pair of bright red swim trunks, and Aaron could see that he was getting sunburned. *If we aren't careful, he thought, the kid'll get sunstroke—just like that time when . . .*

"I just said how beautiful it is here, that's all," Stevie interrupted his train of thought. The child continued to work at his hole. "I don't ever want to leave."

Aaron laughed as he knelt down beside the boy. The surf flowed over his bare feet, so warm. "We have to go home sometime," he said as he ruffled the boy's blond hair. "Don't you want to see Mom and Dad again?"

Stevie turned and pointed up the beach. "They're over there," he said. "I can see them anytime I want."

Aaron looked up and saw Lori and Tom Stanley sitting in beach chairs beneath a large, yellow umbrella, a red and white cooler between them.

They'd bought Dr Pepper, he unexpectedly recalled, the first and last time they had ever used the red and white cooler. Something had been left inside it after the beach trip, and it had spoiled, leaving behind a nasty odor. They were never able to get the smell out of it, so they'd thrown the cooler away. Aaron tried to remember how long ago that had been. It was the same trip that Stevie got sunstroke.

Lori and Tom waved happily from their beach chairs, and

Aaron tentatively waved back, suddenly overcome with a sadness he couldn't comprehend.

"Don't feel sad," his foster brother said, filling his pail with sand. "There's nothing to be sad about here."

"How did you know I was feeling sad?" Aaron asked.

Stevie did not answer, and continued to dig in his hole—making it larger, deeper.

Aaron stood and gazed out over the ocean. Dark clouds were forming off in the distance—perhaps a storm coming in. "This all seems so familiar," he said, more to himself than to Stevie, as the wind ruffled his dark hair.

"And is that so bad?" the boy asked.

Aaron glanced at his little brother and saw that Gabriel now sat beside the child, tail wagging as Stevie patted his head. "Hello, Gabriel," Aaron said to the dog.

The dog wagged his tail in response, panting happily. He had been running in the water and was soaking wet, sand sticking to the fur on his legs.

"What's the matter with you, Aaron?" the child asked. "Everything here is so perfect—so peaceful. Just let yourself accept it."

The sky was darkening as the clouds drifted closer to the shore.

"I want to," Aaron replied, a feeling of pure joy beginning to bubble up within him, but he forced it back. "I really, really do—but this feels wrong. Like I lived it before."

"But you were happy then, right? And you can be that way again. It's a gift for all you've had to endure." Stevie was suddenly standing in the middle of the hole he had been digging. "Let me take your pain away." He stretched his sunburned arms toward his older brother, a smile on his face.

It seems simple enough, Aaron thought as he watched the gray clouds billow offshore. They seemed to be changing direction, leaving the sky over his head perfect, unblemished by the storm. All he need do is accept this time, this place, as his reality, and everything would be fine.

But it wouldn't.

"This is all wrong," he said aloud with a furious shake of his head. He gestured to the ocean and the world beyond it. "This isn't right, this moment has passed. It's a memory from three years ago."

"Stop it, Aaron," Stevie demanded. "Don't spoil what I've made for you."

Aaron stared at the angry child as the clouds again tumbled in from the sea, low and dark, pregnant with storm. A distant, threatening rumble of thunder shook the air. "This is all a dream—a nightmare, really."

"Aaron!" the boy screamed, stomping his foot.

"What are you?" Aaron asked, a powerful wind suddenly whipping at his clothes. "Stevie never talked like this—he barely talked at all." Aaron looked at the dog, who continued to wag his tail happily even though the wind was blowing sand into his lolling mouth. "And this isn't Gabriel. It just looks like him." Aaron stepped closer to the child. "I'll ask you again," he said grimly. "What are you?"

It was suddenly black as night on the beach, and arcs of lightning coursed across the sky as thunderclaps boomed. The ocean had been whipped into a frenzy by the tempest, with waves crashing violently on the shore.

"You can be happy again!" the child shrieked over the storm. "All you need do is—"

"What. Are. You?" Aaron spat. From the corner of his eye he could see the ocean waters, in the distance, begin to froth and boil.

"I have existed since the fifth day of creation," Stevie said in a chilling voice not his own.

Something moved beneath the roiling waters. Something large.

"I was that spark of uncertainty in the Creator's thoughts as He forged the world—that brief moment of chaos—before Genesis."

A monster emerged from the depths of the sea, skin blacker than the darkness that now surrounded them. It seemed to be at least a hundred feet tall, its wormlike body swaying above the storm-ravaged sea. Hundreds of tentacles of varying degrees of thickness and length grew from its body, writhing in the air as if desperate to entwine something in their embrace. Aaron could not pull his eyes away from the nightmarish visage as it undulated across the thrashing sea toward the beach.

"The darkness of the ocean became my dwelling," said the thing that resembled his brother. "And there I thrived, hidden beneath the waves—until the Lord God sensed my greatness and sent His angelic messengers to snuff out my glorious light."

The monster was closer now. Large, opaque sacks dangled hideously from its glistening body, swaying like pendulums as it lurched closer to land.

Aaron was unable to take his eyes from the horribly awesome sight, surprised that he could even think, let alone speak. "You're so wonderful that God decided to take you out?"

The Stevie-thing ignored his question. "The ocean was my domain, and any who dared traverse it were subject to my wrath—and I soon developed a taste for the lives of those the Creator sent to destroy me."

The enormous sea beast loomed above Aaron. Even from this distance, he could see that its mass was covered in rows of fine scales that glistened with the colors of the rainbow. If it weren't so outright hideous, he might have found it beautiful. There was a blinding flash of lightning, followed by an explosion of thunder—and the pregnant clouds opened up in a deluge of thick, driving rain.

"That's what has kept me alive over the millennia, and what will eventually free me from my prison beneath the sea."

The viscous torrents coated Aaron's body, forcing him down upon the sand. The ground could not absorb the thick, milky fluids, and they pooled around him, ever rising.

The beast reached the shore, hundreds of tiny muscular appendages propelling the nightmare up onto the beach. "I sense in you a power that both frightens—and excites," the monster said, its voice now coming from two places, his little brother and the thing upon the shore, a perverse stereo effect echoing through the air. "Never have I encountered one such as you."

Aaron fought to stand, but he felt the ground beneath him shift, rising up to hold him fast. The foul rain continued to fall, coating his body in a layer of slime. "What is this place?" he frantically asked the doppelgänger of his brother.

"It could have been your individual paradise," the entity explained, its voice a disgusted rumble. "Like a bee to the flower, I used the promise of personal heaven to lure you to me. A place where you would have been content until your final days." Stevie shook its head in disappointment. "But you have rejected it."

"It's not real," Aaron spat, attempting to keep the fluid that rained from the sky and flowed down his face from entering his mouth. "It's a lie."

The thing that had taken on the guise of Stevie scrambled from its hole and walked casually toward the gigantic behemoth that had emerged from the sea. "Be it lie—or truth," it said, approaching the front of the beast. The creature responded to the strange child's approach by opening its cavernous maw.

The rain of slime was falling all the harder now, and Aaron felt himself violently sucked beneath the surface. His arms became trapped in the rising mire that accumulated upon the ground, and he thrashed in a futile attempt to free himself from the hungry earth, but to little avail.

Stevie had entered the mouth of the sea monster; the circular opening was ringed with razor-sharp teeth. It reminded Aaron of the mouth of a piranha fish. The boy stood there, peering out as it slowly began to close. "It all ends the same," he said from within the monster's maw. "You within the belly of the beast—food for Leviathan."

The final words ringing in his ears, over the storm's rage, the great beast snapped dosed its mouth, reared backward— and threw its mass back into the roiling sea.

Aaron struggled; it seemed as though the harder he fought, the faster he was pulled deeper. *It all ends the same,* he heard the inhuman voice reverberate in his mind, his head beginning to sink below the surface. He tried to scream, to bellow his belief that this was all some twisted mind manipulation, but it was cut short—abruptly silenced as a mixture of the sand, and the slime that fell in torrents from the black sky, flowed into his mouth and down his throat. *You within the belly of the beast,* the monster had gurgled.

Food for Leviathan.

* * *

The beast that was Leviathan reclined its massive shape against the cramped confines of the cave wall, where it had been trapped for countless millennia. The monster was content for now, for many of the digestive sacks that dangled from its body were filled with angelic life—brimming with power that would bring the dark deity to eventual release.

Its latest feed—the half-breed—the Nephilim, fought mightily to be free of Leviathan's hungry embrace, his mind filled with panic.

"Your struggles are futile." The monster wormed its way into Aaron's frenzied thoughts. "Take comfort in knowing that the power that resides within you—now flowing into me—will be used to reshape the world. Through the eyes of my minions I have seen what the Creator's world has become: a place teetering daily on the brink of chaos."

Leviathan showed the young man within its belly disturbing images of the world at large. Scenes of war, wanton violence, and death flashed before the Nephilim's mind's eye, a world seemingly touched by madness.

"This is what *God* has done," the beast growled. "*I* can do better. When I am finally free from my prison beneath the earth and sea, I will use your power, your marvelous strength, to push this place toward pandemonium. And then I shall mold it in my glorious image."

Thousands of Leviathan's black-shelled spawn writhed

eagerly beneath the protective cover of its scales. It would be they that would carry out the will of the beast, changing and twisting the existing fauna—from the inside out. The idea of being unleashed upon the planet made them chitter in happy anticipation.

The Nephilim continued to fight, refusing to allow the digestive nutrients to begin the process of his absorption. This annoyed the great beast, and again, it delved into the captive's mind. Indelicately it tore into his memories, and found the recollection of a life most mundane—or it was, until the power of Heaven inside his frail human shell awakened to pursue some long-forgotten, ancient prophecy of redemption.

Leviathan had no time for prophecy; it had a world to conquer.

The one called Aaron thrashed and bucked as Leviathan picked unmercifully through his memories. The beast saw the awakening of the angelic nature, the resurrection of his pet—imbibing the lowly animal with a life-force that it was currently finding most delicious—the death of his parental guardians, and the furious battle with the leader of the Powers' host, Verchiel.

The monster writhed within its prison of rock. Long had it anticipated Verchiel, and those who followed him, to seek out and attempt to eradicate the glory that was Leviathan in the name of God—but it never came to be. For some reason, it had been spared this attack. Leviathan continued to exist, feeding on prey that would allow it to survive, drawing those of an angelic nature to it. Like the cunning anglerfish, the sea beast psychically dangled the tantalizing promise of bliss before the pathetic creatures of Heaven, and it was only a matter of time before they were ensnared, resting inside its ravenous digestive sacks.

When it was finally able to emerge from its underground prison, Verchiel and the Powers would need to be dealt with. And they would feel the ferocity of Leviathan's wrath and know its insatiable hunger.

The picture of a small child—the Nephilim's sibling— flashed within the monster's mind. It was the boy-child it had used to bring the Nephilim here to Blithe. But the Nephilim saw through the ruse, and attempted to free himself—unsuccessfully.

Leviathan would do everything in its power to keep the half-breed as his own. The life-force within him was strong, intoxicating, and it would serve the behemoth well in its eventual dominion of the world.

It could sense that the Nephilim was thinking of the child again—the child in the clutches of Verchiel. This agitated the Nephilim, made him struggle all the more, interrupting the pleasures of the digestive process. Leviathan was annoyed, and again forced his way into the angelic being's thoughts. It would need to assure the youth that any hope of rescuing his brother from the clutches of the Powers was futile.

"Give up," said Leviathan to the Nephilim. "Your struggles are all for naught."

The great beast painfully recoiled, the mental activity of the angelic being frantically struggling within one of his many bellies, causing renewed discomfort.

In the youth's mind there was a thought, an image of a blinding light, a light so bright that it could pierce even the most infinite of stygian depths. And the light, that horrible, searing light, had begun to take shape, becoming something that filled the ancient deity with a feeling of dread.

The light in the Nephilim's mind had become a weapon, a weapon Leviathan had not seen since the fateful battle that had trapped it in the underground cavern.

The light had become a sword—the sword of God's messenger.

Aaron was drowning.

He tried with all his might to fight it, to keep the foul liquid from inside his body, but there was a voice, a calm, soothing voice that attempted to convince him that this was the wrong thing to do, that the fight would only prolong his pain.

Then the silky smooth tones inside his head, which promised him the end to his suffering if he would only give up, told him that his little brother was dead, that the angel Verchiel had destroyed the child soon after he was taken, that the fight was all for nothing.

And there was the overpowering sorrow of this knowledge, combined with the weighty sadness he had already been carrying: the death of his parents, being forced to flee the life he'd built for himself—to leave Vilma—it was all too painful. He had almost started to believe that it was best for him to submit, to allow the milky solution to fill his mouth and flow into his lungs.

But then the sword was there—the mysterious weapon seemingly forged from the rays of the sun, piercing the darkness of his innermost misery, burning away the shroud of sorrow and despair that enveloped him to reveal the truth.

The truth.

Aaron screamed within the membranous sack, expelling the foul liquids that had managed to find their way into his body. The sword was in his hand, as it had been that night in his dream, glowing like the new dawn, revealing the true nature of the nightmare that had taken him captive. He drew back the sword of light and cleaved his way through the fleshy, elastic wall of his prison. In his mind he heard a scream—the shriek of a monster in pain.

The fluid immediately began to drain from the open cut in the digestive organ, and he was able to breathe. The stench of the air within the sack was foul, but it was what his aching lungs craved nonetheless. He gulped greedily at the fetid atmosphere, like a man dying of thirst, coughing up remnants of the invasive liquid.

The fleshy chamber, in which he was still imprisoned,

began to buck and sway, bellows of rage and pain thundering around him.

He had to get out, to escape the grabbing, organic confines, and he threw himself at the gash he had cut into it. It was what he imagined birth to be—squeezing his head through the slice, which had, miraculously, already begun to heal. Aaron tumbled from the wound, falling a great distance, before landing upon a floor of solid rock with a jarring thud. Stars exploded before his eyes, and for a moment he thought he might lose consciousness, but he shook it·off, scrambling to stand, the weapon of light still in hand.

He looked around and saw that he was in a vast, underground cavern. The place was eerily quiet except for the distant thrum of the pounding surf. Thick patches of a luminescent fungus grew on the walls, throwing a sparse and eerie green light about the sprawling cave.

The blow came from behind. His mind likened it to the approach of a freight train, hitting him with such force that he was thrown through the air to land against a far wall. His head was ringing, and the bones of his back and legs screamed their protest as he struggled to regain his footing. He was bleeding from a dozen places, but still managed to hold on to the sword of light and brandished it as he fought to stand erect.

"The sword of the messenger," something bellowed from within the darkness of the cave, and then it leaned toward him, revealing itself, its tubular body so large, it was barely able to move. "I would have thought it impossible for one such as you to wield a weapon so mighty."

Though his body continued to protest, Aaron held the blade tighter as the black-scaled monster loomed above him. He studied the details of the creature that could only be Leviathan. Its body was covered in fine, interconnecting scales, like chain mail, and it swayed snakelike above him. Repulsed, Aaron could see things living beneath its body armament, familiar spidery things that would have liked nothing better than to crawl down the throats of every living thing upon the planet.

It lashed out at him with a tentacle as thick as a tree trunk, and Aaron scrabbled quickly over the cave floor. It was like the deafening crack of the world's largest bullwhip, the fleshy appendage fragmenting the rock where he once had stood.

Leviathan shifted its great size within the cavern to follow Aaron's progress, the top of its head rubbing against the ceiling as it attempted to maneuver its enormous mass in the confining space. "Where are you going, Nephilim?" it asked in its horrible, thunderous voice. "You cannot escape me. Surrender to the inevitable."

Some of the black-shelled spider things fell from the monster's body and eagerly scuttled across the cave floor to get at him. The blade of the messenger—as Leviathan had called it—made short work of the crawling things.

As he dispatched the spawn of the monster, something

began to bother him. Since awakening within the digestive sack of the monster, he had not felt the presence of his angelic power. As he destroyed more of Leviathan's pets, he tried to remember when last he had felt the force, always so eager to be unleashed. It had been back in the tunnels, when he had been attacked by Katie McGovern and the residents of Blithe. It had screamed to be free and he had rebuked it, pushing it away as he had done since that first battle with the angel Verchiel.

Leviathan squirmed its bulk closer. Had the great monster somehow sucked it away? Aaron wondered as another of the Leviathan's tentacles reached down to ensnare him in its grasp. He swung at the muscular appendage, and it recoiled from the blade, hovering in the air before him like a cobra waiting for its opportunity to strike.

"Where are you?" he whispered to the presence that should have stirred inside him. "I really could use your help around now," Aaron said, alert as the monster's tentacle again attacked. There was no answer, and Aaron felt a wave of despair wash over him as he threw his diminishing strength into fighting the plentiful appendages that reached for him. He brought the blade down and watched as it dug deep into the black, muscular flesh of the beast.

"Yarrrrggghhhh," Leviathan roared as it violently pulled the injured limb away—and with it, the sword of the messenger. Aaron watched dumbfounded as the tentacle thrashed, dislodging the annoyance—sending it hurling across the cave, far from his reach, where it disappeared in a blinding flash. Panic set in. *Without any contact with the angelic nature, is it still possible for me to defend myself?* he wondered frantically.

He pressed his back to the cave wall and attempted to conjure a weapon of his own creation. Aaron breathed a sigh of relief as a blade of fire, puny in comparison with the splendor of the sword of the messenger, began to form in his hand. At least that power had not been taken from him.

Leviathan wasted no time and again attacked. The behemoth twisted within the confines of the cave, bringing its enormous mass down toward Aaron. The sword of flame sprang fully to life in his grasp, and he was raising the blade to defend himself against this latest onslaught, when his attention fell upon the many, fleshy sacks that hung obscenely from the front of the descending beast.

Aaron froze as he stared into the contents of the sea beast's numerous stomachs: the missing Camael, his poor Gabriel, one of the ugly little creatures that had attacked them on their way to Blithe—and so many others, all trapped within the bellies of the beast. The horror of it all was almost too much for him to stand.

"The sight of me—of my magnificence—it fills you with wonder," Leviathan said, reaching down to claim Aaron as its own.

Its writhing body shifted, and a rain of tentacles fell

from above to ensnare him. Aaron slashed at the relentless onslaught, the fiery weapon severing many of the limbs. The beast shrieked in pain, but still it attacked.

And as he fought Aaron could not help but return his gaze to a mysterious being he saw floating within one of the digestive sacks. He knew—somehow, *instinctively?*—that this was an angel, but that same something also told him that this was an angel of enormous prestige and power. *An archangel.* Through the opaque skin and milky fluid he could see the ornate armor that hung from the emaciated body of the heavenly being.

"Look upon those that fell before my might, Nephilim," gurgled the monster, assaulting his ears and mind. "He was the Archangel Gabriel—the messenger of God, an extension of the Creator's Word—and he was vanquished as easily as the others."

Aaron's mind was suddenly filled with images of the monster's battle with God's messenger. He saw the winged warrior descend from the heavens, his golden armor glistening beautifully in the dimness of the primordial world. The angel dove beneath the churning waves to confront his quarry, wielding the awesome sword of light.

The battle that Aaron bore witness to could only be described as epic in proportion: a force of the purest light against unfathomable darkness—two opposing powers coming together in a conflict that quite literally rocked the world. The ocean waters around them boiled and churned, kicking up rock, dirt, and silt. Great undersea mountains quaked and crumbled, then the ocean floor split apart, a yawning chasm appearing beneath the opponents, still lost in the midst of conflict. And they rumbled into the gaping abyss, swallowed up by the cataclysmic fury unleashed by their struggle.

The vision came to an abrupt end with the disturbing and final sight of Leviathan engulfing the diminished angel Gabriel within its cavernous mouth. The messenger of God struggled pathetically as he was gradually drawn down the gullet of the beast—immured within one of the behemoth's many stomachs; eternal food for the beast, trapped in a cave, far beneath the sea.

Leviathan laughed within Aaron's mind, a low, gurgling sound, filled with a perverse confidence. *Not even a messenger from God Himself could defeat the monster,* Aaron thought as he continued his battle with the writhing tentacles. *What chance do I have?* he wondered, his efforts against the behemoth beginning to slow. He knew this was what the monster wanted, but he couldn't shake the sense that his struggles against the beast were not going to be enough.

Leviathan's attack was relentless, and it wasn't long before one of the tentacles ensnared the wrist that held his weapon of fire. He tried to pull away, to somehow use the flaming blade against the slimy black limb, but it was to no effect. There was a sudden sharp snap and blinding pain as his wrist was broken. Aaron cried out in shock, watching the sword fall from his grasp, evaporating in the cold, damp air of the cave before it could even touch the ground.

Aaron struggled in the monster's grasp as tentacles wrapped themselves around his arms, his legs, and waist, constricting almost all movement. He found himself lifted from the ground and borne aloft.

Drawn upward to the monster's mouth.

CHAPTER ELEVEN

Leviathan's muscular tendrils hauled him closer. Aaron tried to squirm from their strangling grasp, but the monster's hold upon him was too strong. The sea beast attacked his mind as well, weakening his resolve, taking away his desire to fight back. The spider-things living beneath the behemoth's armored scales chittered and hissed as Aaron's body was drawn steadily upward.

He was almost to Leviathan's mouth, a yawning chasm of razor-sharp teeth, when he heard another voice in his head. It was soft at first, a soothing whisper, like the sound of the wind moving through the trees on a cool fall night. He focused on this new, not unpleasant, tickle and struggled to stay conscious.

He opened his eyes and found himself gazing into one of the many opaque sacks hanging from the gigantic beast—the one that held God's messenger. The Archangel Gabriel's eyes opened, and Aaron knew it was *his* presence within his mind.

"I have long awaited your arrival," whispered a voice that sounded like the most beautiful of stringed instruments.

The voice of the monster was suddenly silenced, drowned out by the enlivening sounds of a cosmic symphony—and despite his dire predicament, Aaron reached out to communicate with this latest entity in his teeming mind.

"How is that possible?" Aaron asked. *"How could you know that I would be here—that I would come?"*

Aaron could sense Leviathan's growing annoyance. Something was blocking its access into his mind, and the monster did not care for that in the least.

"I knew that my torment would not last an eternity," said the angel Gabriel, the celestial music inside his head building to a near deafening crescendo. *"That my successor would eventually come and complete the task assigned to me,"* the angel's voice crooned.

Aaron didn't completely grasp the meaning of the Archangel's words. *"Successor?"* he questioned. *"I don't understand."*

The angel's eyes again began to close. *"There is no time for misunderstanding,"* the angelic being whispered, the sound of his voice growing steadily weaker. *"You are as I was,"* he said. *"A messenger of God."*

"Wait!" Aaron screamed aloud as he was dragged away from the digestive sacks and up toward the monster's face. He squirmed in the tentacles' clutches, the broken bones in his wrist grinding together painfully as he tried again to establish contact with the Archangel. "What do you mean?" he shouted. "I still don't understand!"

A tentacle, its thickness that of a tree trunk, reached down from above the struggling youth and snatched him away from the lesser appendages, drawing him upward.

Aaron found himself hanging upside down by the leg in front of Leviathan's monstrous countenance. The bulging eyes on either side of its head studied him with great interest; its enormous circular mouth puckered and spat as it spoke. "What is there to understand?" asked the horrific sea deity, its voice like the last gasp of a drowning man echoing inside his head. "Your struggles are futile. Surrender to my supremacy and know that it was your life essence, and those of your companions, that finally enabled me to procure my freedom."

Somehow, Leviathan had not heard the angel Gabriel's words. The monster did not hear the angelic warrior proclaim him as a messenger of God, and Aaron began to wonder if it all wasn't some kind of perverse trick on the part of the sea beast—to give him the slightest glimmer of hope and rip it savagely away.

He was brought closer to the gaping hole of a mouth, and Aaron saw himself pathetically reflected in the glassy surface of its bulbous, fishlike eyes, dangling upside down, waiting to be dropped into the cavernous mouth of the ancient, undersea behemoth. *Messenger of God my ass, I don't have a chance in hell,* Aaron thought as he prepared to be consumed.

"That is what it wants you to believe," said the barely audible voice of the Archangel Gabriel. *"That is how it has defeated us all, by making us believe that which is not true."*

Aaron squirmed, the angel's words chasing away the monster's infusion of self-doubt.

"When will you realize the futility of your actions?" Leviathan asked, giving him a violent shake. "Why do you fight when you cannot win, little Nephilim? The time for struggle is past. Now it is time to surrender.'"

Aaron found the words streaming from his mouth before even realizing what he was going to say.

"I will not surrender to you," Aaron said, a powerful anger building up inside him. He began to thrash, attempting to free himself from the ancient beast.

Leviathan laughed, tightening its grip upon his leg and lowering him toward its yawning mouth. "Courage even in the face of the inevitable," it gurgled. "Perhaps it shall make your life stuff all the more sweet."

The stink that wafted up from the monster's gullet was enough to render a body unconscious, and Aaron tried desperately to hold his breath. The flesh of the sea monster's tentacle was slimy beneath his clawing fingers, and he could not get a good enough grip upon the skin to render any damage. He felt the appendage's hold upon him loosen, and prepared for the fall into oblivion—when the angel Gabriel spoke again.

"I give again to you, my weapon of choice. Take it now as you took it the first time you struggled within the grasp of nightmare. I give to you Bringer of Light—use it well, messenger of God."

Aaron felt the blade of the messenger, Bringer of Light, appear in his hand, and the sharp, grinding pain from his broken wrist immediately eased as the bones miraculously knitted themselves back together.

"What is this?" Leviathan growled, its enormous eyes attempting to focus on him and the weapon that sprang to brilliant life in his grasp.

Aaron felt invigorated. The shroud of despair that had held him in its grasp dissipated like the morning fog in the presence of the rising sun. He swung his body out and swiped his blade across one of the fishlike eyes that ogled him. Bringer of Light cut across the wet surface of the bulging orb, slicing open the gelatinous organ. Leviathan screamed in a mixture of agony and rage—and Aaron was released from its hold.

The monster continued to shriek in pain, its gigantic mass thrashing in the close quarters of the undersea cave. Aaron landed precariously atop the cluster of sacks hanging from the front of the raging Leviathan. He tried to grab hold, to keep from being thrown from the swaying stomachs. His body slid across the rubbery surface of the digestive organs, sounding much like it did when rubbing a hand upon an inflated balloon. Aaron sunk his fingernails into the fleshy surface and held on.

The sea monster was bucking, bellowing its rage throughout its cave domain, its injured eye swollen closed, weeping streams of thick yellow fluid that resembled egg yoke.

"You shall suffer for that, Nephilim!" it screamed as it bent its body in an attempt to locate him with its remaining sensory organ. "I shall make your internment within my hungry stomach last an eternity. You shall be my favorite meal, and I will savor the taste of you for a very long time!"

Aaron began to slip, his purchase upon the tumorous sacks insecure. His face pressed against the surface of one of the opaque membranes, and he again found himself peering into the wan face of the Archangel Gabriel, floating within the digestive fluids of the behemoth.

"Messenger," a voice probed weakly within his brain, *"free me."* And the angel opened his eyes, their intensity inspiring him to act.

Aaron pulled back his arm with a yell and brought it forward, hacking at where the digestive sacks connected to Leviathan's chest. The heavenly blade passed through the connective tissue with ease, and the dangling organs fell from the monster's body like ripened fruit from the tree.

Leviathan continued to bellow, throwing its body against its stone prison, causing parts of walls and ceiling to crumble, raining rubble down onto the cave floor.

Aaron let himself fall. He had done his best, cutting away as many of the stomach prisons as possible, but there were just too many and he could not reach them all. Landing atop a pile of the fleshy sacks, he began to cut into the fluid-filled organs, attempting to free those trapped within before the beast overcame its fury.

Thick, milky liquids drained from opened casings, coating the ground in a layer of foul-smelling digestive juices. Leviathan moaned woefully, its great, serpentine mass leaning against the undersea cave's wall, seemingly thrown into a kind of shock—*perhaps as a result of being cut off from its food source,* Aaron guessed wildly, but he knew deep down that the beast would not remain docile for long. It was only a matter of time before its anger would fuel it to strike back at the one who hurt it so.

"You have hurt the beast," a voice said from behind him. Aaron turned to see the emaciated form of the angel Gabriel. His once glorious armor was now the color of a dirty penny, hanging large upon his dripping, skeletal frame. The Archangel swayed, barely conscious, in a puddle of viscous fluid. "Now you must finish the task we failed to complete." He gestured with a skeletal hand to the other sacks, and those still lying within. Bracelets that were probably once worn tight upon thick, muscular wrists jangled loosely, threatening to slip off. "In the name of the Creator, slay the beast Leviathan."

Aaron came toward him. "I . . . I can't do that," he said. He offered Gabriel the sword. "Here," he said. "You do it."

The angel fell to his knees upon the fluid-saturated ground. "That is not possible," Gabriel wheezed. "To do battle with the monster would only quicken my inevitable demise."

Aaron returned to the digestive sacks. "Maybe one of the others could help you," he suggested, fitfully gazing down at the still forms of the other angelic beings that had been held captive in the bellies of the fearsome monster. Many had curled into the fetal position, trapped within a world of Leviathan's making.

"Most are in as dire condition as I am," Gabriel wheezed in response.

Aaron knelt down beside two sacks, which contained his dog and Camael. "Will they be all right?" he asked, laying a trembling hand upon the Labrador's side, feeling for a heartbeat or any sign of life.

"They have not been prisoners of the beast for long," the Archangel said. "They will survive—if Leviathan does not reclaim them."

The monster stirred, a low, tremulous moan echoing throughout the underwater cavern.

Aaron stood, Bringer of light still clutched tightly in his hand. "Do you have any idea what you're asking me to do— you want *me to* kill *that?*"

Gabriel tilted his head to one side. "Do you have any idea the extent of power within you?" the angel retorted.

"Nephilim!" the monster raged, its muscular body stretching as high as the ceiling would allow, its injured eye swollen closed and dripping. Its head moved from left to right as it searched for its prey. "I will find you—and all that you are shall belong to *me!*"

Aaron stood rooted, watching as the enormous, sluglike monstrosity began to undulate in his general direction, its tentacles writhing in the air, as if somehow replacing the sensory organ that had been violently stolen away.

"Even the monster knows what resides within you," the angel Gabriel said. "And still you deny it."

Leviathan shambled closer, its tentacles lashing out, snatching at the air as it attempted to find its quarry. "Where are you, Nephilim?" it spat.

"The power I had inside me . . . I think it's gone," Aaron stammered, eyes upon the sea beast. "I've tried to communicate with it, but it doesn't answer. I think Leviathan might have done something and—"

"Is that what you wish happened?" the Archangel asked. "Or is that what actually occurred?"

At first, Aaron didn't understand what the angel was suggesting, but the meaning was suddenly clear.

"I've been inside your mind, Nephilim," Gabriel said, touching the side of his own head with a long, delicate index finger. "I've seen the fear that fills your thoughts."

"I . . . I don't think I'm strong enough to control it," Aaron said flatly, watching with terror-filled eyes as Leviathan drew closer.

"And if it were gone," suggested Gabriel, "you would no longer have to be afraid."

Aaron nodded, ashamed of his fear and that it would allow him to put the lives of his loved ones—as well as the fate of humanity—at risk.

"The power of Heaven is your legacy," the angel explained weakly. "It is this might that exists within you that will allow you to perform your sacred duties as messenger." Gabriel again climbed unsteadily to his feet. "It belongs to you—you are its master."

And Aaron came to the realization that his angelic power had not gone away, but had been there all along, hidden beneath the shroud of his uncertainty—waiting patiently to be unleashed.

"Own this power," the angel said, turning his attention from the boy to the quickly approaching foe. "Show that you are an emissary of Heaven."

Leviathan was almost upon them, and Aaron closed his eyes and looked upon what he had created to keep the power at bay. He imagined standing before a gigantic gate of his own construction, made from the logs of some mighty tree. It was like something he'd seen in the movies used to keep King Kong on his side of Skull Island. Within the face of the gate was a lock, and in the center of the lock, a keyhole. He produced an old-fashioned skeleton key and tentatively brought it toward the keyhole. The gate rattled and shook, as if something of enormous size were waiting on the other side, eager to be set free. He could hear it breathing; slow, steady breaths like a locomotive gradually building to speed.

Tentatively he brought the key to the lock. He knew that this was what had to be done—he could no longer be afraid of the force that shared his body; there was too much at stake for fear. With a deep breath, Aaron turned the key and listened to the sound of the lock as it came undone with a tumbling *clack*.

The slow and steady breathing on the other side of the gate came to an abrupt stop. He could feel its anticipation grow as it suspected what he was about to do. Without further hesitation, Aaron threw open the great wooden gates and set his power free.

Aaron gasped as the archaic markings began to appear upon his flesh. They burned from the inside out, rising to the surface to erupt smoldering and black on the skin of his body. He had no idea what the strange sigils were for, or what they meant, but they were the first sign that the ancient inner power residing within him was about to be unleashed.

The sensation was far less painful this time, and not entirely unpleasant. *It's like the world's biggest head-rush,* he thought as he was caught up in the transformation of his body. Muscles that he'd only recently become aware of contracted spasmodically, pushing the latent wings furled beneath the flesh of his back toward the surface. Aaron winced as the skin split and tore, the feathered appendages that would allow him flight emerging. He flexed the sinewy cluster beneath the skin of his back and felt the strength within the mighty wings as they began to flap.

The power was intoxicating, and Aaron felt himself caught up in the enormity of its strength. It wanted nothing more than to explode out into the world, to vanquish the enemy before it—and then to move on to the next. It was a power of battle that had become part of him, and it reveled in the art of war.

The transformation nearly complete, Aaron gazed with new eyes upon the weapon still clutched within his hand. "This isn't mine," he said, his voice like the purr of a jungle predator. He tossed the blade of light to its originator, the Archangel Gabriel—who caught the sword with ease, taking strength from contact with the radiant weapon.

A sword of Aaron's own design came to life in his hand, and he gazed at the weapon with a growing sense of anticipation. "*This* belongs to me," he said, admiring the blade's potential as it sparked and licked hungrily at the air.

"Yes," Gabriel said with a nod. "I believe it does."

The power sang within him, and Aaron found it hard to remember what exactly he had been so afraid of—but only for the briefest of instants, for the monster Leviathan attacked.

"I've found you, Nephilim," it growled, its ruptured eye still dripping thick streams of yellow fluid, the other wide and bulging. "And what I see, can be made mine."

Before he could act, Aaron felt his mind viciously assaulted, and his perceptions of the here and now suddenly, dramatically altered. He was no longer standing in an underwater cave, sword of fire in hand, a monster of legend looming above him; Aaron now stood in the middle of the playroom of his loving home in Lynn, Massachusetts, his foster parents familiarly nestled into their appropriate pieces of furniture. It was Friday night—movie night at the Stanley household.

"Are you going to sit down and watch the flick, or are you going out?" Tom Stanley asked from his recliner, the plastic box for the DVD rental in his lap.

Aaron smiled sadly at his foster dad, a mixture of happiness and sorrow washing over him—and he didn't quite remember why he would feel that way.

A new feeling forced its way to the surface of his soul, violently attempting to tear the heartfelt emotions away. Aaron actually twitched, eyes blinking severely, the level of feelings washing over him so intense. *What's going on?* he wondered, too old to blame it all on puberty.

"It's the new Schwarzenegger," his dad said, holding up the plastic case. "The one where his family is killed by terrorists and he gets revenge." There was an excited grin upon his face.

"He always liked those kinds of movies . . . ," said a voice

inside his head that sounded more like an animal's growl than his own. And again he shuddered.

"Are you all right, hon?" the only mother he had ever known asked from the corner of the couch. She put down her latest in a long succession of romance novels. "You look a little out of it," she said with genuine concern. "Why don't you sit down, watch the movie, and I'll make you up some soup."

The growling voice inside his head was back. *"That was her first line of defense against all kinds of illness,"* it said, letting the meaning of its statement begin to permeate. *"It didn't help her a bit against Verchiel."*

An anger fueled by sorrow ignited in his chest, and the palm of his right hand began to grow unusually hot, tingling as if asleep.

Lori Stanley got up. "Go on," she said, touching his shoulders. "Sit with Stevie and Gabriel and I'll make you something to eat." She headed for the kitchen.

For the first time, Aaron noticed his foster brother sitting on the carpet surrounded by blocks of all sizes and shapes. The dog was sleeping soundly beside him, his breathing rhythmic and peaceful. Aaron scratched at the tingling sensation in the palm of his hand and wondered where he had heard the name Verchiel before.

"I really think this is going to be a good one," his dad said excitedly from his recliner, staring at the picture on the front of the DVD case. Distracted, Aaron gazed down to see that the little boy was spelling something out in the letter blocks upon the carpet. But that was impossible; he knew Stevie could barely talk, never mind spell.

Aaron knelt down beside the child, his body torn by a maelstrom of emotions that were attempting to take possession of him. He hadn't a clue as to what was wrong with him—until he read what Stevie had spelled out upon the floor.

Your mother and father are dead, it said in multicolored plastic letters, which he unnecessarily remembered had magnets on the back of them so that they could be stuck to the refrigerator.

Aaron sprang to his feet, and a fire sparked in the center of his hand as his mother returned to the room with a steaming bowl of soup. Aaron was holding a sword of fire now, and he gazed in awe upon it as if he had never seen its like before.

"Sit down, Aaron," his dad said as he motioned with his hand for him to get out of the way of the television. "This is going to be the best movie night ever." Again, Tom motioned for him to sit, to forget all the conflicting emotions running rampant through him—to forget that he was now holding a flaming sword.

"Here's your soup," Lori said, holding the bowl out to him. "It's chicken with stars," she said.

This was what he wanted, more than anything, but something inside him—something very angry and quite powerful—told him that it wasn't to be, that it was all a lie.

He again looked down at the words spelled out in plastic letters.

Your mother and father are dead. The words were like the powerful blows of a sledgehammer, breaking away the false facade of a world that no longer existed, and Aaron began to scream.

He lashed out with his sword of fire, giving in to the rage that tried so hard to show him the deceit of it all. Aaron felt nothing as the weapon of fire passed through the form of his mother. She wailed like the mournful screech of breaks on a rain-soaked highway. His father cried out as well, still eagerly holding on to the DVD case as his body slumped to one side, consumed by fire.

"It's all a lie," Aaron bellowed, letting the living flame from his weapon extend into the playroom, burning away the untruth—and the screams of the unreal grew all the louder.

Aaron became conscious in the grip of Leviathan, the monster recoiling from the ferocity and violence of his thoughts. This was the personal heaven of his angelic nature unfolding within his skull that the sea beast now bore witness to. A heaven consisting of untruths burned away to reveal reality, the enemy vanquished—consumed in the fires of battle. It was a version of Paradise that Aaron doubted the great beast had ever created in the minds of its prey—a perfect bliss that involved its very own demise.

And it could not stand the thought of it.

The monster howled its displeasure and hurled him away. He could not react fast enough, his wings crimped from being entwined in the multiple tentacles of the beast, and bounced off the cave wall, falling to the rocky floor.

"What's the matter?" Aaron asked as he struggled to his feet and slid across the loose rock. He flexed his ebony wings, their prodigious span fanning the stale air of the undersea cave. "See something you didn't like?"

He sensed that the power within him had a streak of cruelty; exploiting the weaknesses of his enemy, prying away at the chinks in its armor, and that it would stop at nothing to achieve its victory. Aaron wondered exactly how far it would go—and, if it became necessary, was he strong enough to stop it? He would just have to hope that he was.

Aaron spread his wings and sprang into the air, sword at the ready. A savage war cry escaped his mouth that both frightened and excited him with its ferocity. He flew at the swaying monster, ready to bury the flaming weapon into the creature's flesh and end the nightmare's threat to the town of Blithe—as well as to the world.

He slashed at the half-blind beast, his sword of fire connecting repeatedly with the body of Leviathan. Sparks of flame leaped from the weapon's contact with the monster's scaled flesh, but to little avail. The scales were like armor, protecting the ancient threat against his attack. His angelic nature yowled with displeasure, and he attempted to push aside the overwhelming bloodlust so that he could rethink his course of action, but the ferocity was intoxicating, and he continued with his fevered assault upon the beast.

"Strike all you wish, little Nephilim," it gurgled as sparks of flame danced into the air with each new blow upon its seemingly impenetrable scales. "It matters not to me."

One of Leviathan's multitude of limbs lashed out, wrapping around one of his legs. Before he could bring his blade down to sever the connection, the monster acted, whipping him back against the wall with savage ferocity. His head and upper body struck the side of the cave wall, and he felt himself grow numb from the impact.

"They have all thought themselves superior," the monster continued, slapping him against the opposite side of the cave with equal savagery. "The righteous against the wicked—is there ever any doubt against the outcome?"

Leviathan then threw him upon the ground, and it took all the inner strength that he could muster not to slip away into unconsciousness. The inner angel struggled, but it, too, was fighting not to succumb to the ferocity of the attack.

Aaron heard the gigantic animal shift its mass closer—and then what sounded like the fall of heavy rain. He could not begin to discern the source of the sound until he felt the chitinous limbs of one of Leviathan's spawn scurry across his outstretched hand. Its spidery children were crawling out from beneath their master's scales to pour down upon him. Aaron could feel them moving across his back and legs and was filled with revulsion.

"They never could imagine the strength that I amassed," the behemoth boasted. "Overconfidence has always been their downfall."

Aaron felt it again attempting to intrude upon his mind and he blocked it, temporarily locking it behind the fortified fence that he had mentally erected to keep his newly awakened angelic nature isolated. He needed to think, to come up with a way to vanquish the monster before it had a chance to do the same to him, but time was of the essence.

Aaron picked himself up from the ground, the hissing spidery abominations clinging to his clothing, attempting to reach his mouth where they could crawl inside, making him docile enough so that their progenitor could consume him with the least amount of effort. He would have none of that; tearing them from his body by hand and spreading his wings, beating them furiously.

Leviathan loomed closer and opened its damaged eye to glare at him. The injured orb had begun to heal, but the reminder of his sword's cut across it could still be seen.

"Nowhere for you to run, nowhere for you to hide," cooed the beast. "Others far mightier than you have tried to destroy me—and look what has befallen them."

Aaron's glance shot to the severed digestive sacks. He could see that many still lay within the protective cocoons of oblivion, while others, he believed, were most likely dead, their life forces drained away by the nightmare before him.

Leviathan slithered closer, and Aaron gazed up into the monster's flapping mouth, staring into its soft, pink gullet—and an idea began to coalesce.

His angelic nature had received its second wind, and surged forward eager to continue the struggle. Aaron gritted his teeth with exertion, placing a mental choke chain around the powerful force's neck and drew it to him. The power of Heaven fought, wanting to ignite a sword of fire and again leap into the fray—wanting him to battle against the ancient evil from the primordial depths.

But that was not his plan, even though holding back was probably one of the most difficult things he had ever had to do. Aaron stifled screams of pain as the essence of his angelic nature fought against him to be released.

"Not yet," Aaron whispered through gritted teeth, as the monster shambled closer to where he crouched. The beginnings of a heavenly blade sparked in his grasp, but he wished it away, turning, his entire attention to the beast that now lorded over him.

"What shall the game be this time, Nephilim?" Leviathan asked, obviously expecting their conflict to resume.

Aaron shook his head, gazing up into the face of the horrific nightmare that was Leviathan. "No games," he told the beast. He held up his empty hands to the behemoth, showing the monstrosity that they were empty of weapons. "I can't fight you anymore."

Leviathan laughed, a horrible, rumbling gurgle. "How sensible of you, Nephilim," it said, tentacles squirming in the air with anticipation.

Aaron stood beneath the monster and spread his arms in a show of surrender. His body was still racked with pain as he tried to contain the furious forces that fought desperately to emerge and to defend itself; but he held it back, for it was not yet time.

"Take me," he told the wormlike creature that had existed since the dawn of time.

And Leviathan entwined him in its clutches, pulling him up toward its hungry mouth. "I shall use your power well," it said, staring at him with its cold, unblinking eyes, viscous saliva beginning to pour from its circular orifice to run down the length of its black, glistening body.

"Eat me," Aaron shouted. "And I hope you choke!" he added as the muscular appendages shoved him into its gaping maw, and he was swallowed up whole.

The first thing that Aaron noticed was the unbelievable stench. It stank even worse on the inside. He recalled the putrid aroma of a single mouse that had died in the kitchen wall of the Stanley house, and how he had thought nothing could smell as bad.

He couldn't have been more wrong.

He would rather have been wearing the dead rodent around his neck as jewelry for the rest of his life than endure the overwhelming stench of Leviathan's insides.

If it wasn't for the thick lubricating fluids that flowed upon him as the muscular throat of the beast contracted, sending him down toward its stomachs, there was the chance that the aroma of the monster's internal workings could very well have rendered him unconscious.

The excretions of Leviathan's digestive system were beginning to have their effects upon him also. His skin burned, and he felt a wave of undeniable fatigue attempting to purge the fight from his spirit. Even the angelic presence became increasingly docile, and Aaron knew that it would soon be time to put his plan into effect.

The interior of the beast gurgled and spat as it moved his mass through a series of powerful, muscular spasms—down what Aaron believed to be its esophagus—on his way to one of the still remaining digestive sacks hanging from Leviathan's body. It was getting difficult to breathe, and he felt his eyes grow heavy. Aaron wrestled with the idea of taking a bit of a nap before continuing with his course of action, but thought better of it, remembering the fate of the angelic beings that had been food for the great evil.

Perversely enough, the trip down the monster's gullet reminded him of one of those amusement park water slides as he attempted to bend his body in such a way that he could see where he was going. It was black as pitch within the monster's stomach, and Aaron managed to summon a ball of fire and maintain it as he continued his twisting journey to the belly of the beast. Half of him wished he didn't need the source of light, for the insides of a creature of chaos was not the most pleasant of places to see.

There was an abrupt turn in the food tube, and Aaron suddenly found himself about to be deposited within one of the remaining digestive organs. This was not part of his plan, and he summoned a knife of fire, stabbing it into the fleshy wall of the digestive passage, halting his progress. He felt his surroundings roil, and knew he had caused the great beast discomfort. *The son of a bitch doesn't yet know the meaning of the word,* he thought, releasing his hold upon the power within him—and even though more manageable than it had been before he was eaten, it took full advantage of a chance for freedom. If his plan was successful, Leviathan would have much more to worry about than simple discomfort.

An incredible surge of energy coursed through his fluid covered body, and he felt his lethargy immediately burned away. He positioned himself within the stomach passageway and unfurled his wings as far as he possibly could; still holding on to the knife blade that acted as an anchor, preventing him from being pulled further into Leviathan's stomach. Now wielding the full extent of his latent power, Aaron conjured an awesome sword of heavenly fire, illuminating his nauseating environment—and immediately began to put his plan in motion.

He was about to show Leviathan the disastrous effects of eating something that did not agree with it.

If it were capable, the beast Leviathan would have smiled.

As it swallowed down its latest morsel, a wave of contentment passed through the monster the likes of which it had never experienced. Leviathan could feel the pulse of the Nephilim's power within it, and knew that this source of strength would be what would finally allow it to emerge from its prison of rock, and claim the world above as its own.

It watched the others that had once been part of its nourishment, the angelic creatures, useless husks, drained and sprawled about on the floor of its prison, and realized that none had made it feel as glorious as it did now. The spawn moved excitedly beneath their parent's protective scales, sensing that it would soon be time to leave the cave and emerge out into the world, where its reign would commence.

It imagined that the Creator, in all His infinite wisdom, would send others to smite him—soldiers of the heavenly realm—that would all meet a similar fate as those who had come before. With the Nephilim's strength, there was nothing that could stop Leviathan from recreating the world in his own likeness.

Sated by the mere promise of new angelic energies, Leviathan prepared itself for the transforming influx of power that would soon awash it. It leaned its colossal, wormlike bulk against the cave wall and imagined what was next in its future. After countless millennia, it had the means to be free. The denizen of the depths would send its spawn out of the cave, to the settlements beyond, bringing the inhabitants, now under its control, to Blithe. Now it would have the substantial numbers and tools needed to be liberated from its rocky prison.

And then its work would begin.

The monster fantasized of a world transformed—sculpted as a representation of its own chaotic nature. It saw a place covered with churning seas, most of the landmasses swallowed up by volcanic upheaval, the skies gone black from volumes of ash expelled into the atmosphere to blot out the hated sun. And all the life upon the new world, that teemed upon what was left of the blighted land, and swam beneath the dark, ocean depths, would praise its name in Worship.

"Leviathan," it imagined they would proclaim. "How blessed we are that you have touched us with your resplendent glory. Praise be the Lord of the deep, hallowed be thy—"

It felt a sharp twinge of pain in the lower internal regions of its mass, a burning sensation that seemed to be growing. The monster removed itself from the wall where it had reclined, its head scraping the roof of the undersea cavern as it rose.

"What is this?" it asked in a sibilant whisper full of shock and surprise as the discomfort intensified. "What is happening?"

Never had it experienced such agony; it was as if there was a fire raging within its body—*but how is that possible?* it wondered. The heat of its pain was intensifying, the blistering warmth expanding up from the nether regions of its serpentine trunk to spread throughout.

"This cannot be happening," Leviathan exclaimed as the first of the remaining digestive sacks exploded, the fluids contained within brought to a boil from the raging internal temperatures of its body. Leviathan moaned in agony, powerless to act. Another of the sacks ruptured, spraying the walls in a bubbling stream—followed by another, and then another.

The monster swooned, its pain-racked form crashing into the rocky surface of the cave walls. The spawn, normally protected beneath its armor of scales, rained down to the cavern floor, scampering about in frenzied panic—driven to madness by the pain of their progenitor.

Leviathan wanted nothing more than to flee its prison, to have an opportunity to show the Creator that it, too, had a reason to exist. In its fevered thoughts it saw the glimpses of a paradise of its own design fading quickly away. It saw the black, roiling oceans full of life that it had helped reconfigure—a world of chaos that looked upon it as God and Master.

"It would have been magnificent," Leviathan moaned as the sword of fire erupted from the center of its body—and something that burned like a star emerged from the smoldering wound.

CHAPTER TWELVE

Camael slowly removed himself from the ruptured digestive organ and gazed about his foreign surroundings with a cautious eye.

While trapped within the prison he was made to believe that he had found the angelic paradise that was Aerie—and all the centuries of isolation and conflict he had experienced had come to an end. The prophecy had occurred: The fallen angels of Earth forgiven by Heaven. It was bliss.

As he looked around the subterranean cave, the reality of the situation was driven painfully home. He had not found Aerie, and where he now stood was the farthest from Paradise any angel could possibly be.

A mournful wail rose in intensity, reverberating around the cavern, awakening the angel further to his environment. Camael turned to see the monster Leviathan in what appeared to be the grip of torture. The sea behemoth thrashed, its body viciously pounding off of the cave walls as it shrieked in pain.

A sword of fire grew in his hand, a caution in case he should need to defend himself.

"He is accomplishing what we could not," said a voice nearby, and Camael turned to the Archangel Gabriel, withered and wan, leaning back against the stone wall.

Camael bowed his head, recognizing the angel for what and who he was. "Of whom do you speak, great one?" Camael asked, returning his attentions to the flailing beast.

"The Nephilim," the desiccated emissary of Heaven whispered. "The latest messenger of God."

"Aaron," Camael gasped as Leviathan continued its dance of agony. He watched awestruck as the skin of the beast smoldered, the protrusions that dangled obscenely from the monster's front, and of which he had been captive within, exploding, their contents spraying the air with a steaming mist.

"It would have been magnificent," he heard the creature of nightmare rattle as a weapon of fire suddenly tore through its midsection, and a warrior angel—one he first bore witness to only a few weeks ago—stepped from the gash in what seemed a mockery of birth.

He was about to call out to the Nephilim, but something stayed his tongue. Camael observed the half-breed, the offspring of angel and human, and was startled, and perhaps even a little concerned by what he saw.

The Nephilim jumped from the wound in the sea beast's stomach, his black-feathered wings flapping furiously, attempting to dry away the internal fluids that stained their sleek ebony beauty. In his hand he held a sword of fire—a weapon so fierce that it could rival those carried by the elite soldiers of Heaven. This was not the newly born being of angelic power that erupted to life mere weeks ago to avenge loved ones viciously slain, Camael observed. This was something all together different.

Camael watched as the transformed youth rose into the air before the agonizing beast, his mighty wings beating the air, lifting him to hover before the face of his enemy.

Leviathan lashed out at the Nephilim, its whiplike tentacles attempting capture, but falling upon empty air, the angel's movements were so swift.

"Damn you," Leviathan roared, its thick, green life stuff draining out from the gaping stomach wound to pool upon the cave floor. "Damn you—and the master you serve."

Aaron hovered before the snarling face of the beast, sword poised to strike, and Camael marveled at the sight of it.

"Got a message from the big honcho upstairs," Camael heard the Nephilim cry as he brought the flaming blade down in a powerful arc aimed at Leviathan's head. "You're dead."

The fire blade cleaved through the incredible thickness of the sea beast's skull with a resounding *crack*—the majority of the fearsome weapon buried deep within its monstrous cranium. It thrashed wildly in a futile attempt to dislodge the flaming weapon, but then grew impossibly still.

Aaron withdrew the sword and held it proudly above his head, powerful wings beating, holding him aloft. A fearsome cry of victory filled the air, and Camael stared in awe as the gigantic body of the ancient sea deity began to burn. The first flames shot up from Leviathan's head wound in a geyser of orange fire, the ravenous heat spreading down the length of the monster's enormity—its scaled flesh, muscle, and bone food for the heavenly flames.

Aaron flew down to the cave floor just as the monster's body collapsed in a gigantic pyre of smoldering ash, and strode menacingly toward Camael. The spawns of Leviathan scrambled about the cave floor, their shells aflame—the final remnants of the ancient sea monster left alive—but not for long.

Camael clutched his own weapon, unsure of the Nephilim's true intentions. It would not be the first time that he had borne witness to a half-breed's descent into madness after manifesting the full extent of its heavenly might.

Aaron stood before him, heavenly armament in hand, and he studied the fearsome countenance of the Nephilim. In his weakened state, Camael wasn't sure if he could survive a battle with such an adversary, but prepared himself nonetheless. Neither spoke, but the angel warrior watched for the slightest hint of attack. If there was to be a battle, his first strikes would need to be lethal.

"That thing really pissed me off," Aaron said as a small smile played across his warrior's features. "Glad to see you're all right."

And Camael lowered his sword, confident that the Nephilim's mental state was still intact—at least for the moment.

Aaron placed his hand on Gabriel's side, watching the rise and fall of the dog's breathing. The Labrador's yellow coat was saturated with slime. "Hey," he said softly, giving his best friend a gentle shake. "It's time to get up."

At first, the animal did not respond, his mind still in the embrace of doggy paradise. Aaron shook him again a bit harder. "Gabriel, wake up."

"I am awake," replied the archangel wearily, still resting his emaciated frame against the cave wall.

Aaron looked up. "I was talking to the dog," he told the messenger of God. "His name is Gabriel, too." He smiled briefly and looked back at his friend, who was finally beginning to stir. "Hey, pally, you awake yet?"

The dog stretched his four limbs and neck, emitting a low, throaty groan that began somewhere in the lower regions of his broad chest. Then he sighed, his dark brown eyes coming open. *"I was having a dream, Aaron,"* he said sleepily. *"I was chasing rabbits and having lots of good things to eat."*

Aaron stroked the dog's head lovingly. "You can do all that stuff out here—without being eaten by a sea monster."

The dog lifted his head and gazed about. *"Where are we?"* he asked, sitting up. *"The last thing I remember . . . the old woman,"* he said, a wide-eyed expression of shock on his canine face. *"She spit something at me, and it made me numb."*

"Yep, I know," Aaron nodded. "But I think we've taken care of that," he said, and looked in the direction of the still smoldering remains of the mythological sea monster.

"The spawn cannot continue to exist without the beast's mind," Camael said, standing over the fleshy sacks that Aaron had liberated from the monster's body. He was checking to see which of the captives of Leviathan were still living. "They were all part of one great beast—and the parts cannot survive without the whole."

Gabriel stiffly climbed to his feet and shook, spattering the surrounding area with the digestive juices that still clung to his fur.

"Watch that," Aaron said, covering his face, his wings reflexively coming around to block the spray. "I've got enough of that crap covering me."

"Then you won't notice a little more" the dog said, and smiled that special smile unique to the Labrador.

"Maybe there's still a chance I can shove you back into one of those stomachs," Aaron grumbled with mock serious-ness, giving the dog a squinty-eyed stare. Gabriel barked and wagged his tail, none the worse for his experience being captive in the gut of a sea beast.

"Who's he?" the dog suddenly asked, coming forward, his nose twitching.

Aaron noticed the angel Gabriel now stood by him, and seemed to be studying his dog of the same name.

"Gabriel," Aaron said to the animal, "this is Gabriel." He motioned toward the archangel.

Gabriel padded closer, nose still sniffing, tail wagging cautiously. *"That's a very handsome name,"* the dog told the angelic being.

The archangel looked from the dog to Aaron, a quizzical expression on his gaunt features. "You named this animal—after *me?*"

Aaron shrugged his shoulders. "Not specifically. It's just a very regal-sounding name. When he was a pup he looked like a Gabriel to me, that's all."

"I was quite adorable when I was a puppy," the dog said with a tilt of his blocky head.

The still weakened angel carefully walked toward the dog, reaching out a trembling hand to touch the animal's head. The Lab seemed to have no problem with that, licking the angel's hand affectionately.

"This animal has been changed," the archangel said, stroking the fur on the side of Gabriel's handsome face. "It is not as it should be." The angel looked back, as if seeking an explanation.

"Gabriel is very important to me," Aaron began. "He was hurt—near death. I saved him."

"You saved him," the angel repeated, holding the dog's face beneath the chin and gazing into his dark chocolate eyes. "And so much more."

"He did," Gabriel said, looking back.

"What other wonders can you perform, Aaron Corbet of the Nephilim?" the angel Gabriel asked, fascination in his tone.

Aaron didn't know what to say, feeling self-conscious beneath the scrutinizing eyes of the messenger of God. "I really don't know, but . . ."

"He is the chosen of the prophecy," Camael spoke up. The former leader of the Powers was kneeling beside the now deflated digestive sacks, and the remains of the angelic beings they contained. He gazed at the bodies of the heavenly creatures, many just barely alive——on the verge of death. "What other wonders is he capable of?" Camael asked sadly among the desiccated and the dying. "He can send our fallen brethren home."

Aaron remembered what he had done for the dying Ezekiel—how his newly awakened power had forgiven the fallen angel of his sins and allowed his return to Heaven. This ability, this power of redemption, was what the ancient prophecy that had taken over his life was supposedly all about, and whether he liked it or not, it was his job to reunite the fallen angels of Earth with their Creator.

He found himself drawn to the dying angels, his entire body beginning to tingle as if some great electrical charge were building in strength inside him. Aaron was becoming familiar with these feelings. He moved amongst the withered bodies, their life forces taken by the voracious appetites of a creature of chaos, and felt an incredible sadness overtake him. *How long— how many centuries has the monster been drawing them here?* he wondered gazing down at what were once things of awesome beauty—now nothing more than empty shells of their former glory. Those that had fallen from grace, soldiers in service to the Creator, twisted mockeries of angelic life created for servitude: They were all here, lying amongst one another, all desperately in need of one thing that he was capable of bestowing upon them.

Release.

Aaron felt their great sadness—their disgrace, as the churning supernatural power inside him settled in a seething ball at the center of his chest. He knew precisely what to do; it now felt like second nature to him—like breathing, or blinking his eyes.

He laid his hands upon them, one after another—the vortex of power swirling at his center coursing down the length of his arms into his hands. Whether they be Orisha, fallen, or heavenly elite, Aaron touched them all, igniting their dying essences with the force of redemption. "It's over now," he said to them, their bodies glowing like stars, fallen from the night skies to show the fabulous extent of their beauty.

Camael stepped back, bathed in the radiance of their

transformation, and Aaron wondered if it was only awe that he saw expressed upon the angel warrior's face, or was it envy?

What the angels had become, as sustenance for a monster's hunger, was no longer a concern—burned away to expose the final flames of divine brilliance that still thrived in each of them.

"You're free," Aaron said as they hovered above the cave floor, reveling in the experience of their rebirth. He spread his wings of shining black and opened his arms. "Time to go home," he proclaimed, and with those words spoken, the dank, eerie darkness of Leviathan's lair was filled with the light of the divine, and any trace of evil still alive within the monster's dwelling was routed out and annihilated in purging rays of heavenly brilliance.

The vivified angels gravitated toward the Archangel Gabriel, orbiting around the messenger of God, bathing him in their luminous auras—and through the light, Aaron could see that Gabriel was growing stronger, gaining sustenance from his angelic brothers.

Aaron felt at peace as he watched the long-suffering creatures of Heaven reunite, and let his angelic countenance recede back into his body—sated, for now. The arcane sigils that were etched upon his skin started to fade, and his wings furled, gradually withdrawing beneath the flesh and muscle of his back. Both Camael and his dog had joined him, not wanting to interfere in any way with the once-imprisoned angels' communion.

"They're very happy to see one another again," the dog said, tail wagging happily.

"They have been too long without the company of their own kind," Camael said, his eyes riveted to the scene before him, and Aaron questioned if the warrior was not in some way speaking for himself as well.

The Archangel Gabriel was restored to his true glory, armor glistening as if freshly forged and polished, wings the color of a virgin snowfall opening from his back. The wingspan of the messenger was enormous, and he curled them around the children of Heaven, drawing them closer to him.

"We have much to thank you for, fellow messenger," the archangel said in a rich, powerful voice that vibrated in the air like the lower notes played on a church organ. "The monster has been vanquished—and our freedom regained."

Aaron was speechless; even after all that he had seen over the past life-changing weeks, the sight before him filled him with awe. They all floated in the air now, Gabriel as the center of their universe, all those who had survived their ordeal, enwrapped in his loving embrace. He was taking them back— the Archangel Gabriel was escorting them home.

"Know that my blessing goes with you on your perilous journey, brave Nephilim," the angel continued, "and that your acts of heroism shall be spoken of in the kingdom of God."

His dog nudged his hand with his head. *"Did you hear that,*

Aaron?" he asked excitedly. *"They're going to be talking about you in God's kingdom."*

Aaron petted his ecstatic friend, still mesmerized by the awesome vision before him.

"With these acts, you have done much to expunge the sins of the father and to fulfill the edicts of prophecy—"

Aaron was so caught up in the melodious sounds of the angel's proclamation of thanks that he didn't immediately catch the meaning of the last sentence—but it gradually sank in, permeated his brain, and alarm bells began to sound.

He hadn't even heard the final words of gratitude spoken by the messenger. The Archangel Gabriel had lifted his head toward the ceiling of the cave, the heavenly glow about them all growing in intensity. Bringer of Light had appeared in his hand, and he pointed the mighty blade toward the cave roof— toward their celestial destination beyond the ceiling of rock and the world of man above.

Aaron charged forward, shielding his eyes from the blinding light of their ascension. "Wait," he cried as he tried to find the Archangel within the radiant spectacle. "Did you say the sins of the father?"

He could just about make out the outline of the angel messenger at the center of the expanding ball of light. Through squinted eyes he saw that Gabriel was looking at him. "My father's sins?" Aaron asked, wanting desperately for the emissary of Heaven to clarify what he had said. "Do you know who my father was? Please . . ."

The light burned so brightly now that he had no choice but to turn away, or go blind.

"You are your father's son," Gabriel said within the light of Heaven. "At first I did not see it, but then it was oh so obvious."

His back to the departing creatures now seemingly composed of living light, Aaron begged for answers from the messenger. "If you know who he is, can't you tell me something—anything . . . please!"

Aaron could feel the pull of the celestial powers as the angels were drawn up to Heaven. He wanted nothing more than to turn around and throw himself into the light, to prevent Gabriel from returning to God's kingdom—until the Archangel told him what he knew.

There were sounds like the world's largest orchestra tuning their instruments all at the same time—and he knew that it was only a matter of seconds before Gabriel and the others were gone from this plain of existence, taking their valuable knowledge with them.

Aaron fell to his knees upon the cave floor, both physically and emotionally drained.

"You're the messenger," he said, holding out all hope that he would be heard. "Give me a message . . . give me something."

There was a sudden flash of brilliance—and the cavern was filled with an eerie silence as the denizens of Heaven returned to their homes, but not before he heard the whispering voice of the Archangel Gabriel in his ear. "You have your father's eyes."

CHAPTER THIRTEEN

The people of Blithe were vomiting—and Aaron imagined he knew exactly how they must feel. No, he didn't have some crablike creature living inside his chest, but he had just received the very first pieces of information he had ever learned about his *real* father; that the prophecy had something to do with his father's sins, and that he had his father's eyes. He thought he might be sick.

Aaron, Camael, and Gabriel moved through the winding passage that led up from Leviathan's lair to one of the many chambers that had been excavated out of the rock by the townspeople under the sea monster's thrall.

"Gross," Gabriel said, and Aaron couldn't have agreed more. The people, who up until Leviathan's demise had been busily clearing away tons of rock and dirt in an attempt to free the beast, had stopped their work. They had dropped their tools

and were bent over in obvious pain—their bodies racked with vomiting and throwing up the horrible things that had crawled inside to control their actions.

"Are they all right?" Aaron asked, wrinkling his nose in disgust at the repellant sounds of people in the midst of being sick.

"Their bodies are rejecting Leviathan's invasive spawn," the angel warrior said, rather blasé. "I would imagine they will be fine—as soon as the dead creatures and their nests are expelled from the body."

The floor of the smaller chamber was puddled with all manner of foulness, and the already decaying remains of the spiderlike things that had taken up residence in their bodies.

Aaron wasn't exactly sure how he felt about what he had learned; it wasn't as if he had been given a phone number or a home address. The identity of the man—*angel*—that had sired him was still a complete mystery, and one that he really couldn't afford to think about right now. He decided that he would deal with it later, when things had calmed down—when things were back to normal. He laughed to himself, as if his life could ever be that way again.

"I wonder how long those things have been inside them?" Aaron asked to distract himself as they proceeded from the smaller cavern, his level of disgust quickly on the rise.

"Most likely since Verchiel wholeheartedly abandoned his holy mission and became obsessed with preventing the prophecy from becoming a reality," Camael said as they walked a tunnel that would, he hoped, take them to the surface.

"So this is something else I can be blamed for?" Aaron asked, feeling the dirt pathway of the tunnel beneath his feet begin to slant upward. They continued to pass the people of Blithe, many of them passed out from the exertion of purging the foreign invaders from their bodies.

"In a way, yes," the angel said. "By ignoring their tasks, the Powers have allowed the forces of chaos to take root in the world, growing in strength, unabated. I shudder to think of what other malignant purveyors of wickedness are hiding in the shadows of the world."

"Great," Aaron responded with a heavy sigh. "Wouldn't want to be let off easy or anything. I wonder if I have anything to do with global warming?" he asked, his words dripping sarcasm. "We might want to look into that."

Gabriel ran up ahead of them and had begun to bark excitedly. *"We're almost to the surface,"* he cried, waiting until they caught up, and then running up ahead. The dog was as sick of being underground as they were, Aaron imagined, and wanted nothing more than to breathe in some nice fresh air.

They emerged from the tunnel out into the main excavation in the heart of the former boat factory. Aaron noticed that the heavy digging machinery had been silenced, and the only sound that could be heard throughout the air of the place was that of retching. Everywhere he looked, somebody was being sick or incapacitated as a result of being sick.

"This is just too much," Aaron said, taking it all in. "Those things must have been living inside just about everybody in town."

An angled road of dirt had been constructed on the floor of the dig so that trucks and such could be driven down into the hole, and Aaron and his companions used the packed-earth path to ascend to the lip of the excavation at ground level.

As the three moved toward the door that would take them out of the factory, and walked around the violently ill, being careful to step over the reeking puddles that contained the decomposing corpses of Leviathan's children, Aaron caught sight of Katie McGovern and went to her. "Katie," he said as he approached. "Are you all right?" His guess about the filthy man in the cave veterinary clinic had been correct, for her former boyfriend Kevin was with her, and they both gazed at him slack-jawed, their bodies racked with chills. Aaron saw no recognition in Katie's eyes, and he began to feel afraid.

"What's the matter with them?" he asked Camael, who now stood by his side staring at the two as he was.

"Shock, I'd imagine," the angel said. "Their minds are attempting to adjust to the horrors they have experienced. The human mind is a wondrous invention indeed," he said as he stepped closer to Katie's former fiancé. Camael reached out and grabbed the man by the chin, looking deeply into his eyes.

"By the morrow they'll have only the vaguest idea that something had happened to them at all," he said, as if attempting to get a glimpse of the inner workings of a human being. "To most, it will become the distant memory of a horrible nightmare." He let Kevin's face go and proceeded to the door. "Such is the coping mechanism of the mortal brain."

Aaron and Gabriel followed the angel out into the early morning dawn. Outside the door, Chief Dexter leaned against his patrol car. He had thrown up onto the windshield, and it looked as though he wasn't quite finished yet. Aaron quickly looked away. "So they won't remember any of this?" he asked the angel who was now striding toward the parking lot.

Gabriel sniffed around the tires of the parked cars, completely disinterested in their conversation. There was valuable sniffing time to be recouped.

"They'll remember, but their minds will shape the event into something that they will be able to accept—no matter how odd or unlikely," Camael answered. "It's how their minds work—how they were designed. And those that do remember the reality of the situation, and dare to speak of it, will be ostracized and labeled as insane."

"Nice," Aaron said, a little taken aback by the angel's cold interpretation of the human psyche. He was silent for the moment, digesting the angelic warrior's words, and decided that he didn't buy it. "If that's how our poor human brains work, then how come I didn't chalk up all this angel crap to eating bad tuna or a high fever due to some rare African virus?"

The angel stopped and turned to stare. "You are Nephilim," Camael said, as if that would be more than enough of an answer.

"Yeah, but I'm still human, right?" Aaron said, staring at the angel and gazing into his steely gray eyes.

On the outskirts of the parking lot, he waited for the angel to respond. Camael remained silent—but the lack of an answer spoke volumes.

"What are you trying to say?" Aaron asked nervously.

It was then that the angel spoke. "You were sired by an angel. You are no more human than I am."

It felt as though he'd been struck. Even though deep down inside, Aaron already knew this, hearing it come out of Camael's mouth was like a whack with a two-by-four between the eyes.

I'm not human, he thought, letting the concept rattle around inside his brain. Could his life be any weirder?

He again heard the Archangel Gabriel's final words to him—before the angel had taken the express bus to Heaven. The words about his father.

"The Archangel Gabriel said that what I was doing—the prophecy?—was somehow connected to the sins of my father," Aaron said to his angel companion as they reached the pad-locked gate.

"Yes," Camael said as a sword of flame came to life in his hands and he severed the chain with a single slice. "And he also said that you have his eyes." Camael pushed open the gate and strode through onto the road.

Aaron held back, waiting for his dog to finish sniffing around a patch of weeds.

"Do you know who he is, Camael?" Aaron asked as his dog trotted over to join him. "My father—do you know who my father is?"

The angel had continued to walk up the road, but he stopped and slowly turned. "I do not, no," he said, shaking his head. "But what I do know is that he must have been an angel of formidable power to have sired one like you." Camael then promptly turned away, continuing on his journey.

"I think he just paid you a compliment, Aaron," Gabriel said as he walked alongside him.

Aaron smiled slightly. "I think you might be right there, Gabe."

Berkely Street was deathly quiet in the early morning stillness, as was the rest of Blithe. Aaron removed a pair of sweatpants and shirt from the backseat of his car and prepared to put them on over his filthy and ripped clothing.

"I think I might have an extra sweatshirt," he said to Camael, gazing at the angel's filthy suit with a wrinkled nose.

"That will be unnecessary," he said.

And Aaron watched with amazement as the accumulated dirt and grime on his companion's suit faded away before his eyes, leaving it as if it had just come from the cleaners. The angel then adjusted his tie, glancing casually in his direction.

"Let me guess," Aaron said as he pulled the sweatshirt down over his head. "I could do that, too, if I just applied myself."

Camael was about to respond, but Aaron put up a hand to silence him; he didn't have the time or energy for a dissertation right now. He finished putting on the rest of his clean clothes and checked out his reflection in the side mirror of his car. It would have to do for now. That was all he needed, for Mrs. Provost to see him looking like he'd been through World War III. It was going to be hard enough to explain what had happened and how she had come to be locked in the cellar.

Camael studied the quaint house with squinted eyes. "And you say that the old woman attacked you?"

"Yeah," Aaron said as he combed his unruly hair with his fingers. "I knocked her out and put her in the cellar. I didn't want to take the risk of her letting the other people in town know I was on to them."

"I'm very hungry after being inside the belly of a monster," Gabriel declared, and hurriedly headed up the walk to the front door. *"I wonder if she'll have any meat loaf?"*

"Not if she's been locked in the basement all night, pal," he said, coming up behind the dog and reaching for the doorknob.

It was unlocked, and Aaron swung the door wide—and

was immediately hit with the smell of something cooking, something that made his belly ache and come to the realization that Gabriel wasn't the only one who was very hungry.

"Mrs. Provost?" he called out, looking around the foyer and the area around it. Strangely enough, it showed no sign of their struggle. They all moved toward the kitchen, toward the wonderful smell of breakfast cooking, Camael bringing up the rear.

"Mrs. Provost?" he said again as he came around the door frame and saw the older woman at the stove. She was wearing an apron and was frying up some bacon. The old woman turned momentarily from her cooking to give him a smile. "Morning," she said, reaching up with a white bandaged hand to brush away a stray whisp of white hair from her forehead. "Knew the smell of cooking would get you in here." She went back to work, carefully favoring the injured hand.

"What happened to your hand?" he asked her, knowing full well that she had burned it on his sword during their scuffle. She was placing some strips of bacon onto a folded paper towel on the stove, and Gabriel went to her, tail wagging. She was careful to finish up what she was doing before petting the animal with her good hand.

"I'm not really sure," she said, rubbing the dog's ears. "Think I took a bit of a spill down the cellar steps last night," she said kind of dreamily, straining to recall what had happened to her. "Must've knocked myself senseless and touched something hot on the furnace."

She peeled some more strips of the breakfast meat out of the package and laid them in the greasy pan. "Even found a way to lock myself inside," she said with a laugh. "Good thing I found a spare skeleton key down there or I'd still be locked up." The old woman was making sure that the bacon was lined up straight in the pan. "Probably should go see the doctor to rule out concussion or anything," she added. Gabriel lay down on the floor at her feet, gazing up at her adoringly.

Aaron turned and looked at Camael behind him. The angel had been precisely right. Mrs. Provost's brain had done exactly as he described. It had attempted to rationalize the bizarreness of the situation, steering clear of anything that would be too difficult to explain or comprehend.

Mrs. Provost placed her fork down and walked to the refrigerator, all the while under the watchful eye of his Labrador. "I was just about to cook up some eggs," she said, pulling on the fridge door to open it. "My father always used to say that a big breakfast could cure what ails you." She removed the carton of fresh white eggs. "Thought today might be a good day to take his advice."

Camael had not willed himself invisible this time, and Aaron caught her staring at the large, older man behind him— too stubborn to ask his identity. She would wait until he got around to explaining who Camael was.

"This is my friend," he said in introduction. "The one who had some business up in Portland?" She nodded slowly, remembering the conversation that they'd had the first night over supper. "He just got back this morning," he explained.

Camael was silent, studying the old woman just as she was studying him.

"Is he staying for breakfast?" she asked, taking the eggs with her to the stove.

Aaron was about to answer for the angel, when Camael suddenly spoke for himself. "I will have French fries," he said, stunning Aaron with his answer.

Mrs. Provost, completely unfazed by the angel's request, reached down to the stove and pulled it open. A new delicious aroma wafted out of the oven with a blast of heat. There was something cooking inside on a metal sheet.

"Don't have any French fries, but how about home fries—will they do?" she asked. "My husband, God rest his soul, used ta tell me that I made the best home fries in New England." She used an oven mitt covered in a pattern of bananas to remove the hot pan of browned, chopped potatoes from the stove.

"If you like French fries, you're going to love these," Aaron told the angel, his mouth beginning to water.

"Then I will have—home fries," he said, eyeing the breakfast dish now resting atop the stove.

It was all pretty strange and quite amazing, Aaron mused as he finished giving Gabriel his breakfast and watched the kindly old woman expertly crack the last of the eggs into the frying pan, making breakfast as if it were just like any other day of the week. It was hard for him to wrap his brain around the concept. Less than two hours ago he had been fighting for his life against a force that could very well have threatened the world—but here he was now, about to sit down to a big breakfast of bacon, eggs, and home fries. The realization that his life had dramatically changed was again driven home with the force of an atomic blast—and with every new day, it seemed to change more and more. Aaron wondered if he'd ever get used to it, if it would ever seem as mundane as sitting down to eat breakfast.

Shaking some salt onto his eggs, he watched the angel Camael take a tentative bite of the home fries and begin to chew. A look that could only be described as pleasure spread across his goateed face, and he greedily began to eat.

Will my life ever seem so mundane again? he wondered, watching as an angel of Heaven consumed a plate of home-fried potatoes beside him.

He seriously doubted it.

Miss you. Love Aaron.

Aaron sat back in the desk chair, contemplating the last words he had typed in his e-mail to Vilma. is *it too strong?* he wondered, fingers hovering over the keyboard as he tried to decide. His feelings for the girl back home hadn't even come close to changing, and the more he thought about her, the longer he spent away from her—the stronger they seemed to become.

An all too familiar sadness washed over him as he wondered if he would ever see the pretty Brazilian girl again. He knew it was for her own good that he stay away—Verchiel would certainly think nothing of using her to get to him—but a selfish part of him wanted to be with her, no matter the consequences.

Aaron read through the e-mail again, smirking at how boring it all sounded—if only he could write even a portion of what he'd been experiencing.

Miss you. Love Aaron.

He wondered what Vilma was doing just then. It was early Sunday morning, and he guessed that she probably wasn't even up yet. He wouldn't have been, either, but they had to get going and continue his search for Stevie. He always loved sleeping late on Sundays, reading the *Globe* with a big glass of milk and a couple of Dunkin' Donuts that his foster dad would buy. But that was then.

Aaron read the e-mail one last time and deemed it perfectly fine. *What do I have to lose?* He clicked on the Send button and watched his letter disappear into the electronic ether. *No turning back now,* he thought, in more ways than one. There was only the road ahead of him now, and at the end of that road he hoped to find his little brother, and maybe a chance at a normal life—if fulfilling an ancient prophecy didn't get him killed first.

Gabriel and Camael had started loading the car. Aaron was just about to shut the computer down when Mrs. Provost appeared in the doorway to the tiny office. "Don't shut that off right yet," she said. "I was thinking of maybe sending a note to my son."

Aaron got up and motioned for her to take the chair. "That would be nice. I'm sure he'd like to hear from you." He suddenly wondered if it could have been Leviathan that had kept her from leaving Blithe all these years.

"Damn thing'll probably blow up in my face," she said, scowling at the computer as she took a seat in front of the monitor.

"You'll do fine," he said. He then remembered that he hadn't paid the woman yet for his stay, and reached into his pocket for the money there. "Oh, before I forget," he said handing her the stack of bills. She took it from his hand and began to count it.

"Gave me too much," she said, handing back more than half the cash.

"You said that it was—"

"Are you calling me a liar, Corbet?" she interrupted with a scowl worse than the one she had given the computer.

Aaron knew he was on the edge of real trouble here. "No, it's just that you said—"

"Never mind what I said. This is plenty." She held up the money she had kept, then folded it and stuck it inside the front pocket of her ancient blue jeans. "I enjoyed your company—and your dog's, too, even though he's a bit of a pig, if you ask me."

Aaron laughed. "You don't have to tell me! The boy's been

like that since he was a baby. His stomach's a bottomless pit."

They both laughed.

"Well, I gotta hit the road," Aaron said. "You take care of yourself, Mrs. Provost," he said, waving good-bye as he left the office doorway.

"Same to you, son," she said. "You and that dog of yours stop by again sometime, and bring your handsome friend along too."

Aaron headed for the front door, listening to the old woman's fingers tentatively moving on the keyboard. It sounded as though she was doing just fine, but as he opened the door, he heard her curse and threaten the computer with being tossed out with the trash. Laughing softly to himself, he stepped from the house to join his friends.

Aaron was passing beneath the flowered archway to go to his car when he saw Katie McGovern. She was dressed in a baggy white T-shirt and some running shorts. The vet was patting Gabriel, checking out his bite wound. Aaron noticed that her hand was bandaged as well. "Hey," he said, approaching them and his dog.

"Hey, back," she answered. "Was out running and saw Gabriel in the yard. He begged me to come pet him. Healed up pretty fast, didn't he," she pointed out, running the flat of her bandaged hand along the dog's flank.

"I didn't tell her anything" Gabriel grumbled, looking at him guiltily, tongue lolling.

Aaron ignored the dog. "I don't think it was as bad as it looked—and plus, he had the best vet in town looking after him. How could he do anything but miraculously heal?" he asked, chuckling. They were both patting the Labrador now, and the animal was in his glory.

"So you're leaving, huh?" she said, eyeing his vehicle. He looked where she was staring and saw that Camael had already taken up his place in the front seat, patiently waiting.

"Yeah, got some things to take care of," he said, stroking Gabriel's side. "Thought I'd get an early start."

"Is that the friend you were waiting for?" she asked, motioning with her chin to the car, and the back of Camael's head.

"That's him. Got back from Portland yesterday," he lied.

"Nothing I could say to get you to stick around and help Kevin and me with the practice, is there?" she asked half-heartedly, already expecting that she knew what his answer would be.

"You and Kevin, eh?" he questioned, a sly smile creeping across his face.

"Yeah," she said, now rubbing Gabriel's ears. "Since he got back, we've been spending a lot of time with each other and have decided to give it another go." Katie shrugged. "We're taking it a day at a time—see what, happens. So I guess your answer's no?"

Camael turned around in his seat and gave him an intense stare. *Even an angel's patience has its limits,* he thought, moving gradually toward the car. "Sorry," he said, opening the back door of the Toyota for Gabriel. "Still got something I have to do, but thanks for offering." He thought of his little brother still in the clutches of killer angels and he felt his pulse rate quicken. The dog jumped into the backseat, and he slammed the door closed.

"You're good, Aaron," she said, hands on her hips. "If you ever need a letter of recommendation for school or anything, be sure to look me up, okay?"

"Thanks," he said, opening the driver side door. "You take care now. I hope everything works out between you and Kevin."

Aaron sat behind the steering wheel and was just about to slam the door of the Toyota closed when Katie abruptly stopped him.

"The other night," she said, her eyes wide. She licked her lips nervously. "You know what happened then—don't you?" Katie nervously played with the bandage on her hand.

Aaron looked into her eyes and told her that he didn't know what she was talking about, but he suspected that she didn't believe him.

"There's a little voice in the back of my head telling me that I should be thanking you for something—but for the life of me I don't know why."

He turned the key in the ignition and started up the car. "You don't have to thank me," he said, shaking his head, feeling a little sad that he was leaving. The town of Blithe had really started to grow on him. His own little voice—the selfish one again—was telling him that he should turn the car off this instant, accept Katie's offer, and take up permanent residence in the now peaceful town—to turn his back on the prophecy.

"Never ignore the little voice in the back of your head, Aaron," she said, leaning into the open window and giving him a quick peck on the cheek. But he knew that it wasn't to be; that if he had listened, it would be no better than the false peace that he had known in the belly of Leviathan.

"Thank you," she said as she withdrew herself from the car.

"You're welcome," he responded, and she turned from the car with a final wave and continued with her morning run.

He had responsibilities now, he thought as he watched Katie recede down Berkely Street, duties that extended far beyond his own personal satisfaction and happiness. It was a lot to cope with, but what choice did he have, really? He'd tried to deny it, to keep it locked away, but that had almost got him killed. Begrudgingly, he was beginning to accept it was all part of what he had to do—the job he had been chosen for.

"*I like her,*" Gabriel said as Aaron put the car in drive, beginning the process of turning the car around on the dead-end street. "*Even if she is a vet.*"

"I like her too," Aaron said in the midst of completing a three-point turn, his mind already elsewhere. He thought about his brother, and the dangers that were obviously to come—and he thought about his father.

He began to drive up Berkely Street, and on reflex turned on the radio. Paul McCartney and the rest of the Beatles were singing "Yesterday." It had always been one of his favorite oldies, and listening to the words now, it had new meaning for him. He turned the volume up a bit and felt Camael's burning gaze upon him.

"I want you to listen to this," he said, glancing over at the scowling angel as he took a left off Berkely and headed back through the center of town. "Don't think of it as a song—think of it as poetry."

"I despise poetry," the angel growled, looking away from him to gaze out the passenger window at Blithe passing by.

"Bet you thought you hated French fries too," Aaron said, chuckling.

Would his life ever again be filled with lazy Sundays reading the newspaper, drinking milk, and eating doughnuts? Aaron had no idea what the future held, but he *did* know it would certainly be interesting; it was in the job description.

What else would one expect as a Messenger of God?

EPILOGUE

It was a dream—but it felt like reality.

The night was cool, although she could feel the heat from the sand, warmed by the day's relentless sun, beneath her bare feet as she fled across the ocean of desert.

It seemed so real, as if part of a life lived in the past. Long, long in the past.

Her heart beat rapidly in her chest, and she turned back to gaze at the city burning in the distance—somehow she knew that its name was Urkish. The sky above the primitive desert-city had turned black, as smoke from the burning buildings of straw and mud rose to hide the stars.

She could hear a sound, a high-pitched, keening sound, and even at this distance, she had to cover her ears against it. It was like the cries of birds—hundreds of angry birds.

Each night the dreams became more vivid, and she found

she was beginning to fear sleep. She would have given anything for a dreamless night of rest. But it wasn't to be.

Someone called to her, and she remembered she wasn't alone. Eight others had fled Urkish with her—eight others had escaped from . . . from what? she wondered. A girl no older than she was, wrapped in a tattered cloak and hood, motioned frantically for her to follow. There was fear in her eyes, fear in all their eyes. What are they afraid of? What has driven us from the city? She wanted to know—she needed to know.

"Quickly," said the girl in a language the dreamer had never heard—yet could comprehend. "We must lose ourselves in the desert," the girl said as she turned back to the others, her ragged cloak blowing in the desert breeze. "It is our only chance." They started to run, fleeing across the dunes—but from what? the dreamer wondered again.

She turned her attention back toward the city. Was the answer there? The fires burned higher, and any semblance that a civilization had once thrived there was lost—consumed in the rising conflagration.

The others called to her, their voices smaller in the distance, carried on the wind. They pleaded for her to follow, but she did not move, her eyes fixed upon the city in flames.

Sadness enveloped her as she watched the city burn—as if Urkish was somehow important to her. Was it more than just a place she dreamed about? Did it actually have some kind of a special meaning for her?

She stamped her foot in the sand, frustration exploding within her. "I want to wake up," she shouted to the desert. "I want to wake up now." She closed her eyes, willing herself to the surface of consciousness, but the world of dream held her in its grasp.

The horrible cries again rang in her ears, and she opened her eyes. She saw them flying up from the fires of the city, their wings fanning the billowing black smoke as they rose. There were hundreds of them, and even from this distance she could see that they were clad in armor of gold.

She knew what they were. Ever since she was a child, they had filled her with wonder and contentment. She had fancied them her guardians, and believed they would never let any harm befall her.

Breathlessly she watched them fly now, dipping and weaving above the burning ruins of the city. She knew she'd been in this dream before, but for the life of her, could not remember why the heavenly beings had come to Urkish.

"They've come to kill you," said a whisper from the desert, and she knew the voice was right.

They were flying beyond the city now, out over the desert waste—searching. Searching for her.

She started to run, but the sand hindered her progress. Her heart hammered with exertion as she attempted to catch up with the others. She remembered now. She remembered how the creatures had dropped from the sky, fire in their hands—and the killing. She remembered the killing. Her thoughts raced with images *of violence as she struggled to climb a dune, the sand giving way beneath her frantic attempts.*

They were closer now—so very close. The air was filled with the sounds of pounding wings, and the cries of angry birds.

No, not birds at all.

She reached the crest of the dune. She could just about make out the others. She cried out to them, but the sound of her voice was drowned by the beating wings. She turned to look at them—to see how close they were.

And they were there, descending from the sky, descending from Heaven—screeching for her blood.

Angels.

How could she have ever loved creatures so heartless and cruel?

Vilma awoke from the nightmare, a scream upon her lips. She could still feel the wind on her face as they carried her up into the night sky, the swords of fire as they pierced her flesh.

She began to sob, burying her face in the pillow so her aunt and uncle would not hear her. They had already caught her crying twice this week and were beginning to worry. She couldn't blame them.

Getting a hold of her emotions, Vilma lifted her face from the pillow and caught something from the corner of her eye. Outside her bedroom window was a tree, and for the briefest moment there was something in that tree, something disturbingly familiar, and it had been watching her.

It was then that Vilma was convinced her aunt and uncle were right: She *did* have some kind of mental problem, and should probably seek help. Why else would she be having such horrible dreams—

And see angels outside her window.

His body covered in armor the color of blood, Malak the hunter crept through the beast's lair, searching for the scent of his prey. He removed the gauntlet of red from his hand and knelt before the ashen remains of the sea monster. Malak plunged his bare hand into the remnants of the beast, and just as quickly removed it. The hunter sniffed at the residue clinging to his fingers—his olfactory senses searching for a trace of the one his master sought. He hunted a special quarry, one that had meant something important to him long ago, in another life—before he was Malak.

There was a hint of the hunted upon his hand—but not quite enough.

He sensed that there were magicks in the air—spells to mask his enemy's comings and goings, but not enough to hide him from one as gifted as he was. His master Verchiel had blessed him with the ability to track any prey—and the myriad skills to vanquish them all. He was the hunter, and nothing would keep him from his quarry.

Malak stood and walked around the cave. He tilted his head back, letting the fetid air of the chamber fill his nostrils.

His powerful sense of smell sorted the different scents, until he found the one he sought.

The hunter moved across the cavern, zeroing in on the source of the prized spore. He found it upon the wall of the cave, the tiniest trace of blood. He leaned into the wall, sniffing, but the blood had dried, which had taken away some of its pungent aroma. Malak leaned closer, his tongue snaking out from within the crimson facemask, to lick at the stain—his saliva reviving the blood's sharp, metallic stench.

The smell flooded his preternatural senses, and the hunter smiled. He now had the scent.

It was only a matter of time.

AARON'S JOURNEY AND
THE GREAT WAR OF HEAVEN
CONTINUE IN

THE FALLEN 2

AERIE AND *RECKONING*

C an I take your order, sir?" asked the cute girl with the blond ponytail and a smile wide enough to split her face in two.

Aaron Corbet shook himself from his reverie and tried to focus on the menu board behind her. "Uh, yeah, thanks," he said, attempting to generate interest in yet another fast food order. His eyes were strained from hours of driving, and the writing on the menu blurred as he tried to read it. "Give me a Whopper-with-cheese value meal, and four large fries to go."

Aaron hoped the four orders of fries would be enough to satisfy Camael's strange new craving for the greasy fast food. Just a few days ago the angel had given him a song and dance about how creatures of Heaven didn't need to eat—but that had been before he sampled some of the golden fried potatoes.

Angels addicted to French fries, Aaron thought with a wry shake of his head. *Who'da thunk it?*

But then again, who could have predicted this crazy turn his life had taken? he thought as he waited for his order to be filled. The angel Camael had become his companion and mentor since Aaron's realization that he was born a Nephilim. He remembered how insane it had all sounded at first—the hybrid offspring of the mating between a human woman and an angelic being. Aaron thought he was losing his mind. And then people he cared about started dying, and he realized there was much more at stake than just his sanity.

Aaron turned away from the counter and looked out over the dining room. He noticed a couple with a little boy who appeared to be no more than four years old. The child was playing with a blue plastic top that he must have gotten as a prize with his kid's meal. Aaron immediately thought of Stevie, his foster brother, and a weighty feeling of unease washed over him. He recalled the last time he had seen his little brother. The seven-year-old autistic child was being dragged from their home in the clutches of an angel—a soldier in the service of a murderous host of angels called the Powers. The Powers wanted Aaron dead, for he was not just a Nephilim, he was also supposed to be the chosen one spoken of in an angelic prophecy written over a millennium ago, promising redemption to the fallen angels.

At first it had been an awful lot to swallow, but lately Aaron had begrudgingly come to accept the bizarre twists and turns that life seemed to have in store for him. Camael said that it was all part of his destiny, which had been predetermined long before he was born.

The child had managed to make the top spin and, much to his parents' amusement, clapped his hands together as the plastic toy careened about the table top.

The prophecy predicted that someone very much like Aaron would be responsible for bringing forgiveness to the angels hiding on Earth since the Great War in Heaven, that he would be the one to reunite the fallen with God. It's a big job for an eighteen-year-old foster kid from Lynn, Massachusetts, but who was he to argue with destiny?

The spinning top flew from the table and the little boy began to scream in panic. Again Aaron was bombarded with painful memories of the recent past, of his foster brother's cries as he was stolen away. "I think I'll keep him," the Powers leader, Verchiel, had said as he handled the little boy like some kind of house pet. Aaron's blood seethed with the memory. Perhaps he *was* some kind of savior, but there was nothing he wanted more than to find his brother. Everything else would have to wait until Stevic was safe again.

The child continued to wail while his panicked parents scrambled to find the lost toy. On hands and knees the boy's father retrieved the top from beneath a nearby table and brought the child's sadness to an abrupt end by returning the toy to him. Though his face was still streaked with tears, the boy was smiling broadly now. *If only my task could be as simple,* Aaron thought wearily.

"Do you want ketchup?" he heard someone say close by, as he turned his thoughts to how much farther he'd be able to drive tonight. He was tired, and for a brief moment he considered teaching Camael how to drive, but that thought was stricken from his mind by the image of the heavenly warrior in the midst of a minor traffic altercation, cutting another driver in two with a flaming sword.

Aaron felt a hand upon his shoulder and spun around to see the girl with the ponytail and the incredibly wide smile holding out his bags of food. "Ketchup?" she asked again.

"Were you talking to me?" he asked, embarrassed, as he took the bags. "I'm sorry, I'm just a bit dazed from driving all day and . . ."

He froze. His foster mom would have described the strange feeling as somebody walking over his grave, whatever the hell that meant. He never did understand the strange superstitions she often shared, but for some reason, the imagery of that one always stuck with him. Aaron missed his foster parents, who had been mercilessly slain by Verchiel, and it made his desire to find his brother all the more urgent. He turned away from the counter to see a man hurriedly going out a back door, two others in pursuit.

The angelic nature that had been a part of him since his eighteenth birthday screamed to be noticed, and senses far beyond the human norm kicked into action. There was a trace of something in the air that marked the men's passing as they left the store. It was an aroma that Aaron could discern even over the prominent smells of hot vegetable oil and frying meat. The air was tainted with the rich smell of spice—and of blood.

With a polite thank-you he took his food and left the store, quickly heading to the metallic blue Toyota Corolla parked at the back of the lot. He could see the eager face of his dog in the back window. Gabriel began to bark happily as he reached the car, not so much that his master had returned, but that he had returned with food.

"What took so long?" the dog asked as Aaron placed the bags on the driver's seat. *"I didn't think you were ever coming out."*

Being able to understand and speak any form of language, including the vocalizations of animals, was yet another strange manifestation of Aaron's angelic talents, and one that was both a blessing and a curse when it came to his canine friend.

"I'm starved, Aaron," the dog said eagerly, hoping that there would be something in one of the bags to satisfy what seemed to be a Labrador retriever's insatiable urge to eat.

Gabriel also loved to talk, and after Aaron had used his unique abilities to save the dog after a car accident, the Lab had suddenly become much smarter, making him quite the dynamic personality. Aaron loved the dog more than just about anything else, but there were days that he wished Gabriel was *only* a dog.

"I'd really like to eat," he said from the backseat, licking his chops.

"Not now, Gabe," Aaron responded, directing his attention to the large man sitting with his eyes closed in the passenger seat. "I have to speak with Camael." The angel ignored him, but that didn't stop Aaron from talking. "Inside the restaurant," he said. "I think three angels just went out the back door and . . ."

Camael slowly turned his head and opened his steely blue eyes. "Two of them are of the Powers; the other, a fallen angel"—he tilted back his head of silvery white hair and sniffed, the mustache of his goatee twitching—"of the host Cherubim, I believe. I was aware of their presence when we pulled into the lot."

"And you didn't think it was important to say anything?" Aaron asked, annoyed. "This could be the break we've been waiting for. They might know where Stevie is."

The angel stared at him without emotion, the plight of Aaron's little brother obviously the furthest thing from his mind. With Camael, it was all about fulfilling the prophecy—that and finding a mysterious haven for fallen angels called Aerie.

"We have to go after them," Aaron said forcefully. "This is the first contact we've had with anything remotely angelic since we left Maine."

Gabriel stuck his head between the front seats. *"Then we really should eat first. Right, Camael?"* he asked, eyeing the bags resting on the seat. *"Can't go after angels on an empty stomach, that's what I always say."* The dog had begun to drool, spattering the emergency brake.

Camael moved his arm so as not to be splashed and glared at the animal. "I do not need to eat," he snarled, apparently very sensitive to the recent craving he had developed for French fries.

Aaron opened the back door of the car and motioned for Gabriel to get out. "C'mon," he said to them both. "We have to hurry or we'll lose them."

"May I have a few fries before we go?" the dog asked as he leaped from the car to the parking lot. *"Just to hold me over until we get back."*

Aaron ignored his dog and slammed the door closed, anxious to be on his way.

"Do you think this wise?" Camael asked as he removed himself from the front seat of the car. "To draw attention to ourselves in such a way?"

Aaron knew there was a risk in confronting the angels, but if they were ever going to find his brother they had to take the chance. "The Powers answer to Verchiel, and he's the one who took Stevie," Aaron said, hoping that the angel would understand. "I don't think I could live with myself if I didn't at least try to find out what they know."

Camael moved around the car casually buttoning his dark suit jacket, impeccable as always. "You do realize that this will likely end in death."

"Tell me something I don't know," Aaron said as he turned away from his companions and followed the dwindling trail of angel scents into the dense woods behind the fast-food restaurant.

* * *

No matter how he tried to distract himself, Verchiel found himself drawn to the classroom within the St. Athanasius Orphanage where the prisoner was held.

Standing in the shadows of the room, the angel stared at the huddled figure feigning sleep within his prison, and marveled at how a mere cage of iron could contain an evil so vast. Verchiel would destroy the prisoner if he could, but even he was loath to admit that he did not have the power to accomplish such a task. He would have to take a level of satisfaction from the evil one's containment, at least for now. When matters with the Nephilim and the accursed prophecy were properly settled, then he could concentrate on an appropriate punishment for the captive.

"Am I that fascinating a specimen?" the prisoner asked from his cage. He slowly brought himself to a sitting position, his back against the bars. In his hand he held a gray furred mouse and gently stroked its tiny skull with an index finger. "I don't believe we saw this much of each other when we still lived in Heaven."

Verchiel bristled at the mention of his former home; it had been too long since last he looked upon its glorious spires and the memory of its beauty was almost too painful to bear. "Those were different times," he said coldly. "And we . . . different beings." The leader of the Powers suddenly wanted to leave the room, to be away from the criminal responsible for so much misery, but he stayed, both revolted and mesmerized by the fallen angel and all he had come to embody.

"Call me crazy," the prisoner said conversationally as he gestured with his chin beyond the confines of his prison, "but even locked away in here I can feel that something is happening."

Verchiel found himself drawn toward the cage. "Go on."

"You know how it feels before a summer storm?" the prisoner asked. "How the air is charged with an energy that tells you something big is on the way? That's how it feels to me. That something really big is coming." The prisoner continued to pet the vermin's head, waiting for some kind of confirmation. "Well, what do you think, Verchiel?" he asked. "Is there a storm on the way?"

The angel could not help but boast. His plans were reaching fruition and he felt confident. "More deluge than storm," Verchiel responded as he turned his back upon the captive. "When the Nephilim—this Aaron Corbet—is finally put down, a time of change will be upon us." He strode to a haphazardly boarded window and peered through the cracks at the New England summer night with eyes that saw through darkness as if it were day.

"With the savior of their blasphemous prophecy dead, all of the unpunished criminals of the Great War, driven to despair by the realization that their Lord of Lords will *not* forgive them, will at last be hunted down and executed." Verchiel turned from the window to gaze at his prize. "That is what you are feeling in the air, Son of the Morning. The victory of the Powers—my victory."

The prisoner brought the mouse up to his mouth and gently laid a kiss upon its tiny pointed head. "If you say so, but it doesn't feel like that to me. Feels more special than that," he said. The mouse nuzzled his chin and the prisoner chuckled, amused by the tiny creature's show of affection.

Verchiel glided toward the cage, a cold smile forming on his colorless lips. "And what could be more special than the Nephilim dying at the hands of his sibling?" he asked the prisoner cruelly. "We have spared nothing in our pursuit to destroy him."

The prisoner shook his head disapprovingly. "You're going to use this kid's brother to kill him? That's cold, Verchiel—even for someone with my reputation."

The angel smiled, pleased by the twisted compliment. "The child was a defective, a burden to the world in which he was born—that is, until I transformed him, forged him into a weapon with only one purpose: to kill the Nephilim and every tainted ideal that he represents." He paused for dramatic effect, studying the expression of unease upon the captive's gaunt face. "Cold?" Verchiel asked. "Most assuredly, for to bring about the end of this conflict I must be the coldest one there is."

The mouse had defecated in the prisoner's hand and he casually wiped it upon his robe of heavy brown cloth. "What makes this Nephilim—this Aaron Corbet—any different from the thousands of others you've killed over the millennia?"

Verchiel recalled his battle with this supposed savior, the ancient angelic sigils that covered his flesh, his ebony wings, the savagery of his combat skills. "There is nothing special about this one," he sneered. "And those of the fallen who cling to the belief that he is the savior of prophecy must be shown this."

He remembered how they battled within the storm he himself had conjured, weapons of heavenly fire searing the very air. It was to be a killing blow; his sword of fire poised to sever the blasphemer's head from his body. And then, inexplicably, lightning struck at Verchiel, and he fell from the sky in flames. The burns on his body had yet to heal, the pain a constant reminder of the Nephilim, and how much was at stake. "With his death," Verchiel continued, "they will be shown that the prophecy is a lie, that there will be no forgiveness from the Creator."

The prisoner leaned his head of shaggy black hair against the iron bars of his prison as the mouse crawled freely in his lap. "Why does the idea of the prophecy threaten you so?" he asked. "After all this time, is absolution such a terrible thing?"

Verchiel felt his anger blaze. His mighty wings unfurled from his back, stirring the dust and stagnant air of the room. "It is an affront to God! Those who fought against the Lord of Lords should be punished for their crimes, not forgiven."

The prisoner closed his eyes. "But think of it, Verchiel: to have the past cleared away. Personally I think it would be pretty sweet." He opened his eyes and smiled a beatific smile that again reminded Verchiel of how it had been in Heaven—and how much had been lost to them all. "Who knows," the prisoner added, "it might even clear up that complexion of yours."

It was a notion that had crossed Verchiel's mind as well—that his lack of healing was a sign that the Creator was not pleased with his actions—but to have it suggested by one so vilified, so foul, was enough to test his sanity. The leader of the Powers surged toward the cage, grabbing the bars of iron.

"If I have incurred the wrath of my heavenly sire, it is for what I failed to do, rather than what I have done." Verchiel felt the power of his angelic glory course through his body, down his arms, and into his hands. "I did not succeed in killing the Nephilim, but I have every intention of correcting that oversight."

The metal of the cage began to glow a fiery orange with the heat of heavenly fire, and the prisoner moved to its center. His robes and the soles of his sandals began to smolder. "I deserve this," he said, a steely resolve in his dark eyes. "But *he* doesn't." He held the mouse out toward Verchiel and moved to the bars that now glowed a yellowish white. He thrust his arm between the barriers, his sleeve immediately bursting into flame, and let the mouse fall to the floor where it scurried off to hide among the shadows.

"How touching," Verchiel said, continuing to feed his unearthly energies into the metal bars of the prison. "It fills me with hope to see one as wicked as you showing such concern for one of the Father's lowliest creatures."

"It's called compassion, Verchiel," the prisoner said through gritted teeth, his simple clothing ablaze. "A divine trait, and one that you are severely lacking."

"How dare you," Verchiel growled, shaking the bars of the cage that now burned with a white-hot radiance. "I am, if nothing else, a spark of all that is the Creator; an extension of His divinity upon the world."

The prisoner fell, his body burning, his blackening skin sending wisps of oily smoke into the air as he writhed upon the blistering hot floor of the cage. "But what if it's true, Verchiel?" he asked in an impossibly calm voice. "What if . . . it's all part of His plan?"

"Blasphemy!" the angel bellowed, his anger making the bars burn all the brighter—all the hotter. "Do you seriously think that the Creator can forgive those who tried to usurp His reign?"

"I've heard tell," the prisoner whispered through lips blistered and oozing, "that He does work in mysterious ways."

Verchiel was enjoying his captive's suffering. "And what if it *is* true, Morningstar? What if the prophecy is some grand scheme of amnesty composed by God? Do you actually believe that *you* would be forgiven?"

The prisoner had curled into a tight ball, the flesh of his body aflame, but still he answered. "If I were to believe in the prophecy . . . then it would be up to the Nephilim . . . wouldn't it?"

"Yes," Verchiel answered. "Yes, it would. And it will never be allowed to happen."

The prisoner lifted his head, any semblance of discernable features burned away. "Is that why I'm here?" he croaked in a dry whisper. "Is that why you've captured me . . . locked me away . . . so that I will never be given that chance?"

Verchiel sent a final burst of energy through the metal of the cage. The prisoner thrashed like a fish pulled from a stream and tossed cruelly upon the land. Then he grew very still, the intensity of his injuries sending him into the embrace of unconsciousness.

The Powers' leader released the bars and stepped back. He knew that his captive would live, it would take far more than he could conjure to destroy something so powerful, but the injuries would cause him to suffer, and that was acceptable for now.

Verchiel turned from the cage and walked toward the door. There was still much to be done; he had no more time to concern himself with prisoners of war.

"As does the Lord," he said to himself, "I too work in mysterious ways."

The power of Heaven, tainted by the poison of arrogance and insanity, flowed through his injured body, bringing with it the most debilitating pain—but also sweet oblivion.

The prisoner drifted in a cold sea of darkness and dreamed.

In his dreams he saw a boy, and somehow he knew that this was the Nephilim of prophecy. There was nothing special about the way he looked, or the way he carried himself, but the Powers captive knew that this was the One—this was Aaron Corbet. The boy was moving purposefully through a thicket of woods; and he wasn't alone. Deep within the womb of unconsciousness the prisoner smiled as he saw an angel walking at the boy's side.

Camael, he thought, remembering how he had long ago called the warrior "friend." But that was before the jealousy, before the war, before the fall.

And then he saw the dog; it had gone ahead into the woods, but now returned to tell its master what it had found. It was a beautiful animal, its fur the color of the purest sunshine. It loved its master, he could tell by the way it moved around the boy, the way it cocked its head as it communicated, the way its tail wagged.

It would be easy to like this boy, the prisoner guessed as the sharp pain of his injuries began to intrude upon his insensate state. He pulled himself deeper into the healing embrace of the void. *How could I not like someone who has caused Verchiel such distress?* the prisoner wondered. And besides, Aaron Corbet had a dog.

I've always been a sucker for dogs.

ABOUT THE AUTHOR

THOMAS E. SNIEGOSKI is the author of more than two dozen novels for adults, teens, and children. His books for teens include *Legacy*, *Sleeper Code*, *Sleeper Agenda*, and *Force Majeure*, as well as the series The Brimstone Network.

As a comic book writer, Sniegoski's work includes *Stupid, Stupid Rat-Tails*, a prequel miniseries to the international hit *Bone*. Sniegoski collaborated with *Bone* creator Jeff Smith on the project, making him the only writer Smith has ever asked to work on those characters.

Sniegoski was born and raised in Massachusetts, where he still lives with his wife LeeAnne and their Labrador retriever, Mulder. Visit him on the Web at www.sniegoski.com.

LEVIATHAN

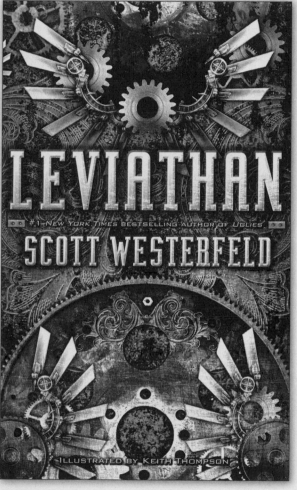

— FROM —

SCOTT WESTERFELD

THE BESTSELLING AUTHOR OF THE UGLIES SERIES

FROM SIMON PULSE

PUBLISHED BY SIMON & SCHUSTER

"A spellbinding story about loss, rebirth,
and finding out who we really are inside.
This intense and moving novel will wind up under your skin."

—SCOTT WESTERFELD

New York Times bestselling author of the Uglies series,
on *Skinned*

THE FIRST TWO BOOKS IN A GRIPPING TRILOGY

From Simon Pulse | Published by Simon & Schuster

SiMON TEEN

Simon & Schuster's **Simon Teen**
e-newsletter delivers current updates on
the hottest titles, exciting sweepstakes, and
exclusive content from your favorite authors.

Visit **TEEN.SimonandSchuster.com** to
sign up, post your thoughts, and find out what
every avid reader is talking about!

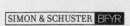